THE
INCREMENTALIST
A Novel

Endless money forms the sinews of war.

Marcus Tullius Cicero
The Philippics

THE INCREMENTALIST
A Novel

Ian McKercher

for Patrick —

Enjoy!

Ian McKercher

Burnstown
Publishing
House

**Burnstown
Publishing
House**

5 Leckie Lane
Burnstown, Ontario K0J 1G0
www.burnstownpublishing.com

Copyright © 2016

Ian McKercher

THE INCREMENTALIST: A Novel

ISBN: 978-1-77257-111-0 (PB)
ISBN: 978-1-77257-112-7 (eBook)

Editor: J. Karchmar
Cover and Interior Design: W.D. Clements

Published and Printed in Canada.

*THE INCREMENTALIST is a work of fiction
wound loosely around historical events and personages.
Names, characters, places, and incidents are products
of the author's imagination, or have been used fictitiously.*

For Amelia

Contents

OTTAWA 1939

August 28:

> *The Canadian dollar began to fall vis-à-vis the US dollar, dropping 9 per cent in value to 91 cents U.S. by September 15.*
>
> (Powell, 31)

September 3:

> *The Defence of Canada Regulations were promulgated under the War Measures Act, granting the government sweeping powers to intern people without trial, restrict free speech, and detain anyone acting "in a manner prejudicial to public safety."*
>
> (Cook, 213)

Not even Charles Dickens would have confused it with the best of times.

It was the demise of the Depression;
    it was the birth of blitzkrieg.

It was the triumph of dictatorship;
    it was the trial of democracy.

It was the twilight of innocence;
    it was the dawn of holocaust.

It was the end of appeasement;
    it was the beginning of blood, sweat, and tears.

War (noun): a crucible in which humanity is either reduced to ash or forged into steel.

The choice was simple enough.

PART
ONE

Canada was ill-prepared for war. In 1933, the annual defence budget had fallen to $13 million. By 1939, as a result of a decade of neglect of its military, the country could not defend its own coasts, let alone dispatch fully equipped and trained forces to help Britain.

(Bryce, 12)

MISS BRISCOE

September 9:

> *The Canada Parliament voted to declare war on Germany.*
>
> (Granatstein, 17)

September 15:

> *The Foreign Exchange Control Board* [FECB] *was established to prohibit the withdrawal of capital from Canada and scrutinize all foreign exchange transactions. Bank of Canada Governor Graham Towers was named chairman.*
>
> (Fullerton, 119)

Under the capable direction of Captain Hyland, the Canadian Pacific freighter *Town of Mont Royal* crept unobtrusively into Halifax Harbour at dusk to tie up at a remote pier beside an abandoned railway spur. Scotty Meldrum, the deputy governor of the Bank of Canada, had wired ahead to insure that an armoured train and twenty Royal Canadian Mounted Police officers were waiting on the quay. With the moon down over the blacked-out port, only the occasional squeal of a winch evidenced the transfer of forty million dollars in Polish gold from the *Mont Royal*'s hold to the waiting armoured freight cars.

Scotty Meldrum, Frances McFadden, and Paul Roderick were ensconced in the caboose when the train rumbled out at midnight without a departing whistle. The track had been cleared completely of rail traffic for the slow grind westward. During essential stops to take on water and coal, ten Mounties armed with Thompson submachine guns silently patrolled each side of the steel-plated boxcars. The train, compromised by its weighty cargo, didn't arrive in Ottawa until nightfall. Under cover of darkness, a circuit of Brinks trucks ran a relay the short distance down Wellington Street between

Union Station and the loading docks at the Bank of Canada. Just after two a.m., Frances was finally freed from her duties to go home to her Balmoral apartment and sleep for the first time in a nation newly at war.

The war changed everything. Everything except Miss Briscoe. Other tides surging to other moons changed Miss Briscoe.

Mid-September found the two Bank of Canada secretaries in adjoining rooms in the East Block of Parliament Hill. Deputy Governor Meldrum was to chair a meeting of deputy ministers while Governor Towers would work with Mackenzie King's war cabinet next door. At 8:00 a.m., Frances was distributing agendas when Miss Briscoe appeared at the open door.

"You're an early bird, Miss McFadden."

"As are you, Miss Briscoe," returned Frances with a smile.

Miss Briscoe lingered. Unusual. She did not waste time with gossip or chat about the weather. "We are both booked here all day. The governor and the deputy governor will be invited to lunch in the Parliamentary dining room. The invitation will not extend to us." She hesitated. "Would you care to join me at the Chateau Laurier?"

"Will we have time?" asked Frances, although it was less than a five-minute walk.

"The ninety-minute lunch is sacred on Parliament Hill."

"Even during wartime?"

"If the troops in the field are to be supported, the home fires must be fuelled. They'll break at twelve, and what with cigars and port, won't be back before one thirty."

"Then the Chateau it is. Shall I wait for you?"

"Go ahead. Find a quiet table. I'll join you as soon as I can."

A quiet table?

In five years at the Bank of Canada, Frances had never shared coffee with Miss Briscoe, let alone a meal. She couldn't remember ever seeing her in the Bank's cafeteria. Did the woman eat? What would they possibly talk about at *the quiet table?*

Miss Briscoe had come to the Bank of Canada with Graham Towers from the Royal Bank's head office in Montreal back in 1934. A magisterial aura exuded from her like a rich, subtle fragrance. This grace shone from within and owed nothing to her position with the governor. She was always well dressed, although her wardrobe displayed a restrained range in the colour spectrum, running to charcoals and blacks. Frances thought she looked like a nun trying not to look like a nun. An enigma. Not a fraternizer. *And now lunch?*

The maître d' at the Chateau's Canadian Grill beamed. "Ah, Mademoiselle McFadden! So good to see a cheerful face, given the times. Your window table?"

"*Non merci*, Raymond. I need something more private. Governor Towers's secretary will join me shortly."

Along the east wall of the dining room, half a dozen discreet tables hid in deep nooks. Generous swag drapery hung down to cloak diners in shadow and to mute power cliques colluding over cocktails.

Miss Briscoe arrived breathless. "I hope you won't think me unprofessional, Miss McFadden, but I absolutely need a restorative to pace me though the day. Will you join me in a gin and tonic? I have an expense account that I seldom use. I'm happy to treat."

Alcohol? At noon on a workday?

Frances wondered about the effects on her note-taking, but didn't wish to appear prudish. Henri took their orders and twirled away like a toy top.

"How was your morning?" asked Miss Briscoe. A detached lethargy in her eyes suggested that the answer didn't much matter.

"Much wailing and gnashing about the new Foreign Exchange Control Board," replied Frances. "The mandarins think it's hopelessly bureaucratic. And this from bureaucrats? At the Bank we've been working on emergency planning for over a year, but the concept of war governance seems to have poleaxed the deputy ministers. No contingencies and little deftness at adjusting to changed circumstances."

"Much the same with the war cabinet. The declaration of war, the grand gesture, was the easy part. The cabinet is clearly unsure what 'at war' really means. Most particularly, what it will cost, and how to pay the piper."

When the drinks arrived, Miss Briscoe cut in the tonic and a squeeze of lime with a surprisingly practised hand before sipping deeply. Women of Miss Briscoe's demeanour didn't smack their lips, but a rejuvenated glimmer was allowed to creep into her eyes.

"Now, Miss McFadden, I have a twofold purpose for asking you here. May I count on your usual discretion?"

"Certainly, Miss Briscoe."

"It is not my custom to chatter about personal matters, but some background is necessary. Remember when I went into the hospital during the summer with food poisoning, and you covered my desk for two weeks?"

"Of course."

"For good or ill, I was taken to the Civic, which is a teaching hospital, and Dr. Pagliarello used me as a specimen for his student residents. The diagnosis was plain to me, but this gaggle insisted on examining every cell in my body."

Frances swallowed a smile imagining the prim Miss Briscoe being prodded like a voodoo doll by earnest interns.

"They found something."

"That you had food poisoning?"

"Yes, and something else. I have a tumour. On my hip. They did more tests in September. It's malignant. I'll need surgery, and a long convalescence, if I live through the surgery." Miss Briscoe drained a third of the gin and tonic in a single swallow.

Frances gasped. "I'm so sorry."

A demure wave dismissed the comment. "I am no longer young, Miss McFadden. Cancer plus age are two strikes against me. Thankfully, I'm in no pain. However, I have become exceedingly fatigued of late and have lost my appetite."

Henri arrived with two plates of poached salmon and assorted greens. He cocked an eye at Miss Briscoe's empty glass. She hesitated but declined. "I used to find the thirty-minute walk to the Bank of Canada from my Glebe apartment a pleasant morning tonic. I enjoyed climbing the four flights of stairs to my office. Since September, I take a taxi and use the elevator."

"Does Governor Towers know?"

"Last week I finally accepted the fact that I can no longer carry out my duties, and told him. It's not a question of will, Miss McFadden. I have the will. I do not have the capacity. I have submitted my resignation."

Frances blinked. "How will the governor ever function without you?"

Another dismissive wave. "No one is irreplaceable. I feel bad letting the governor down as a war begins, but quality work is now beyond me. It would be disloyal to continue. My final duty is to prepare the transition as best I can."

"That won't be easy," reflected Frances. "There are capable secretaries at the Bank, but none with your experience. There might be possibilities from the business world, but they'd lack your grasp of central banking."

"The governor has done me the courtesy of soliciting my opinion on the matter." She paused and Frances looked up. "My opinion, Miss McFadden, is that you would be the best candidate."

Frances's fork of poached salmon froze in transit. "You can't be serious! You've been with the governor since before I was born. I've never worked as a private secretary."

"To be frank, Miss McFadden, the governor and I discussed several options. Where character, discretion, and work ethic were considered, no one came close to you."

"Well, I'm floored. If the governor thinks so highly of me, he's certainly kept it to himself."

"He would never show favouritism. Bad for morale. Besides, should you decline him directly, it might compromise your future working relationship." Miss Briscoe took a deep breath. "I realize this must be a surprise, but the governor needs to know your answer soon. I gave my two-week notice last Friday. That leaves eight days."

She drained her gin and tonic. "I have relished every minute of my career. But please understand, being secretary to the second most important man in Canada will affect your every waking hour. How old are you?"

"Twenty-two."

"I'm almost three times your age. You do everything as well as I do."

"Miss Briscoe!"

"I do not play false with the truth, Miss McFadden," she said, dropping her napkin on the untouched plate of salmon. "I am convinced that you are the best person for the job, and so is the governor. Think about it. Sleep on it. Although please don't discuss it. Tomorrow afternoon the boardroom is not booked. Let's meet there at 1:00 p.m."

Sleep on it? Frances often slept poorly. She was haunted by nightmares of one-armed Max Kessler—her friend Anna Deloitte's supposed fiancé. Was he a spy? A double agent? He had been on the train carrying the Polish gold reserves from Warsaw to the port of Gdynia with her and Scotty Meldrum in late August. One second he was there, arguing with them on the small platform between train cars, and then suddenly, when the train entered a tunnel, he disappeared, like a Houdini trick. Fell? Was pushed? Jumped? It all happened so quickly in the dark. She couldn't tell whether she had contributed to this departure, and, worst of all, she couldn't tell Anna. Anna understood Max to be in Western Canada, visiting fall fairs and selling farm equipment.

After the chat with Miss Briscoe, Frances was now torn by dreams of blind alleys and futile searches for misplaced mittens. She didn't know the governor personally, although her every interaction with him had been pleasant and professional. He had a quiet sense of humour and always demonstrated a deep well of reflection before speaking. He seemed shyer than Scotty Meldrum, the deputy governor, who had a bear-like personality.

At 1:00 p.m., Frances entered the massive boardroom doorway to find Miss Briscoe toiling amid a ream of papers at the far end of the long mahogany table. The north light from the windows that overlooked the Gatineau Hills was not gentle on her face. A pen went down and her eyebrows went up. "Well?" she queried as Frances sat down.

"Well, I have two concerns, Miss Briscoe. As I said yesterday, I have no experience at all being a private secretary."

Miss Briscoe's delicate hand closed over Frances's wrist. "Fiddlesticks! You'll be fine. I've seen how quickly you solve new problems. There is honestly no one else. Secondly?"

"I don't wish to sound immodest, but I'm working twelve-hour days on several special projects that the deputy governor feels are vital to the survival of democracy." She smiled. "His words. These files are top secret. It would be irresponsible to turn them over holus-bolus to someone new. I can't continue those tasks and become the governor's private secretary as well."

"Mere logistical problems, Miss McFadden, that play to your greatest strength. I remember the archives you set up in advance of the governor's appointment back in 1934. Thirty filing cabinets full of cross-indexed resource material. Astounding! And I've seen the effortless way you organize the governor's annual Christmas tea for three hundred staff."

She paused. "You are aware of the difference between power and influence?"

"Aren't they much the same?"

"Not at all. Power is the authority to make decisions. The governor has power. Influence is much subtler, a capacity to achieve results by indirect means. The governor's secretary has influence. More than almost anyone else in Canada."

"How so?"

A rare smile lit Miss Briscoe from within. "You'll see. You must be careful not to abuse it. I'll schedule you in to meet Governor Towers tomorrow morning at ten. Present your concerns. Suggest solutions. He's not unreasonable. Should you take up the mantle, we will need a deeper discussion. No list of duties adequately describes what you're in for."

2

THE GOVERNOR

*Graham Towers, a man of acute intelligence and cool judg-
ment, was a source of advice to the finance minister, the
prime minister, and occasionally to cabinet as a whole.*

(Bryce, 3)

*Interest rates affect virtually every aspect of our existence:
what we buy, where we live, how we save. Thus the person
who moves these rates, the Bank of Canada Governor, is
the most important non-elected official in the country, and
arguably can affect our lives more than the prime minister.*

(Babad and Mulroney, 49)

Frances McFadden never thought of herself as "a central banker,"
yet the Bank of Canada was as central to her life as the cross
was to Christianity. She had worked at the Bank for five years, almost
a quarter of her life, but she still found economics confounding.
Its governing principles were not like the law of gravity, which never
varied. She had observed that economists used the conjurer's trick
of distraction, "other things being equal," when forecasting. But
other things were never equal. Social, economic, and political forces
did not holiday while some economic theorem was acted out in
a vacuum.

At 9:55 a.m., Frances arrived in Miss Briscoe's office. At 9:58,
Miss Briscoe pressed a green button on her desk. Exactly two minutes
later, she knocked twice on the connecting door to the governor's
office and ushered Frances in. "Miss McFadden for your ten o'clock,
Governor," she said, and withdrew, drawing the heavy oak door
closed.

"Miss McFadden," said Graham Towers, rising from his desk. "How
good of you to see me on short notice."

Frances laughed. "Well, sir, Miss Briscoe can be quite insistent. I was shocked to hear her news. Her departure will be a great loss to the Bank."

The governor blinked several times and turned quickly to look out the window at the blue haze over the Gatineau Hills. "Miss Briscoe and I have worked hand-in-glove for over two decades. She deserves at least half the credit for whatever I have accomplished during those years. But life goes on, as she would be the first to say. I asked her to recommend a replacement. It's a terrible job. Long hours. Endless details. Demanding people." The governor looked chagrined through a veil of cigarette smoke. "Miss Briscoe feels that you are the only person she would trust in the position."

"I'm honoured by the recommendation, Governor, but I have some concerns."

"There are a few perks. A raise. A private office. An expense account. Although I believe Miss Briscoe rarely used the latter."

"My reservations are more practical than personal. To date, all my clerical duties at the Bank have been very general in nature. I have no experience as a private secretary. And secondly, this 'special assignment work' I've been doing for the deputy governor over the past year: Who would take that over if I were to leave it? Mr. Meldrum believes it to be crucial to the war effort. Please understand. I'm for the Bank. I'm just not sure where I can be of best service to the Bank."

Graham Towers leaned back, reflecting. "I don't doubt your ability to serve as my secretary. Experience is helpful, Miss McFadden, but enterprise is essential. Based on your past performance, I'm confident that you would grow quickly into the role.

"Your second point is another issue. Miss Briscoe believes you can do anything, but clearly you can't do everything. There aren't enough hours in the day." He shook his head. "I've often seen this very problem in other organizations. Beleaguered secretaries so over-whelmed that office work grinds to a halt." He cleared his cigarette ash. "Since you framed the question so precisely, have you an opinion?"

"I have. You may not like it."

"Perhaps you shouldn't be too quick to judge my likes and dislikes, Miss McFadden." Graham Towers smiled. "Yet."

"Well, sir, the only solution I could come up with would be costly and disruptive."

"Wars, Miss McFadden, are disruptive. And our first duty when defending the nation is to expedition, not to expense." He gave a mock grimace. "Don't quote me on that. Well?"

"My thought is that you are not in need of a secretary, but a team of secretaries."

"A team?"

"Yes. A team of office assistants to cover the work that Miss Briscoe and I are currently doing and deal with all the new tasks wartime will surely bring us."

"How big a team?"

"I think five would do."

"Five?"

"You need a personal secretary. The secret internal Preparation-for-War Committee I've been working on now needs a full-time secretary, as does the Government Department Coordinating Committee. These names will likely change, but the responsibilities will continue and increase. Add in the new Foreign Exchange Control Board."

"That's four."

"Do you doubt that new challenges won't present themselves daily? And everything we do has to be thoroughly cross-referenced in a coordinated filing system. Filing sounds insignificant until you need to find something quickly. As well, we should have a contingency person to fill in when anyone is ill or double booked. Deputy Governor Meldrum told me that you two now have identical job descriptions. For backup. We need the same mutual support. Each of the five needs to learn the five jobs, so service never falters."

"It sounds a little redundant."

Frances smiled. "Is a deputy governor redundant?"

Governor Towers laughed. "Okay, Miss McFadden. I'll find the money. What do we call these people? Can't call them a team—sounds like a sports event."

"How about 'the Governor's secretariat'?"

Graham Towers lifted a dictionary from the bookshelf behind his desk. "Let's see. Sometimes the word 'secretariat' in government parlance refers to administrative officials." He read, "secretariat, *noun*: the officials or office entrusted with administrative duties, maintaining records, and overseeing or performing secretarial duties. A group or department of secretaries.' I guess no one would confuse your group with the Bank Executive Council. All right, then, but where do we house this secretariat?"

"In the lobby right outside your office door."

"Is there room?" He walked over to his office door and looked out. "Not much privacy." The hall was a lengthy, sky-lit passage over thirty feet wide stretching from the elevators to the boardroom at the front of the Bank. A dozen leather wing chairs and side tables huddled like sheep in small groupings.

"We can easily fit in five desks and still leave channels to your office and the boardroom. I'll park right in front of your door. If anyone needs privacy, we can use Miss Briscoe's office."

"I guess the space *is* underutilized," said the governor. "Still, we don't want a rabbit warren out here. I'm partial to Cuban mahogany for the furniture, but walnut would do in a pinch. Now, where do we get the new people?"

"May I recruit Bank staff?"

"Probably shouldn't tap Cricket Crabtree. Doug Marble is still growing into his job and needs her. I know you're friends with Mary O'Brien—sorry, Mrs. Bedford—in the library archives, but she's now married and might … have expectations … at any moment. Other than that, help yourself. Anyone in mind?"

"I've always liked Bridget Stanton, Mary's assistant. She's a little unpolished, but she's gritty and will walk through fire. The Carnation Girls who worked with me on your annual Christmas Tea were all go-getters. Claire Allen from the Securities Department would be my first choice. And a male perspective could be helpful—just to keep us from becoming giggling idiots. We might entice Brendan McGuire away from the catering department."

"Excellent choices. I do sometimes worry that we're a little insular," mused the governor. "What do you think about bringing in one person from outside the Bank? For perspective?"

"Good idea."

"Oh! Do you perchance own cats?"

"I do not. Is that a job requirement?"

The governor laughed again. "Miss Briscoe has two cats, Rosencrantz and Guildenstern. I do not fault her in any way professionally, but the care of these felines meant that she could never leave Ottawa on Bank business when I travelled. Miss Briscoe claimed that she was more valuable here, feeding the cats and guarding the office. But with a secretariat …"

"And no cats."

"And no cats, could you travel when duty calls?"

"Certainly. Back in the early days, when Dr. Grace was setting up the Bank archives, he took me to meetings in Toronto and Montreal, and I spent close to three weeks in Europe on the Polish gold issue."

"Good. I'll probably have to go to the United Kingdom this fall and I'd like you along. There will be detailed negotiations, and we'll need meticulous records."

"Negotiations about … ?"

"Financing the war effort. The British suffer from exaggerated expectations about how much Canada can contribute."

"Don't most Canadians believe it our duty to aid Britain?"

"They do. And we will, but there's a finite limit to our resources. We won't be any help to Britain if we bankrupt ourselves in the process."

"I helped type the new Foreign Exchange Control Board guidelines and supervised having them printed, but I must confess that I really didn't understand how the FECB contributes toward the war effort."

"Economic systems crave stability. Wars are disruptive. Cautious money can scurry to safe havens such as the United States. The production costs of the Canadian war effort will be enormous. To finance them, we need to prevent capital flight. That will be the main job of the FECB."

"Does that mean a factory that builds airplanes can't buy parts in the USA?"

"Not necessarily. We'd like manufacturers to make purchases in Canada where possible. Keeping the cash flow internal protects foreign exchange reserves. Jobs are created here that will generate tax revenue. But right now, Canada has absolutely no infrastructure for producing war materials. We desperately need to build planes, so if a fellow has to buy parts or tools outside the country, the FECB would approve the transaction."

"But if he wants to build bird cages …"

Graham Towers smiled. "You catch on quickly, Miss McFadden."

Frances nodded. "Back to travelling. Sometimes my presence was frowned upon when Dr. Grace took me along. He had to be very persuasive to get me in the door. Won't they be sticklers for protocol in England?"

"The United Kingdom desperately needs Canadian financial support to pay the war bills. They won't slap the hand that writes the cheque." He lit a cigarette. "So then, are you willing to become governor's secretary and major-domo of this fledgling secretariat? For better or for worse?"

"For richer or for poorer? I guess so."

"Wonderful!" He blew three perfect smoke rings in celebration. "Any other concerns?"

"Miss Briscoe warned me to beware of an all-consuming job, lest I be consumed. Two nights a week, I leave at six o'clock; and Saturday at one, I'm done for the weekend."

"Fine with me. I'm in at eight on the dot every morning and I leave at five-thirty sharp every evening. If Canadian monetary policy is under control after the stock markets close on Friday, I don't come in on Saturday. You'll know where I am, but I value my privacy."

"What if there's an emergency? Dr. Grace used the code 'Culloden File'—after the great Scottish disaster in 1746—to signal that some cataclysm demanded immediate attention."

"Use it often?"

"Only once."

He shrugged. "Let's try it."

Governor Towers stood up. "Thank you, Miss McFadden. I leave it to you and Miss Briscoe to work out the details of the transition. In the meantime, the war goes on."

3

INFLUENCE

September 18:

> *The chiefs'* [Canadian army, navy, air force chiefs of staff] *estimated costs for the first twelve months of the war would total $492 million. Governor Towers told the cabinet that he doubted we could contemplate an expenditure of over $250 million without materially affecting the credit of the country.*

(Bryce, 22–23)

September 28:

> *The last remnants of the Polish army defending Warsaw capitulate to the Germans.*

(Hastings, 19)

At the Metcalfe Street Bridge Club, tradition was under siege. "Isn't playing bridge a bit frivolous now that war has been declared?" asked Margery Davies, who had a colour portrait of George VI over her living room mantle.

For Betsey Knowles, the childless doyenne of the club, her card tables were her legacy. She was not the type of woman to let a world war erode her empire. "We've weathered both the Roaring Twenties and the Depression. We have a moral duty to continue." As the new currency controls would end her annual winter escape to Bermuda, Betsey felt she was sacrificing more than enough to the war effort.

"But shouldn't we be helping the Red Cross at the military canteens, or rolling bandages?" asked Sarah Dawes, who flirted with being a Quaker when it suited.

"We only play bridge twice a month. You ... we have time for both."

"Remember," added Nora Ray, worried that her relentless championing of German culture might call her patriotism into question, "It's the Nazi Party that is the enemy! Not Bach or Beethoven."

"I don't know why we're in this mess because of *Poland*," blinked Debra Semple. "What's Poland to us, or us to Poland?" Of the forty-five-year-old Semple twins, Debra and Clarissa, who always dressed identically, Debra was known as "the simpler Semple."

"Great Britain has a mutual defence treaty with Poland," explained Frances's friend and Balmoral neighbour, Anna Deloitte. She had lost her British husband in the Great War. "Poland was attacked, so Britain was honour-bound to help. Britain is the mother country, so Canada is obliged to assist." Playing the war-widow card purchased Anna latitude for a developing interest in a certain German tractor salesman.

"But Great Britain wasn't attacked."

"And has done precious little to help Poland in the meantime."

"I *beg* your pardon! Britain declared war on Germany!"

"How many Polish lives did that save?"

"It's all so convoluted!"

"I still don't understand," continued Debra. "Did the British government consult Canada before signing that treaty with Poland? I mean, if your mother lends a hundred dollars to a friend, and the friend loses the money, is it up to you to repay your mother?"

Audrey Beauchamp was by far the best bridge player in the club, and the only French-Canadian. Out of respect for her card-playing skill, no one corrected her when she said "two no-trumps" instead of "two no-trump." During war talk, she strategically said nothing.

"One spade!" snapped Betsey Knowles, closing debate on the digression.

"Although torn about abandoning ship in heavy seas, Miss McFadden, I am much consoled to know you will take over," said Miss Briscoe.

"I just hope that I'm equal to the task."

"Do not doubt yourself for a minute! Now, next Friday, the governor will announce my retirement. There will be no hoopla. I will give you my home phone number in case you have questions. But my operation takes place the week after I leave, and I'll be hospitalized for some time—if everything goes well. If things don't go well ... well, you'll be on your own."

Frances fumbled to change the topic. "What's your best advice, then?"

"Your first duty is to shield the governor from the legions who want to waste his time. Guardian at the gate. Your second priority is to follow up his big strokes with the finishing touches on every file. He has a brilliant overview of situations, but minutiae are not his long suit. Finally, you need to protect the governor from himself. I admire him more than any man on Earth, but he has his weaknesses. Do the best you can."

Miss Briscoe hesitated for a moment. "You know, of course, that Ottawa is a city where power is exercised. Power structures are pyramid-shaped, with the prime minister, or whomever, at the top. Always a man," she sighed. "The top dog can prevent change, but he can seldom make change happen on his own. Your job is to craft the details of execution. This is the influence I spoke of earlier. You help the governor organize his meetings and agendas. You prepare files for his viewing. You draft letters and memos for his signing."

"Where's the influence in that?"

"You control access. You don't always choose who gets an audience, but you schedule the sequence. You decide who sees the governor when he's in a generous mood, and who sees him when he isn't. You select which files and correspondence he sees first, and which he might not look at until next week. His day is filtered through your eyes."

Frances thought this sounded more like interference than influence, but she didn't interrupt.

Miss Briscoe continued philosophically. "Remember, progress is rarely gained by thunderbolts. Enduring change is achieved by small, subtle increments. Like a kitten's growth." She nodded her head in silent emphasis.

"Now, I arrive at 7:30 every morning to prepare for the day. I set a pot of coffee on to perk so it's ready when the governor arrives at eight. He takes milk but no sugar. Two cups. Help yourself to the rest. At 8:20, we meet for ten minutes on the day's schedule and any items on the near horizon.

"The governor prefers holding meetings in his office so as to not waste travel time, but will accommodate the minister of Finance or the prime minister if necessary. His day is tightly scheduled. Five minutes before a meeting is to end, I buzz his desk to shoehorn out the stragglers. At noon he takes lunch in the executive dining room, often with other senior staff. His appointment book is clear between twelve and one-thirty."

"He takes a long lunch?"

"No. He eats in thirty minutes and then has an afternoon nap in the bedroom off his office. Only the deputy governor and I know this. He brooks no disturbance during that period except from the two of us. Not from the prime minister or the governor of the Bank of England. If the building were on fire, I'd wake him, but otherwise I let him be. When robbed of that nap, he's less focused in the afternoon.

"Oh. Sometimes the governor will put a question to me about economics or politics, knowing that I understand little of either. He's just curious what an average person might think about some abstraction he's dealing with. The experts, he's fond of saying, often 'focus on the freckle and miss the frown.' I just give an honest answer. I suggest you do the same if the occasion arises.

"The governor is tremendously efficient. He rarely takes work home from the office. His wife looks after his social life. Mrs. Towers is …" a rueful smile. "Well, I'd best let you form your own opinion. I usually stay until seven to tend to details and prepare for the next day. On Tuesdays and Fridays, I leave when the governor does."

Frances smiled. "You have time for a private life?"

Miss Briscoe looked over her glasses at Frances. "If that's what you'd call the United Church Women's Mission Committee or meetings of the Imperial Order of the Daughters of the Empire." She sat back. "Do you have a private life, Miss McFadden?"

"I play bridge every second Tuesday, and attend Knox Presbyterian Church Sunday morning."

"No romantic interest?"

Frances blushed. "Well, just recently I've been seeing a young engineer from the Department of Agriculture. We usually take in a movie Saturday night."

"Is it a serious relationship?"

"He's a very nice man, but it's too early to tell."

"I only ask, Miss McFadden, because I did not find it possible to be the personal secretary to the second most important man in Canada," she repeated for emphasis, "and have time for any … emotional distractions."

Those cats don't count?

It did prod a thought. "Who assists the prime minister?"

"Ah!" snorted Miss Briscoe. "Dear Mr. Heeney. I certainly won't miss dealing with *him*."

"Oh?"

Miss Briscoe sighed. "I know it's unchristian to be critical. 'Judge not,' etcetera. Mr. Heeney is a Rhodes Scholar, so can't be stupid, but I found him impertinent and condescending. He would call up and say, 'The prime minister wishes to see Governor Towers this afternoon at two. Please inform him.' Then hang up. No, 'Is the governor available?' Just a summons to the Star Chamber. I appreciate that Prime Minister King is a busy man, but so is the governor. I don't know how many times I had to cancel other meetings and reschedule appointments to suit the whims of dear Mr. Heeney." Miss Briscoe's lips pursed. "I grew to despair at the sound of his voice. Slimy, like a snake oil salesman."

"What was he like in person?"

"Oh, I never actually met the man. I saw him at meetings, hovering behind Mr. King like the Holy Ghost. He does not reflect well on the prime minister at all. And *I'm* a Liberal." The fury died down in Miss Briscoe's dark eyes and she shrugged her shoulders. "They say 'a new broom sweeps clean.' Good luck."

Frances reflected. "If you were starting over, would you do anything differently?"

"I would have taken more holidays. I have hundreds of days banked." She snorted. "A lot of good they are now. And there's over a thousand dollars in my expense account. I might have indulged myself. I'll sign that over to you next Friday. I focused on serving the governor to the exclusion of all other things. I remember your invitation to represent the Bank with those secretaries of the senior government deputy ministers. I might have learned how Ottawa worked a little better had I taken that up."

"Why didn't you?"

"I have no patience for prattle. I felt if you attended, you would keep Mr. Meldrum apprised of news from government departments. Nor did I reach out to other Bank staff. When Sir Nigel Holmes was deputy governor, his secretary was a man, and British, and quite full of himself. Nothing to be gained there. Mr. Meldrum's secretary, Mrs. Hewitt, was, well … words fail me, but we were not cut of the same cloth at all. So, I stayed aloof from the fray and shielded the governor's door."

"Yesterday you mentioned 'his weaknesses'"?

Miss Briscoe's mouth twitched. "You are young, Miss McFadden. Are you familiar with the appetites of men?"

"I know that Dr. Grace and Deputy Governor Meldrum share a tremendous appreciation for single malt Scotch during working hours."

"You disapprove?"

"I come from a teetotal Presbyterian home. Liquor was the devil's toxin. I was shocked at first, but imbibing never seemed to impair their performance. Does the governor drink?"

"Never during working hours. No, he has other appetites that the United Church Women would take exception to. However, they don't render the service to the country that Governor Towers does, so they don't need to know. It is not my place to censure. He was always loyal and forgiving. I returned the favour."

Miss Briscoe looked exhausted and left it at that.

4

MADDIE HALL

The war threatened to destabilize international trade and Canadian prosperity. The prospect of military blockades, trade restrictions, and currency controls worried nations like Canada that relied on imports of capital and technology and exports of natural products and other goods.

(Bryce, 30)

Dr. Wilbur Grace, who worked for the Department of Finance, had been Frances's first boss. He was wise and witty, and she had blossomed under his mentorship. They no longer worked together, but she enjoyed his company and still often sought his counsel. He usually wore his tallness with casual dignity, but today Dr. Grace sat stooped over as if the high-ceilinged Rideau Club dining room weighed him down. "The mythic grandeur of war is quite deceitful," he said, as he flushed soda over the ice in his double Macallan. "As though wars were all about noble causes achieved through valour in triumphant battles."

"They're not?"

"No. They're all about money. Whoever has the most wins. Did you ever read Cicero's *Philippics*?"

"Nope. For some reason Roman philosophers were not featured in the High School of Commerce curriculum."

"Well, the old boy hit the nail on the head way back when. 'Endless money forms the sinews of war,' he wrote."

"Would the Canadian General Staff agree?"

"Not likely." He inhaled commodiously of the Scotch. "That doesn't change the truth."

"Is the Finance Department out robbing piggy banks so we can throw back the Nazi aggressors?"

He sighed. "Must we dwell on it? It seems I spend every waking moment scrounging for clever ways to pay for barracks and uniforms and airplanes."

"Well then Doctor, I have another topic for you, but it is tippy-top secret. Can you be trusted?"

Dr. Grace threw her his mock squint-eyed stare. "You didn't finagle an invitation to the Rideau Club just to chat about the war? *Quelle surprise.*"

"You are only the fourth person on earth to hear this, and it has to stay that way for another seven days. Agreed?"

"When I hired you back in 1934 to run the start-up office for the Bank of Canada, we agreed that 'off the record' means the same as 'never happened.' That still stands with me."

"It's good to know that the war hasn't altered everything."

"So?"

"I'm changing jobs," Frances said coyly.

"Abandon the Bank of Canada? The love of your life? Has Mackenzie King offered you a seat in the cabinet?"

"No, silly, I'm not leaving the Bank. The governor has asked me to become his private secretary."

Dr. Grace raised his Scotch in silent salutation, then drained the Macallan in Frances's honour. "What happened to the dour Miss Briscoe? Did she turn out to be an enemy agent? I always thought she had a shifty look."

"Goodness, you have a vivid imagination for someone raised in Rosedale. No again. Miss Briscoe has some unfortunate health issues and is taking early retirement. Not very early—she'll be sixty-five in the spring."

"And you're stepping up to the plate?"

"I am, and I need your advice."

"Didn't Miss Briscoe give you any?"

"She did. She fears my youthful impetuous nature," Frances smiled, "and cautions an incremental approach."

"I think you should hold out for all that overtime pay the Bank owes you. Are you still tracking it like I told you?"

"A pointless exercise, Doctor, although I have continued it for the accounting practice. After five years, the Bank of Canada, in theory, owes me $10,120 for 6,543 hours of overtime at time-and-a-half, plus 3 per cent on the unpaid balance. Which is, of course, the total balance."

"Good Lord! We won't be able to finance the war if you insist on a payout."

"Two chances of that—fat and slim. Anyway, I'm setting up a small secretariat of five people in the Governor's office."

"Five people! From one? You call that 'incremental'?"

"Miss Briscoe neglected to advise Herr Hitler on the value of the incremental approach. In the Bank's response to his war, we need a small army in the governor's office. The workload is now quite beyond the capacity of one person."

"Even the Herculean Frances McFadden?"

"Frances McFadden knows nothing better than her own limitations. Thanks particularly to you for regularly pointing them out. The governor has suggested that I bring in at least one person from outside the Bank. A fresh perspective. Are there any bright lights in the Department of Finance? Besides you, of course."

"A wide range of wattage exists at Finance. I would be disloyal if I allowed you to steal the best, and it would betray our friendship if I saddled you with a dim bulb."

"That's not much help. The governor is quite keen on Bank staff, but fears we're a bit incestuous."

"Ah!" Dr. Grace pensively swirled the ice in his empty glass. "Incest, metaphorically speaking, brings to mind my young cousin, Madeline Hall. She graduated from the University of Toronto in the spring. A real firecracker. Ran a camp in Muskoka all summer almost single-handedly. Was engaged to be married in the fall but it fell through. She needs a distraction. The Bank of Canada might be a good fit."

Frances' eyes narrowed. "The Bank of Canada's charter does not extend to therapy for the lovelorn. I don't do marriage counselling, lacking expertise in the area."

"Why not reserve judgment, Miss McFadden, until you've met her? She's coming up to Ottawa on Saturday for a little repose. I could set up a meeting."

At noon on Saturday, Raymond guided Frances through the linen archipelago in the Chateau Laurier's Canadian Grill to Dr. Grace's table by the window overlooking the Ottawa River. Sitting across from him was a pert young woman sporting a ponytail. A splashy cocktail with floating fruit and a tiny umbrella sat untouched in front of her. Dr. Grace performed introductions, embellishing both their biographies. Miss Hall was a pretty, slight, blonde with dark circles under youthful eyes. She looked drained, like a dancer in a four-day marathon.

"Miss McFadden needs to hire staff and Madeline is currently unemployed. This double coincidence of wants encouraged me to bring you together. Now, as the war is no respecter of weekends, I only have time for a quick lunch. Let's dine and I'll leave you two to discuss details."

Madeline Hall had an erect posture and very good table manners. She took tiny forkfuls so her mouth was never full when she had to answer a question. Both women relaxed under Dr. Grace's teasing wit. He signed for the cheque and left them to coffee and dessert.

"I know this meeting was not your idea, Miss Hall. Please do not feel compelled to be interested out of duty to your cousin. Dr. Grace is a sweet man, but he is a bachelor, and the preferences of women are often lost on him."

A toothy grin shot across the table. "Please call me Maddie, Miss McFadden. Quite honestly, I did not come to Ottawa looking for a job. I just had to get out of Toronto for a while to clear my head."

"Some grief?"

A sigh. "Short-sightedness more than anything. But it has left me a bit … well, unfocused, as I consider the future."

"Let me outline the position we have. The Bank of Canada's responsibilities have grown enormously in recent weeks. The war requires massive funding while the country is still climbing out of the Depression. We are reorganizing day-to-day, trying to financially cope with the appetite of a growing military. I have been asked to set up a new secretariat in Governor Towers's office to support his added responsibilities. There will be five of us to begin with. The others are internal appointments, but the Governor suggested that an outside perspective might provide balance. I need someone who is very flexible and resourceful in addition to having top-notch secretarial skills."

"My father thought it was a complete waste of money sending a girl to university. He willingly supported my two brothers, but insisted that I take night courses in typing and shorthand so I could get a job if I dropped out. I resented this at the time, but both skills were very useful in college."

"Grigg or Pitman?"

"Pitman."

"Typing speed?"

"Eighty words a minute."

"Spelling?"

"Always an A."

"Your degree was in?"

"English and French."

"Bilingual?"

"I read and write French better than I speak it. Not much occasion to practise French on the streets of Toronto."

"Work experience?"

"I worked at Eaton's on weekends during university. My father, who is not poor, is not indulgent. He offered to match anything I saved toward my university education. He assumed I would fritter my wages away on clothes and ice cream sodas. I surprised him. To his credit, he lived up to his bargain in spite of his attitude toward educating women."

"And in the summers?"

"Since the age of nine, I have attended Camp Cairnaway in Muskoka. I love the outdoors. Canoeing, sailing, swimming. The crackling fire at close of day. When I was sixteen, I took junior counsellor training and have moved up the staff hierarchy ever since. I was hired as deputy camp director this past summer, which included staffing interviews, supply contracts, and program planning. The week before camp started, the camp director, Betty Eligh, who had run the place for thirty years, was in a serious traffic accident in Toronto. She survived, but was in traction and plaster casts all the hot sticky summer. I essentially ran the camp of four hundred campers and fifty staff myself."

"Quite the challenge."

"Well, a timely distraction." She paused. "I'll spare you the details. I'm surprised Willie hasn't told you. Simply put, I was engaged to be married Labour Day Weekend. Then, I wasn't engaged anymore."

There was a moment of reflection, while coffee cups clicked on porcelain saucers. "It was my decision. I wasn't jilted."

"No chemistry?"

"Oh," she laughed, "Derek and I had the chemistry. We just didn't have the physics. No shared principles, I realized almost too late. Derek was childlike—an endearing feature in children—but not what you want to marry. He really didn't value anything beyond money and having fun.

"Losing the approbation of family and friends was painful. Fortunately, I had canoe trips to plan, and a drunken cook to replace, and bats in the craft cabin, so I was successfully diverted. However, I had not planned a future beyond Labour Day. We were supposed to go on a European honeymoon, then move to Vancouver so Derek could take up a management position in his father's company. I have a hope chest full of linens, crystal, and silver plate and nowhere to use them." Maddie Hall rubbed her forehead and looked down.

Frances finished her apple pie and rested her fork. "Does Bank of Canada work interest you?"

"Frankly, Miss McFadden, any work that I could pour myself into would interest me. The more significant question, I suppose is, 'Would the Bank of Canada be interested in me?'"

Frances smiled. "Well, Maddie Hall, I like the cut of your jib. Dr. Grace has never given me bad advice in the five years that I've known him. He is not one to hurl blandishments of praise about lightly, and he speaks highly of you. I'll have to test your shorthand and typing skills, but if you're willing to suffer those indignities, I'll hire you for a three-month trial. A good fit would lead to a permanent contract."

Madeline hesitated. "Excuse my impertinence, Miss McFadden, but you must be younger than I am. How is it that you hire for the Bank of Canada? Isn't there a personnel department? Forms to be filled out in triplicate?"

Frances laughed. "The pace of the war leaves no time for such formalities. So I'm in charge of this little bailiwick. Here's my card. Think it over. Call me on Monday with your decision. If you pass the typing and shorthand test, you'll start work in a week. Fair enough?"

"Fair enough," agreed Madeline Hall, raising her coffee cup to toast the deal.

5

LOVE AND BEETS

Neither the Canadian foreign service of External Affairs nor the military services of National Defence were organized or staffed to act without relying on the British services for information, contacts, leadership and equipment.

(Bryce, 12)

The word "love" did not figure prominently in Frances McFadden's formative years. Her Victorian-era parents' use of vocabulary was starched and corseted. The senior McFaddens were given to neither verbal nor physical exuberance. Although cared for and provided with the necessities, Frances had never been told by either parent that she was loved. That label was reserved for inanimate objects: "Don't you love the view?" "I just love Clara's blueberry cobbler!"

Frances loved … well valued deeply, her friendships with Mary O'Brien (now Mary Bedford) and the crazy Deavy sisters, Dorothy and Katie (now Katie Warren). Chums since Grade 2, they had played doctor together under the Deavys' front porch, acting out the heroic roles of nursing sisters at the Ypres Number One Casualty Clearing Station. The Matthews twins, Harvey and Harry, bribed with candy, played injured officers. Hospital protocol required they be stripped naked and closely examined for wounds. They were model identical patients, except that one was turgid, the other flaccid. The licorice jujubes prescribed for their wounds distracted both boys from any embarrassment. The nursing sisters concluded that no amputations were necessary.

Neighbourhood youths flashed dirty postcards at them, rifled from the sock drawers of older brothers. The quick-witted Deavy sisters shared a natural gift for neutralizing hooligans.

Larry Brewster: "Hey, Deavy. How much for a piece of ass?"

Dorothy: "Once you've learned to count past ten without taking your socks off, Brewster, we can negotiate."

Jake Dineen dramatically holding his head: "Ow! I called Katie Deavy a two-bit whore and she socked me in the face with a bag of quarters!"

Katie: "Jakie, it's almost two o'clock. Won't your mother want you home for your nap?"

Billy Nesbit dropping his drawers: "Take a gander at this whopper, Deavy."

Dorothy: "Gosh, Billy! It looks just like a penis, only smaller."

The friends had giggled their way to school together thousands of times, sharing intimacies and infatuations. When their stick figures rounded into adolescence, Mary O'Brien filled out like sand in an hourglass. Boys began calling her "Tits" O'Brien, partly to taunt, mostly in awe. Mary, from a strong Catholic upbringing, wretchedly hid her shame in loose clothing.

Dorothy lived with her parents on Bell Street and taught Grade 3 at Connaught Public School. Newlyweds Katie and Kevin Warren both worked at the D. Kemp Edwards Lumber Yard in Mechanicsville. Mary O'Brien, the Bank archivist, met her husband in the Bank cafeteria and had just become Mrs. Nathan Bedford.

Frances loved (valued deeply) her job at the fresh, young Bank of Canada. The electric excitement of a fall fair throbbed through the place daily, forging a collegiality that she had never experienced at home or at school. What a joy to be on the crest of all the newness! It was the ecstasy and terror of tobogganing down a dark hill on a winter's night.

Of course she loved her rambling three-bedroom apartment on the top floor of the Balmoral Arms. Skylights and large, leaded windows flooded sunlight into every nook. Mitzie Gibson, a lumber heiress with money to burn, had furnished it in a lavish art deco style. Miss Gibson abandoned it all (along with thousands in unpaid bills) to marry into European aristocracy. The apartment was a foundling, and Frances found it. She took shelter in the quiet patina of the woodwork and the deep-cushion comfort of the furniture.

She'd never seen anything like the bathroom. It was designed for the use of two people at once! Twin sinks spaced on a marble counter. A Louis Quinze chair where company could relax and chat with a bather. In her childhood home on Rochester Street, the bathroom was a cramped, dark space ashamed of its functionality. A narrow, pebbled-glass window guarded modesty in a blurred light. There had been a thundering toilet, and taps that squeaked reluctant threads of water into a rust-stained sink. Her Presbyterian mother had maintained that more than four inches of bath water was criminally lascivious.

In 7 South West, an immense stand-alone tub commanded the bay window from which vantage a bather could spy on street traffic while submerged to the shoulders. You could shampoo an elephant in the shower area, an ellipse more than a dozen feet across and nearly as deep. Twin showerheads as big as platters dropped a gentle rain in front of a birch grove mosaic that covered the curved back wall. Sunlight poured through a skylight, bathing a bather twice.

An alcove contained a mahogany-seated toilet and a companion bidet. Bidets were new to Frances. When she had given Dr. Grace and Dr. Skelton an apartment tour before signing the lease, Dr. Grace had marvelled at it: "Ah! How civilized! When I was doing post-doc work at La Sorbonne, my apartment had a bidet. I used it to chill my wine." Frances had to check the dictionary to ascertain its other functions.

In three directions, her apartment windows were four floors above the nearest buildings, guaranteeing privacy. Her kitchen and den windows could be viewed from 7 North West across the Balmoral courtyard, but these windows had gauze half-curtains that hid everything below her chin. On Rochester Street, Frances had journeyed to the bathroom either fully clothed, or in her flannel dressing gown. The liberation of living alone! One Sunday, she absently ate a post-shower lunch completely naked, only noticing her state when she swept a hand down to brush off some breadcrumbs.

Frances had limited experience with the opposite sex—most of it embarrassing. Geordie Hilton. Student council president. Handsome, polite, well groomed. Bought her Cokes after Presbyterian Young Peoples' Meetings and solicitously walked her home. He clearly wanted *her* to be *his* girlfriend. Other girls would have killed for a knowing wink from Geordie Hilton. However, for Frances, proximity stirred no spark.

Buddy Drury, the grocery boy at the corner store. Raw, uneducated, uncouth. High cheekbones and deep-set eyes. Wore a green pack of Export A's tucked into the upturned sleeve of his T-shirt. Greased his dark hair into a ducktail like a hoodlum in training. Walked with a tight-bum swagger. Far too presumptuous with his comments and his hands. Somehow he ignited a wild, confusing rush that surged through Frances in shameful ways, especially in dreams where she imagined the unimaginable. She had never confessed this frailty to anyone, most particularly Buddy Drury.

And now Paul Roderick, an engineer with the Department of Agriculture. A farm boy with an aw-shucks grin and intelligent eyes. They'd met in Poland in August. He was there to close a deal for a hundred thousand dollars' worth of Krupp tractor parts. She was there to help Scotty Meldrum sneak the Polish gold reserves out to safe haven in the Bank of Canada vaults before the Nazis invaded. Gold heists can be bonding experiences. She liked him. Did she love him? Frances's upbringing left her bereft of the vocabulary to clearly categorize her emotions.

Safely back in Ottawa, Paul invited Frances out to see *The Wizard of Oz* at the Capitol Theatre. She accepted. Movies became a regular Saturday night routine. He'd meet her in the lobby of the Balmoral Arms. They'd walk to the Imperial or the Regent or the Rialto for a double feature, followed by a hot dog at the Honeydew or a toasted western at the Tic Toc Café. Then he'd escort her back down Metcalfe Street to her apartment building. On the second date he kissed her on the check. On the third date, he kissed her on the lips. Gently. On the fourth date she held his arm as they walked downtown, and their hands colluded in the dark of the movie theatre.

On the fifth date, after a lengthy snuggle in the Balmoral lobby, she said, "I'd like to invite you up to my apartment, but I don't know if it would be appropriate."

"I can wait until you're sure it's appropriate," he smiled. "I promise to be on my best behaviour."

Respect. Frances liked the respect.

"Maybe I don't want your best behaviour."

So bold!

Frances phoned Paul at work. "Want to celebrate with me this Saturday?"

"What's up?"

"Can't tell you until Saturday, but I think it justifies dinner at my apartment. There's just one problem."

"You can't find a chaperone?"

"No, silly. I can't cook."

"Not at all?"

"I can scramble an egg. I can open a can of soup. I can make toast. A limited repertoire for a special occasion." Frances's mother had used cooking as a private therapy to work off her anxieties, and had not welcomed her daughters in the kitchen except as dishwashers.

Frances really didn't need to cook. She always ate a hot meal at noon in the Bank cafeteria—quality fare generously subsidized.

"Then I'll cook. If you can scratch together some cheese and crackers I'll look after the rest."

"You can cook?"

"You'd be surprised what talents farm boys from Ilderton have at their command. Do you have a stove and a frying pan?"

"Yes. And a fridge to boot."

"We're in business. Oh. Is there food you don't like?"

"Only beets."

"What's wrong with beets?"

"My mother used to buy bushels of them on sale every fall. We ate them three times a week for five months. Disgusting little vegetable."

"How about pickled beets?"

"Rotten beets disguised with vinegar? No thanks. I've had enough beets for three lifetimes. But I'll eat anything else."

6

CHANGING THE GUARD

Prime Minister Mackenzie King's position was that Canada should not exceed its resources [in funding the war]. *King did not want to repeat the experience of World War I when the government ran up huge deficits to cover the cost of the war, leading to post-war instability and dislocation.*

(Bryce, 41)

On Friday morning, October 6, Governor Towers, Deputy Governor Meldrum, and Associate Deputy Governor Soulière met with Mackenzie King's war committee in the East Block. The prime minister wanted to know how to beg or borrow enough money to fund the war. Miss Briscoe took notes, and Frances managed the confidential files. The discussion ranged over taxation issues and war bond possibilities but was inconclusive.

At noon, Graham Towers escorted the Bank people to a private dining room at the Chateau Laurier. After cocktails were served, the governor stood and spoke.

"I have been honoured to work in tandem with Elizabeth Briscoe for twenty years. She took me under her wing at the Royal Bank head office in Montreal, and mercifully agreed to follow me to the Bank of Canada in 1934. Out of respect for her modesty, I will not detail the contributions she has made to my work over those years. A private secretary likely knows a man better than the man himself. Through all this, Elizabeth was the soul of discretion, worked like a Trojan, and somehow kept me in harness.

"Two weeks ago, she handed in her notice, announcing that she would be retiring today. I don't think I'm betraying confidences to say that only pressing health concerns have forced this decision. I know she feels bad leaving the Bank at this critical time. She has typed a memo to be distributed this afternoon announcing that effective at

5:00 p.m. today she would be retiring and that the position of governor's secretary would be assumed by Frances McFadden. I would like to thank Miss Briscoe for her unflinching support and present her with a small token of the Bank's esteem for services rendered."

To warm applause, the governor pulled a blue Birks box from his briefcase. Miss Briscoe wordlessly opened the gift to reveal a double pen set flanking a sterling silver model of the Bank of Canada. Her name and dates of service were engraved on the walnut base.

The stoic Miss Briscoe blinked away tears as she unsteadily stood up. "Governor, gentlemen, Miss McFadden, I feel deeply honoured. I did not work at the Bank with any thought of reward other than the satisfaction of service well done. I know that's true of you all. I would not leave you at this distressing time, except that to stay would be a betrayal. My doctors have me scheduled for surgery next week to be followed by a lengthy convalescence. The single solace in my departure is that I was able to convince Miss McFadden to take over my desk at the governor's side. It has been a privilege to work with all of you in forging the highest standards of central banking. The Bible admonishes that 'Pride goeth before a fall,' but I was proud to be part of it." She picked up her gin and tonic. "Governor, Gentlemen, Miss McFadden, I give you the Bank of Canada."

Everyone rose and echoed, "The Bank of Canada!"

Then the governor said, "I give you Miss Briscoe," and a chorus replied.

The lunch was convivial. Even M. Soulière, who was mute as a tomb at meetings, was solicitous to the honouree. It was Miss Briscoe whispering something about afternoon appointments that forced an end to the revelry at 1:30. She and the governor returned to the Bank by taxi. Frances took the ten-minute walk up Wellington Street with Scotty Meldrum.

"Well, lass," said the deputy governor in his broad Scottish brogue, "the heartiest of congratulations. The governor told me about your secretariat idea. Excellent concept."

"Thank you, Mr. Meldrum. Now I need to bend your ear on another topic. My good friend Anna Deloitte has been getting mail from all across Canada."

"How nice for her. Will this help us finance the war?"

"The mail is from Max Kessler."

"Aha!" he said with his tongue stuck thoughtfully in his left cheek. "Well, we know you threw him off a train in northern Poland, so it's unlikely ..."

"I did *not* throw anyone off a train! The train lurched in a tunnel. I stumbled and bumped something, and when we emerged into daylight he was gone."

"Fishing, perhaps?"

"Stop it! It is unmannerly to suggest I killed the man. What is more, it's beside the point."

"And the point … ?"

"Anna Deloitte is getting postcards from Toronto and Sudbury and Winnipeg that say things like, 'Having a wonderful time, wish you were here.'"

"Not very original. Or very romantic."

"Not bad for a dead man. There may have been steamier stuff, but she didn't share those with me."

"Did you recognize his handwriting?"

"No, but Anna would. They must be authentic."

Scotty lit a cigar and inhaled deeply. "Herr Kessler did his homework. Wrote these little missives before he sailed for Europe. Somebody accompanying the Krupp farm implement display to all the fall fairs out west must have laid the false trail. Postcards travel delightfully slowly as third class mail. They take weeks to arrive back in Ottawa."

"Krupp wouldn't want their goods impounded once war was declared, would they?"

"Certainly not. There will be a final postcard from somewhere like Fargo, North Dakota, stating that Herr Kessler has moved to neutral territory to avoid incarceration as an enemy alien and warning that contact might be disrupted for a while."

"Perhaps for an eternity," said Frances with chagrin.

Scotty Meldrum roared with laughter.

Miss Briscoe's retirement memo went out at 3:00 p.m. and Frances immediately began recruitment. Brendan Maguire looked a little harried when she cornered him in the boardroom kitchen. "Do you have time for a private word?" she asked.

"I'm up to my elbows in cucumber sandwich trays and a rebellious coffee urn. Later, perhaps?"

"Say, 4:30 in my office?"

Brendan smiled his antic smile and nodded.

Bridget Stanton liked her work in the library archives with Mary Bedford and Mr. Mueller. "It's so peaceful up there compared to my home. Mary and Mr. Mueller rarely scream or throw dishes. They're considerate and easy to work with. Not that you weren't," Bridget added hastily.

"I'm glad you think so, Bridget, because I want you back with me in the new governor's secretariat."

"Holy cow," Bridget said with genuine surprise. "I'm kind of rough-edged for the executive suite, don'tcha think?"

"You're an excellent worker grounded in solid common sense."

"Don't you have the choice of the whole Bank staff?"

"I do. I chose Bridget Stanton. What do you say?"

Tough, street-wise Bridget Stanton had to bite her lip. "Oh, Miss!" was all she managed.

Claire Allen in the Securities Division was one of the original Carnation Girls who had helped organize the governor's staff Christmas tea since 1935. Frances went downstairs and knocked on the open door of George Pike's office. The head of Securities was a rumpled scarecrow with a high forehead and mischievous eyes.

"Mr. Pike, may I have a moment?"

"Of course, Miss McFadden, please come in. Congratulations on your promotion."

"Thank you," said Frances, walking in and closing the door behind her.

George Pike gave a mock grimace and whispered, "A closed-door conference with the governor's secretary? Am I being fired?"

Frances laughed. "Things are on the move on the fourth floor, but the governor and I have decided to keep you where you are for the duration of the war."

"Is that a blessing or a curse?" he said while loading his pipe. "What's up?"

"The governor's secretarial work has grown tremendously since the outbreak of war. He needs a small army up there. I'd like permission to poach Claire Allen from your department."

George Pike exhaled a cloud of smoke before replying. "It's the governor's bank. He could poach whomever he pleased."

"He could. We both know he wouldn't."

"Miss Allen is smart as a whip. I can see why you'd want her. What do I get in exchange?"

"Your choice of replacements. The envy of the other department heads at having your protégé elevated. And Claire as your personal mole in the governor's office. What a deal!"

"You have a wonderful way, Miss McFadden, of taxing people so subtly that they think they're being done a favour. Very well. Go speak to Miss Allen. If you can convince her that the fourth floor throne room is more attractive than being holed up down here with the bean counters, she's yours."

Claire Allen, who was quite the athlete, checked that they were alone before turning a very revealing cartwheel in the hall corridor.

Brendan showed up at 4:40. "Sorry," he said. "They stayed late and left a mess. Oh, and congratulations." He extended his hand with a conspiratorial smile.

Brendan had a secret hold over Frances going way back to the early days when they shared catering responsibilities at the Bank. He had come to clean up a lunch one day when he found Frances wrapping a sandwich in a napkin to take home for a cold dinner.

"Purloining Bank of Canada assets, are we then, Miss McFadden?" he had said with raised eyebrows.

Frances felt guilty for about half a second. "Well, Brendan, it seems to me that any use the Bank might have had for these stale sandwiches has now passed, and I was just helping you clear the debris. Wouldn't you be throwing it out anyway?"

"A few stale crusts I'd chuck in the garbage. If the leftovers are substantial, I box them up and send them over to the Union Mission or the Sally Ann soup kitchen. But I suppose the charity of the Bank could extend to its foremost employee."

"It would be corrupt to pilfer Bank property, Brendan, and I don't wish to take food out of the mouths of Ottawa's needy. I shall desist. Thank you for the edifying lesson in professional ethics."

From that day on, Frances stayed away from the detritus of abandoned sandwich trays. From that day on, a brown paper bag with F. MCFADDEN printed in block letters appeared every afternoon in the staff refrigerator. Inside, carefully wrapped in waxed paper, were fresh sandwiches and several cookies.

Magnanimity is an underappreciated virtue.

"So?" he inquired.

"You've been in charge of catering for over three years. Would a change of venue interest you?"

"You don't think I do a good job?"

"*Au contraire.* You have an excellent command of detail, can deal with multiple challenges at the same time, and always stay under budget. All admirable traits. There's a new position opening in the governor's office, and I was wondering if you'd be interested."

"But you're the new governor's secretary, right?"

"Yes, and without the word of a lie, there's enough work up there for five people. The other four will be women. Can you handle four women at once?"

A double entendre tempted Brendan. He let it pass behind a smile that betrayed his thoughts. "Who?"

"This is hush-hush until a memo goes out from the governor on Monday, but Bridget Stanton has agreed to come up along with one of the Carnation Girls."

"Which one?"

"Does it matter?"

"I've squired a few Carnation Girls out to the movies. They're great fun after hours, but working beside one all day is a different situation."

"Well, well, Mr. McGuire, I didn't realize you were such a social butterfly."

"You're not exactly a recluse yourself, Miss. Two weeks ago I saw you feeding popcorn to a young man at the back of the Somerset Theatre when you might have been watching John Wayne in *Stagecoach*."

"I'll add discretion to your resumé of outstanding traits, Brendan. Have you ever dated Claire Allen?"

"No."

"Don't you like her?"

"I do. She's too smart for me."

"A good attribute in a professional colleague, *n'est-ce pas*?"

"*Oui*. Who's number five?"

"An outsider. Woman from Toronto named Madeline Hall. You'd like her."

"To work with or take to the movies?"

"Let's start with a working relationship. If a torrid affair develops, you can move back to catering."

"So what does this five-some do for the governor?"

Frances held her hands out wide. "Everything that needs to be done. Grease the cogs. Track the details. Keep the shop running tickety-boo. Intense, but could be fun. Want to join?"

"This is all a bit sudden. Can I think it over?"

"Do you have reservations?"

"No. You've just caught me by surprise." His mischievous smile again. "Who would pack those mystery lunches for you?"

"There's a war on, Brendan. We all have to make sacrifices."

7

SEVEN SOUTH WEST

Quebec Premier Maurice Duplessis called a provincial election for October 25. He cited proclamations made under the War Measures Act as a federal invasion of provincial rights encroaching on the freedoms of Quebecers.

(Nolan, 22–23)

"It is a diabolical act on Duplessis' part to have made the issue Provincial autonomy verses Dominion Government." [Mackenzie King diary] *Mackenzie King realized that systematic opposition from a provincial government in Quebec with a fresh mandate from the people would frustrate the effective prosecution of the war.*

(Pickersgill, 35)

Home from work, Frances came through the front door of the Balmoral Arms, hesitated in front of the elevator, then walked down the corridor off the lobby to knock on Miss Gilhooly's door. Her former typing teacher beamed on hearing her news.

"I'm just surprised the Bank took so long to recognize your talent, dear," she said, pouring cups of Earl Grey into her best bone china. "You are *la crème de la crème*." At the High School of Commerce, Miss Gilhooly, aloof and imperious, controlled her students with an iron hand. Outside the classroom, Frances discovered her to be warm and effusive. They lunched together on the last Saturday of each month at Murphy-Gamble's Department Store, and crossed paths every second Tuesday at bridge club.

"You are too kind, Gladys. It seems quite a leap from obscurity into the limelight."

"Come, now. Did this Miss Briscoe prance on centre stage?"

"No. She much preferred the shadows."

"Well, you could be the same if you chose, although I would say it's not your style."

"I have style?"

"Frances! You need to step back occasionally and look at your own accomplishments."

"Right. I dropped out of Grade 11."

"Mr. Forestall practically railroaded you out of school into the job at the Bank. He wanted an inside agent to scavenge future positions for High School of Commerce girls. I thought it most unprincipled for a principal."

"It worked. There must be thirty Commerce grads down at the Bank now."

"The man had more brains than I gave him credit for. And you've performed extraordinarily well for a dropout." She chuckled. "Maybe we should toss more students out the door in Grade 11. Seems to breed success."

The Balmoral Arms elevator was elegantly trimmed in brass fittings. It was self-operating, the first such device Frances had ever used. One simply pushed a numbered button, the elevator door slid closed and the car trundled silently to the desired floor. Like magic.

Only three other apartments shared the top floor. Betsey Knowles, mistress of the Metcalfe Street Bridge Club, was directly across the hall from Frances in 7 SE. Sir Lyman Duff, chief justice of the Supreme Court, lived on the north side of the courtyard from Frances in 7 NW. Senator Cairine Wilson and her family rounded out the northeast corner. Only Frances's apartment had a rooftop terrace, with a glass gazebo full of cushioned wicker, a shallow reflecting pool, and a firepit, legacy of Mitzie Gibson. A private circular stairway led up to the terrace from just inside Frances's apartment door. She often ventured up in her robe to bask by the shimmering pool in the sunlight.

Weekly cleaning service was included in the rent. Every Thursday, two phantoms addressed the refrigerator defrosting, the bathtub ring, and the dust that never sleeps. The ghosts left telltale scents. A pervasive body odour unadulterated by deodorant lingered in the kitchen and bathrooms. Frances imagined a swarthy Bertha—short, wide of girth, swabbing toilets and scrubbing floors on her hands and knees. The scent of lily of the valley trailed from whoever did the dusting and vacuuming. The cheap perfume lingered particularly in the folds and pleats of Frances's work wardrobe. The cleaning was not fastidious. A feather duster had etched fleeting traces around the mantle clock and had darted lightly between the deco vases. Frances turned a blind eye, thankful not to have to deal with it herself.

At 5:05 p.m., Paul arrived with a bulging A&P shopping bag. "Gosh!" he exclaimed. "You live in digs like these, you should be dating cabinet ministers."

"None have asked. I'm quite happy with a representative from the Department of Agriculture." She gave him a welcoming hug and a kiss. "Like a tour?"

The bathroom impressed him the most. "You could stable two workhorses in this shower stall. It has two sets of faucets! My God!"

"Yes, the former tenant seemed to have led an unconventional lifestyle. Her hospitality apparently extended to shared showers."

"Not exactly what I'd expect from a Presbyterian Bank of Canada employee, Miss McFadden."

"I took the place as I found it. I did not order a double shower."

"Ever used it?"

"Do I inquire about your hygiene habits, Mr. Roderick? The girls —Mary and Dorothy and Katie—have been here for a couple of sleepovers, and shared showers have been taken. Mary, who has by far the best figure of the four of us, is the shyest about displaying her torso. There is nothing shy about the Deavy sisters."

"And how shy is Frances McFadden?"

"Time to get back to the kitchen, Mr. Roderick," Frances gave him a push out the bathroom door. "We're getting a little too personal here."

Paul dug out a bowl and bathed a pork tenderloin in chutney sauce. He chopped up potatoes, carrots, and onions into wedges and cubes, then tumbled them in an olive oil slurry. The vegetable mixture went onto a cookie sheet and he set the oven for hot. "In an hour, I'll braise the pork in the frying pan, then build a cream and wine sauce with the drippings. We can relax until then."

Frances had picked up some Stilton and a well-aged cheddar at the Ottawa Dairy and two kinds of crackers from the Elgin Grocery. She arranged the spread on an art deco platter while Paul opened a bottle of white wine. "German Riesling," he said. "Sweet and fruity. Perfect with cheese. Uh-oh. I didn't think! Is it disloyal to drink German wine these days?"

"Probably. We'd better destroy the evidence before the Mounties show up."

"Now, Miss McFadden, do tell how a bank clerk can afford to live in a palace like this? You sneaking gold bars out of the vault in your lunch box?"

"How does an engineer from Ilderton become a master chef?"

"Suburban Ilderton, actually. Our farm was on RR#3."

"You're evading the question."

"As are you. The apartment fit for the Queen of Sheba?"

"My mother's small estate came to me when she died. Coincidentally, the owners of this apartment building were on the verge of defaulting on their mortgage. They offered two years' rent for the price of one to tenants with cash up front. I invested my inheritance in a long-term lease, even though I can barely afford new light bulbs."

"And the furniture?"

"The previous tenant was young, but came from old money. Had a New York designer outfit the place. She skipped the country to marry some European count. Just walked away, leaving six month's rent unpaid. I covered the rent in return for the furniture. Now, back to cooking, Mister engineer."

"My two older brothers are big brawny guys. They gave Dad all the support he needed to run the farm. Mom had arthritis, and I helped in the kitchen until my kid sister was old enough to be of any use. I started with peeling potatoes and worked my way up to sous chef. Cooking is a lot like engineering. You build a meal out of various raw products, apply heat, and presto—edible art."

Paul was easy to listen to. He spoke knowingly, but didn't brag. His work focused on improved machinery to harvest Canadian crops. "Half our farmers are still using horses to pull their ploughs and harrows," he sighed.

"So? Horses don't need to be gassed or oiled."

"True, but they do need oats and hay. A farmer can use up to forty acres to feed and graze a pair of workhorses. On a hundred-acre farm, that cuts seriously into the acreage left for cash crops. Using a tractor frees up a lot of space."

"Why don't they switch then?"

"Farmers are hard workers, but are not the quickest to jump at innovation. They know animals. Horses, cows, and chickens haven't changed a lot in two hundred years. New-fangled machines are expensive to buy and tricky to maintain. Still, I tour fall fairs to demonstrate how modern equipment would help them save time and money. They always remind me that they need to spend money to save money. It's somewhat Sisyphean." He poured more wine. "Enough about me. What are we celebrating?"

"New job! At 5:00 p.m. yesterday I was appointed secretary to Governor Towers."

Paul lifted his glass of Riesling in a toast. "Congratulations! What exactly does the governor's secretary do?"

"I typed six letters this morning. Took minutes at two meetings. Did a lot of filing. Pretty exciting, eh?"

"But you're right there at the top of the Bank. You must see some interesting stuff."

"Frankly, I don't understand much. Economics and monetary policy are very convoluted."

"Aren't they primarily concerned with financing the war effort?"

"True. There are endless discussions about options. What the consequences of one policy over another might be."

"Like what, for example?"

Frances poked Paul's chin with her forefinger. "Listen mister, I signed the Official Secrets Act. I'm not supposed to discuss anything I do at work with anybody."

"You think I'm a spy?" He poked her back.

"I think it unlikely, but when you go out with the guys for a beer after work, you might say, 'You'd never believe the crazy things my girlfriend says they're doing at the Bank of Canada.' Ottawa is a small town. Word gets around."

"So you're my girlfriend?"

"Well, I am a girl. We are friends, aren't we? How else would you define the relationship?"

"Let me show you, Miss McFadden."

8

FEAR

Mackenzie King genuinely believed and frequently said that the real secret of political leadership was more in what was prevented than in what was accomplished.

(Pickersgill, 10)

Bedsheets thrashed into a rat's nest. Since her luncheon date with Miss Briscoe, solid sleep had eluded Frances. After fleshing out her secretariat team, she suffered several sleepless nights. To the nightmares about stumbling in the dark on a swaying train toward Max Kessler was added a new element of anxiety. The canyon of her incapacity yawned before her. Aide-de-camp to Graham Towers? "The second most important man in Canada?" How could she possibly learn that job while simultaneously shaping the new secretariat? It was like trying to build a skiff while sailing it at the same time. Her sleep came in small bouts of fitful tossing. She went to work dazed, blinking through the day.

In the dark muddle of her third sleepless night, Frances drifted to the dining room credenza where Mitzie Gibson had stored her liquor. In two years, the cupboard had only been opened for company. Dusty spirit tombstones hunched in the dark. She opened a bottle of brandy, her mother's secret drink. It smelled repulsive.

She found a bottle of forty-year-old Graham's Douro port, and poured a sampler. It sampled very well. She sipped the glass empty and topped it up again. The port had a soothing, caramelly feeling in her throat. With a third glass, she watched the moon tumble behind the clouds until she drowsed down in a wing chair in the dark living room.

Sunlight startled her awake at 7:00 a.m. She jumped up and needed to call Murray at Red Line for a taxi to avoid being late for work. She was a little disjointed throughout the day, but the sleep helped. That night, three crystal goblets of port by 9:30 helped her sleep right through the night. She awoke feeling fuzzy-mouthed and guilty. The ghost of Vera McFadden raised a glass to her.

On Wednesday morning, a call went out to Dr. Grace. "Can we meet for lunch? I'm at my wits' end."

Dr. Grace was well into his double Macallan and a deep conversation in French with Henri, his favourite waiter at the Chateau Laurier, when Frances crumpled into the chair across from him.

"Well, Miss McFadden," he said. "You look like you've been rode hard and put away wet. A little oh-be-joyful freshener? Henri, a single Macallan on the rocks for the lady."

Frances winced, but didn't refuse. When Henri left she whispered "Do you drink alone?"

Dr. Grace reflected. "Only when there's no one around."

"Seriously! At home do you drink by yourself?"

"Maybe an occasional nightcap. You doing a survey?"

"I haven't been able to sleep properly for over a week, so I started to have a glass or two of port at night. It was very tasty. I shouldn't be drinking alone, but I've got to get eight hours of sleep or I'm a cripple at work. I'm turning into my mother."

"You're too hard on your mother. Give her some credit for the excellent way she raised you. Why can't you sleep?"

"I can't sleep because I'm taking on two new jobs and don't know how to do either of them."

"Pish. You've taken on lots of new jobs over the last five years. You always figure things out."

"That was minor league. Miss Briscoe thinks of the Holy Trinity as God, Mackenzie King, and Graham Towers. Not necessarily in that order. I'm in way over my head."

"A little perspective, *ma chérie*. Did you apply for the job?"

"No."

"No. The job applied for you. Graham Towers is getting exactly what he wants—Frances McFadden, bunions and all. Let *him* lose sleep if it worries him. I'd bet it doesn't."

"But I don't have a clue what he expects from his secretary. There's a war on! I don't have time to learn this by trial and error. And secondly, I have no idea how to get the members of this secretariat singing from the same songbook."

Henri arrived with their lunch and swept away.

"Have you ever heard the expression 'Truth to Power'?" asked Dr. Grace, while peppering the lamb chops.

"No." Frances shook her head, too tired to untangle metaphors, too impatient for poetry.

"It's a Quaker saying. My father once represented a poor Quaker family during World War I. They were pacifists and wanted their three sons recognized as conscientious objectors to avoid conscription. This right was guaranteed in legislation dating back to 1873, but was overlooked in the jingoistic enthusiasm to fight the Hun. Their three boys were incarcerated for refusing military service. Father took the case pro bono. He won, because the law was on the books and he knew the law. His victory garnered him disparaging stares around the Toronto courthouse, as though he were aiding the enemy.

"The mother gave Dad a framed needlepoint that said in bold gothic script, 'Truth to Power.' It hung in his law office for years and later in his judge's chambers as a reminder that it takes courage to do the right thing when the going is unpopular."

"So? I tell the truth. How does this solve my problems?"

"Where's the power?"

"Governor Towers."

"Right. So ask him how he wants the shop run. He hired you. He trusts you. It may not be clear to him what instructions you need."

"But it sounds so idiotic. ''Scuse me, Governor. How do you want your letters formatted?'"

"Have you looked through Miss Briscoe's files?"

Frances sighed. "Yes. They may have made sense to Miss Briscoe, but they're a hopeless morass to me."

"She always struck me as so orderly."

"Orderly in a disorderly way. She clearly had a penchant for geography. She has a file titled 'Americans' and all the Americans she dealt with are in there. Another file titled 'British' and a third for 'Scottish'. If the Governor says 'Could you please get me the Robertson file?' I don't know whether Robertson is Latvian or Venezuelan, so it takes me an hour to find it.

"And you wouldn't believe the minutiae she recorded from meetings, or the number of drafts she did of a three-sentence letter. I don't have time to do all that."

"My mother used to say, 'It's an imperfect world,' by which she meant, I believe, that when there isn't time for perfect, aim for good. How would you do the filing?"

"Alphabetically by proper name or topic."

"Why not just reorganize the files?"

"That would take a month. And what would Miss Briscoe say if I destroyed her system?"

"Miss Briscoe is beyond caring. You've got a new team keen to show how good they are. Have them all pitch in and you'll have the reorganization done in a few days. They'll love being involved in creating the new filing system. The governor has accepted your advice on the secretariat. Ask him how he wants the help to help. My guess is that he'll tell you to do what you think best."

"That doesn't solve the issue of organizing the secretariat."

"In the private secretary role, Governor Towers is the power. In the secretariat, who's the power?"

"Well, on paper it looks like I am. But if I can't harness the team effectively, we're not going anywhere."

"Maddie and Bridget and Brendan and Claire—the team really are the power. Admit it to them. Everything is new, but every decision isn't your responsibility. Say, 'Here's the problem—what do you think we should do?'"

"Is that leadership?"

"Leadership is overrated. The most important part of leadership is following good advice."

"I don't even know how to organize the office space."

"Ask your team! They're smart. That's why you chose them. They'll work a lot harder on things that they help decide. What gets you out of bed and into the Bank every day?"

Frances reflected. "Well, it's meaningful work. The Bank helps direct the Canadian economy out of the Depression. I'm a very small cog, but I know I contribute to that every day. I can almost feel the pulse of the country growing stronger. The people are smart and nice to work with. It's actually kind of fun."

"Keep your team having fun doing interesting things with nice people. Everything else will work itself out."

On Thursday, Frances was in the Byward Market ordering office supplies when she absently turned a corner and came upon The Bluebird Café. Through the plate-glass window, she spotted the Buddha-like shape of Huey Foo sitting alone in the back booth having a cigarette and a Coke.

"Is this a private party?" Frances asked, sliding into the seat across from him.

"Ah! Miss Fran. So happy see new secretary Governor Tower. Good for you!"

"And how would a cook in a Chinese restaurant learn about staff changes at the Bank of Canada?"

Buddha smiled his cryptic smile. "Like new job?"

"It's exciting, but I have trouble sleeping. I guess my mind doesn't shut down at night."

"Sometime, I have sleep problem. Use Chinese medicine. Always help."

"Chinese medicine? You mean opium?"

"No! No opium. You don't want sleep forever. Chinese doctor have many cure. Herb. Acupuncture. You should try."

"What's acupuncture?"

"Doctor stick many needle in your body. Help energy flow. Bad energy out. Good energy in."

"Sounds painful."

"No pain. Little sting, like mosquito."

"I should probably see my family doctor, but I'm sure he'd just tell me to take two aspirin and get lots of sleep. Which, of course, is the problem in the first place."

"Western doctor treat one thing. Have sore stomach, he treat stomach. Chinese doctor treat whole body. Stomach feel pain, maybe cause in kidney. Headache? Maybe liver too hot. Needle tie many body channel together."

"But if I can't sleep, is that in my head or my elbow?"

"You talk. Chinese doctor listen. He solve. Give herb. Give needle. You sleep."

Frances looked dubious.

Huey Foo pulled a pencil out of a pocket in his sauce-splattered apron and scribbled an address on a napkin. "Dr. Wei very good. Office above Lee Kim laundry on Albert Street. He my doctor. He fix your sleep. Guarantee."

A mysterious medicinal odour permeated Dr. Wei's office. He was a slight man of indeterminate age who spoke English with a Scottish accent. "I attended Mission school in Hunan for twelve years," Dr. Wei explained. "All the missionaries were from Scotland."

Frances described her problem. The doctor directed her to lie down on a padded table in a small alcove off his office. He put a pillow under her knees and gently massaged her shoulders and neck with something that had the eucalyptus aroma of Vicks VapoRub. Very relaxing.

She barely felt the pin pricks to her forehead, ear lobes, wrists and ankles. Maybe twenty needles all together. "Just rest now," said Dr. Wei, putting on a record of what she assumed was Chinese music to play faintly in the background. "I'll come back in half an hour."

Frances fell sound asleep, and only awoke when the doctor coughed politely. All the needles were out. "If you come back once a week for a month, we can restore the balance of yin and yang in your body. Your natural rhythm of sleep will return."

Could the cure be any worse than Douro port?

9

ESPRIT DE CORPS

In the 1939 fiscal year, the overall cash requirements of the Canadian federal government were $573 million. By 1944, they would be $5,779 million.

(McIvor, 173)

Governor Towers surveyed the outer office/hallway now that the wing chairs had been cleared away. "Phone John Robson at the Experimental Farm and ask him to lend us some indoor plants so the place doesn't look so sterile. Wanted to do that years ago but Miss Briscoe had allergies. Do you have allergies?" he asked as an afterthought.

"No cats. No allergies," said Frances, while making notes. "I've been looking through Miss Briscoe's files of minutes and letters. Do you want me to follow her models?"

The governor reflected as he lit a cigarette. "Miss Briscoe tended to embellish my correspondence. She did this, I think," he smiled, "out of a misplaced sense of the exalted position of governor of the Bank of Canada."

"It is exalted."

"I hope that after five years in business, we've established that, and can let the letterhead speak for itself."

"Sparser style, then?"

Graham Towers absently moved his jaw around while pondering. "Let's say polite but succinct. Most government communications are godawful ponderous. We're at war. Time is an enemy. Short and pithy should be our theme. Miss Briscoe was a martinet for exacting form. This is admirable, but often it took her days to get minutes drafted to perfection. Let's live with the occasional comma splice in return for alacrity. The people at a Wednesday meeting will need to know the decision of a Monday meeting to move projects forward. Polite, pithy, quick. The rest I leave to you."

With replacements trained and former desks cleared out, the secretariat gathered together for the first time at 11:00 a.m. on Friday, October 13. The sleek new furniture sat uncrated in a corner. Frances introduced Maddie Hall. "As you can see, we're setting up office in a hallway. It's a generous space, but it has to hold us and still function as a hallway. The governor doesn't want a hodgepodge."

"Will you be using Miss Briscoe's office?" asked Brendan.

"No. We'll all be out here together. My desk should probably be right beside the governor's door. We'll reserve Miss Briscoe's office for meetings. Where would you like your desks? If we can get things in position before lunch, they can install the phones this afternoon."

"What if we put them in a row along the far wall," said Claire, pointing.

"Yeah," said Bridget. "The wall kind of anchors us and leaves the centre open to traffic."

"Maybe," suggested Maddie, "we should have one reception desk out in the centre facing down the hall toward the elevators."

"Kind of exposed out there."

"Look," Maddie continued, "I don't know the nuts and bolts around here yet. I could be the receptionist. I can learn the names of everybody that comes by and direct phone calls and shepherd lost souls so the rest of you aren't bothered."

No argument there.

"Okay," said Frances. "Let's set the place up."

Everyone pitched in, enjoying the physical activity. In twenty minutes they had carved up the hallway into U-shaped fiefdoms of desks and credenzas. "Great," said Frances, slapping her hands, spit-spot. "Lunch at the Chateau Laurier is our reward." Frances had booked the same private room that Governor Towers had used to honour Miss Briscoe's retirement. When they arrived, the sideboard held pitchers of ice water, orange juice, and two ice buckets containing open bottles of white Burgundy. A platter of assorted hors d'oeuvres sat on the dining table.

"When Dr. Grace interviewed me to help set up the Bank of Canada back in 1934," said Frances, "we met for lunch in the Canadian Grill downstairs. My first introduction to wine. I was half-crocked by the end of the meeting. A wonderful beginning. Ladies and gentleman, a toast to the birth and success of the secretariat."

Glasses clinked.

"Wow!"

"Holy crow, that's smooth!"

"Liquid sunshine."

"Will we be here every Friday for lunch?" asked Brendan.

"Enjoy the moment. It may be a while before we get back. Check the menus and I'll call room service."

"Christmas! There are no prices on this menu."

"Either a terrible oversight or terribly classy."

Frances phoned down the orders to Émile. They sat down at the table drinking and nibbling. "It might help us work together if we knew a little bit about each other," she said. "I'll start. I love movies and popcorn. Those are weaknesses, I guess. My greatest strength is that I usually know what I don't know, and I feel no shame in asking for help."

Claire went next. "Well, my weaknesses are sports. I'm the short-stop on the Bank's women's baseball team. I love tennis and badminton. I suppose my strength is exacting detail. I learned that down in Securities where that every penny had to be accounted for."

Brendan said, "I have a weakness for beautiful women." He spread his arms inclusively wide. Everyone laughed. "You could add golf and crossword puzzles to my list of frailties. My strength is probably logistics. In catering, I learned to keep six plates spinning at once. It sounds like we're in for lots of plate spinning."

"I really like singing," confessed Bridget Stanton. "Particularly Irish ballads. *Oh, Danny boy, the pipes, the pipes are calling,*" she trilled in a magnificent alto. She reflected a moment. "Mary Bedford has drilled me on filing and cross-indexing. That's where I can help the most. Neat, tidy, and easy to find."

"I love the outdoors. Camping, canoeing, swimming, sailing," said Maddie Hall. "My mother used to say that I'm relentless at solving problems. I keep trying new approaches until something works out."

Émile arrived, pushing a wagon filled with domed serving dishes. He sorted them out while Brendan poured a final round with the second bottle of Chardonnay. "Thank you, Émile," said Frances. "Better send up another bottle of wine. This is a thirsty crowd."

When the third bottle of wine was demolished, Frances felt they were relaxed enough for thinner ice. "We're embarking on brand-new territory, and, frankly, I'm a little frightened at the prospect. I'm going to need your help. I've never been a private secretary and I've never run a team of five. It occurred to me that you all may have some misgivings as well. Anyone? Let's be frank."

With inhibitions mellowed by wine, there was only a brief lull before Brendan took the initiative. "*Frankly*, Miss, back in catering I was king of the castle. I'm not sure if this chain gang approach isn't going to chafe a bit. Nothing personal, mind."

"When I was up in the library archives," said Bridget, "I was pretty much out of sight. It didn't matter what I wore. This was good, because, *frankly,* I have two work outfits. I wash out one every night and hang it to dry while I wear the other next day. My wardrobe looks a little frayed beside all that Cuban mahogany."

"I may have a university degree," continued Maddie, "but, *frankly*, I don't know a thing about banking. When you guys talk shop, it all sounds like Swahili. I feel like I'm walking blindfolded through a jungle."

Claire closed out the confessional. "Dealing with the ledgers down in the Securities Department was crisp and clean. Debit. Credit. The end. *Frankly*, this new job sounds like working inside a popcorn popper."

Frances took a deep breath and smiled. "I'm so happy to have you all with me! This is going to be fun. There'll be mistakes. Let's try to make each mistake just once. Our mission is simple—"

"To have as much fun as possible?" put in Brendan.

"Correct. And serve the governor as best we can." She handed out a typed sheet. "Here's a list of the key responsibilities he wants covered. Can everybody choose something you find interesting? We'll all have secondary responsibilities, to understudy each other, so eventually, each of us can do every job in the office."

They each picked up a primary duty for one of the big committees, and backup on a second committee, and backed up the backup on a third. Bridget volunteered to take charge of the filing system. "If you guys can help me rejig Miss Briscoe's files, I can keep things organized from there on in. It might make sense for me to take the back desk close to the file room."

Claire said, "I can look after the office financial accounts if you like. It should be a piece of cake after dealing with securities ledgers."

Maddie said she would handle the mail as well as the reception desk.

Brendan agreed to be in charge of logistics and contingencies. "I can set up a wall chart in Miss Briscoe's office tracking everyone's schedule and organize backup if anyone gets double-booked. There should always be at least two of us holding down the office. We'll have to arrange lunch break and out-of-office duties around that. Maybe I should take the front desk in the row against the wall. Close at hand in case any ruffians try to run roughshod over Miss Hall."

Frances volunteered to build protocols on minutes, memos, letters and cables. "Everything going out of this office under the governor's signature has to be one hundred per cent error free. No typos. No grammar errors. No smudges."

"Should all outgoing correspondence be proofread by someone else?" asked Bridget.

"At least in the beginning," agreed Claire.

Wardrobe was a delicate issue. Frances knew how little they were paid. "We are the new face of the Governor's Office. Everyone that comes to see him—cabinet ministers, senior bureaucrats, officials from other countries—will all walk right past us to get to him or to the boardroom. I chose you as the best possible support for the governor, but we dress a bit like Hal Roach's Little Rascals."

"Our Gang?" laughed Maddie. "Do you think Spanky, Alfalfa, and Buckwheat would have us?"

"You never look scruffy, Miss," said Claire.

"When I first started working for Dr. Grace before the Bank of Canada was set up, I was very nervous. A dropout from the High School of Commerce suddenly meeting all these high- flyers. He advised me that if I wore quality apparel to work, people would defer to the clothes. Camouflage fear under duds from Holt Renfrew. It worked."

"You want us all dressed the same? Like bellhops or the Dionne Quints?" asked Brendan.

"No. But we are now the governor's window dressing, so we need to dress up the windows."

"Miss ..." pleaded Bridget.

"I don't expect you to bear all clothing costs yourselves. I inherited an expense account from Miss Briscoe. I'll allocate seventy-five dollars to each of you to upgrade your office wardrobes. We'll finish early today. Maybe Bridget and Claire and Maddie can go clothes shopping together. Share advice on fashion choices and not buy identical outfits by accident."

"What am I?" asked Brendan. "Chopped liver?"

"The girl talk would bore you silly, Brendan," said Bridget.

"Oh, come with us," invited Maddie. "We'll get you outfitted first so that women will find you irresistible. Then you can go play golf for the rest of the afternoon."

10

BEGINNINGS AND ENDINGS

The concern for national unity that had been demonstrated by Canada's separate declaration of war on September 9 would continue to dominate Canadian policy. Nowhere was it more prominent than in the first few months of the war when Canada engaged in a series of difficult negotiations with London on military and economic matters.

(Granatstein, 42)

"It is amazing how these people … from the Old Country … seem to think all they have to do is tell us what is to be done. No wonder they get the backs of people up on this side." [Mackenzie King diary]

(Granatstein, 48)

On a crisp Sunday in mid-October, Anna Deloitte had Frances down to her apartment on the sixth floor of the Balmoral Arms for pumpkin muffins and coffee before they walked over to Knox Presbyterian Church together. Anna had started to wear reading glasses, which she took off the second she wasn't reading. She was very attractive in a refined way, and Frances thought the glasses made her look more intellectual. "I just had a letter from Max in Chicago. Well, the letter was mailed from Chicago—heaven knows where he is now. He had to leave Canada, of course, before war was declared, or they would have locked him up. It's so unfair! My gentle Max—what threat is he to anyone? He says he might be out of touch for some time. He's awaiting instructions from head office and might have to go back to Germany by some circuitous route."

"I'm sorry," said Frances, who was sorrier than she could ever let on. "I guess that will put your plans on hold for the time being." Not exactly a lie, but evading the truth with a good friend was a burden of shame.

It was a circus, although a well-dressed circus, as the secretariat slowly invented itself. Traditions took root. Their jury-rigged home in the hall quickly came to be called the "outer office." Out of a sense of history, Miss Briscoe's former office became the MBO (the Miss Briscoe Office), used for meetings or a quiet retreat for anyone working on a complicated issue. They took breaks in there—Claire set up a jigsaw puzzle on a card table—and sometimes lunch, out of sight, but close at hand. Although there were bumps, blips, and miscues, Frances was heartened by everyone's willingness to come to each other's aid. Roughed-out routines smoothed down with repetition. Incrementally, cohesion was forged.

It helped that Bridget and Brendan were quick with the quips. Claire had a generous laugh—a welcome audience. Once Maddie understood that Brendan's tone was primarily ironic, she overcame an initial restraint. Brendan always had the crossword puzzle from the *Ottawa Citizen* on the go when he had a spare minute. Looking perplexed, pencil in mouth, he would wonder out loud, "Six down: ten-letter word for sexual union with a four-legged animal? B-e-s-t … ?"

"Bestiality," threw out Maddie without looking up from her typing.

Brendan made a theatrical display of surprise that such a word would be in her vocabulary. "Six-letter word for female genitalia? v-a-g-blank-blank-blank?"

"Brendan! Those words are *not* in the *Ottawa Citizen* crossword!" said Claire.

"Nine across. Three-letter slang expression for a woman's breast?"

Madeline stopped typing. She glanced around to see Claire mouthing "No!" at her and Bridget, grinning, shaking her head. Madeline composed herself. "It's 'tit,' Brendan. If you could ever get a woman to go out with you, you might get to touch one."

Bridget and Claire roared. Brendan clutched his heart, mortally wounded by the shaft, and collapsed on his desk.

Frances accompanied a team member to each of the major committees for a working tutorial. Both took shorthand notes and both drafted the minutes before comparing results. There were few discrepancies. After two runs with training wheels, Frances freed them to go it alone. Maddie, the best educated, was the most unsure of herself at first, as the Bank jargon was so unfamiliar. "Marginal propensity to consume?" "Increasing returns to scale?" She quickly caught on.

The governor wanted verbatim shorthand transcripts for reference, but succinct minutes recording active direction: "It was resolved that ..." or "PMO was requested to respond to ..." A conscious effort was made to erase personal styles from minutes, memos, or letters to standardize anything that carried the governor's name. Without the telltale initials at the bottom, it became impossible to know who had drafted a document. They called it "hiding in the bushes" and made a game of it.

Whenever possible, they each covered only one major meeting a day. Minutes could then be drafted immediately, proofed, put in the governor's inbox for his signature, and then distributed, all within twenty-four hours. Polite. Pithy. Quick.

The Momsies were a special case. The personal secretaries of the federal government's six senior deputy ministers met every second Tuesday at four. In theory, they were coordinating common office practices to improve intra-department communications. In fact, they enjoyed a collegial respite from hectic responsibilities, over tea. Each was a veteran of at least twenty years of government service. Collectively, they knew every player, every hair-brained plan, and every closeted skeleton. Frances had been introduced to this powerhouse five years earlier and stayed with them by volunteering to act as secretary. She recognized the Momsie meetings as a privileged portal on government personnel and practices, but she no longer had time to do the minutes. She phoned Rose Malone, secretary to Mr. Clark, the deputy minister of Finance.

"Congratulations on your appointment, dear," said Rose. "You really belong with us now."

"I'd like to continue attending, Miss Malone, but I'm afraid I can't carry on as the secretary, what with my new responsibilities." There was a jarring silence on the phone line. "Could I bring someone from our new secretariat to take minutes? That would free me to be more actively involved in the discussion."

Relief! "I'm sure there will be no objection, dear. Just let me check with the others."

The others were happy to recognize Frances's new status, and happier still not to have to take turns doing the minutes. Whom to delegate? Brendan and Bridget were a little too flip. Claire was too high-energy for the sedate pace of elder stateswomen. Maddie, then. Maddie was respectful, asked intelligently for clarifications, and could refill the teakettle without missing a beat.

In alphabetical rotation, the four took turns covering Frances's desk when duty called her elsewhere. One Tuesday morning while Frances was taking minutes at the Bank Executive Meeting, Bridget took a message from the Civic Hospital Intensive Care Unit. Frances had taken flowers in to Miss Briscoe the week after the surgery, to find that the patient was sedated but resting peacefully. What with getting the secretariat running and learning the governor's preferences, Miss Briscoe had slipped from her field of vision.

"A Nurse Butler at the Civic asked that you call right back," said Bridget.

Frances phoned, then immediately dialled Murray at Red Line for a taxi. She met Miss Butler at the nursing station by the elevators on the third floor.

"Miss Briscoe asked that I contact you," said the businesslike senior nurse. "The surgery went as well as could be expected, but tests showed the cancer was quite advanced. She knows the prognosis. She insisted that we stop administering morphine three days ago. Said it made her feel dopy. It does, but that's the price of countering the pain. I'll take you to her room."

Miss Briscoe was lying on her side facing away from the door. Frances could hear a plaintive murmuring when she entered. "Meow, meow?" She stopped and listened. Miss Briscoe was whispering, "Ow, ow, ow, ow, ow," like a quiet mantra.

Frances backed out of the room and took two deep breaths. Then she knocked loudly on the door frame and called out, "Miss Briscoe?"

Slowly, the body in the bed turned face up, then a head inched across the pillow to face the door. A shrunken voice whispered hoarsely, "Miss … McFadden?"

Frances barely recognized the ravaged face. She picked up Miss Briscoe's cold hand and stroked it softly. Bird bones beneath withered skin.

Miss Briscoe could squeeze out only two or three syllables between laboured breaths.

"Thank you … for coming … How's … the Bank?"

"We are doing our best to keep our collective heads above water. The governor now has five people doing the work that you used to do all by yourself."

Miss Briscoe's mouth opened but no words came out, just a laboured breathing, and the corners of a distant smile. Finally, with great effort she rasped, "The governor?"

"He misses you, of course. In the middle of dictating a letter he'll suddenly stop and turn to look out the window toward the Gatineau

Hills. He appreciates that we're all trying hard, but we are not what he is used to. We are not Miss Briscoe."

"Thank you … for taking … over … Protect him … and … the Bank." She closed her eyes to regroup. "Remember … small in … cre … ments …" Beads of sweat bathed Miss Briscoe's forehead. Frances stood beside her for several minutes, softly stroking the emaciated hand. There were no more words. Miss Briscoe's small ribcage shook with every breath. A laboured intake and a terse exhalation. A pause. A breath. A longer pause. A shallower breath. A long, long pause. A sip of air. And no more. Frances ran to the nursing station. "Miss Butler!"

They hurried back to the limp form that had been Elizabeth Briscoe. Nurse Butler scrambled to find a pulse, then bent down to listen to the lungs while watching for chest movement. After a minute she stood up, turned to Frances, and shook her head.

11

MR. HEENEY

October 25:

The Duplessis Union Nationale government was defeated, losing all but 14 seats in Quebec. "It is a great wish for the allied cause," King mused. "Had the results gone the other way, Germany would have felt dismemberment of the British Empire had already begun. [King Diary] *Bruce Hutchison said in 1952, "In retrospect, it may be considered the most important election in modern Canadian history."*

(Nolan, 32)

The outer office settled into a semblance of order, and, with some trepidation, Frances turned her attention to another front.

October 30, 1939

Dear Mr. Heeney,

I have just taken over as Governor Towers's secretary. The prime minister and the governor would likely be best served if we consulted on the scheduling process when they need to meet. Any thoughts?

Yours respectfully,

Frances McFadden

Office of the Governor of the Bank of Canada

November 1, 1939

Dear Miss McFadden,

Thank you for your note of October 30th. Congratulations on your appointment and my condolences on the passing of Miss Briscoe.

Familiarity with each other's office practices would indeed be beneficial. Would you be free to join me for lunch at noon Friday in the Parliamentary Dining Room?

Yours respectfully,

Arnold Heeney

Principal Secretary

Office of the Prime Minister

The Parliamentary Dining Room on the fourth floor of the Centre Block was not as elegant as the Chateau Laurier, but it had a special cachet. It was not a public space. It served only the elected and the selected. Frances wondered if the invitation would give Mr. Heeney home field advantage in any negotiations.

A friendly commissionaire decked in a rainbow of service medals greeted Frances at the west door of the Centre Block and directed her to the elevator. Frances mentioned Mr. Heeney's name to the maître d', and he escorted her across the dining room, negotiating between laden linen tablecloths where conversations buzzed in pools of cigar smoke. Mr. Ralston, the new Finance minister, and his deputy, Mr. Clark, glanced up as she passed their table. Frances smiled and nodded.

The maître d' stopped by a corner table, and a handsome man stood to greet her. "Miss McFadden? Arnold Heeney. Pleased to meet you." Eye contact was maintained during a firm but not oppressive handshake. They sat down. "May I order you a drink? Mr. King has given up alcohol for the duration, with the implication that patriotic Canadians on his staff will do the same. That doesn't mean you have to suffer as well."

"Are you suffering, Mr. Heeney?"

He laughed. "I had found that an occasional libation could stoke the boilers during a long work day."

"I grew up in the household of an abstemious Presbyterian mother, who, mind you, kept a supply of medicinal brandy in the upstairs linen closet. I found that an iced tomato juice with Worcestershire sauce accompanied by a vodka sidecar gave all the appearances of sobriety with no telltale vapours."

"Really?"

"Really. And Mother had a bloodhound's nose for infractions. Cover never blown once."

"Really!"

"Really. This is off the record, of course."

"Well then, Miss McFadden, will you join me in a tomato juice with extensions?"

"I'd be delighted, Mr. Heeney."

Mr. Heeney recommended the fish and chips for lunch. "It may sound pedestrian, but it's the unsung star of the menu. The cook is from Cape Breton. He flies fresh cod in by floatplane every other day to the base at Rockcliffe. His breading batter is as light as angel's breath."

The conversation was genial and general until they settled into a crème brulé with coffee. "I must confess, Miss McFadden, that my relationship with the late Miss Briscoe was frosty, to say the least." He paused. "The fault may well have been my own. Mr. King works fourteen-hour days, although not always the same fourteen hours. He expects his staff to be on deck and ready to go pretty well around the clock. If he takes a fancy to speaking to the governor general at midnight on affairs of state, I don't believe it occurs to him that the GG might be sound asleep or otherwise engaged. He has the same attitude toward everyone in public service."

"And you make the phone calls?"

"I do. The shortcoming to otherwise interesting work. Now, when the prime minister wished an audience with Governor Towers, I often had to negotiate between Mr. King's insistence and Miss Briscoe's intransigence. She treated your governor like a sequestered monk who could not be disturbed for anything short of the Second Coming. Mr. King would be arching his eyebrows, silently shouting, 'Why isn't he here yet?' and Miss Briscoe would be stonewalling. Harried and sleep-deprived as I often was, I may have come across as abrupt."

"Perhaps we can work out a protocol, then, Mr. Heeney. You know your employer; I'm getting to know mine. I'm sure they both wish Canada to prosper and the war to come to a quick and victorious end. Wartime has greatly expanded the responsibilities of both. We each have some input into weekly agendas. Could we anticipate a regular meeting every third Thursday or something?"

"Good idea, Miss McFadden. That should work, 90 per cent of the time. What about the other 10 per cent?"

"I appreciate that the prime minister has the woes of the entire country in his hands, while Governor Towers is merely concerned with finding the money to bankroll the war. Would you ever suggest something like: 'I can contact Governor Towers's office, but we must remember he is working day and night to cover the war debt, and we wouldn't want to distract him needlessly from that task.'"

"You know, that might work. Mr. King is not *consciously* inconsiderate. I'll give it a try. But if that fails …"

"Then call, and I'll do my very best, knowing that you've done your very best."

They were toasting their cleverness when a man with an unruly shock of hair and pince-nez glasses strolled up to their table. Mr. Heeney stood to make introductions. "Miss McFadden, may I introduce Jack Pickersgill, my colleague in the PMO? I wanted you two to meet. If the prime minister has me out running errands, which happens most of the time, Jack's your man." Mr. Heeney checked his gold wristwatch. "Speaking of … I must fly. I'll leave you two to get acquainted. Miss McFadden, this has been the most profitable lunch I've had in months. We will have to do this more often. Jack, please get the chit."

He bowed with mock formality and a light smile. Mr. Pickersgill sank down in the vacant chair and signalled the waiter for coffee. Where Mr. Heeney was tall and wore his three-piece pinstripes with distinction, Mr. Pickersgill was short and pudgy, wrapped in a rumpled brown suit that looked as though it had been slept in for several days. A quizzical grin covered his face as though he were planning an elaborate prank.

"And what is your role in the prime minister's office?" asked Frances after a certain silence.

"Arnold Heeney is the brains," Mr. Pickersgill replied. "I am the brawn." He drank his coffee black and quickly. "I mostly take the blame for things that go wrong."

"The brawny blamester," mused Frances. "An interesting job title."

"I actually have a business card," he said, pulling a tattered pasteboard out of his suit coat pocket and handing it over. "It doesn't state a title, just 'PMO.'"

"That still probably opens a lot of doors."

"Perhaps … should I be interested in having doors opened. I'm usually trying to close them while leaving no traces. Mr. King's office structure is somewhat amorphous. I mostly do backdoor things. Write reports and speeches. Arnie handles the front door."

"Have you worked for Mr. King for long?"

"Two years. I'm actually a third secretary with the External Affairs Department. Mr. Skelton, our under-secretary, sent me over to the PMO. Mr. King is his own minister of External Affairs, and I'm the go-between. 'Look up the capital of Mongolia' sort of thing. I've become very adept with an atlas. But enough about me. Tell me about yourself, Miss McFadden. You seem quite young to be running the Bank of Canada."

"I'm new to the governor's office. It's a little premature to say that I'm completely in charge. In fact, my job description is much like your own. We're currently setting up a new secretariat to deal with the war workload, so everything is in flux."

"Do you come from a long line of bankers?"

"No. I was a student at the High School of Commerce without so much as a bank account when Dr. Grace at the Department of Finance shanghaied me back in 1934. He wanted to get a head start organizing things before the Bank Act legislation actually passed."

"Willie Grace? Know him well. We're both at the Five Lakes Fishing Club. Has quite a fondness for the Macallan. A very distinguished credential for a government bureaucrat."

"More distinguished than a Ph.D. in Economics?"

"A Ph.D. is a matter of application and perseverance. An affinity for single malt Scotch and an aptitude for fly-fishing are proficiencies one must be born with. A good man."

"Agreed."

"So you are his acolyte. That's quite a distinction. But that alone wouldn't get you parked beside Graham Towers's door."

"I was asked by Dr. Grace to help set up the Bank of Canada. I was asked by Governor Towers to take over when his secretary retired. All I did was say 'yes' twice."

"Ah! You have that wonderful Canadian modesty, Miss McFadden, that conceals everything but the truth."

"I think we are cut of the same cloth, Mr. Pickersgill. Please call me Frances."

"All right, Frances, if you will call me Jack."

"Before you arrived, I was discussing with Mr. Heeney how best to keep our respective lords and masters aligned with each other. I recognize that the prime minister pulls rank on a mere Bank governor, but if he pulls too hard and too often, things might chafe."

"No one is served if that happens," said Jack, draining his coffee cup. "And while the official order of precedence at a state occasion would recognize privy councillors and Supreme Court justices ahead of the governor of the Bank of Canada, no heartbeat is more vital to the prime minister than that of Graham Towers."

"More important than the Finance minister?"

"Mr. Ralston was reluctantly pressed into service as Finance minister just six weeks ago, and is still figuring out where the washrooms are. The job almost killed Charles Dunning before he limped into the wings in September. So Governor Towers is the crown prince of Canadian monetary policy and, if I may say so—off the record—he is very highly respected on the Hill."

"Speaking of 'off the record,' may I assume that any conversation between us is off the record to anyone? Excepting Mr. Heeney, of course."

"Certainly. You are a signatory to the Official Secrets Act?"

"I am."

"As are Arnie and I. This compromises the free flow of information somewhat," he sighed. "The governor and the prime minister are on the same side and seem to respect each other. Mr. King believes absolutely in himself as prime minister and in the Liberal Party as the best possible governing agent to bring Canada successfully through the war. As you know, the last federal election was in 1935. He will soon need to go to the people of Canada for a mandate. Political expediency might not always parallel the governor's preferred monetary policy. This is likely the only area of possible disharmony between the two. Perhaps if we notice a negative situation developing, we might unobtrusively bring it to each other's attention. That would hardly be a breach of the Official Secrets Act, would it?"

"I think not. Do you foresee any problems on the horizon?"

Jack Pickersgill flashed the wryest of grins. "In order to form the government, Mr. King needs the support of Quebec members of Parliament. In the 1935 election, the Liberals won fifty-nine out of sixty-five Quebec seats. Ninety per cent. Mr. King likes that ratio. However, Quebecers demonstrate a pronounced lack of enthusiasm for dying to save George VI's empire. Some are pacifist. Some felt betrayed by the conscription issue in the last war. The Catholic Church, a very strong opinion-swayer in Quebec, is vehemently anti-communist. There are murmurings that if Herr Hitler is also anti-communist, can he really be all that bad?

"Quebec premier Maurice Duplessis played to these sentiments in the recent provincial election. He challenged the prime minister directly on aspects of the War Measures Act that he felt curtailed Quebec's legal prerogatives. Had Duplessis been re-elected, he would have had the bully pulpit to crow against the war effort and divide the nation."

"But he lost. Badly."

"That's because Messieurs Power, Lapointe, and Cardin from Mr. King's cabinet jumped into the fray and carried the provincial Liberals, a very weak lot, to victory. The election boiled down to a simple question: Did Quebecers want three strong anti-conscriptionists in the federal cabinet, or did they want Duplessis as their premier?"

"And Quebec answered."

Jack Pickersgill nodded. "French Canadians have always known which pot the pea soup is bubbling in. They've needed to be astutely pragmatic to survive as a cultural minority in an anglophone sea for one hundred and seventy-five years." He signed for the dinner chit. "Are there any reluctant warriors at the Bank of Canada?"

"There's a very small francophone contingent headed by M. Soulière, the associate deputy governor. I don't know him very well. He's virtually mute at executive meetings. It's hard to tell if politics or economics are his first interest."

"Keep your ear to the ground."

12

POTLUCK

Combined personnel in the Canadian army, navy and air force in August, 1939 totalled 10,602 men. By 1945 manpower in the combined services had grown to 1,029,510.

(Stacy, 4; 590)

While the German army's Polish campaign had been wrapped up by October, the refitting of the army for the Western front against France was taking longer than anticipated. Western journalists reduced to covering the war from the pubs of London and the bistros of Paris peevishly dubbed the stalemate the Phoney War, or the Sitzkrieg.

(Nolan, 35)

Of Frances's childhood friends, Mary was the most beautiful, Dorothy the most intelligent, and Dorothy's sister Katie the most brazen. Mrs. Katie Warren, who never called Frances at work, called Frances at work. "How ya doing, slug? You know, married life is a slice o' heaven, but I do miss the old gang. What if we all got together for a potluck dinner this Saturday?"

"Great idea. Where?"

"Well, Kevin and I squat in a tenement above a fish store. Mary and Nat rent a shoebox apartment on Somerset. Dorothy still lives at home with Mom and Dad. What does that suggest?"

"My place?"

"Great idea!"

"But it's a little embarrassing."

"Because it's a palace?"

"It's a little ostentatious for a bank clerk from Rochester Street."

"You don't want to share your good fortune with your friends?"

"Of course."

"Then indulge us. If it makes you feel better, we'll pretend to be unimpressed and whisper catty comments."

"Won't Kevin be heartsick spending a Saturday evening without you?"

"I'll bring him along. Mary can bring Nat. Dorothy has some secret admirer that I'd like to flush out into the open. And, it's time I met this engineer of yours to see if I approve."

"Four couples? For dinner? I can't cook."

"Potluck! We'll all bring something. You can pick up some dessert at Fenton's Bakery and make the coffee."

"Won't the guys be bored by all the girl gossip?"

"All men need is a couple of beers and a chance to brag, and they're happy as clams. Just throw out a line like, 'How 'bout those Montreal Canadiens, eh?' and they'll talk for hours."

The men hit it right off. Kevin and Paul shared a bawdy sense of humour, especially for limericks.

"There once was a fellow named Sweeny,
Who spilled some gin on his weenie ..."

"There once was a plumber from Lee,
Who was plumbing his girl by the sea ..."

Nat Bedford, who looked like a Sunday school teacher in his wire-framed glasses and close-cropped hair, giggled like an eight-year-old at the ribaldry. Dorothy's man, George Holland, was older and more reserved than the others. He relaxed as the evening wore on. The copious supply of beer and the wine may have helped.

War was on everyone's mind. "You guys are in no rush to enlist and fight for king and country, I see," observed Katie.

"You want to pack me off to the wars from our brief-warmed marriage bed?" asked Kevin with a clownish pout.

"You don't need to be in khaki to serve the cause," said Paul.

"No," added George. "The war started the first week of school. Is it better that I teach my chemistry classes the periodic table or that I join up and march endlessly around some drill hall?"

"At the Bank of Canada," put in Nat, "we're working like crazy to figure out where the money will come from to equip and pay for the armed forces. Governor Towers would consider it treasonous if I left to join up."

"You're all strapping young bucks. Aren't you worried about what people might say?"

"Well, no one has called me a shirker to my face," said Kevin, who was a well-muscled six-foot-three. "Down at the lumberyard we've never been busier. All this new construction for headquarters, offices, and barracks has us working overtime. Mr. Edwards thinks we should set up our own construction company and bid on some of these government contracts. He'd shoot me if I joined the army."

"Nothing's happening overseas anyways," said Dorothy. "Tough on Poland, but it's not likely that the Germans are about to dive-bomb Halifax harbour."

"Canada needs us working right where we are," said George. "Unemployed fellows who want a job and three squares a day can join up. The services are all competing for recruits. There are work opportunities like we haven't seen in ten years."

"If you did join up, which service would you choose?" asked Mary.

"Air force, of course!" said Nat. He broke into song, "Off we go, into the wild blue yonder ... Climbing high into the sun!"

"Navy for me," said Kevin. "See the world."

"Army's where the real work is done," said Paul.

Everyone looked over at George who sat in silence.

"If you had to choose?" prodded Katie.

"I'm not much of a shoot-'em-up type," said George. "I guess it's part of being a teacher. You help bring kids into a better understanding of themselves and the world. You don't want to raise killers. Joining in the slaughter seems like a betrayal of first principles."

"But you don't want them to be victims, either. Look what happened to Poland," said Mary. "What if the Huns were marching down Rideau Street?"

"Come on, Georgie, gun to your head."

"Then I guess I'd join Nat in the air force."

"For the glory?"

"For the company. And the view."

The men did the dishes while the women took advantage of the unusually mild night and adjourned to the roof terrace.

"So, tell me about married life," said Frances. "What am I missing?"

"Try buying a vacuum cleaner these days," said Mary. "Impossible."

"I had no concept of the laundry a man creates," said Katie. "Or the mess they make in the bathroom. Father was neat as a pin."

"It is strange," added Mary, "learning to live with someone new. You're familiar with your own family's quirks after a lifetime. Ned's differences are, well, different."

"How?"

"He likes his food well-seasoned. Salt and pepper were about as spicy as we got at home. Nat's mother was Italian and used garlic and basil and oregano all the time. He compliments my cooking, but asked me to kick up some of my recipes."

"Kevin treats anything in the icebox as fair game for snacking. I can't count the times he demolished something I was saving for tomorrow's supper. Now I put 'Eat this and die' notes on things."

"You two are so lucky," said Frances. "Married and established so young."

"Well, middle-class morality dictates that a good girl *has* to get married these days to access the amenities, so to speak," said Katie.

"And are you?"

"I am!"

Mary blushed scarlet before adding, "We're trying to have a baby."

"You are?" shot back Katie. "We're trying *not* to. Can't afford to have kids yet. But Kevin's one randy animal. Buys rubbers by the dozen. Needs the extra-large size," she said with a wink.

"This has been great fun," said Dorothy, moving the conversation to safer ground. "Georgie is a little quiet, but everyone's friendliness has put him at ease. Can we do this again?"

"How about a rematch in three weeks?" said Frances. "November 25? Give us all time to recover and work on new recipes."

Paul stayed behind to help clean up. "Your friends are nifty," he said, giving her a squeeze.

"You were a big help," replied Frances. "They loved your mixed greens. I've never had oranges and nuts and onion together in a salad before. You didn't learn about that combination down on the farm."

"They do sell cookbooks, you know, Miss McFadden."

"I heard you joshing George about the Queen's–Western football rivalry. Seems like a nice enough fellow. Dorothy's tentative about him for some reason. Kevin was the only man without a university education, but he didn't seem out of place."

"Kevin's a riot. I don't think it's possible to have a great sense of humour without being intelligent. Maybe he didn't go to university, but he's sure sharp with the quips. He was very impressed by the range of wood types used in your apartment. Gave us a complete tutorial."

Frances snuggled under his chin. "I'm glad you had a good time."

"Oh! I just had a letter from my mom asking about my Christmas plans."

"Will you be heading down to Ilderton to be with your family?"

"Yes. What do you usually do for Christmas?"

"Now that I'm an orphan? Well, the O'Briens usually have me over on Christmas Eve, and the Deavys invite me for dinner on Christmas Day."

"You're not really an orphan. Your dad is out there somewhere, isn't he?"

"The last I heard from him was a two-sentence condolence telegram when my sister died in 1934. For all intents and purposes, I'm an orphan."

"Christmas is on a Monday, and we get Boxing Day off as well. I have some holidays left over, so I'm taking the whole week off." He took a deep breath. "I was wondering if you might like to come down to the farm for Christmas. See the bright lights of Ilderton."

"I … I … wow! This is quite a step."

"They're just family. That's where you're supposed to be at Christmas. I know you'd be welcome."

"Are you sure it wouldn't be any inconvenience?"

"I haven't broached it with Mom yet. I wanted to see if you were interested. She likes to take in strays for the holidays—the bachelor bank manager, the maiden schoolteacher, the new priest. There's always plenty of food. Her Christmas larder could feed an army. What do you say?"

It was a plunge. "I'd say that I'm speechless."

"You have many characteristics, Frances McFadden, but speechlessness is not one of them." He ducked a swat from a tea towel. "You have a beautiful bell-like voice and I'd like my family to hear it."

"Why don't you check it out with your parents. If they'd like to host a bank clerk from Ottawa, well, I'd be delighted."

Paul took her in his arms. "You'll probably sleep in my sister Jenny's room. She has bunk beds, and that's where the overflow goes."

"How old is she?"

"Fourteen."

"An impressionable age. I might be a bad influence on her."

"I'd rather that you be a bad influence on me."

13

MOLLY TOWERS

Financial problems between Canada and Great Britain developed early. They included the financing of British purchases in Canada, sharing the costs of the British Commonwealth Air Training Plan, the price of Canadian wheat, and prospective British cuts in buying Canadian products [due to foreign exchange controls in Britain].

(Fullerton, 124)

A woman in a tailored fox fur jacket and a smart black hat swept resolutely around the left edge of Claire's reception desk and flitted across the outer office like a steel Tinkerbell. Hand on hip, Mae West fashion, Tinkerbell gave Frances the once-over. "You the new girl?" Bright red lipstick blossomed on her alabaster skin. "I'm Molly Towers. I'm here to see Graham."

If the governor was expecting his wife to drop by, he hadn't told Frances. "He's with the deputy minister of Finance right now, Mrs. Towers, but if you'd—"

Molly Towers had no-nonsense edgy blue eyes. "Clifford? Oh good. I want to see if the Clarks can come to dinner on Saturday."

Mrs. Towers moved to the governor's door and opened it without knocking. "What are you two bad boys up to?" she was heard to say before the door closed on the outside world. The outer office entourage paused and eight eyes moved to Frances. She acknowledged them with hands wide, facing upward, semi-crucified, before going back to work. In ten minutes, Mr. Clark left, and shortly thereafter the Governor buzzed Frances to come in. Mrs. Towers was fitfully punishing a cigarette.

"Miss McFadden, you've met my wife?"

"Yes, sir."

"And what was your first impression?" he asked with a twinkle in his eye.

"Very fetching hat," said Frances. "And I doubt that the fur looked nearly that good on the fox."

They both smiled. "Quick recovery after having been bowled over in the outer office," said the governor. "Mr. Clark has just given me my marching orders for England. Negotiations on war financing are floundering. I'd like you along. Can the secretariat carry on without you?"

Abandon her Little Rascals?

Frances's jaw twinged. "I'm confident they'd be fine."

Graham Towers flashed a discount grin, but it was the answer he wanted.

Truth to power? Sure thing.

"Good," he said. "We use Altman's on Rideau Street to book steamship passage. Miss Briscoe would have left a travel file somewhere. Get us out of Quebec City late next week on one of the Canadian Pacific Empress fleet. Molly and I will need a two-bedroom suite in first class."

"Get cabins just front of midships," added Mrs. Towers, exhaling a stream of smoke. "Minimizes the ocean swell."

"Book a one-bedroom suite for yourself," added the Governor. "One with a wall safe for the code books."

Frances stopped taking notes and looked up. "They have suites in steerage?"

Mrs. Towers laughed.

"We all travel first class," said the governor. "We represent the government of Canada. The suites are our offices on board. Molly sleeps late and I rise early, so we need two bedrooms. I'll use the living room for meetings. We'll have to host a couple of cocktail parties on the way over."

"I don't need to travel first class," said Frances. "My last trip across the Atlantic was on a freighter. Shared a bathroom, but it was fine."

"Won't do. You need access to the first-class dining room and all the lounges. I might need your living room for business if Molly is entertaining in our suite. You'll be working full out from dawn to the last dance in the ballroom."

"At?"

"Gathering information. Discreetly of course. Finding out who knows what and how they found out. It's a little game. Pick up the most, give away the least." He smiled. "Scotty Meldrum says you're a natural."

"I dance like a cement mixer, and I can't lie without blushing."

"The pros never lie, although they are quite agile at deflecting direct questions with partial truths. You can say you work at the Bank of Canada, and if pressed, in the governor's secretariat. All true. Have business cards printed up that say something like, 'Secretariat Director, Bank of Canada.' The British respond particularly well to a title."

Frances's Presbyterian thrift provoked a thought. "Isn't first class passage rather expensive?"

"This war is going to cost Canada ten billion dollars if it costs a dime. Our travel expenses won't amount to chump change."

"Have Altman book us into the Dorchester Hotel in London," threw in Mrs. Towers.

"Yes. Same deal—a two-bedroom suite for us, and a one-bedroom suite for you close by. Phone Arnold Heeney in the PMO and borrow a private railcar for the trip to Quebec City. The cabinet uses several, but they're all chained to Parliament Hill with the House in session."

"Can you call Altman's now?" pressed Mrs. Towers.

Frances retreated to her desk phone and was back in ten minutes. "Mr. Altman says that the CP Empresses are all being requisitioned for war service. The *Empress of Britain* makes its last run out of Montreal on November 23. He can get us over on that, then she's going to Greenock to be refitted as a troop carrier. The only way he can get us back to Canada is on one of CP's smaller Duchess liners or flying through the Azores."

"Oh, God!" exclaimed Molly Towers. "The Rollicking Duchesses. They're round-bottomed and leap like broncos on the slightest wave. But I'm sure as hell not flying," she declared, stubbing out her cigarette.

The Governor rocked back in his swivel chair. "All right, get us all out on the 23rd. We'll book return passage later from England. We don't know how long things will take over there. I'd like to be back to host the Christmas Tea on December 22. Prep your team to carry the show until the end of December in case we're held up."

"Yes, sir. One other item. I don't own much that would pass as first-class cabin clothes."

"Miss Briscoe claimed she drew little from the expense account you've taken over. Use it. Men get by with a few business suits, three tuxedos and two sets of tails. It's a little more complicated for women. They seem to change clothes about five times a day. Molly?"

Mrs. Towers liked having her advice sought. "I could give your wardrobe a quick look," she purred.

"Thank you. When would—"

"Let's get it over with," she said, standing up. She walked over and gave the governor a proprietary peck on the cheek. It was a warmthless second-cousin kiss, just marking territory.

"Remember tonight, Gray. Cocktails at six with the Binkleys. Don't be late." She marched out the door, and Frances scampered after the restless spirit.

Molly Towers drove a large Buick too fast down Metcalfe to the Balmoral where they rode the elevator up in silence. Her eyes widened upon entering 7 South West. She struggled to pretend that she wasn't too impressed. "Lovely spot," she observed. The "for a bank clerk" was left unsaid. Eyes flicked over the four-poster bed and the marble fireplace mantle as they passed through the master bedroom to the dressing room where sunlight filtered through the skylight. She sat down at the vanity table and lit a cigarette. Frances opened the louvered closet doors and began bringing clothes to her like tribute to a queen. The queen sat there regally dispassionate, like one compelled by duty to perform a pedestrian task.

"Your professional clothes are fine. That black cocktail dress is good, and could be worn a couple of extra times with floral scarves. You'll want at least four more short dresses. Stick to solid colours. Elegant, but not flashy. You'll need three floor-length gowns with matching gloves for evening wear. Keep the gowns simple. Understatement is the best strategy for a young woman with a good figure.

"It will be cold and damp on board and in London. Bring slacks and sweaters. A lined raincoat and an umbrella. Get good footwear. Five or six pairs. The British are snobs about shoe leather."

"And where can I get all this? We leave in ten days."

"Montreal. French Canadians are light-years ahead of the rest of the country in style. Marie-Paule Nolin has her own fashion boutique at Holt Renfrew's. That's probably your best bet for ensembles. She'll make sure all the pieces talk to each other. You can look in at Gaby Bernier and Ida Desmarais, who are first-class couturieres, but may not be able to give you a quick turnaround, as they make everything by hand.

"Get yourself a matched set of luggage from either John Pound or Louis Vuitton. You'll need a steamer trunk and at least three large suitcases. Quality clothing suffers when packed too tightly."

Molly Towers stood up, the powwow over. "Drive you back to the Bank?"

"Thank you, no. I'll walk back later. I appreciate the help." Frances saw her to the elevator then phoned Anna Deloitte downstairs in 6C.

"I need a fashion consult. Can you spare a half hour? I'll make some tea."

Anna Deloitte was fifteen years older than Frances but their kindred spirits provided an easy bond. Anna appreciated distractions. She was still quietly anxious that her German gentleman friend, Max Kessler, had "gone missing" after war broke out. Anna did not know that Frances had ever met Max. Frances knew full well that Herr Kessler had suddenly left a moving train in Poland, not likely of his own volition. She hated herself for it, but did not know how to tell Anna. "So," Anna smiled, "Molly Towers has taken you under her wing. Interesting."

"Wouldn't want her husband's secretary looking like she just fell off the turnip truck, would she?"

"Molly Towers has made a career of securing her own advantage."

"There is a twitchiness about her, like she's skating over thin ice. 'Not comfortable in her skin,' my mother would have said. Do you come across her much at Ottawa social events?"

"As often as she indulges society with her presence. She looks calm, although you're right—her eyes dart around like a cornered ferret. I think she's insecure. The Anna Deloitte Theorem on Aberrant Social Behaviour—from braggarts to wallflowers—everything stems from insecurity."

"Why would she be insecure? She's attractive. Intelligent. Being the wife of the governor of the Bank of Canada must place her high on the pecking order in Ottawa."

"True. Just below the privy councillors' wives and the old money."

"Know much about her?"

"Upper-middle-class Montreal background. Father was vice-president of the Montreal Steel Works. Mother a Molson cousin by marriage. Plays golf and doubles tennis decently. No children. Reputedly finds Ottawa dull and slips away to Montreal or their summer place at Murray Bay as much as she can. Then it's the Jupiter Club at Hobe Sound in Florida every winter. Socializes with a very small circle of friends. The Scotty Meldrums, the Clifford Clarks, the Norman Robertsons, and a few others. Is seen as a little stand-offish. Refuses to flirt with other women's husbands."

"That's bad?"

"Every married woman fantasizes that her spouse is both immensely loyal and immensely attractive to other women. It's a little insulting when someone doesn't bother flirting with your husband."

"This is because she's so smitten with Graham Towers?"

"Don't think so. Their partnership seems sexless to me, like a brother and sister duo. No teasing innuendo or spontaneous hugs. There are rumours that she has 'outside interests' in Montreal. Not male."

"You're kidding!"

"Rumours. There's always a degree of cattiness in woman's rest-room chat that needs to be discounted. And she's never put her hand on my thigh—so it's either spurious gossip, or I'm not her type."

"Here's her clothing advice for first class travel to England. What do you think?"

Anna examined the list. "A little restrained. I wonder if she advises 'simple' and 'understated' attire because she doesn't want competition. She's quite the clothes horse. If she's advising three gowns for evening wear, you can bet she'll bring six."

"I'm not the governor's wife. I don't want to compete. Being a wallflower is fine. I'm going to have enough trouble carrying off 'first-class behaviour' as it is."

"If the governor wants you on the travel team, he wants you looking good. Why don't we go shopping in Montreal this weekend? Doll you up. Create an Eliza Doolittle mystique that will enchant every man in first class."

14

BON VOYAGE

The cost of the Canadian war effort had two principal components in that first war year: Canada's own military bill, and the cost of carrying the British deficit [for military supplies] *with Canada.*

(Fullerton, 127)

Mr. Mueller covered Frances's desk in the secretariat so she could take the Little Rascals to lunch at Murphy-Gamble's. Reggie Armstrong was happy to see her again and found her a table for five.

"Cheers!" she said, lifting her glass of Coca-Cola. "It's not the Chateau Laurier, but we have to work this afternoon and should hold back on the white wine. A great first month! We have the outer office shipshape and we're firing on all cylinders. Congratulations." She drank deeply and set her glass down. "Now, a new challenge."

"Nazi attack?" queried Brendan. "Maybe we should order quickly."

"No. Although the Nazis are indirectly responsible. This is completely confidential Official Secrets Act time. Not a peep to loved ones or family."

"Interesting semantics," observed Maddie, "suggesting loved ones *aren't* family."

"Thank you, language police. Governor Towers is leaving for England next Thursday and he wants me to accompany him. We might be gone three or four weeks. He asked if the secretariat could function in my absence. I gave him my unqualified assurance."

"What!" exclaimed Maddie.

"But who's in charge when you're gone?" asked Claire.

"The very question we are here to consider," said Frances. "Let's order lunch first. The chicken pot pie is delicious."

"How about rock-paper-scissors?" said Brendan.

"I'll take the potpie," said Bridget.

"Why don't you just appoint one of us?" asked Claire.

"I think you four should decide. You have to live with the new Pooh-Bah while I'm in merry old England. I'm confident each one of you could do the job."

"*Come on!*" said Maddie. "We're spirited, but we are not Frances McFaddens."

"And lucky you're not," replied Frances. "What if you shared the job on rotation? Pooh-Bah-for-the-day?"

Brendan winced. "Too short a rotation. It would be chaotic. Like that Abbott and Costello skit—*Who's on First?*"

"I barely know how to work the pencil sharpener," said Maddie. "I can't be in charge."

"You're the only one of us with a university degree," countered Claire.

"Yeah. That and a nickel will buy you a coffee," replied Maddie. "I know nothing—*nothing* about the Bank of Canada—compared to any of you."

"I've been here for over three years," said Bridget. "But I'm not the leader type. Following is my strength. I'd follow any one of you."

Frances nodded. "Valid points. That doesn't mean that I don't still have confidence in you both. Brendan and Claire: Would you two be willing to split the job up?"

A mute pause, then Brendan suggested, "What if I were the big cheese for one week, and then Claire took it for a week. Bridget and Maddie watch, then take turns batting cleanup. Everybody shares part of the load."

"Fine by me," said Frances. "Brid and Maddie?"

"You both would be fine," confirmed Claire. "We've been under-studying each other in every role."

"Still sounds scary. What does the Pooh-Bah have to do?"

"You see me at work every day. It's not complicated. I delegate new business and make sure the workload is evenly balanced. I arrange relief if someone looks overwhelmed. I'm the point person if the governor isn't here, but I'll be with the governor, so that won't be a problem. If anything serious comes up, just pass it along to the deputy governor. And I'm just a telegram away. You'll have to code all cables being sent to the governor. Keep them short. I'll have to decode them."

"Aren't you worried about your safety?" ask Brendan. "Nearly ninety ships were attacked by U-boats in September and October. Over 400,000 tons of shipping lost."

"Lots of boats are still getting through. The governor is comfortable enough to bring his wife along."

Frances was sleeping better. Max Kessler still occasionally entered her dreams, but as a grainy sidebar, not the feature story. Acupuncture treatments from Dr. Wei had done their work. He'd given her chrysanthemum tea to drink before bedtime. It wasn't as tasty as the port, but there was no fuzzy morning-mouth and a lot less guilt.

Frances told Miles, the Balmoral doorman, that she would be away for several weeks on holidays, and asked him to put her mail on the dining room table. Gladys Gilhooly would forward her apologies to the Metcalfe Street Bridge Club. She warned Anna Deloitte that she wouldn't be in church for a while. Dr. Grace knew where she was going and why. "I've seen cardsharps working these transatlantic ships," he cautioned. "They draw suckers into bridge or poker games. It starts all friendly penny ante where the sucker wins big for the first hour. Then the stakes rise and suddenly the tables turn. Be careful. I don't want to have to come over and bail you out of debtors' prison."

Breaking the news to Paul Roderick was going to be ticklish. They'd shared several lovely Saturday evenings since his mother had confirmed the invitation to the farm for Christmas. Frances invited him to dinner at the Chateau Laurier.

She was late arriving and was surprised to see Paul conversing in French with Henri, their waiter. "Where do farm boys from Ilderton learn to speak French so fluently?" she asked when they'd ordered.

"Mademoiselle Gagné, my high school French teacher, was a saint. French from France. Her passion for the language was infectious. She claimed I had been gifted with an excellent ear for languages. Most of the farm boys dropped French as soon as they could. The class got smaller and smaller up through the grades. Only three of us left by Grade 13. Like a personal tutorial. She played records of French songs, making us write them out then sing the lyrics. We did crossword puzzles and acted out plays in French. We discussed the news in French. It was insidious. I started dreaming in French. It brought her great joy to plant these seeds in rural Oxford County. The 93 per cent I got on my French departmental helped me win a scholarship to Western."

Paul was so animated and cheerful that she put off telling him until coffee and dessert. "Bad news, I'm afraid. I have to leave Ottawa next Thursday on Bank business. Return date unknown. I can't count on being back for Christmas. I'm going to have to bow out of your invitation to Ilderton for the holidays. I'm sorry."

The sparkle drained out of his eyes. "Where are you going?"

"I can't say."

"Will you be travelling with Governor Towers?"

"I can't say."

"And you have no idea when you'll be back?"

"The Bank of Canada has one staff party a year. The Governor's Tea on December 22. I'd like to be back for that."

"That'd be too bad. If you missed the tea."

"Listen. I truly am sorry. I was looking forward to meeting your family. It's out of my hands."

Paul's face sagged. "I bragged about you so much that Mom made my brothers give Jenny's bedroom a fresh coat of paint." A rueful laugh. "I guess I misunderstood how much I meant to you."

"Hey! Not fair. You mean a lot to me. We've grown very close in a short time."

"Not so close that you'd tell your boss you have plans for Christmas."

"There's a war on! I was asked to help. You'd do the same."

"Surely you're not the only secretary at the Bank of Canada that can do whatever it is? Take minutes? Type letters?"

Frances hung her head.

"Well, that's all you ever say about your job. Write memos. Do filing. Yet this ... this clerical stuff is more important than your personal relationships? How about your friends? Do they count? You've invited everyone to dinner at your apartment next Saturday."

"Oh Lord! I forgot. I'll call Katie. You're all still welcome to use my apartment."

Paul looked pained and pale. "This pretty well takes the wind out of the evening. We might as well call it a night."

"Paul, I invited you here to celebrate. How many times can I say that I'm sorry? These are desperate times. I'm just trying to do my bit."

"Let's get our coats. I'll walk you home."

"Are you going to sulk all the way?"

"I'm a little down. Still, it's my duty. I'll walk you home."

"Oh? I'm an obligation you have to discharge? Like putting out the garbage?"

"Come on. There are lots of soldiers on the streets letting off steam before they're shipped out. You shouldn't walk home alone."

"I can take a taxi."

"Is that what you'd like?"

"I'd like a little understanding of my position."

"Your position?" He snorted. "You've sold your soul to the Bank of Canada. I hope it was a good bargain."

Frances stood up. "Good night, Mr. Roderick!"

"Goodbye, Miss McFadden."

Governor Towers thought it would be good for morale if they came into the office for two hours on the morning that the *Empress of Britain* sailed. It gave Frances a chance to run over final details with the Rascals, whose eagerness was compounded with apprehension. Anxiety didn't keep them from purchasing a travel gift for her, a pair of fine leather gloves. It was so thoughtful and unexpected that Frances almost cried. "You'll be fine. I'll miss all the fun." She wanted to hug everyone.

"Right," said Brendan. "After the bright lights of London, you'll barely remember our names." Brendan was taking the first week at her desk, leaving Claire free to finalize plans for the governor's Christmas Tea with the Carnation Girls. Three hundred and forty staff, and possibly no governor. "We hope to be back by December 22, but we just don't know. Have contingencies."

The governor gave the Executive a final briefing, and then met for an hour with the ten department heads. At 10:15, Frances left for home. At 11:30, she called Red Line, and Murray had the taxi at the door by the time Miles had dollied her luggage down to the lobby. Murray whistled on seeing the steamer trunk and the huge suitcases. "You goin' to the moon, Frances?" he asked.

At Union Station, it took three redcaps to transport everything to the governor's rail car. Molly Towers was engrossed in a fashion magazine and acknowledged Frances with the barest of eye flickers. The governor was more welcoming. "We'll have lunch en route at 12:15, then I will need a nap and suggest you take one, too. We can get a little work done between two and four. We should be in Quebec City by five and on board in time to change for dinner at seven."

"What colour gown are you wearing tonight?" asked Molly from behind her magazine.

"Haven't given it a thought."

"Well, I'm wearing my coral lamé. Stay away from that hue or we'll look like the Bobbsey Twins."

There was absolutely nothing Bobbsey about Molly Towers. Burrs seemed to slip easily under her blanket. Was she anticipating being seasick for five days? Or was she reluctant to take the trip at all? Or unhappy that Frances was along? Double Bloody Marys during lunch mellowed her. "There will be a surfeit of men on board the *Empress*," she said. "When submarines lurk, women tend to stay home. The men have little to amuse themselves and see single women as fair game."

"Game?"

"For shipboard romance. Short, torrid, and so long forever. Upper-class Englishman can be quite appealing for an intense little tryst. Enjoy, but don't flatter yourself into thinking that you'll ever see these men again once the ship docks at Southampton."

"By the way," said the governor. "Did you tip anyone on your freighter trip?"

"No. Mr. Meldrum gave Captain Hyland a case of Macallan."

"Well, be prepared to tip on the *Empress*. Your room steward and your dining room waiter will be expecting at least $10 in an envelope on the last day. Their wages are low. They survive on patronage. You'll be dealing with the ship's telegraph operator every day. Tip him up front and get our cables sent first. Put this all on your expense account."

"Do you have seasick pills?" added Molly.

"No."

"Get some. It can be a rough ride on the North Atlantic. There's a drugstore at the train station in Quebec City. You won't earn your passage if you're lashed to a toilet for the trip."

Molly Towers had a talent for disparaging largess.

Bon voyage? A litany of cautions about U-boats, seasickness, card sharps and romantic bounders. All this on top of a chilly estrangement from Paul and a galling sense she was forsaking her secretariat before it had jelled. Frances wondered if the acupuncture and chrysanthemum tea would be enough to balance her yin and let her rest. Who was it that said, "The purpose of life is the search for a good night's sleep"?

15

EMPRESS OUTBOUND

King went on to say that Canada would not go beyond her resources and would proceed [in supporting the British] *subject to the advice of the Minister of Finance. Finance Minister Ralston asserted that Canada's fiscal capacity would not enable her to come "within shooting distance" of the figures suggested by the British …*

(Bryce, 45)

After so many warnings about the perils of ocean travel, Frances found the Atlantic crossing a little anticlimactic. Fortunately, she had brought along *Pride and Prejudice* to reread, and in the train station bookstore had picked up a Penguin pocketbook edition of Shakespeare's *Antony and Cleopatra*.

In the first-class dining room, eight tables were headed by a ship's officer. Governor and Mrs. Towers sat at the captain's table with four other couples. As the rank descended through executive officer, second officer, doctor, chief engineer, purser, etc., so did the status of the passengers. Frances was seated with seven others at the table of young Second Lieutenant Hastings, the fourth officer. Wide ears bracketed a freckled, boyish face. They shared the table with two RAF officers, a Toronto businessman and his nervous wife, a Red Cross nurse, and a Dominican nun.

The RAF men knew Lieutenant Hastings as "Wingnut" from their days together at Harrow. Flying Officer Smalley and Flying Officer Radcliff had been in Canada working under Lord Riverdale on the logistics of the British Commonwealth Air Training Program. "The RAF is only twenty-one years old," FO Radcliff explained. "Younger than me! The commanding officer was to be known as 'Marshal of the Air,' but King George felt that sounded too much like it encroached on the attributes of God, whom he did not wish to offend, so the CO was named Marshal of the Royal Air Force."

"Anyone I've ever met from the RAF," countered Lieutenant Hastings, "emulates a close kinship with God."

"Come now, Wingnut," said FO Smalley, "we're not that snotty. We've been known to dine with fourth officers from the merchant marine."

Lieutenant Hastings left before dessert to return to duty.

"Isn't it a little mean to call Lieutenant Hastings 'Wingnut,' Frances asked, "just because his ears stick out a bit?"

"Old-school tradition, Miss McFadden. Everybody had a nickname at Harrow," replied FO Smalley.

"Dated from 1572 when the place was founded," confirmed FO Radcliff. "It was a badge of honour. Meant you belonged. Smalley here was known as 'Smalls'—British slang for women's knickers."

"Yes," said FO Smalley. "And Radcliff has been known as 'Leaky' since Lower School. Was so excited when we beat Eaton at cricket that he pissed his pants. Wingnut got off rather lightly."

"What was your school nickname?" asked F.O. Radcliff.

"Didn't have one," said Frances. "No one did."

"Ah! Lovely country, Canada," mused FO Smalley. "Earnest, congenial citizens. Perhaps a little short on metaphor. And tradition."

"The perfect place to have one's servants raised," concluded FO Radcliff.

After dinner, Frances found the telegraph office, an overheated, charmless closet below the bridge. Able Seaman Neilson explained the system. "There's someone on duty twenty-four hours a day, Miss. Three of us work four hours on and eight hours off. Louter and Munro are the other chaps. Very reliable fellows."

"I'm travelling with the governor of the Bank of Canada, who may generate a lot of telegraph traffic. I'll drop down frequently. Please find me if something urgent comes in." Frances handed him six one-pound notes. "Kindly share this token with your colleagues and convey how much I appreciate their service."

"Yes, ma'am!"

Frances's cabin was a confusing trek from the Towerses' suite through a labyrinth of twisting halls. A shipboard routine was quickly established. Frances picked up incoming telegrams at 7:00 a.m. and decoded them in her suite over coffee delivered by Jackson, her steward. She slipped them under the governor's door by 8:00 and headed up to the dining room. Breakfast was casual, buffet style.

Her tablemates drifted in and out, which lent itself to informal conversations.

Sister Servacia reminded Frances of her friend Mary, a guileless font of unintentional double entendres. She was returning to France to oversee an orphanage run by their Mother House in Reims, having superintended a similar operation near Lake Megantic for seven years. "Warriors reap what they sow," said Sister Servacia. "The fruits of war are orphans. I return for the harvest."

The nurse, Mabel Wilson, was going to England to set up a convalescent hospital for Canadian officers at Garnons in Herefordshire. A dozen other nurses would follow her in January.

Thomas Tanner was vice-president of a tool-and-die factory in Hamilton. He was heading to Manchester to finalize the negotiations of contracts related to artillery parts. His wife, Laura, had never been on a ship before. Her green face was a meld of motion sickness and fear.

Conversation was cordial but circumspect, prodding Mabel Wilson to acknowledge with a smile, "Loose lips sink ships."

"And let's not forget that we *are* on a ship," Laura Tanner reminded those who might have forgotten.

Frances was able to get away with admitting to employment with the Bank of Canada, and the need by Governor Towers for administrative support when he travelled.

"I'm surprised that you travel first class," said Mr. Tanner.

"Me, too," admitted Frances. "Governor Towers wanted me close at hand."

"I'm sure Miss McFadden understates her services to the governor," Sister Servacia said with a Delphic ambiguity that could imply Frances was either a modest secretary or the governor's mistress. Sidelong glances shot around the table indicating how widely the latter interpretation was considered.

At 10:00 a.m., Frances knocked on the governor's door, and they worked until noon. They caught up on correspondence and worked on details of the first war bond issue that was due out in February. The bond float was worrisome.

"We need vast quantities of money to pay for this war," said the governor. "But if the issue doesn't sell out, it will be a terrible blow to morale. However, a small loan, say a hundred million dollars, would last only about six weeks. It would hardly be worth the paperwork."

Brief answers were dictated to incoming cables. Few other messages were sent. Graham Towers was enjoying a relaxed holiday before the heavy lifting began in England.

"When we get there, I will be harassed for more money to support the war effort. I will assure all petitioners that each concern will be drawn to the attention of the prime minister through daily reports back to Ottawa. The British will find this unsatisfactory and will press for hard cash and a signed agreement. They will be eager to interpret, or misinterpret, any nuance as a commitment. There will be no official minutes of these sessions, so you will need to keep meticulous verbatim records. Can't have recriminations later with the 'but you promised' sort of thing. We are all on the same side, after all. Mr. King has allowed me the latitude of throwing them a bone before we leave, perhaps guaranteeing some level of funding for six months."

The governor sent Frances to the head steward for a passenger list, and Molly culled through it for two cocktail parties they would host on successive nights. Prominent Canadians would be invited to one and the international banker-business crowd to the other. "You're welcome to come if you wish, Miss McFadden, but these are not command performances."

"Could I be of any help?" asked Frances.

"You might benefit from meeting the financial community. I'll be corresponding with many of them later, and you can put names to faces."

It was time lost to reading Shakespeare, but it was worth the cost of admission to watch Molly Towers in action. Her public persona was witty and gracious. She listened attentively, circulated to include everyone, even taking Frances by the arm and introducing her. "This is Frances McFadden, Graham's chief factotum during business hours. After work she hands what's left of him over to me," she'd say with a conspiratorial smile, as though they were partners in crime. A virtuoso performance, and most definitely not the Molly Towers Frances had seen offstage. Who was the *real* Molly Towers?

It did beg the question: "Is there more than one Frances McFadden?"

Every evening after dinner, the Layton Swing Band entertained in the ballroom. The seasoned musicians mixed the tempo to suit all ages and temperaments. Another surprise: Molly and Graham Towers danced exquisitely together to every imaginable rhythm: the waltz, the tango, the foxtrot. Even the Charleston. Nothing in Graham Towers's shyish Bank of Canada demeanour gave any hint of his talent on the dance floor.

There were few single women on board, making Frances and Mabel Wilson popular in the ballroom. FOs Smalley and Radcliff adopted them as mascots, and generally kept them whirling to ward off predatory males. Lieutenant Hastings was deemed safe and scored as many dances with her as he could. Frances's dance experience had been limited to partnering with one of the Crazy Deavys and lurching around to Saturday night radio tunes on the Deavy living room linoleum. She kept an eye on the Towerses for pointers and sat out the faster numbers.

During a band break, Frances was ensconced in a bathroom stall, when she heard two women enter the Ladies and heels click toward the row of sinks. The voice of Molly Towers piped over the running water. "If I can keep him to two drinks before dinner, he behaves himself. The meal soaks it up. It's the early third drink that launches his libido downward. Can I borrow your rouge? I must have left mine in our cabin."

"Here … How's the new girl?"

"Seems sensible enough. I had a fearful moment when I heard that the old battle-axe was retiring. I shouldn't speak ill of the dead, but she would *never* put my calls through. This one is barely out of bobby socks. Gray's recreational tastes run more to ripe and worldly. Anyway, she's someone else's sugarplum. You should see her penthouse at the Balmoral Arms. Chock-a-block with art deco furniture. On a bank clerk's salary? I don't think so."

"Any ideas?"

"I asked Betsey Knowles. She gave me some cock and bull story about an inheritance. From a mother who was a night shift nurse? Or a father who went west looking for work years ago and never returned? No, she's latched onto somebody with deep pockets who fancies them young."

"So, who?"

"Probably some lumber money with a boring wife."

"She doesn't look the ingénue type. Attractive enough, but a very plain dresser."

"Yes, well, she asked my advice and I gave it to her."

"Unfair!"

"She's young. She has lots of time. I don't need any more competition than I already have."

A laugh. "Is the pot calling the kettle black?"

"At least I'm discreet."

"Was that weekend at Montebello discreet?"

"Nobody's perfect."

"Was Graham furious?"

"What could he say, really? All things considered?"

By tradition, on the second night at sea, R.N. Stuart, VC, Commodore of the Canadian Pacific fleet and commanding officer of the *Empress of Britain*, hosted a pre-dinner reception for allied commissioned officers from all services. They numbered over forty, including the ship's complement. Unattached female travellers under fifty were extended courtesy invitations. Wingnut explained to Frances that women called upon to balance the gender ratio at such social occasions were known as "ballast." "No offence," he added.

Lieutenant Hastings pried Frances away from FOs Smalley and Radcliff and introduced her to his colleagues, all resplendent in their formal mess jackets and service ribbons. The second officer, Richards, did a double take on meeting her. "Frances McFadden? Not *the* Frances McFadden?" he asked.

"*A* Frances McFadden. There may well be others. My parents didn't think to copyright the name."

"You're a bank clerk in Ottawa?"

"Yes."

Richards called to the Executive Officer. "Denby! Get over here and see what the cat dragged in." Richards presented Frances like an oyster on the half shell. "Commander Denby, Frances McFadden."

"*The* Frances McFadden?" Denby asked with raised eyebrows as a small crowd gathered around them.

"We've been through this already."

"The Frances McFadden who killed a German spy with her bare hands?" continued Denby.

Frances tried for composure. "Wherever did you hear such a story?"

"From Jiggs Hyland, Captain of the *Town of Mont Royal*. In the back room of the Green Parrot in Quebec City," said Richards smugly. "A little gin joint near the docks where all the Canadian Pacific line officers hang their hats when in port."

"Ah," said Frances, as the lights went on. "The good Captain Hyland. I am much in his debt for getting me safely back to Canada in September. As I recall, he had a gift for hyperbole. The truth was often a casualty, especially when there was liberal access to Jamaican rum."

"That's Jiggs all right," said Denby. "A hard man to out-drink or beat at spinning a yarn."

"But you don't deny it," pressed Richards.

"A double agent, wasn't it?" added Denby.

"Captain Hyland was in the wheelhouse around the clock getting the *Town of Mont Royal* out of submarine range as war broke out. He must have been near comatose when we finally docked."

"He claimed," continued Denby, "that a scruffy little bank clerk from Ottawa named Frances McFadden did the dirty on a Nazi spy in Poland. 'With her bare hands,' he said."

Frances froze. "Did he say anything else?"

Denby reflected, "You know, I think there was some other gem he was dying to share, but he bit down on it."

By this time, a dozen partiers had surrounded them, like moths drawn to a porch light. A tight spot to escape from, incrementally. Then an arm with gold braid half way to the elbow reached into the scrum and gently turned Frances' palm face up for all to view. "Doesn't look like the hand of a murderer to me," said Commodore Stuart with a congenial smile.

"Thank you, Commodore," said Frances. "An officer *and* a gentleman."

"But you don't deny it," repeated Richards.

"Richards, you're becoming a bit of a bore," said Denby. "Fetch Miss McFadden a rum punch."

In the lexicon of British insults, Frances had noted that "bore" was the supreme reproach, well beyond "bastard" or "coward." Richards slunk away.

"Miss McFadden, are you free to join my table for lunch tomorrow?" asked Commodore Stuart.

"It would be my pleasure," said Frances, "if Wing … if Lieutenant Hastings can spare me."

16

HIGH COMMISSIONER

Mackenzie King reflected that it was "really shameful the way in which the British Government in these matters seeks to evade and undo and to change the meaning of the most definitely understood obligations."

(Pickersgill, 49)

Crerar's talk about wheat with the British had gone nowhere. Crerar had proposed a bulk contract to the British of 150 to 180 million bushels of wheat at a price of 93.5 cents per bushel. Ottawa thought Crerar's price too low, but the British thought it far above the prevailing market price.

(Fullerton, 128)

The *Empress of Britain* was met at the Southampton docks by a man whose business card read "Lester Bowles Pearson, Second Secretary, Canadian High Commission." He was a cheerful man in a bowtie. His puckish smile was hail-fellow-well-met, with warm handshakes and cheek kisses, and "Mike" and "Molly" and "Graham" all round. Mr. Pearson was also well known at the customs shed, and their baggage was whisked through without inspection. In forty minutes, they were settled into a first-class carriage on the London Express.

"We'll be at Waterloo Station by noon. Why don't you go right to the Dorchester to check in and have a bite to eat, then come around to Canada House for 3:00 p.m. The high commissioner would like to have a strategy session. A heavy round of meetings has been set up with people from the Bank of England, the chancellor of the exchequer, the Dominions Office, and the foreign secretary. They'll all be pleading for money, of course, and it's best to have a battle plan. We're all shoulder-to-shoulder to defeat Hitler, but opinions vary on who is carrying the heaviest load."

"Do they think Canada is shirking?"

Mr. Pearson smiled. "They see Canada as a broad dominion teeming with vast resources. They wonder out loud when they might see some of these resources over here in the front lines."

Graham Towers shook his head. "They called this war without giving us much notice. We're doing damn well by them under the circumstances."

"Did Prime Minister King give you instructions?"

"He did. Surely he cabled them to Canada House as well."

Mr. Pearson gave a rueful smile. "Mr. King shares very little with Mr. Massey, other than complaints."

"Doesn't trust him? Why did he appoint him high commissioner, then?"

"Vincent Massey was president of the Liberal Party during the 1935 federal election. The Liberals won. Mr. Massey was owed a favour." Mr. Pearson laughed. "As well, Mr. Massey did such a wonderful job as Liberal president that there was some chatter about his becoming Liberal leader. The Liberal leader was not amused."

"So Mr. Massey was exiled to London?"

"Something like that. Mr. King barely needs a Canadian high commissioner; he has so many other channels open to him. He can speak to the governor general or the British high commissioner in Ottawa. Over here, he can deal with the Dominions Office. He can chat up Mr. Chamberlain, prime minister to prime minister. Ultimately, he's a first minister of King George, and he has no hesitation talking directly to his sovereign."

"King to king."

"Exactly. At the High Commission, we're always hunting around for 'the news from Canada,' as we often are the last to hear anything."

Graham Towers digested this all before continuing. "Essentially, Mackenzie King wants the purse tightly latched. He's very concerned that the demands of war will quickly outpace our ability to pay for them. Mr. Ralston at Finance whistles the same tune. That attitude shouldn't be much of a surprise."

"No," replied Mr. Pearson, "but it's a beggars' opera over here. Endless pleas."

"Sounds tedious," said Molly Towers. "I'll spend the afternoon at Harrods while you duke it out."

"Fine," said the governor. "Miss McFadden and I will see you at Canada House at three, then."

Mr. Pearson had a smile for every occasion. "I'm not sure that Mr. Massey expects Miss McFadden to be present at discussions," he said.

"Miss McFadden will attend all meetings with me. The British can conjure innocuous comments into iron-clad agreements. I want my own record of proceedings."

"Not unreasonable," agreed Mr. Pearson. "Still, it will be a surprise to the high commissioner. He's a man who doesn't like surprises."

When they were ushered into the high commissioner's office, Vincent Massey frowned at Frances as though a street urchin had slipped past the guard at the door.

"High Commissioner, may I present my personal assistant, and director of the secretariat at the Bank of Canada, Frances McFadden. Miss McFadden, the Canadian high commissioner."

Mr. Massey scrutinized Frances before a regal hand drifted toward her. "Miss McFadden," he said through thin lips in a cadaverous face.

"High Commissioner," Frances responded. His hand was as cold as his smile. He reminded Frances of the Lord high executioner in *The Mikado.*

The governor and the high commissioner demonstrated a long-standing familiarity, taking social liberties not presumed by others. "Do you *really* need to bring your own secretary to these meetings, Graham? A lot gets accomplished informally over port and cigars."

"Formal or informal, Vincent, I can get caught up in the heat of the debate, and not recall every detail. I have no wish to be compromised by some innocuous comment that was misinterpreted. Miss McFadden will take things down verbatim."

"Even off the record?"

"Anything that is aired, is aired to a purpose, on the record or off. We're dealing with billions of dollars, here. Very little of it is flowing toward Canada."

A butler in morning coat and striped pants poured tea into delicate Belleek cups while they waited for the others to arrive. Mr. Massey took the governor over by the fireplace for a quiet word. Frances wandered the room looking at the art—bold canvases by Group of Seven painters. She leaned in close to one particularly vibrant piece, trying to read the artist's scrawl in a lower corner.

"Careful, there," admonished the high commissioner from across the room. "These are exceptional pieces of Canadiana that came to me at exceptional prices." A vacant smile flashed brief as lightning before he resumed conversing with the governor.

Mr. Pearson arrived with Colonel Vanier, the first secretary, and Mr. Crerar, Canadian minister of Mines and Resources. They eased into a semicircle of chairs facing the fireplace. "This is off the record," said Mr. Massey. "Considerable pressure is going to be put on Governor Towers this week to be quickly forthcoming with cash and war materials. Montague Norman at the Bank of England will be wringing his hands. The chancellor of the exchequer will cry that their cupboard is bare and Anthony Eden in the Dominions Office will hammer on duty to ..." He stopped in mid-sentence and glared at Frances, who was taking down his comments in shorthand. Every head turned to follow his gaze, and when Frances eventually looked up into the silence, Mr. Massey's civility was castigating. "I said this conversation was off the record. Do you understand English, girl?"

Frances dismissed him with a blink and looked over at Governor Towers. "It would be very helpful to me, Vincent," said the governor, "if I can have Miss McFadden's transcripts of all meetings. I can review them later when my head is clear. Nothing said will go beyond me, except for updates back to the prime minister."

Mr. Massey's face inadequately hid his feelings on the topic. In a failed attempt at the graceful gesture, he surrendered with a wave of his hand.

"Loan negotiations have stalled, in spite of my best efforts during the last month," said Mr. Crerar. "Discussions are circuitous. They have no concept here of the balance of powers in Canada between federal and provincial governments, especially regarding taxation. There are no provinces in England, and they don't understand how this complicates funding the war. We have eleven million people; they have forty million. They have nearly four times the number of taxpayers to cover the tab."

"In their plight, the British fail to realize that Canada has limited resources and is staggering out of the same Depression that has crippled the United Kingdom," added Colonel Vanier. "We're madly ramping up our own war effort—enlisting soldiers and sailors, building barracks and airbases, letting contracts for uniforms and munitions—all to help them. It's a huge strain on our economy."

"The British also fail to appreciate that Mackenzie King has to go to the people for a new mandate very soon," continued Mr. Pearson. "They criticize his caution. They don't grasp how supportive he really is, or his need *not* to alienate Canadian voters who might have reservations about any war commitment at all."

"What if Great Britain bought more Canadian wheat?" asked the governor. "Bring some money back our way."

"That would be ideal," agreed Mr. Crerar, "but there are foreign exchange restrictions here, too. They're deathly afraid of spending a farthing outside the country and undermining the pound sterling. Canadian wheat sells for ninety-three cents a bushel, and they can still buy it on the world market at seventy-four cents a bushel, so they won't commit to a contract." He threw up his hands.

Colonel Vanier outlined Britain's needs from a military perspective. "The first Canadian expeditionary force of twenty-five thousand troops will arrive in the UK before Christmas. We're still working on where to house them. The details of the British Overseas Air Training Plan are almost finalized. Over a hundred airports will be set up across Canada to train pilots and aircrews from the Commonwealth.

"Mr. King insists that Canadian air squadrons are to be kept as unique fighting entities when they go into service. A sticking point. The British want to fit in the trainees wherever they're needed, regardless of country of origin. Also, Mr. King wants British ground crews to service Canadian squadrons, whereas the British want the Canadians to bring their own ground crews, which is another way of saying we should pay for the maintenance of our own planes. Mr. King definitely does not want a repeat of the situation in the Great War where Canadians were sent to the front as cannon fodder without any recognition of nationality, other than 'soldier of the British Empire.' That no longer washes."

Mr. Massey outlined the week of meetings and social events that Governor Towers would be attending. When they finished, they all stood up and stretched. Frances gathered up teacups to put them on the tray on a side table.

"Please don't touch the china," said Mr. Massey. "It's fragile, and you're taking a job away from the help."

It would have been hard for Frances to say which she disliked the most, pickled beets or Vincent Massey. The high commissioner continued a flow of advice as the butler assisted Governor Towers into his coat. On the other side of the entrance hallway, Mr. Pearson held Frances's coat out for her. She was so exasperated that she could barely get her arm in her coat sleeve. He slipped something into her hand. "Here you go," he said.

It was the thick paper label from a container of Marmite. Frances had seen the distinctive jars on the breakfast table every morning on the *Empress of Britain*, alongside Keiller's Dundee marmalade. A red V was superimposed on the centre stoke of the golden M. Underneath was the slogan "To Victory with Marmite!" The label had been pruned so that only the medallion showing the V over the M remained. She turned the token over in her hand. "What's this?"

"It's the Vincent Massey medal," Mr. Pearson explained, sotto voce. "Awarded only to those wounded in the line of duty." His puckish smile. "Colonel Vanier has four. I have nine."

17

BUCK HOUSE

Towers stated clearly that it would not be feasible for Canada to finance the whole of the UK's net adverse balance of payments to and from Canada; Canada would need payment in gold or US dollars to meet the cost of increased imports of defence supplies into the country from the United States.

(Bryce, 54)

After two weeks of futility, they were back in Vincent Massey's office at Canada House. Along with tea, oven-fresh scones were served with butter and strawberry jam.

"Molly and I have been sumptuously banqueted," Graham Towers said to the high commissioner and Mr. Pearson, "but negotiations show scant progress. I see no reason to stay longer. Molly enjoyed the soirees, but was tremendously bored by the rest of the goings-on. She left last night on the Edinburgh Flyer to visit friends in Scotland for ten days. She'll make her own travel arrangements to Ottawa in the New Year, but I should be getting back to mind the store. Frances, can you book us out through Portugal and the Azores on the first available flight?"

Frances rose to go to the phone in the hall just as the butler ushered in Captain Campbell, the King's equerry. "I've come directly from the palace," said the captain, a handsome man with a debonair moustache. "The king and queen would like to host Governor and Mrs. Towers at family tea tomorrow afternoon. An informal reception with a few other Canadians."

"Well, well, well," mused the high commissioner. "They're putting their number one salesman on the case. They're desperate to salvage something."

"What does 'informal' mean for tea at Buckingham Palace?"

"No uniforms or court dress. Three-piece suit will do. You'll meet the princesses. Lovely girls."

"Well, by now Molly's in the Outer Hebrides and could never get back by tomorrow. I should probably pass," said the governor.

Vincent Massey's eyebrows lifted. "Turn down a personal invitation from your sovereign? To whom we have all sworn an oath of allegiance? He's a rational man. You might have an easier go with him than you've had with the Exchequer people or the Dominions' Office. Unfortunate about Molly's absence. I'm told the queen wearies of the male preponderance at these functions. Isn't there someone else in London you could escort?"

Graham Towers lit a cigarette and thought for a long moment, then turned toward Frances. "Miss McFadden, how would you like to meet the king?"

Frances was dumbstruck, giving the high commissioner a chance to interject. "Be serious, Graham. This is Buck House for tea with the royal family. It's you he wants to talk to."

"Meeting a few ordinary Canadians might help their royal highnesses understand how ordinary our financial resources are. If the king wants to grill me for millions over tea, I'll need Miss McFadden to record any developments."

The governor turned to Captain Campbell. "Could you check to see if Miss McFadden might be substituted in place of my wife? Otherwise, we both should pack up and head for home."

Mr. Pearson escorted the captain to the hall phone and they were back in three minutes. "Miss McFadden is welcome. The Masseys and the Pearsons and the Crerars are also invited. Tea at four tomorrow."

"Could you fetch my wife, please?" the high commissioner said to Mr. Pearson, displeasure colouring into voice. "She's at breakfast in the conservatory." He turned to Frances. "Alice will give you a quick lesson in court etiquette. Most importantly, girl, never touch a royal. And it's a damn good idea not to touch anything else. The palace is full of priceless antiques."

"What if I'm offered a handshake?"

"Kings shake hands with lords and archbishops and Victoria Cross winners, not ..." His mind was churning for a diplomatic term for bank secretary, when Alice Massey arrived.

"Bit of a crisis here, Lal. This ..." he made a nuanced wave at Frances without looking at her ..." girl will accompany Graham to tea at the palace tomorrow and needs a quick deportment lesson. Can you run her through the basics so no one's too badly embarrassed?"

Frances wanted to stab him with the butter knife. "I have no wish to be a liability to the Bank or Canada or the war effort," she said. "I will not go to tea."

"Excellent idea," said the high commissioner with ill-concealed relief.

"But the invitation has been confirmed," countered Captain Campbell. "Miss McFadden is obliged to go, unless she falls ill or has a tragic accident."

Vincent Massey's narrowing eyes were considering which of these options would be most easily arranged when Alice Massey cut in. "Oh, Vin, it will be all right. I'm sure Graham's people are only the best. We'll just run over a few items, and she'll be fine." She took Frances by the arm and led her down the hall to the conservatory.

"You mustn't mind Vin. He works very hard at promoting Canadian interests here. He's a perfectionist. That's his strength and his weakness. Now, dear, a few basic rules should get you through tea. It comes down mostly to common sense: respect for the dignity of the king and his family. Have you ever met members of the aristocracy?"

"Yes. Lord and Lady Tweedsmuir at Rideau Hall."

"Good. The same considerations apply. Show me your curtsey. Right foot behind your left heel. Excellent! They will likely meet us in one of the smaller drawing rooms on the main floor. The upstairs rooms are cavernous. After we've all arrived, the royal family will come in. Everyone will be presented in order of precedence. You will be last, so you can watch the others. When you're introduced by Captain Campbell, you step forward, stopping about five feet from the king. You curtsey, eyes down, and say 'Your Majesty.' Wait until the king has responded with 'Miss McFadden,' then rise from the curtsey, and make brief eye contact. Realign with the queen, who will be on his left, and curtsey again, saying, 'Your Majesty.' With Princess Elizabeth and Princess Margaret, repeat the curtseys and address them each as 'Your Royal Highness.' Then prepare to take five or six steps backward. Do a little shoulder check to make sure you don't knock down a side table. Never turn your back on a Royal until you're at least a dozen feet away and out of their conversation zone.

"One does not initiate conversation with a royal. After the first salutation exchange, if you are engaged in further discourse, it's 'Sir' to the King, and 'Ma'am' to the queen and the princesses."

"I call a girl half my age 'Ma'am'?"

Alice Massey shrugged. "I don't make the rules."

"What does one wear to tea?"

"Cocktail dress. Knee length. Not flashy. No cleavage showing. Definitely not sleeveless, or you'll freeze to death. Buckingham Palace is godawful frigid. Stand near the fireplace if you can, but cede it to any royal who approaches. Don't carry a purse. There's nowhere to put it when you're handling a teacup and a sandwich plate. Go to the bathroom ahead of time. It's bad form to ask for the nearest loo."

"Bad form?"

"It suggests that their majesties may occasionally use such a convenience themselves."

"But …?"

"In an emergency, best not to pee on the Persian carpets. Ask the butler, and he'll discreetly have a footman escort you. It may well be a hundred yards away down a labyrinth of corridors." She sighed. "I didn't eat or drink for a full day before the king's coronation in 1937, knowing two thousand of us would be crammed into Westminster Abbey for five hours with hopelessly inadequate facilities.

"This whole show won't last an hour. We'll meet here at 4:00 p.m. and go over in two cars. We'll be in place by 4:20, and they'll come in right on time. There will be tea and these ghastly tiny sandwiches—cream cheese and pimento sort of thing. Oh! They have these damn dogs that race around wreaking havoc. Do *not* feed them, even though they will lunge at an unprotected sandwich in your hand. Treating the little buggers is a royal prerogative." Mrs. Massey smiled. "You'll be fine. They're just human beings like you and me."

Frances and Governor Towers took a taxi to Canada House at 3:30. In the upstairs library, Frances was introduced to Jessie Crerar and Maryon Pearson. Everyone was a little anxious, as though they were going to the funeral of a friend.

Two Rolls-Royces took them the three-minute drive down The Mall to Buckingham Palace. They whisked through the great wrought iron gates and under an archway into the interior courtyard. Guardsmen in full kit opened car doors and a footman escorted them inside and down the hall to a cream- and-gold-coloured room the size of a tennis court. Beautiful Chinese regency furniture was clustered in conversational groupings. No one sat down.

At exactly 4:30, a well-disguised door in the woodwork opened and a liveried butler announced, "Ladies and gentlemen, His Majesty, King George, and the royal family." Princess Elizabeth wore a Girl Guide uniform, and Princess Margaret that of the Brownies. They stood, ramrod straight, beside their mother, hands carefully tucked behind their backs.

The introductions went off smoothly, after which the king immediately lit up a cigarette. Governor Towers and all the men joined him. A footman carried in a large silver tray holding an elaborate tea service, colourful china cups and a crystal creamer. Another brought in two platters of sandwiches. A butler asked about tea with milk or black. Sugar was not offered, due to rationing. When everyone was served, the butler and footmen left the refreshments on a library table and withdrew.

With the fear of falling on her face during the curtsey over, Frances realized she was freezing, and welcomed the warmth of the tea.

"I have told the king a thousand times that smoking is bad for his health," said Queen Elizabeth. "He has a terrible cough. He says the smoking calms him, but at what a cost!" She sighed. "Kings always seem to get the last word. Men smoke with him as a bond of kinship. Women never smoke in his presence—it's deemed déclassé. Do you smoke, Miss McFadden?"

"No, Ma'am."

"Good. Though it's something of a double standard, don't you think?"

"Double standards are better than no standards at all, Ma'am," replied Frances.

The queen's eyes sparkled and she positively chortled. "How very droll, Miss McFadden! I must remember that one. The United Kingdom is a democracy, of course, but every kingdom needs a king, doesn't it? Aristocracy is, by nature, a hierarchy, yet democracy is all about equality. So we live daily with this double standard, for which I am constantly made to feel guilty."

The queen noticed Mrs. Crerar gazing at a picture on the wall. "Do you like art, Mrs. Crerar? This is van Dyck's portrait of Charles I. Come take a closer look." Mrs. Pearson and Mrs. Crerar drifted off with the queen. Frances edged closer to the fireplace, where Mr. Pearson was warming his back. She noticed Captain Campbell standing near the window, vigilantly on duty, but discreetly apart from the conversations. Mr. Pearson followed her gaze.

"Do equerries have wives?" she asked.

"Do equerries have lives, might be the more pertinent question," Mr. Pearson replied.

There was a sudden small voice at Frances's elbow. "Being from Canada," Princess Margaret inquired, "you probably are not familiar with British butterflies, are you?"

"I am not, Ma'am."

"I am! My collection is right over there." She pointed at a glass-topped table with elegantly carved legs. "Would you like to see it?"

Frances threw a sidelong glance at Vincent Massey. He was in deep conversation with Mr. Crerar, while the king chatted with Governor Towers. The coast was clear. "I'd be delighted, Ma'am," she said.

Princess Margaret pointed to a spray of butterflies pin-mounted beneath the glass top of the table. "Their official name is Lep-id-op-tera," she enunciated carefully. "That is Latin, you know. But they're still butterflies to me. Aren't they beautiful?"

"They are, Ma'am. Which is your favourite?"

Princess Margaret's face was so close to the glass that she misted it with her breath. "I adore this one," she said, pointing to an incandescent pistachio-coloured specimen labelled Green Hairstreak.

Vincent Massey began making guarded glances at Frances, to see if she was pocketing the silverware. The corgis, Gobbler and Dookie, bounded playfully around the room, chasing each other under tables and around chesterfields, yapping joyfully.

Princess Elizabeth was taking the huge silver tea tray around to guests, offering refills and picking up empty dishes. She concentrated on keeping the tray in balance. Having relieved Frances of her teacup, the princess turned toward the fireplace, where the Queen was chatting with the other female guests. Gobbler had liberated a crustless sandwich from somewhere and was tearing away with Dookie in hot pursuit. Gobbler darted successfully between Princess Elizabeth's legs but Dookie's greed got the better of his timing, and he heavily cross-checked the royal shins. Princess Elizabeth stumbled forward, launching the tray of cups, tea pot, and crystal creamer into the air. For a terrifying instant, tray and Princess were suspended in space, floating through the cold drawing room.

Frances stepped behind Princess Elizabeth and grasped her under the arms to arrest her fall. There was a devastating explosion of crystal and china fragments as the tray smashed to the floor. The horrified princess turned from the carnage and clutched Frances. A frightened heart beat wildly.

"Oh, my God!"

"Good Lord!"

"Are you hurt?"

Vincent Massey spun about on hearing the racket. Aghast, he bore down on Frances as Princess Elizabeth disengaged and stood shame-faced. The High Commissioner was in a froth. "I warned you *never* to touch a Royal!" he hissed. "*You have manhandled the heir presumptive to the throne!* You thoughtless—"

He was cut off by the arrival of Queen Elizabeth, who had seen the whole event unfold. "Oh, bless you, Miss McFadden! Such quick thinking! I can't imagine what a mess Lilibet would have made of herself had she landed face first in all this breakage. You have saved her from grievous harm." A gloved hand touched Frances on the arm. "I thank you," she said with a heartfelt smile.

The king arrived. "Elizabeth has been going through a growth spurt. Lanky limbs are all a-tangle." He put his arm affectionately around his daughter's shoulders. "Still, sits a horse beautifully, and *that's* what really counts, after all." He smiled down into quaking eyes.

Vincent Massey backed away to compose himself.

"We are very much obliged to you, Miss McFadden," continued the king. "Could you join us at Sandringham for the weekend?"

"Oh, no thank you, Sir. I have to get back to Canada as soon as possible."

"When are you leaving?"

"I was able to get Governor Towers the last seat out tomorrow on a flight through Portugal and the Azores. I'm trying to arrange my own passage now, but every ship is booked solid."

"Campbell," said the king, drawing his equerry into the conversation. "Miss McFadden needs to get back to the Bank of Canada to keep the money flowing to us." He gave Graham Towers a wink. "Having a little trouble finding a ship. Can you put in a word?"

"I'll see what I can do, Sir."

18

EXEUNT

When war broke out, the British Admiralty requisitioned seventeen Canadian Pacific passenger liners [Canadian Pacific's head office was in London, England]. *The ships were sent to the four corners of the globe with troops, fuel and supplies one way and prisoners of war and refugees the other.*

(Pigott, 130*)*

By VE Day, eight CP passenger liners would be lost to enemy action.

(Musk, 44)

Surprise, surprise.

The Empress of Britain was *not* going to Greenock for conversion to a troop carrier. After the battleship HMS *Royal Oak* was sunk by a marauding U-boat at Scapa Flow, the British Home Fleet retreated to the more sheltered Greenock dockyards. The *Empress* was being sent back to Quebec City for retrofitting in safer territory. Room for one passenger had been found on board.

The *Empress*'s white hull had been completely repainted battleship grey, a colour matching the mood of the small crew. Frances walked up the gangway at the Southampton docks to a decidedly reserved reception. Second Lieutenant Hastings explained: "Canadian Pacific draws almost all officers and crew from here in the United Kingdom. Everyone had been looking forward to being at home with family for the Christmas holidays. Since the *Athena* was torpedoed in September, with a loss of 112 lives, enthusiasm has waned for venturing onto the Atlantic aboard an unarmed ship.

"There weren't supposed to be *any* passengers at all. I was pleased, but a little astonished, Miss McFadden, when word came down from head office that you would be joining us. Coyle, the chief engineer, was to enjoy the luxury of your cabin suite. He's a touch miffed at being bumped."

Commodore Stuart was still gracious. "Welcome back aboard, Miss McFadden. Eliminated any enemy agents while in England?"

"Barely a handful, sir."

"What's your favourite modus operandi? Derringer? Stiletto?"

"I much prefer garrotting, sir," replied Frances. "Pistols are noisy and powder burns can ruin a good pair of kid gloves. Knives—dear me! Not dainty—blood all over the place. Give me thirty inches of piano wire any day. Light weight, coils neatly into your purse, keeps the victim from calling out."

"Should I double lock my cabin door at night?"

"Not unless you're in cahoots with the Nazis. I'm quite selective."

Commodore Stuart laughed. "I must warn you that we are shipping out with a rather sombre skeleton crew. We carried a complement of seven hundred outward-bound from Quebec City to wait on passengers hand and foot. We're casting off with fewer than fifty, most of them needed in the engine room. A dozen officers are going along to supervise the fitting out of the *Empress* as a troop carrier. We need to install five thousand bunks. All the public rooms will become massive dorms. Pity, really. And we're taking a run for it alone, trying not to attract enemy attention."

"Don't ships usually travel in convoys?"

"Usually. There's safety in numbers, and in a destroyer escort. However, the convoy sails at the pace of the slowest ship. They travel in a zigzag pattern to evade torpedo attack, which slows things further. The *Empress* has no armament so our best defence is speed."

"Can you outrun a U-boat?"

"Oh, yes. Full out, we can top twenty-four knots. A U-boat travels at twelve knots max on the surface and only seven knots while submerged. They can still be out there lying in wait, but it's a very big ocean. We'll cast off under cover of darkness. Should be tying up at Quebec City in five days, weather permitting. The dining room is closed, of course. Just one steward serving the officers' mess. You may join us if you wish, or take your meals in your cabin."

"I don't want to get in the way, but I don't really need room service."

"Try us for lunch and make your own call."

Lunch was civil but icy among the half-dozen Canadian Pacific officers off duty. On the first day, conversations closed down to muted civility when Frances entered the officers' mess. It wasn't exactly hostile—more a circumspect neutrality. Eventually, Denby, the executive officer, crossed the conversational gulf to her.

"Quite a surprise to have you with us, Miss McFadden," he said. "A few fellow officers asked to deadhead back to Canada but were refused. You must know Sir Roger Cripps rather well."

"Never heard of him."

"He's president of Canadian Pacific Steamship Lines. He called Commodore Stuart personally asking if we might take you along. Refusing Sir Roger would be like refusing a request from God."

"You must know somebody important, Miss McFadden," said Jackson, the purser.

"My travel plans came up at a tea in London. I'd been able to snag the last seat for Governor Towers on a flight back through the Azores. I mentioned that I was having difficulty booking passage. Someone kindly offered to look into it."

"Someone?" observed Richards, the second officer.

"I had no idea who they got in touch with. I certainly didn't think *The Empress of Britain* would be involved. I'd been told you were heading for dry dock in Greenock."

"Someone?" said Richards, who had a habit of repeating himself.

Frances looked at Richards for a long moment. "You clearly know," said Frances. "So what's the point?"

"Yes. I was officer of the watch when the request came in. I had to roust Commodore Stuart from his sleep."

"Who was it, for God's sake?" asked Cairns, the ship doctor.

Frances and Richards stared each other down.

Finally, Richards blinked. "Herbert Campbell, King George's equerry, called Sir Roger on directions from the king."

"*The king!*" echoed a chorus around the table.

"How the devil does a bank clerk get to know the king?" asked Cairns.

"Mrs. Towers couldn't attend the tea party," said Frances. "They needed another female." She looked Lieutenant Hastings in the eye. "For ballast."

"You must have made quite an impression," said Denby.

"Maybe they just wanted to get you out of the country fast," said Richards. "Before you killed off all the double agents in England."

Wingnut came to her defence. "You'll have to pardon us, Miss McFadden. We're short-handed, and short-tempered. Every jack is doing watch-on-watch. We're all low on sleep."

"Watch-on-watch?"

"Normally we work four-hour shifts, with eight hours off between shifts. Now we're working eight hours on, four hours off. Sixteen hours a day. It's exhausting. And the captain wants the fore and aft crow's nests manned around the clock. We each do a two-hour trick up there each day."

"I thought crow's nests went out with sailing ships."

"Oh, no. The *Titanic* had one. Lot of good it did them. The *Empress* has one forty feet up on the forward communications mast, to watch for ice and flotsam out front. However, we can be attacked from any point on the compass, so we've jury-rigged a second platform on the rear communications mast. They give us good visuals for any nasty business."

"How much farther can you see from the crow's nest?"

"Probably another five miles. But glare and light refraction limit visibility. Submarines lie very low in the water, so they usually see us before we see them."

"The new German VII B submarines are quite amazing," piped up Bryson, the second engineer. "Back in '37 when I was cramming for my papers, I did a three-month stint in the Krupp dockyards at Kiel. I was studying diesel engines, but the U-boat works were just upstream and we would see the VII B's out on the river doing trials. Graceful as swans, they were! Very agile, with two rudders. Five torpedo tubes. Have a range of over eight thousand miles; or so bragged the German engineers after a few beers in the local *Rathskeller*." Bryson's boyish enthusiasm for naval technology regardless of which team it played for was unshared at the mess table.

To lighten the sense of impending doom, Frances said, "I could do a shift in the crow's nest if that would help."

Sidelong glances around the table ranged from amusement to derision.

"It's December in the north Atlantic," said Richards as he crushed a cigarette into a brimming ashtray. "You'd freeze your balls off in sixty minutes."

This was close to the etiquette line for mixed company. Frances's mother, who did not tolerate vulgarity, would have stood up and left in a huff. Eyes turned like gun turrets toward her.

"No sacrifice," reflected Frances, "is too great for king and country."

This drew a ripple of laughter from everyone except Richards.

"A two-hour trick, forty feet up?" Dr. Cairns cackled at the thought.

"You'll need to tell me what to look for," replied Frances.

"The Germans have very few surface raiders out on the Atlantic," explained Denby. "The Royal Navy has blockaded most of them in ports. But submarines are sneaky devils. You'll be looking for periscopes and the V-shaped wake they leave. Difficult to see, even with binoculars. Stare at vast expanses of water for long enough and your eyes play tricks on you."

"Torpedoes, you know, are devilishly clever weapons," enthused Bryson. "They have this clever gauge consisting of a pendulum and a hydrostatic valve to keep them running at exactly the desired depth. Combustion steam fires a four-cylinder engine that can generate forty-four knots. Marvelous technology!" Bryson shook his head in admiration.

"You should be in recruiting for the British Navy," said Richards.

"Only trouble is," continued Bryson, "the spent exhaust gases leave a visible trail of bubbles on the way to the target."

"What a relief," observed Wingnut, then the room fell silent.

"Well, I'm still game to pitch in," said Frances.

"Righty-o," said Edwards, the purser, with a disbelieving smile. "We'll get you some oilskins. Come down to stores in ten minutes. Jenkins," he called to the steward, "splice a thermos of hot tea with rum for the lady."

"Wear your warmest clothes," said Cairns. "All of them. The oilskins will cut the wind and keep the salt spray off, but it'll be bone-chilling cold up there. It's a tiny space. Just a donut around the mast. There's a railing, but it's completely exposed to the wind and rain."

Jenkins handed her the thermos. "Put this right inside your sweater, Miss, like a hot water bottle. It will help keep you alive."

He didn't say "warm."

"Thank you," said Frances, standing to follow the purser down to stores.

"And don't drink it," Jenkins whispered at the door. "It'll go right through you like a hot knife through butter. Make you piss, Miss. It's a long trip from the crow's nest to the head. Richards will rib you from here till Sunday if you leave your post before your replacement shows. Dereliction of duty. All because of nature's call."

Frances thought for a moment. "Wouldn't that be a problem for anyone on duty up there?"

"Oh, yes, Miss, but a man can just yank out his wanker and let fly down the side. The whole upper structure is soaking wet from the rain and the spray. Who'd notice? Harder for a woman, Miss."

19

CROW'S NEST

Between September 3 and December 31, 1939, 156 British and Allied ships were sunk by German U-boats for a total loss of 572,279 gross registered tons [GRT]. During the same period, 9 U-boats were destroyed.

(www.uboat.net)

Lieutenant Hastings accompanied Frances to the base of the rear mast. The smallest set of oilskins in stores draped her body like a collapsed tent. Underneath she wore a blouse, two sweaters, and a coat. Long underwear and slacks under bulky oilskin overalls held her to a shuffle along the spray-dampened deck. She wore a thick woollen toque in navy blue pulled down to cover her ears and eyebrows. With three pairs of socks on, there was still enough room in the toe of each rubber boot for a croquet ball.

"Keep moving round and round," Wingnut counselled. "Lift your knees. Wiggle your toes. Clap your hands. Wave your arms to keep the blood flowing. The railing will be as cold as charity, even through those thick gloves. Keep the binos inside your oilskins until you're ready to use them. Otherwise ice will form on the lenses and the adjusting gear will seize up." He smiled. "Up you go and good luck. There's a phone up there with a direct line to the bridge. Give it a crank if you see anything. I'll relieve you at 1600 hours."

A swaying ladder ran skyward inside a round steel ribcage. Frances clambered slowly up and crawled through a trap door in the nest floor. Tobin, the purser, greeted her with watering eyes and ice stalactites in his moustache. He nodded curtly before beating a hasty exit down the ladder.

The reset trap formed part of the narrow walkway around the mast. A metal cage four feet high was all that kept her from a steep plunge to oblivion. Although the sea was relatively calm, the crow's nest bobbed and weaved like wheat in a windstorm. God bless Molly Towers. Her advice about seasick pills was saving the day.

Frances pulled out the binoculars and slowly scanned the horizon line. How far? Hard to tell. Nothing to give distance perspective but a limitless undulating surface of grey that eventually merged with the sky. She did a sweeping motion with the glasses, zigzagging back in toward the ship. She moved a quarter turn around the mast and repeated. Nothing but a grey quilt of gentle waves occasionally breaking into whitecaps. She did three slow circuits and checked her watch. Twenty-six minutes gone, ninety-four to go.

By forty-five minutes into her shift, Frances was chilled to the bone. Her teeth chattered uncontrollably. She had to rest her elbows on the freezing top railing in order to hold the binoculars steady. When she faced forward, she could see the back of a sailor bundled up in the front crow's nest, too far away to recognize. As she scanned the port side at the sixty-minute mark, a low shaft of sunlight punched through the thick cloud cover. About a mile out, a diamond sparkled on the water and she set the glasses on it. It looked like … a hockey stick? She squinted. Yes. A hockey stick. She swept the glasses left ninety degrees, then right ninety degrees, covering the entire port side of the boat. By the time she came back to recheck, the hockey stick had disappeared.

The phone had a stiff winding crank like a meat grinder. A great crackle of static followed before she heard a faint and distant "Aye, aye."

"Hello?" Frances yelled into the phone. "McFadden in the rear crow's nest. I—"

"This is a direct line, McFadden, for Christ's sake," came back the unmistakable voice of Richards. "There's only one goddamn place you could be. How's the weather up there?"

"Delightful, Lieutenant Richards," Frances shouted into the phone. "Wanted to report that I just saw something about a mile off the port side, mid-ships." Frances was proud of her newly acquired nautical jargon.

"What was it?"

"Well, it looked like a hockey stick glittering in the sun."

She could hear Richards sharing that gem with others on the bridge. "She sees a hockey stick, for the love of God!" Static-strained laughter. "Would that be ice hockey or field hockey?" asked Richards. "Keep us posted on the score of the game." The line went dead.

Frances did two more circuits but saw only the vacant canvas of the sea. Not a seagull. Nothing. The forward lookout turned and scanned the sea on the starboard side of the *Empress*. Seventy minutes gone. She took her arms out of the giant sleeves of the oil skin and clasped the tea thermos tightly to warm her numb hands.

Should she or shouldn't she? With frigid fingers Frances unscrewed the lid and sipped the warm sweet tea laced with rum. Heat surged down to her fingers and toes. Draining the entire thermos revitalized her. However, compounded by the cold and jumping up and down to keep from freezing, Frances' bladder began to whisper, then talk assertively. She looked at her watch. Eighty minutes gone, forty minutes to go. Or, more precisely, until she could go. Could she last forty minutes?

Think about something else. *Haven't sent any Christmas cards. Be too late by the time I get home. New Year's cards? Lame, but better than nothing.* She checked her watch. Thirty-eight minutes left, providing Wingnut showed up on time. Christmas Carol time.

> O little town of Bethlehem, how still we see thee lie,
> Above thy deep and dreamless sleep, the silent stars go by.
> Da-dah-da-dah-da-dah dah, da dah …

Okay. Look for submarines. She did a slow circuit, scanning the horizon with and without the binos, sweeping her gaze left and right back in toward the ship. Nothing but choppy, gray water. Billions of gallons. Unfortunate association. How much does a bladder hold? A pint? Surely not a quart. It felt like five gallons. Ninety minutes gone. She was not going to make it through another thirty minutes to the end of her watch.

So, options. Abandon post and climb down the ladder to the head. Be humiliated by Richards for the rest of the trip. She looked down. It appeared a long, long way on slippery steps. She could barely move her legs, they were so cold and so encumbered in ineffectual clothing. Her fingers were numb again. Could she even hold the handrails going down? Option two. Pee her pants. That *would* warm her up. For about ten seconds. They'd find her frozen to death in a block of urine. An interesting obituary for a bank clerk. Option three. Could she get partly undressed—enough to pee—without freezing her nether regions?

How long does it take to pee? She had done it ten thousand times, but never timed herself. How thoughtless. Katie Warren would know. Scatological details were her forte.

"Women have no friend but resolution …" said Cleopatra. But nobody in a Shakespearean play ever had to pee. Not even in a tragedy.

Not in Jane Austin, either. Mr. Darcy? Miss Bennett? Not once! Who were those people?

So, resolution! Got to be fast. She undid her oilskin coat and turned her back to the wind. She unbuckled her oilskin pants, and tried to roll them, the slacks, the long underwear and her underwear down below her knees. Hopeless. Far too bulky. The whole package bound up in colossal folds on her thighs. Certainly not out of harm's way. She could barely squat at all with the bind of the clothing and the sway of the nest and her numb appendages. Frances stood up again and stepped out of her right rubber boot. It almost fell out of the crow's nest as she stood on it in her sock. Right leg out of oil skin, slacks, long underwear, underwear. With a great torqueing heave, she twisted all the clothing out of the way to the left. A quick shoulder check of the front crow's showed the back of a bundled form. One quarter naked, she looked down at the swaying deck and the ice-crusted superstructure.

What would her mother say?

Frances spread her knees as wide as she dared in a precarious crouch. Ode to Joy. A jet of relief arced out and down toward the cold Atlantic. In twenty-two years, she had never watched herself urinate. War changes everything. Amazing, the propulsion force of a full bladder. A monochromatic rainbow. And just above the rainbow, a thousand yards out, was a sparkle in the low afternoon sunlight. She brought the binos up and focused on the glint of a shining eye staring back.

How rude!

Sated, Frances jumped to her feet and scrambled the goose bumps of her right leg back into her panties, long underwear, pants, and oilskin legging. Her right sock was wet! From the spray? From … ? It didn't matter. The profound sense of relief was a winning trade for a wet sock. She scrunched her right foot back into the giant boot, buckled her pants and re-fastened the oilskin. Then, back to the binos to find the sparkling reflection in the thin breach of sun that cut the clouds. A hockey stick topped with a glass eye gazing at her. She blinked twice, then refocused. It was still there. A little frothy V-wake running out behind.

Frances picked up the phone and cranked the stubborn handle as hard as she could.

"Aye?" came a voice she didn't recognize.

"I see something."

"Another hockey stick for Christ's sake!" After a flurry of background noise, Wingnut took the phone. "Hello, Miss McFadden. What's up?"

"I'm sure there's a periscope off the port side. I saw it glitter in the sun."

"Right," he said neutrally, which could just as easily have meant "wrong." "I'll come up for a gander."

Frances hung up and swept the sea with the binos. Nothing, of course.

They'll think I'm a hysterical idiot. And blind to boot.

In five minutes, Wingnut, swathed in oilskins, was clambering up the ladder. It was wonderful to see that cheerful, wide-eared smile pop through the trap door. He squirmed into the crow's nest. "Now, where was the alleged object?"

"Over there." Frances pointed and they both scanned the horizon with binoculars. Back and forth. Forth and back. Only the wide, anonymous bare Atlantic. "Lieutenant Hastings, Please believe me. I *know* that I—"

"Whoa!" yelled Wingnut. "Trouble!" he shouted, grabbing the phone and cranking like a dervish. Frances followed his arm to an arrow of bubbles, white and effervescent, racing toward them.

"Hard a-starboard!" shouted Wingnut into the phone. "Full speed! Incoming torpedo four points off port amidships. Battle stations!"

The ship began to tilt and Frances grabbed on to the railing to steady herself, all the while tracking the arrow. Four hundred yards. Three-fifty.

"Don't brace yourself!" warned Wingnut. "That's six hundred pounds of TNT coming our way. A hit will rattle the superstructure hard enough to break your arm."

"But I might slip," said Frances, foolishly looking down. With the tilting deck, they were now almost out over the water.

Wingnut opened a supply box and took out a coil of rope. "We're going to tie ourselves loosely together and loosely to the mast. Run this around your waist. Again. And again."

The ship leaned and the klaxon call to battle stations roared over the wind. A hundred yards. Wingnut tied the rope off in a clove hitch. "Flex your knees as though you're going to jump and hang on to me."

The arrow closed. Fifty yards. Thirty yards. Then it disappeared under the port edge of the tilted ship. Frances clutched Wingnut and closed her eyes.

"There! There!" He yelled. "He pointed to the trail of bubbles racing parallel to the ship and then out in front of the bow and then away.

"We did it! We turned in time! Bet that didn't miss us by twenty feet." He grabbed for the phone and cranked it again. "Torpedo passing off the port bow," he shouted down. "You'll see the trail emerge in a second."

He gave Frances a joyous squeeze and kiss, lifting her off her feet. The kiss was a little longer than celebratory. Over his left shoulder, Frances saw a second bubble arrow frothing toward them from the starboard side.

"Look!"

Wingnut gasped, then grabbed the phone again. "Torpedo number two closing from a hundred yards in front of mid-ships starboard. Life jackets, all."

He hung up and grabbed Frances again, holding her against his chest. He counted the seconds off out loud.

"Seven … eight … nine …"

Th-whump. A dull clang. A slight shiver. And nothing.

Frances looked up at him "Th-wump?"

"A dud! A dud! A direct hit and it didn't explode! Poor Bryson will be so disappointed." He loosened the rope that held them together, then did a slow binocular circuit of the horizon. And again. "Coast is clear," he called down to the bridge and hung up. "Your watch is over, able seaman McFadden." He slapped her on the back. "You may retire to quarters."

It took every ounce of Frances's concentration to climb down the ladder. Her fingers and toes screamed with the cold. She could barely move, between her numbness and the bulky clothing. Reach slowly for the step. Bring down the other foot. Slide gloves down the railing. And again. And again. When she finally made it to the slippery deck, she wedged her upper arm over the railing, no longer trusting her fingers. She threw herself at the door, which slowly opened, basting her in warmth. Frances staggered down the hall to her cabin. She started a bath immediately, shedding layers of gear in a careless pile. The warm water brought feeling back to all her parts. She lathered up completely, topping the tub twice as the water cooled. After forty minutes, she felt human again. Frances dried herself slowly and dressed in warm kit before heading to the officers' mess for dinner.

Richards and a dozen officers were there. When Frances walked in, everyone sprang to attention. All saluted, then began a thundering round of applause.

PART
TWO

A good part of America's antagonism toward Britain in the late 1930s stemmed from the British government's sophisticated—and successful—propaganda campaign some twenty years before to draw America into World War I. Many Americans came to believe that their country had entered the war not because its own national interests demanded such action, but because it had been tricked by the scheming duplicitous British. They were determined not to let it happen again.

(Olson, 51)

20

HOMECOMING

December 17, 1939:

The First Canadian Division [of 25,000 men] *began landing in Britain. Canada was to make the announcement after a two-day delay, allowing for complete debarkation in secret. However, Winston Churchill broke the news on December 18. Mackenzie King was indignant at Churchill's pre-emptive action when the Canadian Government was holding back the news at the request of the Admiralty, of which Churchill was the head.*

(Pickersgill, 39)

A driving snowstorm buffeted the *Empress of Britain* as it arrived off Quebec City at 7:00 a.m. on Friday, December 22. Iced-up equipment in the dry dock area delayed the tie-up for three hours.

"Seems capricious to send you off into a Canadian blizzard," Lieutenant Hastings lamented. "Polar bears could be lurking out there, looking for lunch."

"Fear not, Lieutenant," Frances reassured him. "Bears, unlike Canadians, are smart enough to hibernate in this weather." The tiny cab that finally skidded through the slush to the dock already held two passengers for the train station. She squeezed in beside the driver, but there was no room for the Louis Vuitton. Wingnut gallantly undertook to forward her luggage.

Frances had never missed the governor's Christmas Tea scheduled for later that afternoon in Ottawa. Back in 1935, Governor Towers had asked her to organize a celebration of the Bank's first year of operations. A committee of support staff helped sort out logistics. They opted for a casual in-house function instead of a traditional sit-down affair in a rented hall. This freed the entire budget for high-end refreshments. A dozen caterers competed to showcase their delights. Three hundred staff wedged festively into the offices on the executive floor, carousing around bars and food stations. The hosting team wore red carnations for easy identification in the melee. The Carnation Girls propelled the GCT into an annual tradition.

The noon express to Montreal was completely booked, but Frances managed a ticket out on a local train at one. She called the Bank from a phone booth.

"Miss McFadden!" exclaimed Maddie Hall. "Where are you?"

"Quebec City train station. It'll be nip and tuck getting back to Ottawa in time for the tea. Is everything set?"

"Everything but the governor. He's still in the Azores. Fogged in for three days. He could be stuck there for Christmas. Claire has every detail under control. The Rascals all stayed here until nine last night moving furniture and hanging pine boughs trussed up with red bows. Legions of candles are everywhere. We backed our desks against the wall and covered them with oilcloth to protect the mahogany. Caterers are setting up right now. Mr. Meldrum and M. Soulière will each head a reception line. The DG has given everyone Saturday morning off! The Christmas holidays start at the party."

"Give everybody my love. I'll come straight to the Bank from Union Station."

When the conductor's whistle blew on the one o'clock train, Lieutenant Hastings had still not arrived with her luggage. Frances hardly cared. There was something fraudulent about a bank clerk decked out in formal floor-length gowns with matching shoes and gloves.

Snow blotted the landscape as the Montreal local chugged westward along the St. Lawrence River, stopping at tiny villages named for Catholic saints. They pulled into Montreal at 3:40, and she ran to catch the four o'clock express to Ottawa. Hampered by drifting snow, it coasted into Union Station at 6:10, the concourse a thicket of holiday travellers. Frances advised the luggage office about her Louis Vuitton then hailed a taxi.

She stepped off the elevator on the fourth floor of the Bank into a straggle of departing revellers. Scotty Meldrum was standing large by the bar with a small circle of tipplers as caterers cleaned up. "Miss McFadden!" said Brendan with an exaggerated look at his wristwatch, "How timely of you to honour us with your presence."

"I'm truly sorry, Brendan. I feel like a mother who negligently missed the birth of her child. How did it go?"

"Best ever! Economists enjoy a party in wartime. You and the governor were the only truants. No half-filled glass eluded the Carnation Girls. The food was exceptional. Have you had anything to eat?" Brendan took her to the remains of a sculpted ice Christmas tree covered in netting that had once swarmed with shrimp. He speared the half dozen remaining and plated them for her.

Claire came out of the boardroom beaming like the Cheshire cat. "Oh, Miss! We must have had three hundred and fifty here, and people just didn't want to leave! It was the perfect gift to the staff, given the times."

Scotty Meldrum bid his adieus and came over to sweep Frances and Claire into a collective bear hug. "Full marks to your secretariat, Miss McFadden! The governor's Christmas Tea ran perfectly without either you or the governor. Any trouble on the high seas?"

Truth to power?

Frances had no wish to upstage the celebration with U-boat prattle. "One tight spot. Lieutenant Richards, second officer on the *Empress of Britain,* had heard tales from a Canadian Pacific captain about an Ottawa bank clerk disposing of a German spy in Poland. Can you imagine, Mr. Meldrum, where Captain Hyland would ever have heard such a story?"

Scotty's face fell. "Dear Lord! Hyland and I did swap yarns over double shots of the Macallan. That might have slipped out in a weak moment. Sorry, lass. Never took him for a chatterbox. Did he say anything about the Polish gold?"

"Apparently not."

"Thank God."

"Any news of the governor?"

"He got out of the Azores just before noon. Will be in Bermuda tonight and New York tomorrow. Should be home Sunday. Very chagrined to miss his own party."

Frances turned to Claire. "Need any help with the cleanup?"

"You must be exhausted, Miss, and you won't have a thing in your icebox. We can fix you up with some leftovers. I know Brendan put a little smoked salmon away. I think he missed you," she said with a mischievous smile.

"I'm sure," said Frances. "No one to tease. Everything else held together?"

Bridget grinned. "Tickety-boo. Barely needed Mr. Meldrum at all."

"Abandoned as we were by the Queen Mother," added Brendan.

Frances gave them each a hug. Her family!

She hopped the Sparks streetcar to the War Memorial and transferred to the Elgin Line. In the lobby of the Balmoral, Miles caught her up on the gossip while he dusted the snow from her coat. He had taken the liberty of watering her plants when he took up her mail.

There were several dozen Christmas cards waiting on the dining room table: the Momsies, the Bridge Club, Bank staff, her uncle in Strathroy, Prime Minister King (courtesy no doubt of Arnold Heeney), and one from Paul Roderick.

> Dear Frances:
>
> First let me apologize for my behaviour at the Chateau Laurier. I was disappointed when you cancelled our holiday plans. I didn't handle it well.
>
> My mother used to say that we are each responsible for our own happiness, and woe betide the soul who foists that burden onto another. Time for reflection has returned my equilibrium.
>
> You know what brings you happiness. I will attend to mine. My family plays a big role and I'm looking forward to being with them.
>
> Happy holidays and best wishes for the future.
>
> Respectfully,
>
> Paul

Frances could read between the lines … *returned my equilibrium:* "You won't upset me like that again." *Best wishes for the future:* "a future without me."

She sat down. Tears trickled from tired eyes. Gentle, funny Paul Roderick. What had she been for him but boycotter of affections and rejecter of invitations?

Introspection was cut mercifully short by the clamour of the telephone. "Fellow in a uniform here with your luggage," said Miles. "Shall I send it up?"

In two minutes, Miles and Wingnut were at the door manhandling the five pieces of Louis Vuitton. Frances made introductions. "Lieutenant Hastings, the best fourth officer in the Canadian Pacific Fleet, if not the entire merchant marine, let me introduce you to Miles Treleaven, the best doorman in Ottawa, if not all of Canada." They shook hands. Wingnut handed a generous tip to Miles, who saluted and headed back to his post.

"You abandoned ship to bring my bags all the way from Quebec City in a snowstorm?"

"Papal dispensation from Commodore Stuart. He told me to 'do what has to be done' to reunite you and your luggage. You *did* save his ship from a watery grave. Canadian Pacific once lost Lord Camrose's luggage and I had to handle the nightmare of replacing it. Far simpler and cheaper for me to escort your goods back to your doorstep."

"Thank you, kind sir!" said Frances, giving him a hug. "Are you hungry? I have a care package from the tea party I missed."

He accepted a speared shrimp and looked around. "Lord!" he said. "What quarters! Bumping off German agents must pay very well."

Frances narrowed her eyes. "Lieutenant …"

"You never did deny it. When Richards pressed, I noticed you skated discreetly away from the topic."

She sighed. "Didn't Shakespeare write 'The evil that men do lives after them'? Is it true for women, too?"

"I'm prepared to exempt this woman," he said, patting her shoulder. He checked his watch. "I'd better take my leave. I'll just be able to catch the night train to Montreal."

"And sleep on a station bench waiting for the Quebec City Express tomorrow morning? Nonsense! I'm not putting you out on a stormy night after all you've done for me. I have an extra bedroom you could use."

"Housing strange men overnight? Won't your reputation suffer?"

"My reputation? As an assassin? However, if you're concerned for your own safety …"

"There's no one I'd rather be done in by," he said taking off his coat. "Any chance for a nightcap? A man can develop a thirst lugging Louis Vuitton across Canada."

"Certainly. Isn't rum the sailor's poison?"

"Only on the bounding main. On land I'm partial to gin."

Frances went to Mitzie's liquor cabinet. Two gins in evidence. A half bottle of Gilbey's London Dry and a full bottle of Booth's. Did gin go bad? She went to the kitchen and splashed some Gilbey's into a glass. *Hm.* Water with the faintest hint of juniper berries. The same with the Booth's.

Strange.

If her friends had used her apartment for their potluck, would they have nicked her booze and watered the evidence?

"Out of gin, Lieutenant. How about some forty-year-old Portuguese Douro?"

Wingnut winked. "Any port in a storm."

21

LOOSE ENDS

In December, the British Commonwealth Air Training Plan was signed by the United Kingdom, Canada, Australia, and New Zealand. Canada was chosen as the primary training site due to open space and proximity to the war front without threat from enemy attack. By 1945, 167,000 Allied pilots and aircrew would be trained at 107 schools across Canada. Over half the graduates would be Canadian.

(Wikipedia)

The day after Boxing Day, Frances went in to the Bank early, needing the calm of the empty office to work on the five-week backlog. She wasn't early enough. Raised voices drifted through the governor's open door. Frances walked in to discover the governor, the finance minister, and the deputy finance minister all looking weary and rumpled.

"Ah, Miss McFadden! Forgive us," said the governor. "Mr. Ralston had a midnight call from the prime minister. The PM wants guidelines for the new war bond issue prepared for this afternoon's war cabinet meeting. We've been up half the night wrangling over details. Coffee and all the related files would be a godsend."

Frances was back in five minutes. "Coffee is perking," she said, placing a foot-high pile of files on the Governor's desk. He eyed them with trepidation.

"Could you … possibly … summarize the printing status of the bond issue, Miss McFadden? I've been out of the office for five weeks."

And I haven't been?

"Certainly, sir. The British-American Bank Note Company has signed the contract to print the bonds. Designs were approved and the plates engraved. They're just waiting to know the denominations and the quantity required. Information packages are ready to mail to banks across the country as soon as the launch date is set."

"The country's out of money," said Mr. Ralston. "The prime minister wants to launch bond sales by January 15."

"We were discussing the size of the issue and the dollar value of individual bonds when you came in," said the governor, lighting up a Player's Mild.

"The defence minister is being hounded by the chiefs of staff for every possible nickel," continued Mr. Ralston. "He's pressing to go big: five hundred million dollars."

"Wouldn't one hundred million do for now?" queried Mr. Clark.

"A small bond issue might lead the military to think Canadians don't value their efforts," said the governor.

"In the Great War," continued Mr. Clark, "the bulk of the bonds were purchased in large denominations of fifty to one hundred thousand dollars by banks and industrial investors. Should we follow that model or issue smaller denominations so average Canadians can take part?"

"What does the prime minister want?" asked Frances.

The three men exchanged wry smiles. "The prime minister wants success," said Mr. Ralston. "At two o'clock this afternoon, he wants to be told what success looks like."

A twinkle returned to the governor's eye. "What's your opinion, Miss McFadden? You're well acquainted with these files."

Frances cleared her throat. "You three are the nation's economic brain trust. I dropped out of Grade 11."

"Enough with the false modesty. You're steeped in Bank lore. That old saw about not seeing the forest for the trees is painfully true of economists. An objective viewpoint would be helpful."

"I'll mull it over while I get the coffee." Frances did a quick retreat to the kitchen off the boardroom, where the coffee was in mid-perk. She dialed Jack Pickersgill's office.

"Jack! It's Frances McFadden. You're at work early."

"The sun never sets on the prime minister's office. But what are you doing up at this ungodly hour?"

"I need some advice before this afternoon's war cabinet meeting."

"War cabinet meetings are secret. What makes you think there's one today?"

"A very reliable source. Are you familiar with the agenda?"

"The agenda is more secret than the meeting. Mr. King scribbles a few notes on the back of an envelope and wings it."

"Well, off the record, they're discussing the war bond issue."

"Jesus H. Christ! How do you know that?"

"Said source is sitting in Governor Towers's office right now arguing about how big the bond issue should be. The debate ranges between one hundred million and five hundred million dollars. It would seem to me that if we offer five hundred million worth of bonds and sell everything, it's a homerun. If we sell two hundred million, well, it's still second base, isn't it?"

"You forget that perception is everything in politics. If you offer two hundred mil and sell out, that's a triumph. If you offer five hundred mil and sell two hundred, that's a failure. This bond issue is really a referendum on the war. Support the war? Buy the bonds. The Liberals need to win the bond sale referendum and ride it to victory in the next election."

"So, what's a sellout? One hundred million?"

"That would look like you're setting a low bar for fear of losing. Two hundred million is reasonable."

"What if it's oversubscribed? Don't we risk disappointing anxious buyers?"

"An oversell is a clear message that everybody wants to bet on a successful war. Anxious buyers will get in line faster the next time."

"The next time?"

"If this war lasts past April, there'll be many next times."

"Okay. Denomination size?"

"Old Chinese saying: 'Wide net catches many fish.'"

Frances returned to the governor's office with the coffee. The debate was flagging. She set the tray down quietly and turned to leave.

"Not so fast, Miss McFadden," said the governor. "We're waiting to hear your mullings."

Frances looked reflective. "Well, I'd guess that denominations from fifty dollars to fifty thousand will open the game to the widest range of players."

The Governor nodded. "How big an issue?"

"Cautious, but not shy. Say, two hundred million? If that sells out, go bigger later." She cleared her throat. "Now if you'll excuse me, gentlemen, I haven't been at my desk since November."

Frances found her desk in such good order it was frightening. The office log, the budget, the filing were all up to date. The governor's Christmas Tea had run flawlessly.

Was she needed here at all?

A lavender-coloured envelope with a gold crest in the left corner poked over the edge of her in-basket. In place of a stamp was embossed: "On His Majesty's Service." A flowing cursive addressed:

Miss McFadden,
Bank of Canada,
Ottawa, Canada.

Dear Miss McFadden:

Courtesy failed me amidst the shattered teacups at the pre-Christmas tea. Your quick thinking saved me from grievous harm. Please accept this belated note of thanks.

Margaret has <u>insisted</u> that I beg a favour. Could you send her some Canadian butterflies? She wishes to expand her collection to include Commonwealth countries that are so generously supporting us in the war effort.

It was my pleasure (and my good fortune) to meet you.

Best wishes of the season.

Elizabeth

The next day, Frances phoned Katie Warren.

"Well, the gypsy wanderer! Welcome home, slug."

"Thanks Katie. How did my apartment work out for the dinner club?"

"We took a pass. Didn't want to wreck the joint with a wild debauch."

"You needn't have cancelled just because I was away."

"Didn't cancel. Paul invited us to his place."

"Could he accommodate everybody?"

"Sure. You've seen his apartment?"

"Nope."

"You've been dating for three months and Paul's never invited you back to see his etchings?"

"He has etchings?"

"You know what I mean. Get you liquored up and rip your clothes off."

"Katie ..."

"Anyway, he lives right above Drury's Corner Store."

"No!"

"Yup. From whence your old heartthrob Buddy Drury used to bicycle off delivering groceries for his father."

"Buddy Drury was *never* my heartthrob. He took far too many liberties."

"Come now, McFadden! I've seen you drooling at the sight of his tight little bum as he pedalled down Rochester Street."

"Buddy isn't *bad* looking, I'll give you that. But he can barely read a stop sign."

"A literary snob, are we now? Anyway, you've missed your chance to have at him. Buddy and Larry Brewster both got stinking drunk at the Prescott Hotel the Saturday before Christmas. On a dare they hopped the train to Montreal and signed up with the Royal Rifles of Canada. I saw him yesterday strutting down Somerset Street in his natty uniform."

"I hope the army knows what it's in for. Did Paul say anything? About me?"

"Just that you were away on Bank business. We toasted you in absentia."

So, who's watering the gin? Miles? While he's watering the plants?

Although tall and strapping, Miles Treleaven was asthmatic and, to his chagrin, unfit for military service. His once-dashing doorman's uniform had been completely eclipsed by the tide of martial apparel thronging the streets of Ottawa.

"Miles, thank you for looking after things while I was away. Here's a little something for New Year's Eve." Frances presented a bottle of Dom Pérignon.

"Oh, no, thank you, Miss McFadden. I can't … I don't …" He blushed crimson. When he regained composure, he said, "My mother is president of the Ottawa Women's Christian Temperance Union. When I was twelve, she asked me to take the pledge."

"You've never had a drink in your life?"

"No. 'A promise made is a debt unpaid.' I think that's from 'The Cremation of Sam McGee.'"

"But now I have the unpaid debt. How can I thank you?"

Miles' eyes took evasive action again. "Well, Miss, I have a Ford roadster that I love to work on during my breaks. That's hard to do in winter weather."

"So … ?"

"Well, Miss, your apartment comes with an indoor parking spot."

"Oh! Be my guest. Don't own a car. Don't know how to drive."

"Mr. Carlyle wouldn't like me imposing on a tenant."

"Tell him that you're teaching me to drive and you need a car handy for lessons."

Miles smiled weakly. "I don't like to lie."

"Then give me lessons. I'm almost twenty-three. It's time I learned."

On December 31, Dr. Grace always treated Frances to lunch at the Chateau Laurier to honour the passing year. It was a Sunday, and the annual repent-before-the-clock-strikes-twelve sermon at Knox Presbyterian Church went into overtime. The good doctor was calling for a second double Macallan when she sat down opposite him.

"Quite a year," he said, toasting her. "Is this the life you imagined when I whisked you away from the High School of Commerce?"

"I had no comprehension of the havoc that a simple secretary can get into," Frances said, returning the toast. "By the by, I over-heard an interesting tidbit on my trip. Does Graham Towers's marriage have … shall we say … an extracurricular dimension?"

"Would it make any difference?"

"Not fair answering a question with a question."

"Well, would it?"

"Don't know. I grew up in a den of tight-laced Presbyterians. Marriage vows were sacred. I guess I never thought about other alternatives. So, is it true?"

Doctor Grace took a long slow drink of his Macallan. "I've heard spurious gossip about most of the high flyers in Ottawa, from the prime minister on down. If I don't know anything for a fact, I give people the benefit of the doubt. What business is it of mine what a man does outside the office?"

"But doesn't infidelity suggest a weakness of moral fibre? A weak-ness that might impact other areas of life?"

Doctor Grace snorted. "Well, now, Saint Frances, what *is* moral fibre except a fawning adherence to conventions set by others? My mother used to say, 'You don't choose your friends for their faults.' Friends have faults, but it's their strengths that draw you to them. The same is true of professional relationships. Governor Towers is brilliant, competent, and treats you with respect. What else matters?"

It was all too confusing for Frances following so closely on Reverend Stiles's fire-and-brimstone sermon. She changed the sub-ject. "Why do you always pay for lunch?"

"I'm a big shot in the Department of Finance. Money means nothing."

"So are you ferreting away a nest egg to settle down with that perfect someone?"

"I'm likely as settled down as I'm ever going to get."

"You don't like women?"

"I do like women. So much that I wouldn't want to saddle one with my eccentricities."

"You're handsome. You've got a Ph.D. and a pension. I'm surprised women aren't throwing themselves at you."

"A few have—egged on by my mother, whose life's ambition is to get me married. I'm too selfish for all the compromising."

"Marriage is about compromising?"

"That's what I observed at home. You?"

"My mother was prime minister and war cabinet rolled into one. Not much of a compromiser."

"How did your father like that?"

"He didn't argue. He did head west looking for work in 1932 and never returned."

"That makes a statement. How is *your* love interest by the way? Your young engineer?"

"Toot, toot," Frances replied. "His train has moved on down the track. He invited me home to meet his family at Christmas. I backed out, not knowing when we'd return from England. Hurt his feelings."

"Well? Do you like to be jilted?"

"What was I supposed to do? Tell Governor Towers that I couldn't accompany him to England because of an invitation to Christmas dinner?"

"Did you discuss it with the governor?"

"Of course not! My private life isn't his business."

"And *his* private life on the other hand …?"

"Yeah, yeah. Touché."

"Maybe someone else in your secretariat could have covered."

"Look, I'm new to the job, but it is *my* job. The secretariat has made great progress, but the training program hasn't yet covered meeting kings or fending off German U-boats." Frances smiled. "To say nothing of dealing with the Canadian High Commissioner to Great Britain."

"You had a run-in with Vinny Massey?"

"Locked horns the second we met."

"Lord! Is there anything left of the poor man?"

"If condescension were an Olympic event, Vincent Massey would win the gold medal hands down. It would have been cruel and unusual punishment to send one of my Little Rascals overseas to tangle with him. And the Nazis. And Molly Towers."

"Oh-oh. Is Molly in your bad books too?"

"You've met her?"

"Often. Charming hostess. Delightful sense of humour."

"You've met the Dr. Jekyll version of Molly Towers. When the sun goes down and Mr. Hyde creeps out, you'd better keep your back to the wall and your hand on your gun, partner."

"You've met both? Lucky woman."

"It's a privilege I'd swap for a coffee and a crème brulé."

Dr. Grace looked up and signalled Henri.

"By the way, do you know anything about butterflies?" asked Frances.

"Crème brulé is tastier. Thinking of starting a collection? You might try Gerry Scott in the Biology Division at the National Museum. Good sort. Five Lakes Club Member. Spends more time up there with a butterfly net than with a fishing rod. He over-collects doing fieldwork because he's always looking for mutations and new species. Pitches out hundreds of duplicate specimens. He'd be so thrilled at finding a fledgling lepidopterist that I'm sure he'd share his leftovers."

LAST WALTZ

Cairine Wilson was appointed to the Senate of Canada four months after the Judicial Committee of the British Privy Council ruled in the famous "Persons Case" that women were indeed persons and eligible to be members.

When Prime Minister McKenzie King first made the offer, Wilson was highly embarrassed and her husband told the Governor General, Viscount Willington, that the couple did not wish the appointment. McKenzie King prevailed and Cairine Wilson became Canada's first woman Senator February 15, 1930.

(Knowles, 78 and 81)

It was not a complete surprise in mid-January when Betsey Knowles summoned the seventh-floor residents of the Balmoral Arms to an emergency meeting. At bridge club the previous week, she had complained to Frances, "Our rent supposedly includes weekly cleaning but the service is terrible! I've drawn this to Mr. Carlyle's attention time and again to no effect."

Two other apartments rounded out the Balmoral's penthouse floor. Sir Lyman Duff, chief justice of the Supreme Court, lived in 7NW across the courtyard from Frances. He was a short man with a large egg-shaped head and an eccentric disposition. She had occasionally seen him pacing back and forth while waiting for the elevator, talking absently to himself. The Wilson family lived across the hall from the chief justice in 7NE. Mrs. Wilson was a senator. Two Wilson daughters still at home wore the green uniforms and very short skirts of Elmwood, the private girls' school in Rockcliffe. Although polite, the girls were much given to stifled giggles and secretive eye-rolling in the elevator.

Frances was late arriving, a sin Betsey would not have tolerated on a bridge night. When Celeste ushered her into the Knowles living room, the chief justice was holding forth on astronomy. "I'm just an amateur, of course," said Sir Lyman. "But I could scan the sky for hours. My Grubb telescope has a marvellous reflex sight that cancels out most light distortion. Had quite a sensational view of the Quadrantids meteor shower last week. Mr. Carlyle has entrusted me with a key to the roof door, and I tote my Grubb up there every chance I get. It weighs over thirty pounds, case and all, so it's a bit trouble-some on the stairs."

"Frances, do you know everyone?" asked Betsey, rising to greet her. Frances had exchanged pleasantries on the weather the few times she had met either floor-mate in the hall or elevator. She knew who they were from Anna Deloitte, who knew everyone, but had never been formally introduced. Betsey rectified this, stating vaguely that Frances was "with" the Bank of Canada—as though that preposition should resolve any mystery concerning her living in a penthouse apartment cheek by jowl with Ottawa aristocracy.

Betsey's pleasure at hosting a knight in her drawing room was palpable. This exuberance did not extend to Cairine Wilson. The Knowleses were died-in-the-wool Tories, and Betsey thought it déclassé for a woman to show interest in politics. Canada's first female senator remained simply "Mrs. Wilson."

"May I get anyone a drink before we start? Scotch? Sherry? Tea or coffee?"

"Tea, thank you, Mrs. Knowles," said Senator Wilson. "Lyme, won't you join me in a cup?"

Lyme?

"Lyme" suggested a familiarity beyond neighbourliness. Sir Lyman's eyes flittered toward the decanter of Scotch, but he acqui-esced to tea. Frances passed.

"Before Mr. Carlyle joins us at eight," said Betsey, "I'd like your opinions on what passes for cleaning here. I've frankly lost patience. When we lived in Rockcliffe, I had a meticulous Dutch cleaning woman, Fra Vlessing. She washed the light bulbs and dusted the eggs in the fridge. In comparison, Balmoral service is a travesty. These girls are as sullen a couple of gum chewers as you'd ever want to meet. Resistant to suggestions and positively discourteous to my maid. Celeste is forced to take her weekly half-day when they're here to avoid confrontation. Complaining to Mr. Carlyle has been fruitless."

"Our bathrooms get heavy usage," contributed Senator Wilson, "what with the girls grooming themselves for ages. A modest job is done on the mirrors, but clogged drains go untreated. And just before Christmas, Frank's gold cufflinks disappeared. We turned the place upside down but couldn't find them. Last week, the girls passed by Rose's Pawn Shop on William Street, and there were Frank's cufflinks in the window."

"Are you sure?" asked Frances.

"Oh, yes. Had his initials '*NFW*' in italic script. We redeemed them for ten dollars. Mrs. Rose's records indicated a 'Miss Jones' brought them in, no address given."

"Sir Lyman?" Betsey mouthed the title with a rapture that rivalled a grand slam bid then made.

The Chief Justice blinked several times. "I'm a little short-sighted, and could miss a good deal. Mrs. Cann, my cook, has tsk-tsked that the stove isn't given the attention she would like. The girls do seem exceptionally good at cleaning leftovers out of the refrigerator."

Betsey turned to Frances.

"No real complaint," admitted Frances. "I've never met the cleaners but they do leave a distinct aroma after each visit. Lately some bottles in my liquor cabinet seem to have been watered down."

Betsey read back her notes. "Sub-par cleaning all around and indications of pilfering. This should put Mr. Carlyle's feet to the fire."

"Possible pilfering," Frances qualified.

Mr. Carlyle arrived, hat in hand, right on time. His usual gruff manner was mitigated in the presence of the power clique on the seventh floor. He declined a drink. Betsey went on the offensive. "Mr. Carlyle, we have spoken before. My neighbours agree that the cleaning service is far from satisfactory."

"Believe me, Mrs. Knowles, I pass your every concern on to O'Grady Maintenance. Speak directly to Mr. O'Grady."

"To no apparent avail."

"Are there other cleaning services in Ottawa?" asked the chief justice.

"There are," confirmed Mr. Carlyle, "but O'Grady has held the contract since the Balmoral opened in 1932."

"They're resting on their laurels," said Betsey.

"It's a long-standing relationship," defended Mr. Carlyle. "I'd hate to jeopardize it over trivialities."

"Our concerns are trivial?" Betsey's voice rose an octave.

"Oh, no, Mrs. Knowles," said Mr. Carlyle, sweat suddenly glistening on his brow.

"We need to speak directly to this Mr. O'Grady. I want a solution by Thursday afternoon when his girls are back in here."

"They do my apartment Thursday morning," said Frances.

"Can any of you be here?" asked Betsey. "Say, eleven-thirty? To show a united front?"

"Court's in session," said the chief justice.

"The Senate Banking and Commerce Committee is sitting," said Senator Wilson.

"I *might* be able to get away," said Frances. "I'll check my schedule."

Frances did not like taking time off work for personal matters, but felt Betsey's plea for moral support. Her thousands of hours of unpaid overtime should forgive the occasional long lunch.

Frances was at Betsey's apartment at 11:25. Mr. Carlyle arrived at 11:35 with Mr. O'Grady in tow. He was a large, good-looking man with wavy hair and a broad smile. He spoke with a strong Irish brogue. "I apologize for any misunderstandin'," he said. "Your Mr. Carlyle contacts me with a complaint, I get right on it with the girls. Want to keep the customers happy," he grinned.

"Cleanliness, or lack of it, is just one of the problems, Mr. O'Grady," said Betsey. "Your girls treat my maid as though she should be doing their job."

"We don't want no jurisdictional disputes, Mrs. Knowles," said Mr. O'Grady with a conspiratorial wink.

"And personal items have been stolen."

Mr. O'Grady's smile faded. "Now, there's no call attributin' lost property to my cleaners."

"Stolen," repeated Betsey.

"Lost," countered Mr. O'Grady.

A frosty détente settled in the sedate living room.

"Went missing?" suggested Frances. This compromise won a grudging truce.

"These are good Catholic girls," continued Mr. O'Grady when his composure returned. "I don't hire no one without a priest's say-so. Leah and Maeve asked to work together, and 'cause they're troopers, I assigned them to the top two floors here. Whenever I take a suggestion to them, it's 'Yessir, nosir, three bags full, sir.'"

"There is some breakdown then, Mr. O'Grady, because that's not the kind of service we've been witnessing," said Betsey.

Mr. O'Grady's moustache twitched. After a moment he held his arms wide in a placating gesture. "Why don't we get all the cards on the table? Leah and Maeve are over cleaning Miss McFadden's apartment right now. Let's go have us a face-to-face."

Frances led the parade across the hall. Her door was locked, so she dug out her keys.

"Leah? Maeve?" Mr. O'Grady called out. No answer. A mop and pail could be seen down the hall near the kitchen. Music drifted to them through the master bedroom doorway. They entered the bedroom to see a rumpled pile of maids' clothes on the floor and half a dozen of Frances's formal dresses strewn across her bed.

"Odd," said Frances. "I packed these away before Christmas."

The music, louder now, was compounded by the tinkle of falling water. They crossed the bedroom and collectively gazed through the archway into the en-suite bath. The kitchen radio had been moved to the vanity, and the Brox sisters were belting out "Singin' in the Rain." On the seating wall at the edge of the shower, a whisky bottle sat beside two half-full crystal tumblers. Under the showerhead, Maeve and Leah danced naked, eyes closed, locked in each other's arms. The taller woman was good-looking in a ravished sort of way and draped herself around the shorter Rubenesque figure. Mr. Carlyle's mouth dropped open. Betsey's eyes shot triumphantly from the dancers to Mr. O'Grady. Colour mushroomed across his face as he marched over to the vanity and snapped the radio off.

23

HUEY FOO

Loan Response Pleases Ralston

Finance Minister Ralston today expressed his gratitude to the Canadian people whose prompt investment in the first loan of the second Great War enabled him to announce heavy over-subscription for the $200,000,000 loan two days after the books opened. Subscriptions continued to arrive at the Bank of Canada today, particularly from small investors in distant points, and these will be given preferential treatment when bonds are allotted.

(*The Ottawa Journal*, January 17, 1940)

———

Down two, doubled and vulnerable, Mr. Carlyle accepted intercession on the cleaning front. The war front? What of it?

After work, Frances walked east past the Parliament Buildings, then cut through the Byward Market to Dalhousie Street. The Bluebird Café was dimly lit and almost empty, a memory of bygone meals hanging in the air. An ancient Chinese man sat behind the cash register smoking a long pipe. In a booth midway down, a woman with two ketchup-smeared children fussed over the remains of hamburgers.

Frances dropped into a booth along the opposite wall just as a waitress brought coffee and rice puddings through the swinging door from the kitchen. She had Chinese features but very light skin. She pulled a pad from her apron and a pencil from behind her ear. "Chicken-a-la-king is the special today," she said in a melodious though neutral voice.

The menu was printed in English and French. It was all hot turkey sandwiches, grilled cheese, liver and onions. Nothing Chinese at all.

"I'll have the special and a Coke."

In a few minutes she returned with the drink and a platter of unrecognizable lumps in a white sauce over rice.

"Is Mr. Foo in?"

This sparked an inquisitive, sidelong glance before the waitress nodded.

"I'd like to speak with him if he has a moment."

Frances took a deep drink from the Coke. She toyed with her fork while giving the platter a judicious eye. Suddenly, Hughie Foo's hand lifted the plate from the table and returned it to the waitress with a brief direction in Chinese. He slid into the booth across from her.

"Miss Fran. Long time no see." He took a cigarette package out of a pocket in his stained apron. "Enjoy trip to England?"

Frances blinked. "How did you know?" she whispered.

Hughie Foo smiled. "Listen hard, learn much," he said.

She conceded with a nod and a smile of her own. "I didn't get much chance to sample your cooking."

"Never order daily special in Chinese restaurant," he said, dropping a spent match in the ashtray.

"Why not? Dr. Grace always orders the special at the Chateau Laurier. Says it's their showcase item."

"Bluebird Café not Chateau Laurier. At Bluebird Café, always order Jong Foo Chung."

"What's that?"

"Chef Foo's choice. Each day different. Each day best food in kitchen." He took a long drag on his cigarette.

"Why are there no Chinese items on your menu?"

"Canadian want hot dog, fish and chip." He shrugged. "No taste for Chinese food."

"Maybe just no taste," said Frances with another smile. "Don't Chinese people eat here?"

"Oh yes. Order Jong Foo Chung. Always happy." He blew three perfect smoke rings. "You want open restaurant?"

Frances laughed. "The way I cook? No, no. I have a business proposition. Residents on the top floor of the Balmoral Arms are unhappy with the cleaning service. Many complaints, no change. They're looking for alternatives. Are you interested?"

The waitress returned with a steaming plate of greens studded with cashews and tender pork pieces nested on crisp noodles. It smelled wonderful and didn't disappoint.

"Balmoral Arms belong to Irish," said Hughie Foo, continuing with the perfect smoke rings.

"Won't the owners want contented renters?"

"Don't know building owner, but Irish brother, O'Grady, own cleaning. My cleaner not work there."

"The O'Gradys have run into some difficulties. We'd like to change contractors."

Hughie Foo sucked air through his teeth and looked Frances straight in the eye.

"Different people own different building for cleaning. O'Grady brother own some. Italian own some. French own some. I own some. We have agreement. Not compete."

Frances' eyebrows scrunched.

"Ten year ago, Depression start. Fierce cleaning war in Ottawa. Some cleaner beat up. Very sad. One building burn down. No cleaning for anyone. Bad business. So Italian man, Peloso, call meeting of cleaning contractor. We talk how keep worker safe. Keep building safe. We divide city cleaning. Each get some. No fighting. Good business."

"But what if your cleaners are better than the Irish or the Italians? Shouldn't you be able to go after more business?"

"Life about harmony, Miss Fran. Yin and Yang. In competition people hurt. Building burn. No harmony."

"So we're stuck?"

Hughie Foo reflected through a series of smoke rings. "O'Grady very smart businessman, but not very patient man. Maybe he tired of complain, complain. Bad for liver. We respect each other. Maybe we talk. Maybe we trade one building for another building. You like?"

"I like!"

"Must not forget Mr. Carlyle."

"What do you mean?

"Building superintendent get cash from O'Grady brother for cleaning contract."

"He gets a kickback? No wonder he's so loyal!"

"Called incentive. For harmony. Just business."

Coming home from work later that week, Frances turned right when she got off the elevator on the seventh floor and rang the doorbell at 7NW. A dumpling-faced woman with gray frazzled hair and freckles answered the door. "Yes Miss?"

"Mrs. Cann? I'm Frances McFadden from 7SW. I'd like to have a word with Sir Lyman if he's free."

The dumpling processed this for a moment. "May I ask the nature of your business?"

"Astronomy."

The dumpling's eyes brightened. "Ah," she said. "One moment." She left the door slightly ajar, and footsteps retreated down the hall.

Presently, leather slippers shuffled toward her, and the chief justice opened the door. "Yes, Miss McFadden?"

"Good evening, Sir Lyman. I heard you mention at Betsey Knowles's that you often used the roof for stargazing but it's awkward carrying your telescope up the stairs."

"Correct."

"Well, my apartment has access to a rooftop greenhouse and gazebo. If you'd like, you could leave your telescope up there so you don't need to lug it back and forth."

Sir Lyman's jaw moved in animated thought. "That's very considerate, Miss McFadden. The trouble is that the telescope has to be kept in a heated space or the mechanism can seize up."

"There's a radiator in the greenhouse to keep the water pipes from freezing. It's not hot, but it's well over fifty degrees Fahrenheit. Would that do?"

A pensiveness took hold of Sir Lyman's face as if he was considering some fine point of law. "That would do, Miss McFadden. Might I see this greenhouse?"

"Certainly."

Frances escorted him to her apartment and took him up the spiral staircase that opened on the roof inside the greenhouse. She turned on the lights and Sir Lyman looked around.

"Pardon the dust," said Frances. "The cleaning ladies don't seem to have made it up here."

"Perhaps that's a blessing, Miss McFadden." He walked over to the sink and turned the tap. It squeaked but water ran freely. "This might do very well. Are you sure my instrument wouldn't be in the way?"

Katie Deavy's favoured euphemism for male genitalia was "instrument," most particularly in reference to Kevin's pendulous instrument "with which he nightly slakes his carnal lust." There was something magical in the way Katie could render ribaldry in flawless iambic pentameter. Her cat-and-canary grin suggested that lust-slaking might be a two-way street. Frances coughed before responding. "I don't use the greenhouse, except as a passageway, and I don't use the roof at all from November to April."

A boyish enthusiasm overtook the knight. "Why don't I go get the Grubb right now and try it out?"

The chief justice returned in a winter coat and hat, carrying a wooden case four feet long. He was a slight man and struggled with the cumbersome load. He unpacked and set up a tripod stand, then mounted the telescope on top. The covered breezeway between the greenhouse and the gazebo was snow-free, and there he sighted the Grubb with a surgeon's care. "Ah, look at this!" he said and offered the eyepiece to Frances. Orion jumped into focus before her eye.

"Wow!"

Sir Lyman took the eyepiece back and was instantly lost through his portal to the stars. Frances waited a minute before speaking. "Sir Lyman, I haven't had dinner yet, so I'm going downstairs. Stay as long as you wish." A muted "um" escaped the knight, but he didn't look up.

An hour later, Frances heard footsteps descending the metal stairs and walked down the hall to meet him. "Satisfactory?" she asked.

"Quite!" he beamed.

"Let me give you a key to the front door and you can come stargazing whenever you like."

"Oh no, Miss McFadden. I wouldn't want to intrude on your privacy. There was no lock on the greenhouse door. I can go up the central stairs to the roof and walk across."

"The roof can be covered by three feet of snow in winter. Here's a key. Ring the doorbell. If I'm here, I'll let you in. If there's no answer, come and go as you please."

"This is most awfully kind." He paused before confiding, "Astronomy nourishes my soul. It's my one socially acceptable distraction."

The unusual turn of phrase begged the question of *other* distractions. Although curious, Frances let it pass. "Then come and be nourished."

After Boxing Day, Frances had purchased three dozen Christmas cards on sale. Through January, she penned more or less the same thing thirty-six times.

> Please forgive the belated greetings. I've been away from Ottawa since mid-November and my correspondence has suffered.

To Paul Roderick she was a little more detailed.

Dear Paul:

> Thank you for your Christmas card. I trust you had a lovely holiday with your family.
>
> You are wise to seek equilibrium in your life. I'm that fond of you that I would not want to be the source of any disruption.

They say "It takes two to tango," and if your happiness comes from being "untangled," I understand. Frankly, that would not be my personal wish. I've immensely enjoyed our time spent together.

God bless you, Paul, and thanks for all your kindnesses.

Affectionately,

Frances

The week after Sir Lyman Duff's telescope took up residence in her greenhouse, Paul called Frances at work. "Miss McFadden? It's Mr. Roderick. From the Department of Agriculture."

"I only know one Mr. Roderick, Mr. Roderick. How was your holiday?"

"Wonderful. Yours?

"Quiet."

There was a pause as this comment was parsed. Then, "While you were away, the potluck scrum was afraid to use your place out of respect for your furniture. We did not forgo the tradition, however. I offered to host at my place, and we have met twice. We're going at it again on Saturday. Care to join us?"

"I wouldn't wish to upset anyone's equilibrium."

"You look after yours, I'll look after mine. It should be easy. These are all your friends."

"All?"

"All."

"Okay, then. What should I bring? I have a very limited cooking repertoire."

"It's the men's turn to cook. The fairer sex brings liquid refreshment and does the cleanup. That's the system."

24

PAUL'S PLACE

January 18, 1940:

> *Liberal Premier Mitch Hepburn moves a surprising resolution in the Ontario Legislature condemning the weak war effort of the federal Liberal Government. It passes by a vote of 44 to 10.*

(Pickersgill, 62)

January 25:

> *Mackenzie King dissolves parliament and calls a federal election for March 26.*

(Pickersgill, 63)

Seeing a female neighbour walking home from the Brewers' Retail Store carrying a twelve-pack, Frances's mother had once declaimed, "Only a harlot would be so immodest."

The moral high ground goes to the owner of the brandy cache in the upstairs linen closet?

Still, Vera McFadden's influence reached beyond the grave. Frances swathed the Molson's Canadian in tea towels and tucked the bottles snugly into two shopping bags before heading to the potluck. Discreetly laden, she met Senator Wilson waiting for the elevator.

"Good afternoon, Senator. How are the new cleaners working out?"

"Good afternoon, Miss McFadden. They're wonderful! I had no idea how poorly we were served by the dancing lesbians."

"Poor girls," said Frances stepping into the elevator. "Mr. O'Grady didn't need to fire them."

"He certainly wasn't punishing their cleaning skills. Men are hopelessly out of their depth when it comes to non-conforming social behaviour. A woman politician knows that all too well. By the way,

Lyme says you've let him use your terrace to gaze at the stars. Very kind. It's such a healthy distraction for him."

"Have you known Sir Lyman long?"

"Oh dear, yes. We're Laurier Liberals. You don't get to be a Supreme Court justice without some political connections." She laughed. "The same goes in spades for senators, of course. It's been a lonely vigil for Lyme since his wife died in 1925. His sister Annie is usually here to look after him, but she's been called to Toronto to tend to a cousin down with pneumonia."

Paul Roderick's apartment above Drury's Corner Store wasn't two blocks from where Frances grew up. She'd passed the corner a thousand times without giving the second floor a second look. Paul answered the door in an apron. "Reinforcements! Thank God. I'm way behind. The pipes froze last night and I've had a plumber and his sidekick here making a mess since noon. They've just left."

"I'm not much of a cook, but I'm a dervish with a mop."

"Don't you have cleaners do your apartment?"

"I do, forcing me to sublimate my desire to scrub and dust. This is a chance to unleash all that pent-up passion."

They smiled. "I could say something here, Miss McFadden."

"Could you, Mr. Roderick?"

"But we'd better get to work before the crowd arrives."

"That's very Presbyterian."

Paul hung Frances's coat on a brass hook behind the door. A flight of narrow stairs led up to a large open room with a high ceiling. Double-hung windows were spaced evenly along the east and south walls. Windowed double doors centred the west end. The half-wall framing the staircase visually stretched the room wider still. A thick oak trestle table with matching benches separated the kitchen from a lounge area. Tucked in the alcove formed by the stairwell was a studio couch. An orange crate by the pillowed end served as a bedside table. Sparse. It could have been a movie set for a monastery.

"Holy cow!"

"I know. Modest compared to your place, but the rent's cheap and it's close to my office at the Experimental Farm."

"I've never seen anything quite like this."

"Used to be the workshop for Petch Awnings. They made tents and all sorts of canvas goods. When I first saw it, the place was full of huge spools of old canvas that looked like giant toilet paper rolls. Canvas is heavy. They loaded it into the workshop with a hoist outside those double doors," he said, pointing.

What struck Frances instantly was what the space said about Paul, and conversely, how little her own apartment said about her. No frills, although there were plants on the windowsill.

He caught her looking at them. "Forced paper-white bulbs and Christmas cactus cuttings that my mother gave me. I don't have her green thumb, but they're still alive."

"This table," Frances said, rapping it with her knuckles, "is big enough for the Last Supper."

"It used to be twice the size. I cut it down and used the spare wood for the kitchen counter and these benches. Canvas had been dragged across it for thirty years so the top was silky smooth. I scrubbed it clean and sealed it with three coats of varnish."

The only door sheltered a toilet and sink with one tap.

"A cold water flat?"

"Plant Bath is just down the hill. A swim and a shower is only a nickel."

"What if Plant Bath is closed?"

"I can heat a pot of water on the stove in five minutes. Good enough for a quick wash."

Armpits and intimate areas? What Katie Warren called "a whore's bath." Frances wondered how familiar Paul was with the metaphor, or the hygiene of whores. She contained her curiosity.

"Not much privacy for bathing."

"Never been a problem."

"Is that because your company doesn't mind watching you groom, or you don't usually have company when you bathe?"

"We're getting a little personal here, Miss McFadden," Paul said with a wide grin.

"The enigmatic Paul Roderick."

"This from a woman who vanishes for a month at a time?"

"Game, set, and match to you." She turned around. "I love it! My apartment seems so ostentatious by comparison."

"Your place is Versailles. This is humble digs for a working stiff. Glad you like it. Could you live here?"

"An invitation, Mr. Roderick? I thought you were retrenching in the name of emotional stability."

"Just curious about how flexible your life style is."

"Truthfully? I'd have trouble here. No insult to present company, but there's nowhere to hide. My place isn't perfect, but it has lots of rooms. I need space just to get away from myself after a day at work."

"Not perfect? Come on!"

"I took it holus-bolus. As it sat. Someday I'd like to have the same opportunity you've had—to fashion a home from a blank canvas. It says so much about you."

"What does it say?"

"It says practical, masculine, ascetic."

"Maybe it gives too much away," he said with a wink. "Anyway, it was a lucky find. It hadn't been used since Mr. Petch died. Mr. Drury bought the building from Mrs. Petch so he could use the ground floor as a grocery store. His sign in the store window said, 'Space for Rent.' It didn't say 'apartment.' I had just come to town and was holed up in a hot, noisy rooming house on Booth Street. Fighting for the bathroom every morning was a hellish way to start the day. I asked Mr. Drury for a peek at the space. I liked it right away, cobwebs and all. Big and wide with windows on three sides. Kind of heaven for a boy from the country. Rented it for twenty bucks a month. I had to pay for the improvements myself, but Mr. Drury donated a pile of used orange crates for shelving and storage.

"I moved in without one stick of furniture and slept on the cutting table. Rolled up my work overalls for a pillow. Started cleaning and going to church rummage sales to pick up cutlery and dishes. Bought a used icebox and a dinged-up little gas stove from Beach Foundry. Remember those agriculture researchers we met in Poland? Deuteronomy Doyle, and Baily the barley man? Geniuses! Between them, they can fix anything. They plumbed in the kitchen sink and hooked up the stove one Saturday afternoon. Wouldn't accept a penny, but I slipped them each a bottle of Seagram's Crown Royal—you know, that snooty whiskey that comes in the purple sack with gold drawstrings? One of life's mysteries—I've never met a man who admitted to drinking Crown Royal, but I never knew a kid who didn't have one of those purple bags for his marbles."

The gang arrived at six. Ned brought a pan of roasted vegetables. Kevin had picked up smoked salmon and oyster chowder at Warburton's Fish Market. George carried a dark rum cake in a loaf pan. Conversation turned to the federal election that had just been called. Only George Holland had ever voted before.

"How old *are* you, anyway?" asked Katie.

"Old enough to have voted CCF in 1935," he replied with a smile.

"A socialist of indeterminate age," said Dorothy, squeezing his hand.

(Earlier, Dorothy had confided to her sister that she had been seeing a lot of George. "Right," Katie had related to Frances. "I'd like to know just which parts of George she's seeing a lot of. *That* would clarify a few things.")

"I've never voted before," said Mary. "How do you decide?"

"Just follow your conscience," replied George.

"The papers say the CCF aren't keen on the war at all," said Kevin. "The Conservatives want a Union government so we fight the war together, and the Liberals claim only they have experience governing and we should stick with them. What do you think?"

"A Union government didn't work very well during the Great War," said George. "It supported conscription, which soured Quebec. Conservatives haven't had a Chinaman's chance there since 1917."

"Isn't it a principle of parliamentary democracy," asked Paul, "that the party winning the most seats forms the government, and the second most successful party becomes His Majesty's Loyal Opposition? The Opposition holds the government accountable. What happens to accountability in a Union government?"

"I don't see how the Liberals can lose. They clobbered Duplessis in the Quebec election. They should sweep the sixty-five seats there. If they can keep selling wheat, the Prairie provinces will go Liberal. And they have lots of support in Ontario and British Columbia."

"Does it matter down at the Bank of Canada who wins the election?"

"I don't think so," said Frances. "A Conservative prime minister appointed Governor Towers and a Liberal prime minister hasn't raised any fuss over the past five years."

"Enough politics!" said Paul. "I didn't slave over the lamb stew of the century just to let it die on the stove."

25

THE ADMINISTRATOR

In 1930, Lyman Duff's heavy drinking brought on a serious breakdown that kept him in hospital for over three months.

(Williams, 138)

Although he was sober of mind, Sir Lyman Duff's abuse of the bottle and near catastrophic binges almost prevented him from being appointed Chief Justice of the Supreme Court in 1933.

(Knowles, 148–49)

Frances loved three seasons in Ottawa. The sudden greening of spring. The embrace of a hot summer's day. The glorious autumn foliage. Ah, but winter! Her romantic side indulged the first flaky snow-fall and a white Christmas. Romance pales easily. In a perfect world, she would have crocuses poking out of retreating snow by the second week of January. But as Dr. Grace was fond of saying, "It's an imperfect world."

On a brutish February morning, a bitter north wind lashed muffled figures trudging to work. The blanketed horse compelled to draw the Clark Dairy's sleigh stamped his hooves and snorted impatient plumes into the arctic air. Walking up Metcalfe on the way to the Bank, Frances noticed that the flag on the Peace Tower was flying at half-mast. She wondered if a troop ship had gone down on the North Atlantic. Governor Towers broke the news when he arrived.

"Lord Tweedsmuir passed away yesterday in Montreal. He had some kind of stroke last week that Dr. Penfield hoped to treat at the Neurological Institute. No luck. He's the first governor general to die in office since the Duke of Richmond in 1819. A sad day for Canada and his family. The body is coming back to lie in state in the Senate

Chamber. The funeral will be a huge affair at St. Andrew's Presbyterian on Wednesday. You'd better clear my appointments for the whole day."

"When there's no governor general, who signs Parliamentary bills into law? Are they sent to the king in England?"

"Oh, no. There's a contingency plan. An administrator carries out all official duties until the next governor general arrives."

"Who's the administrator?"

"The chief justice of the Supreme Court."

"Sir Lyman Duff?"

"Right."

"Doesn't the chief justice already have a full-time job?"

"It's wartime. Lots of people are doing double duty."

Frances had no idea how much Sir Lyman was making use of her terrace for stargazing. He could be walking across the roof from the main stairs to her greenhouse. He never rang her doorbell, but she was often late getting home and out later still on bridge nights.

The cold was bone-chilling on the walk back from work, and Frances went right in to draw a hot bath. During the day, the sun flooded down through the skylights above her apartment. At night, they were dark, brooding eye sockets. She was adding Epsom salts to the tub when she heard a tremendous crash from above. A glance up at the skylight revealed nothing. Cursed by curiosity, she slipped back into her coat and headed up the spiral staircase to check for damage.

Sir Lyman's felt-lined telescope case was open on a shelf in the greenhouse but the Grubb was gone. Frances stepped out into the winter wind. "Sir Lyman?" she called. It was dark, but the four skylights worked in reverse, drawing blooms of light up from her apartment to the rooftop. In the breezeway between the greenhouse and the gazebo the telescope tripod lay on its side, legs askew, like an upended insect. "Sir Lyman?" she called, a little louder.

Then she saw a pair of shoes jutting out beyond the edge of the skylight. She rushed over to find a body face down in the snow, emitting a low choking sound like a muffled bark. "Sir Lyman? What's wrong?"

The chief justice of the Supreme Court reeked of citrus and juniper berries. He was lying unconscious beside a pool of vomit. A gin bottle sparkled in the snow a few feet away. The gargling sound ratcheted up. Frances struggled to roll the man onto his side and reached in to clear his mouth. She found a moist, dense clump, which she extracted with difficulty. The moaning immediately eased. Sir Lyman Duff's false teeth, once identified, fell from her hand into the snow.

"Sir Lyman!" His breathing steadied, but he was out cold. Very cold, actually, as he wore only a light coat and no hat. Frances attempted to drag the inert body toward the greenhouse. He was not a big man, but the dead weight couldn't be budged through the deep snow. She quickly washed her hands in the greenhouse sink, then raced downstairs, returning with two blankets and a pillow.

Now what?

Downstairs again, she opened her door and peeked into the hall. Empty. She threw a quick glance toward the Knowles's apartment, then ran the length of the hall to Senator Wilson's and rang the doorbell. An agonizing ten seconds later, she knocked frantically. Footsteps.

Janet Wilson, the older, more robust of the two daughters, opened the door in her Elmwood uniform.

"Yes?" she said with a smile.

"Hello. I'm Frances McFadden. From 7 South West. Would your mother be at home?"

"We're just finishing dinner. Could she get back to you in half an hour, Miss McFadden?"

Frances gulped. "Ah … it's something of a rather urgent nature. Could I *please* speak with her?"

Pleading eyes moved the hesitant girl to action. "One moment, please," she said, and leaving the door slightly ajar, retreated into the apartment. Muted voices. Footsteps. Senator Wilson opened the door with both daughters hovering behind.

"Yes, Miss McFadden? Would you care to join us for coffee and dessert? We have Senator and Mrs. Dandurand to dinner."

"No thank you, Senator. Could I … could I have a private word?"

Senator Wilson looked at Frances and glanced back at her daughters. "Hold the fort, girls," she said, and stepped out into the hall, closing her apartment door.

Frances led her a few feet away, throwing a nervous look back down the hall.

"It's Sir Lyman Duff. He's … he's incapacitated."

"Well, I'm not surprised. He must be under enormous stress to suddenly find himself acting governor general on top of his other duties," Cairine Wilson said with a convivial smile. "Is he at home?" She glanced toward his closed door across the hall.

Frances gulped. "He's lying unconscious on the terrace above my apartment."

"Dear God! Did he have an accident?"

"I think … I think he's drunk," said Frances, ashamed that this sounded like an accusation.

"Ah," said the senator as the situation came into focus.

"I couldn't move him by myself. We have to get him off the roof before he freezes to death."

Senator Wilson thought for a moment, then opened her apartment door. Her daughters were standing just inside, looking self-righteous, as though they hadn't been eavesdropping. "Janet, Norma, tell Daddy he's on his own for ten minutes and then come right back."

When they returned, she beckoned them out into the hall. "Emergency, girls. Sir Lyman has had a little problem and Miss McFadden needs our help getting him back home. This way," she said with the confident nonchalance of a scoutmaster leading a hike. Frances took them back to her apartment, up the spiral stairs and out to the unconscious body. The Wilson women showed no surprise at seeing the chief justice of the Supreme Court lying in a snowbank next to his teeth. They rolled him into the blankets and, each lifting a corner, carried him back into the greenhouse.

"We can't get him down the spiral stairs in these blankets," said Frances. "It's too narrow."

"Right," said the Senator. "Jannie, a veteran of the Elmwood field hockey team should be able to lift the shoulders of a man who can't weigh 150 pounds."

"Yes, Mama."

"Be very careful with Sir Lyman's head. He's one of the top jurists in the English-speaking world. Mustn't addle those brains."

"No, Mama."

"Nor, you take the left leg and I'll take the right."

"Yes, Mama," said Norma.

"Miss McFadden, lead the way. Catch us if anyone slips. Ready, then? *Allons-y!*"

As though balancing a platter of Fabergé eggs, they wound delicately down the spiral staircase and emerged in the vestibule, laying the comatose chief justice on the Persian carpet.

"Now, we need another plan," mused Senator Wilson. "If that Knowles woman saw us, the news would be all over town in five minutes. Miss McFadden, do you have any device with wheels?"

"Wheels … wheels." Frances' mind raced through the inventory. "I have a tea cart in the dining room and a desk chair in the den."

"How big a desk chair?"

"Have a look."

Senator Wilson walked past the polar bear rug on the den floor to the desk and pulled out the chair. "Perfect! A good high back. We'll need to lasso Lyme into it. Any rope? A clothesline?"

"No," said Frances. "I have some extension cords."

"Get them."

Frances unplugged three lights in the living room and raced back.

"Good. Lift him gently and hold him steady while we strap him in. There."

"Now, girls," said the senator, "we are in need of one babbling idiot and one clumsy oaf."

Norma deferred to her older sister. "You choose," she said, as though a choice of desserts had been offered.

"I'll be the idiot," said Janet.

"Fine. Miss McFadden, can you lend us a measuring cup?"

Frances fetched a pristine cup from the kitchen.

Had it ever been used?

"Here's the plan," said the senator. "Miss McFadden and I will wheel Sir Lyman down to his apartment at the far end of the hall. It shouldn't take forty seconds. Interlopers can approach from only two directions: the Knowles's suite right across the hall, or off the elevator halfway down. Jannie, take the measuring cup and stand outside the Knowles's apartment, ear to the door. If you hear footsteps approach from within, knock loudly. When the door opens, barge right into the foyer, aiming the measuring cup like a gun. Jabber mindlessly about needing a half-cup of sugar to finish a meringue and could you please borrow one and here is the cup and you'll replace it tomorrow. Look so plaintive that even Tories would be embarrassed to refuse aid to such an imbecile."

Janet nodded. "Got it, Mama."

On the hall table was a clear glass vase containing five inches of white marbles used to anchor plant stems. Senator Wilson poured a dozen marbles out and handed them to her younger daughter. "Nor, I want you to go right down to Sir Lyman's apartment and unlock his door. Here. His keys were in his pocket. Then come back and stand in front of the elevator. If the door opens, spill the marbles onto the elevator floor, saying, 'Oh my God! I'm so clumsy!' Whoever is in the elevator will bend down to pick up the marbles and hand them back to you. Meanwhile you block the view of the hall."

Senator Wilson opened the door and looked out. "Coast is clear. All right, girls. Battle stations."

When the Elmwood uniforms were in position, they rolled the chair into the hall. The wheels dragged on the carpet, but with Senator

Wilson pushing and Frances pulling, they got the chair and the chief justice down to 7NW in less than a minute. No Betsey Knowles. No elevator traffic. The girls, primed for thespian grandeur, barely hid their disappointment.

"Jannie, help me strip the good man to his underwear and get him into bed. Nor, go tell Daddy I'll be delayed a while longer."

Senator Wilson picked up the hall phone. "I'll see if I can get hold of Sir Lyman's housekeeper. Hello, Mrs. Cann? It's Cairine Wilson, the chief justice's neighbour at the Balmoral. Yes, well, he's a bit under the weather. We have him resting comfortably in bed, but I wonder if you could come and spend the night here in the spare room in case he needs anything. Oh, bless you. One of us will stay with him until you arrive." She hung up.

"And bless *you*, Miss McFadden. Sir Lyman Duff is *the* pre-eminent legal mind in Canada. Second to none. Thirty-five years on the Supreme Court. His fellow justices are marginal talents, so he carries the brunt of the work alone. Add to that fifteen years on the Judicial Committee of the British Privy Council. And now acting governor general! It would stagger Atlas.

"When life overwhelms him, Lyme sometimes seeks consolation in the gin bottle." Senator Wilson faced Frances squarely. "This lapse is so trifling compared to his judicial contributions that I feel compelled to overlook it. I trust you will be gracious enough to do the same."

"Of course, Senator," Frances replied. "I should go back up and rescue his telescope from the cold."

"Good idea. Oh! Could you bring Sir Lyman's teeth back down? He'll need them for breakfast."

26

DISCRETION

C.D. Howe, a tough-talking businessman with enormous drive and capability, was essential to the war effort—one in which the supply of munitions and war materiel was to be more crucial than the raising of vast armies, navies, and air armadas. Howe well earned his moniker as "minister of everything," and he would soon oversee all wartime production.

(Cook, 215)

What C.D. Howe's department was doing ... was completing the restructuring of the Canadian economy. Howe's accelerated depreciation programs, Government grants and crown corporations renewed Canada's capital investment after 11 years of depression.

(Bothwell and Kilbourn, 178)

Deputy Governor Meldrum and C.D. Howe, the minister of Transport, had been booked in to see Governor Towers at 10:00 a.m. with no other appointments before lunch. Unusual. The governor did not waste time in meetings, and could dispense with even the loquacious prime minister in half an hour. More unusual still, Frances had not been asked to take minutes, although the governor had requested that she keep herself available.

Keep herself available? The theme of her life.

At eleven, the governor's office door opened and Scotty Meldrum emerged. "Miss McFadden," he purred in his butterscotch highland brogue, "the governor craves an audience if it's convenient." He chuckled. "I'd truly love to stay for this, but I'm already late for the Commons Banking Committee. Good luck!"

Good luck? Taking a memo?

Frances picked up her note pad, signalled for Bridget to cover her desk, then knocked twice on the governor's door before entering.

"Miss McFadden, you know the minister of Transport?" asked the governor as Clarence Decatur Howe rose to shake her hand.

"Only by reputation, Sir. How do you do."

A strong handshake was accompanied by a genial smile. "And how's that reputation?" he asked.

"Stellar. I'm surprised the governor hasn't asked you to leave the cabinet and join us at the Bank." Frances dropped into the still warm seat recently vacated by Scotty Meldrum and flipped open her notepad. She looked up. Graham Towers had two smiles. His "lips smile," as Frances called it, was serene and reassuring—like a Methodist minister at a baptism. His "high-octane smile," which engaged his eyes and put dimples in his cheeks, was the dangerous one. He would tilt his face slightly to the right and throw the smile at you like a curve ball. Smile number two illuminated his face. "Mr. Howe has come in this morning with an unusual piece of business. I'll let him frame it for you."

"Miss McFadden, I fell into conversation with Sir Lyman Duff at Lord Tweedsmuir's funeral last week. Pleasantries and shop talk. I confided to him that I was in need of an unobtrusive woman of complete discretion for a difficult task. He told me point blank that Frances McFadden at the Bank of Canada was the most circumspect female in Ottawa." He paused. "Why do you suppose he would say such a thing?"

"You should probably ask the chief justice."

"I *did* ask. He changed the topic. So I'm asking you."

"Well, Sir, if Sir Lyman Duff didn't care to be more forthcoming, it would hardly be prudent for me to be so."

Graham Towers laughed right out loud. "I told you!" he said, slapping his knee.

"Do you have any idea what Sir Lyman was referring to?"

"I can guess." Frances did not wish to appear coy. "It has nothing to do with the Bank of Canada. Or the Ministry of Transport."

"So it's none of my business?" C.D. Howe asked with a smile.

"I didn't say that."

"You haven't said much at all, Miss McFadden, which makes you an excellent candidate for my proposal. I have a delicate problem," he continued. "I need a completely trustworthy and very discreet person to undertake some business dealings in New York. The governor thinks you're the ticket."

"I suppose I should take that as a compliment," said Frances, "but I have a terrible sinking feeling."

"Here's the situation. The Canadian government has found itself at war without the manufacturing capacity to support a war. One does not build and equip armament factories overnight. The United Kingdom, our largest trading partner, needs every last bolt they produce to meet their own military needs. The United States has ten times our industrial strength, so it would be logical that we purchase combat equipment from them. Unfortunately, their Neutrality Acts prohibit American companies from trade or commerce with belligerents. In addition, there is a vocal isolationist element south of the border paranoid about being drawn into a 'foreign' war."

"So ...?"

"So, we need someone in New York, disguised as a wealthy American, buying American products and shipping them offshore."

"Offshore?"

"They will have a destination for the bill of lading, probably in South America."

"But these products won't be going to South America?"

"No. Once a ship clears the harbourmaster in New York, the American government officially doesn't really care what happens to its cargo. These freighters would have a refuelling stop in Halifax or Sydney on their manifest."

"At which time certain products might be unloaded on dark, moonless nights?"

Mr. Howe smiled the smile of a coach whose prodigy had just won the blue ribbon.

"What kind of products?"

"Aircraft engines, precision machinery, machine tools, rolled steel, brass."

"And how would this someone hide her identity or intent?"

"We do have some American friends. While officially neutral, President Roosevelt is sympathetic to the plight of the democracies in this war. He likes American factories churning out products. Good for the economy. Good for employment. However, it's an election year down there, and he needs to be wary of isolationist politicians who are numerous and vocal. He can't publicly support any foreign belligerent or be seen as leading America toward war."

"So the gatekeeper isn't watching the gate too carefully. Don't you still need a cover story for the manufacturers selling the products?"

"Right you are. We have another friend in Murchison Whitaker, a very wealthy, reclusive industrialist from Minnesota. He is willing to lend us the cover of his business empire and his granddaughter's identity."

"Why would a recluse want this kind of exposure?"

"He doesn't. That's why his 'granddaughter' will act on his behalf. We would create an identity complete with American passport and support paperwork. The story would be leaked in American newspapers that Mr. Whitaker's granddaughter would be representing him in New York on an international business venture.

"The Canadian government has secretly deposited money into a numbered account at the Union Bank of Switzerland. No banks on earth match the Swiss for clandestine financial transactions. The surrogate granddaughter would have signing authority to purchase goods using drafts on that account."

"Well," reflected Frances, "as keen as I am to thwart the Nazis, I see some flaws in the plan. I don't look, act, or dress like the scion of a wealthy American industrialist. I don't know anything about international trade. And most important, I don't like to lie. It's too easy to trip up in a tangle of deception."

"Good points. The scion of a wealthy recluse can dress any way she wants. I was at a wedding recently in Vermont—the granddaughter of very old money, so much money for so long that no one felt the slightest need to dress to impress. The men were almost shabby. The women wore only token jewellery. Whitaker money is old money."

"But I don't know the first thing about business contracts."

"A Whitaker lawyer would be part of the team to handle legal issues, along with an accountant to deal with financial details."

"And why not a man? Won't all these industrialists be men?"

"Yes, but we hope a woman's presence would be enough of a distraction that other details could slip past their notice. Only one little white lie is necessary—the assumed name, which is easy to remember. What other questions would there be? Do you want to buy products? You do. Do you want to ship them offshore? You do. Are you authorized to purchase them on behalf of a Murchison Whitaker company? You are. If you're asked anything personal, just say that you don't mix business with pleasure."

"How long will this take?"

"About a week. The granddaughter should start her trip from Chicago. Mr. Whitaker is taking delivery of a new Pullman coach there and is willing to lend us his old one. He wants to meet the substitute granddaughter."

"Why?"

C.D. Howe looked slightly askance. "Mr. Whitaker is lending us his good name, his business reputation, and one of his companies to cover this operation. Not to mention his granddaughter's identity. Surely he deserves a look at the person he's entrusting with all this?"

"That knife cuts two ways. I deserve a chance to check him out. Quid pro quo."

"*Forbes* magazine lists Mr. Whitaker as one of the wealthiest men in America. His assistance in this enterprise is absolutely vital. He might flinch at a cross-examination."

"I have no ill will toward this Mr. Whitaker. I've never heard of him. However, the mighty can be abusively rude and arrogant. I've experienced it first-hand. I'm not doing that again, even to defeat the Nazis."

C.D. Howe threw an inquisitive look at Governor Towers.

"Ah! The high commissioner," said the governor.

"The far-too-high commissioner," replied Frances.

"Bit of a run-in in England with Vincent Massey," the governor explained to Mr. Howe.

Mr. Howe laughed. "You and Prime Minister King are of like minds. He packed Massey off just about as far as he could send him. He would have sent him to Siberia if he could have. Don't worry. You'll like Butch Murchison a hell of a lot better than Vin Massey. Absolutely no pretence. Butch would never ask you a question he wouldn't answer himself."

This was mollifying. "What would I tell the secretariat?"

"As little as possible. Not even the prime minister knows about this. He gave instructions to get war production geared up quickly and left the details to me. He avoids knowing things that would be difficult to answer to in Parliament."

"I don't like it," said Frances. "Abandoning the office here puts undue stress on my staff. Isn't there anyone else?"

"We can't send someone with a high profile in government or the Bank or industry for fear they'd be recognized. Apparently, you're the most discreet woman in Ottawa. And, you're trusted."

"With the signing authority on a Swiss bank account? How big is this deal?"

"Ten million in American dollars to start. If it works, there could be more."

"What if I skip town with the swag and catch a slow boat to China?"

Graham Towers laughed so hard he almost choked. It was a little annoying to be deemed so guileless. When he regained his composure, he said, "Well, Miss McFadden?"

"It's the craziest idea I've ever heard," Frances replied. "And ever since I joined the Bank, there has been some competition for that honour."

"Are you willing to help out? Discreetly?" asked Mr. Howe.

"I'm willing to think about it."

"We have to move quickly."

"I'll let you know tomorrow."

Frances called Paul Roderick at work. "Hi. I know we don't usually get together during the week, but I need to talk to you."

"Sure. Talk."

"It's not phone talk. How about a Dutch treat dinner at the Honey Dew? Meet you there at 6:30?"

Frances and Paul had restarted their old ritual of Saturday night movies, although a closeness had been sacrificed. He was unfailingly polite and faultlessly friendly, but a new and indefinable caution had crept into his behaviour. He always walked her home to the Balmoral; however, as often as not, he politely turned down invitations up to her apartment. "Once bitten, twice shy," Vera McFadden, queen of the platitudes, would have said. Frances understood that his distancing was defensive and not strategic, but it stirred a yearning in her.

Paul was right on time. They loaded their trays in the cafeteria line and found seats in a back booth. Frances got right to the point. "I was asked this morning to undertake a special assignment related to the war effort. It will take me out of Ottawa."

He smiled his ironic smile. "So?"

"I said I needed to think about it. I wanted to talk to you before I agreed to anything."

"Why?"

"Because I didn't talk to you the last time, and I hurt you. I don't want to hurt you again."

"How long?"

"Possibly seven days."

"What if I said don't go?"

"Here's your chance."

Another smile, no irony. "I've done a lot of thinking since November. It isn't really my prerogative to tell you how to behave. You're 'free, white, and twenty-one,' as my father used to say. You can do whatever you want."

"I want a lot of things. I want to do my job well. I want to help win the war. I want not to hurt you."

"That's nice to hear, but you should make this call without me in the equation."

Frances reached across the table and squeezed Paul's hand. "You're sure?"

"I'm sure. We have a nice relationship, but we haven't made any commitments."

"Yet."

"Yet." He nodded and smiled. "I can probably find some way to amuse myself while you're gone."

"Yeah. That's what I was afraid of."

27

MURCHISON WHITAKER

Stickers declaring KEEP THE U.S. OUT OF WAR adorned car windshields all over America within days of the British and French declaration [of war]. A French journalist based in New York observed: "This country is literally drunk with pacifism."

(Olson, 54)

D etails were ironed out. Frances went down to the Karsh studio on Sparks Street to have several photographs taken. She completed signature identification papers for the Union Bank of Switzerland and signed a ream of other forms without even reading them. A week later, her old friend Inspector Hollingsworth of the Mounted Police arrived at 8:10.

"I'm invited to share your 8:20 with the governor," he said. In the governor's office, he handed her a manila envelope containing an American passport and a California driver's licence with Frances's photographs officially embossed in the name of Melanie Whitaker.

"Nice forgeries," she said.

"They're not forgeries," replied Inspector Hollingsworth. "They're the real McCoy."

"You must have friends in high places."

The inspector smiled. "It's called reciprocity."

The governor passed Frances a file containing Trans-Canada Air Lines tickets and a sheaf of background documents. "Next Tuesday morning, you'll fly from Ottawa to Toronto, where you change planes for Chicago via Detroit. Two Whitaker Consolidated staff will meet you at O'Hare airport. Mr. Dubois is a commercial lawyer and Miss Rutledge is a chartered accountant. They'll take you to meet Mr. Whitaker. You can check each other out."

"What if it's not a match?"

"Go back to O'Hare and fly home."

The Whitaker people were waiting by the luggage claim counter at O'Hare. Miss Rutledge was small as a minute. A brown tweed suit and horn-rimmed glasses gave her an intensely owlish appearance. Mr. Dubois looked as though he had just left his horse tied up outside the saloon. He wore polished cowboy boots and a string tie. A ten-gallon hat stretched him up way over six feet. His weathered face didn't give much away. Mutt and Jeff.

"Hope ya'll had a comfortable trip, Miss Whitaker," the cowboy twanged. "Point out your bags 'n I'll take 'em to the car."

A chauffeur named Neville in green livery held open the door of a Rolls-Royce that matched his uniform. The car purred through the countryside toward the LaSalle Street Train Station. They turned down a side lane and stopped at the end of the train platform beside the steps to a green Pullman car. Green seemed to be a Whitaker theme.

Mr. Dubois helped Neville tote the luggage up the stairs into a lounge-like observation room. It was dated, but comfortably appointed. Overstuffed chairs sat on a Persian carpet in royal reds and blues. A black porter in Whitaker green introduced himself as Charles. "Mr. Whitaker is expecting you, Ma'am," said Charles. "I'll just let him know you've arrived." Charles disappeared through a door in the far end of the car.

"Nice digs," said the cowboy, settling his lank frame into a chair. "A fella could grow used to this."

"This Pullman will be attached to the *20th Century Limited*, which leaves for New York at three," said Neville. "Be at Grand Central Station in sixteen hours."

Charles returned. "Mr. Whitaker will see you now, Ma'am. Alone." The cowboy and the accountant exchanged silent shrugs. Miss Rutledge dropped into another chair and pulled out a Pocket Book.

Frances followed Charles past the bedrooms and out the far door of the Pullman. A wooden gangplank bridged the gap to a similar private car on the next track. "Right this way," he said. The second car had wide aisles and exuded the smell of new upholstery. Charles led her to the lounge, where a large man sat in a wheelchair behind a desk with leather inlay. A tartan blanket covered his lap and legs.

"Pardon my not standing, Miss," said the man. "These legs don't stand much anymore. I'm Murchison Whitaker. Please have a seat. Thank you, Charles. I'll buzz if we need anything."

Frances moved forward, shook the proffered hand, and sat down.

"Not much to you, for all the build-up," he finally said. "Clare Howe said you wanted to check me out." He chuckled. "Pretty gutsy. What'd they tell you about me?"

"Very little. Wealthy. Reclusive. Isolationist. Willing to help."

Mr. Whitaker gave a half chuckle. "Pretty tight resume. You must wonder why an isolationist would want to get involved in this fool war."

"I do," replied Frances.

Mr. Whitaker laughed again. "You sure don't waste time with a lot of jabber. I've got three reasons for pitching in on this scheme. I like Canadians. My family's had a lodge up north of Kenora for sixty years. Grampa bought five thousand acres of wilderness there before the turn of the century. Rocks and trees and a chain of little lakes just as beautiful as the day God made them. I've spent every August up there since I was five years old. Quiet. No Fuller Brush salesmen. Hire locals to keep the place up and Indian guides for fishing and hunting. Never met one try to cheat me or whine about pay.

"Reason number two: I did a lot of business with Clare Howe years back before he went into politics. Goddamn waste of his time, if you ask me. He could have made millions in the grain business. Good man. Honest as the day is long. If he says I won't lose a nickel on this deal and no one will ever know, that's gold standard.

"Thirdly, my son, Laidlaw, used to run our European office from Vienna. Married an Austrian beauty named Zelda Tetenbaum. Cultured. Smart. Jewish. They had problems in '38 when the Germans marched in. Laidlaw had to grease palms to slip his wife and in-laws out the back door to Switzerland. Glad to have them safe, but boy, that left a sour taste. Don't much like paying bribes to racists.

"Clare came up to Minnesota to pitch this idea. Wanted to use one of my companies as cover. I agreed to help, but not in person. Don't like people gawking at me in a wheelchair. That bastard Roosevelt is in a wheelchair, too, although the newspapers only show pictures of him from the waist up.

"Don't want anyone thinking that the Whitaker group of companies is in frail hands. They're not. I could arm-wrestle a bear. Ninety per cent of Whitaker stock is family owned and there's always a Whitaker present to sign off on a contract. Laidlaw's in Geneva with his hands full. My other son, Russell, flits back and forth between San Francisco and Hong Kong handling our far-East interests. No Whitakers available.

"So Clare and I came up with this granddaughter scheme." He shook his head sadly. "I wanted to meet the person who would act as my granddaughter, Melanie. God! What a mess she is. Ever dabbled in drugs, Miss McFadden? Cocaine? Heroin?"

"No, sir."

"Very wise. Half the time Melanie doesn't know who she is. And when she does know, she isn't much fun *to* know. Was the cutest little girl you could ever imagine. Bright. Curly blonde hair. Athletic. Threw it all down the toilet. My own blood. So sad." He shook his head and looked out the window, eyes watering.

"Is Melanie the daughter of Russell or Laidlaw?"

"Neither. Curtis, my youngest son, was her father."

"Was?"

"Was. Bought himself a fancy Mas-er-ati racing car. Proud as punch at how fast the fool thing would go. Raced a train to a level crossing once." A rueful laugh. "Yeah. Once. Not quite as fast as he thought. Wasn't enough left of Curtis to fill a jam jar. You drive, Miss McFadden?"

"Just learning."

"Piece of advice. Don't hit a train. The train always wins."

A brown study clouded Murchison Whitaker's face for a few seconds. "Clare said they'd make up some ID for you. May I have a look?"

Frances took the passport and driver's licence out of her purse and handed them over.

"Like seeing a ghost of what might have been." He handed everything back. "So this project is a salute to my little Mel while she tries to straighten her life out at a clinic in northern California."

"A fourth reason."

"Yeah, a fourth reason. How about your reasons, Miss McFadden?"

"I don't know why they asked me to do this, Mr. Whitaker. I just didn't duck fast enough."

"They sure must trust you. You're handling a wad of dough, and if this story ever came out, I hate to think of the mess."

"Where'd you meet Mr. Howe?"

"Clare Howe saved my bacon big one time. He was a young engineer building grain elevators out of Port Arthur. I closed a big barley and corn contract one spring expecting to use the elevators I had rented for years at Duluth for storage and ship loading. Elevator owner got wind of my situation and tripled the rent. My mistake. Should have sewn up the elevators before I bought the corn and grain. Cost me a few sleepless nights.

"Heard about Clare working up in Ontario and went to see him. Told him I needed some elevators fast. He came down to Duluth and looked around the harbour. Had me buy a hundred acres of swamp. He sent pilings down thirty feet to bedrock and formed an artificial island of concrete on top. Built nine elevators in segments in Toronto and shipped them up by rail. Put it all together in four months, just as the trains were ready to move the grain. Saved me hundreds of thousands. Did a lot of business with Clare after that. Always a square shooter."

"And he recommended me to you?"

"Sure did." Mr. Whitaker took a large manila envelope off a side table and handed it over. There was a cover letter from C.D. Howe on personal stationery—not his office letterhead. Several photographs of Frances that she had no memory of having been taken, and a lengthy missive from Graham Towers dated a week earlier that she had definitely not typed.

"Sounds like a paragon," said Frances. "I think I'm here under false pretences."

Mr. Whitaker chuckled. "Modest, too. It would become the Whitaker name."

"I appreciate that you want to do something in your granddaughter's memory. That doesn't explain why an isolationist wants to get involved in this war."

"Well, Miss, it's the simplest thing. America would be crazy to enter a war three thousand miles away. Doesn't mean I like the Nazis. How to put them in their place without American blood on the line? Help someone else do the job."

"Who will Melanie meet in New York?"

"A couple of dozen businessmen I know back East. They think I'm offering them a chance to get involved in a resource development business in Brazil. There actually is a subsidiary of Whitaker named Amazon Development Corporation. ADC. I've been trying to get something going down there for over five years. Sent in a flock of surveyors and prospectors. Huge bonanza of natural resources there. But no roads, rail lines, shipping facilities, electricity, harbours, all the things you need for resource development. And the political situation has been icy. Just recently that thawed a bit and we have a narrow window to get development going.

"The story I'm giving out, which is close to the truth, is that my assets are invested in thirty-three Whitaker companies around the world. Earning money. Very little liquid jack. I'm in quick need of ADC partners. We'll give these businessmen some corporate bonds at an excellent rate if they invest. Don't want their money. Want their products with as little cash down as possible." He snorted. "I should say that's what Clare Howe wants.

"This crowd you'll meet in New York all went to New England prep schools just like me. Phillips Andover or Groton or St. Paul's. Then Harvard or Princeton or Yale. They're all successful businessmen, although not particularly adventurous. They think I'm coming to New York to make the pitch, but I'm not. You're going to be the Whitaker with the signing pen. I'll telegraph them about the change, but they'll be a bit miffed. I'll provide you with complete files on them and their companies. Your job is to win over as many as you can."

"Isn't this fraud? They think they're investing in ADC, and they're really investing in the Canadian war effort."

Mr. Whitaker laughed. "You're fighting the Nazis, Miss. You think they give a tinker's damn about fraud? Or theft? Or murder? Anyway, the letters patent of ADC are very broad. Cover a wide range of activities. Some of their investment might actually go to ADC. Whatever Clare Howe doesn't need. The Canadian Government will back up the bonds, so they're really taking no risk for a generous return."

"And how much do Miss Rutledge and Mr. Dubois know about all this?"

"They think you're my granddaughter and this deal is legit. Has to be that way. They're my best people. I don't want to confuse them with charades."

He stretched and stifled a yawn. "Well Miss McFadden, you're good enough for me. Am I good enough for you?"

28

20th CENTURY LIMITED

The America First Committee, under the leadership of executive director Robert Douglas Stuart, emerged as the most powerful, vocal and effective isolationist organization in America. One of the group's chief goals was to stop America from going to war, even if that meant Britain's defeat by the Germans. One million people joined America First in the first fourteen months of its existence.

(Olson, 220–27)

The *20th Century Limited* rolled out of Chicago's La Salle Street Station at 3:00 p.m. on the dot. It stopped briefly at Englewood on the south side then ripped east at sixty miles an hour toward Toledo, Albany, and Grand Central Station. In the Whitaker private car, Charles served refreshments to the travellers. "Just iced soda water," said Frances. Mr. Dubois asked for coffee, "paint-peelin' strong." Miss Rutledge ordered bourbon with branch water.

Frances raised her glass. "To a successful journey." They toasted. "Do you two travel much for Whitaker Consolidated?"

"All the time," said the cowboy lawyer. "At our best on the road, wouldn't ya say, Razor?"

"Yep, Duke. Unlike a good wine, we travel well."

"Mr. Whitaker has a mess of lawyers and accountants spread all over the country. God knows how many. Most of the talent rides a short leash. Razor and me, we're tumbleweeds."

"But you do have homes?" asked Frances.

"Got a wife and three boys in Tulsa, Oklahoma," said Duke. "I see 'em about ten days a month."

"Must be hard on family life," said Frances.

"Nah. We're all a little testy, like a nest o' rattlers. Time apart probably saves us from killin' each other."

"Miss Rutledge?"

"Grew up on a dirt ranch in the Texas panhandle west of Amarillo. My brother Vance took over the place when pappy got gored by a bull and bled to death. I wanted to shoot the goddamn animal, but Vance said Cyrus—the bull—was very good at the business of being a bull, rutting cows, even slow-moving steers when he was horny.

"The ranch was two thousand acres of hardscrabble. Took forty acres to feed a cow. Vance said to me one day when the sun was blotted out by dust, 'Ruth-Anne, there is no future here for a sharp cracker like you. Save your pennies, and I'll put aside what I can, and we'll punch your ticket out of here.' I taught in a one-room school for four years to scrape together the money for a business degree from Texas State. Still go home to see Vance and his family at Christmas. Rent a room in Minneapolis where I keep my spare clothes. On the road the rest of the time."

"How did you end up with Whitaker Consolidated?"

"Well," said Duke, "I worked for five years in a dink-ass law firm in Tulsa run by a couple of country club lawyers named Gilchrist and Ellis. They kept bankers' hours and played a lot of golf. I logged ten-hour days waiting to be made partner, but it was always put off for one reason or another. Then a Whitaker company named Oklahoma Oil wanted to get some wells in the ground down by Glenn Pool. It ran into a lot of resistance because the big oil players pretty well had the local politicians in their pocket. So Okey Oil came to Gilchrist and Ellis for legal assistance. The law actually favoured Okey Oil, but it was going to be right gritty. The partners didn't want to ruffle any feathers. Turned 'em down.

"I was bored silly doin' real estate and title searches. Sharpening pencils would have been more excitin'. I bumped into the guy from Okey Oil in the bar of the Mayo Hotel and said if he put me on a retainer, with some share options, I'd quit G&E and do his legal slugging myself. I did. It worked. Made enough to buy a house in Riverview for the family, and Whitaker's been callin' on me ever since when they needed a gunslinger lawyer."

"Miss Rutledge?"

"I started with Whitaker just after America entered the Great War. Whitaker Consolidated had over twenty companies at the time, and things were moving so fast they sometimes ended up bidding against each other for government contracts. They needed a clearinghouse, which I set up for them at the head office in Minneapolis. Saved Whitaker a bucket. Mr. Whitaker sends me all over the country to check on his subsidiaries."

"Looking for hands in the till?"

"Not really. Whitaker people are well paid and loyal. Looking for inefficiencies … better accounting practices. Sharing good ideas. Margins are slim. Try to keep us sailing as close to the wind as possible. I like travel, and the expense account is generous, although I've never ridden in a private Pullman before."

Frances needn't have worried about personal questions from the twosome. Duke and Razor were professionals. They would have listened, but didn't ask. She opened the briefcase full of papers and started going through them. A Whitaker family file gave her enough background to fake things if she was cautious. Other files identified businesses, owners, production records, lots of charts and graphs. Notes in a bold hand were scribbled in the margins. They made little sense to her. "Anticipate any problems in New York?" she asked.

"I'd say no, but it's a very unusual negotiation," said Duke. "Mr. Whitaker took great care hivin' off this little group of dogies from the main herd. He's one of the richest men in America. Has a stellar reputation in the business world. These fellas should feel privileged being let in on this deal."

"What's unusual about it?"

"Normally, a business gets bids on a product from three or four suppliers, chooses one— usually the cheapest—and orders. The product is delivered, and the purchaser is invoiced to pay the full amount in thirty days. In this project, Mr. Whitaker wants the suppliers to partially fund their own deliverables."

"Pay Whitaker to take their product?"

"No. Mr. Whitaker wants them to supply product for 20 per cent down on delivery. He wants the businessmen to take the outstanding balance in Amazon Development Corporation bonds."

"How much interest do the bonds pay?"

"That depends on how big a deposit they want and the term length of the bonds."

"Sounds complex," said Frances.

Duke pulled out a pad of paper. "Say Acme Milling Machines is contracted to sell us ten machines for $10,000 each—$100,000 total. Mr. Whitaker will pay Acme $20,000 on delivery and offer 'em $80,000 in ADC bonds to cover the balance. It's called leveraged purchasing. If they take the bonds for a five-year term, the yield is 5 per cent per year. If they're willing to take a ten-year term, the bonds pay 10 per cent."

"What does 'leveraged' mean?"

"Whitaker gets $100,000 worth of product for 20 per cent of the selling price. The rest is paid for at a later date."

"Why would any business put off getting paid in full for ten years?"

"Lots of reasons. First of all, the selling price isn't the same as the cost price. Maybe it only cost Acme $50,000 to build those ten milling machines. They get $20,000 up front. They're out $30,000. They could get $8,000 in interest per year on ten-year bonds. In less than four years, they have all their costs covered. The rest is gravy. They still have over $48,000 in interest coming to them, and the bonds are redeemed after ten years for $80,000."

"If they can wait ten years."

"Some companies are sleepin' on so much money they're gettin' bedsores," said Razor Rutledge. "Got more cash stashed than Scrooge McDuck."

"During the Depression?"

"This Depression has been hard on some, but parts of the economy are unscathed. Tulsa is doin' fine. People are still buying oil and there are hundreds of jobs related to the oil industry. Many companies have made a profit, but don't know what to do with the money. The stock market's a crapshoot. Government bonds pay a piddly 3 per cent. ADC bonds give an excellent payback.

"They may already have product in inventory. They've paid for raw materials and labour and they're rentin' warehouse space for storage. Or they've got a crackerjack labour force that is only workin' part-time because there are no orders. They don't want their best people to leave because the economy's slow. This is a very good deal for companies with more manufacturing potential or more inventory than they know what to do with. Exactly the people that Mr. Whitaker invited to this meeting tomorrow."

"What if they want 30 percent down and a three-year term on the bonds?"

"We'd probably say no thanks. If they want 25 per cent down and an eight-year term, well, that's Razor's bailiwick," he said with a laugh as Miss Rutledge raised her glass to him. "Razor may look like a scarecrow on a diet," he said with a wink, "but she's the sharpest accountant I've ever met. She can figure out percentages, costs, adjustments, everything in a blink of an eye. Uses one of those Chinese accounting machines."

"An abacus," said Miss Rutledge, pulling out a small wooden frame holding ten metal rods strung with beads. She set it on the table and moved the rows of beads with her fingers while staring at Frances. "Had a Chinese cook on the cattle ranch who used one of these to track expenses. Taught me how to use it during a long, cold winter. It's an amazing tool." She laughed. "And nobody knows what the hell I'm doing.

"Another thing," she added. "The banker for Amazon Development Corporation is in Geneva. These businessmen can take their payouts either at Chase Manhattan Bank in New York or at the Union Bank in Geneva."

"What's the difference?"

"Profits paid into an American bank would have to be reported to the IRS for tax purposes. Profits paid to a Swiss bank may be reported or may not be, and the IRS would be none the wiser."

"They could dodge the tax on the profits?"

"They could, which would of course increase their profit."

"Is this what they call a seller's market?"

"No. Both parties stand to gain from the transaction. Whitaker gets product with a small deposit up front, and these manufacturers get a good, safe return. Whitaker Consolidated guarantees the bonds."

"If Mr. Whitaker is one of the richest men in the United States, why does he need to borrow money at all?"

"His money is tied up. It's not good business practice to have a whack of cash on hand."

"Any weaknesses in our position?"

"Only that Mr. Whitaker usually negotiates these things person-ally. They're expecting him in the boardroom and they're going to get you. He'll let them know you represent Whitaker with full sign-ing authority, but they don't know you. You're gonna hafta do some sellin', Miss."

29

STINKY PHELPS

Charles Lindbergh went before six microphones in a room at Washington's Carleton Hotel to share with the American people his opposition to any U.S. involvement in the European war. Lindbergh was arguably the only man in the country who could rival Roosevelt in commanding the public's attention. The speech was a national sensation. In a matter of hours, Lindbergh became the foremost champion of isolationism.

(Olson, 73)

The Chase Manhattan Bank at 32nd and Broadway had held the Whitaker Consolidated account for forty years and had profited considerably by the relationship. They were happy to lend Whitaker their boardroom for the day. Twenty-four businessmen in leather swivel chairs chatted affably around an immense mahogany table. A wall of windows flooded the room with light. The Whitaker team sat together at the far end of the table. Duke Dubois looked as though he was going to a square dance, but he didn't talk that way. He called the meeting to order at exactly 10:00 a.m.

"Gentlemen, I thank y'all for joining us today. As you likely know, Whitaker Consolidated is the umbrella corporation that oversees thirty-three subsidiary companies around the globe. Whitaker is a private, family-owned business, just like your own companies. This proposal I'm putting to you today is a long-term investment. Long term," Duke repeated slowly. "It will take five to ten years for full payback. A publicly owned company would hear a lotta squawkin' from shareholders demanding quarterly dividends and stock appreciation. No publicly owned companies are here today. While Miss Rutledge from our accounting department hands out individual files to everyone, I'd like to introduce you to Miss Melanie Whitaker, who represents the family interests."

Frances stood up and took a deep breath. "Gentlemen, I bring regrets from Murchison Whitaker. He set up this meeting weeks ago and intended to be here, but he had three reasons for staying in Chicago."

Light laughter tittered around the table, throwing Frances off. *Was her slip showing?* Duke Dubois explained. "Miss Whitaker, your grandfather is known in business circles as 'T.R.' Whitaker because he *always* has three reasons for any decision."

Frances carried on. "He worked out the details in the files before you. He delegated signing authority for any contracts that come out of this meeting to me."

"Excuse me, Miss," said a portly man beneath a walrus moustache. "Legal signing authority for Whitaker Consolidated is completely vested in you?"

"Correct," put in Duke Dubois, holding up a green file of papers. "I have the authorizations documented right here if anyone feels the need to check."

Frances took another deep breath. "Whitaker Consolidated has been active in Brazil for over five years through a wholly owned subsidiary called Amazon Development Corporation or ADC. You each have a copy of the corporate prospectus. ADC is preparing to take a large position in the resource extraction and transportation business in Brazil."

"Five years? What's been the holdup?" asked a balding man on her right.

"When you're trying to set up a business in the middle of the Amazon jungle," put in Razor Rutledge, "there can be complications. This isn't Kansas."

"These complications natural or man-made?" asked a deeply tanned man wearing a pastel tie.

"Some of both," continued Frances. "Ten years ago, the red alluvial deposits along the banks of the Amazon River first came to the attention of a British archaeologist named Michael Dobbin. He was searching for ruins similar to those the Incas left in Peru. He knew enough about geology to realize that somewhere upstream there must be iron ore deposits. He reported his findings in the Journal of the Royal Society in England, but nobody paid much interest until it came to the attention of my uncle Laidlaw Whitaker in Vienna.

"It took some time to get permits to explore. The Brazilian government wants to safeguard their resources for their own citizens and is sensitive about the development intentions of foreigners. A team of prospectors and surveyors was allowed in three years ago. They eventually narrowed the search down to the upper reaches of the Madeira River, a tributary of the Amazon. Ore samples they brought out to be assayed showed very gratifying results. ADC filed for mining rights and permits to use the waterways, build docking facilities, etc. The Brazilian government, ever cautious about exploitation, has been slow to respond."

"Any cannibals down there?"

Mild laughter.

"None found, but the local tribes demonstrated effective use of poison darts to kill birds, snakes, and monkeys. Whitaker employees treat the natives with the deepest respect.

"Brazil is just emerging into the industrial age under the direction of President Vargas. He's a nationalist, and is somewhat apprehensive about foreign investors. However, the depression has left Brazil strapped for cash. A brief window for development partnerships has suddenly opened up. Brazil has given ADC ninety days to demonstrate intent with activity on the ground. That explains the rush. The Brazilian Natural Resources minister is in Chicago as we speak visiting his son, who attends Northwestern University. Grandfather would never seek to unduly influence a government official, of course," Frances said with a smile, "but he has two meetings scheduled with the minister and I'm sure he'll be hospitable."

This brought some chuckles. A man with a crooked nose said, "Butch is a good cajoler. His other two reasons?"

"Murchison Whitaker would never let religion or politics get in the way of a business deal. That said, it won't be any surprise to you that he is a long-time Republican and a strong supporter of the America First movement focused on keeping America out of the European war. He is meeting this weekend with Colonel Lindbergh and Executive Director Robert Stuart to work on strategies to that end."

"Does he have a preference on who wins that particular war?" asked a man with a monocle.

"I'm not going to speculate," said Frances. "He warned me that there would be Democrats and even interventionists in the room today, but that you all were sound businessmen and were invited on that score alone."

"And the third reason?" asked a ruddy faced man near the end of the table.

"You don't run thirty-three companies around the world without delegating authority. He insists that a family member personally take part in all final negotiations. We're running a little light on Whitakers these days, so he sent me here to see if I can hold my own. Any complaints so far?" None were voiced and many heads bobbed. "All right then, gentlemen, let me hand you back to Mr. Dubois."

"You each have a file containing an ADC shopping list for your company's products," said Duke. "You'll find a contract outlining requirements, remuneration options, and delivery dates. Read it over. If you like what you see, book an appointment for Friday with Miss Rutledge, and Miss Whitaker will sign off. If you want to make a counter-offer, I have to have it by 6:00 p.m. tonight. Book a Saturday appointment, and we'll see what we can negotiate. Be aware that Whitaker offices in Geneva and San Francisco are going through identical negotiations simultaneously. If the contract is filled elsewhere, these offers are off the table. The early bird gets the worm."

The room filled with the rustle of turning pages. After several minutes, a robust man in a navy blue pinstriped suit spoke. "Mr. Dubois, I'm Gerald Phelps and I have two concerns. I've known Butch Whitaker since we were floor mates at Andover fifty years ago. I don't question either his integrity or his business acumen. But how do we know that we're really dealing with Butch Whitaker? I haven't seen him in four years. Some say that his health is poorly. I've heard a couple of rumours that he's dead."

There was a ripple of laughter. "Also, this kind of a contract shows no similarity to anything I've ever known Butch to do before. He always dealt with individuals one-on-one. Now we have this shotgun approach and he's represented by a granddaughter whom I'd never heard of. You're asking us to put product on the line and accept corporate bonds from some Amazon enterprise to cover payment. It has a smoke-and-mirrors ring to it. We all could be out a big pile if this is some kind of scam."

"A scam?" repeated Mr. Dubois.

"Yes," said Mr. Phelps. "You and Miss Whitaker and Miss Rutledge all have business cards and fancy looking bonds, but you can buy any of that at a print shop for ten bucks."

Duke's eyes narrowed to rattlesnake width. You doubtin' that we represent Whitaker Consolidated?"

"I'm just saying that I'd be much more reassured taking this gamble if Butch Whitaker were in the room," replied Mr. Phelps.

"He sent his regrets," said Frances. "Entertaining Brazilian officials and keeping the US out of this European war has him tied up."

"These activities of his aren't making the New York Times."

"Mr. Whitaker has never been a man to seek publicity on any issue," said Duke. "If you know him at all, you know that."

"I had lunch with him yesterday in Chicago," said Frances. "He has a pretty good appetite for a dead man."

"No disrespect, ma'am, but I *didn't* have lunch with him, and he isn't here to promote his own project, which severely weakens it in my eyes. Don't know about the rest of you men, but I don't like doing business with a phantom."

Murmurings chased around the table. Not a legal issue. Not an accounting issue. Duke and Razor both turned to Frances with looks that said: "Ball's in your court, kid."

Frances thought quickly. "Would you like to speak with him directly, Mr. Phelps? He hates having his privacy disturbed, but I could call him."

"Any fool could be at the other end of the phone line, Miss. Disguising his voice. How would I know if it's Butch Whitaker if he isn't here in the flesh?"

Silence. A lot of nervous eye flitting.

"Why don't you ask him a question that only Murchison Whitaker could answer?" said Frances. "If you knew him so well fifty years ago, there must be a few old chestnuts you could pull out."

Mr. Phelps nodded his head reflectively. "Yeah. That'd do it. Make the call. Ask him who scored the winning touchdown in the final game between Andover and Essex in November, 1896."

Frances walked over to the phone on the credenza against the wall and dialed. And waited. And waited. "Hello, Lester? It's Melanie Whitaker in New York. We've got a little problem here. Could you put grandfather on the line?"

"I know, Lester. It can't be helped. Please get him. I'll take the can for it."

A long pause. Eyes around the table shifted out the window and to untended cigars and to each other. Finally, Frances spoke into the phone, "Yes, Sir. Yes, Sir. I know. I apologize. Don't blame Lester. We're all at the Chase Manhattan. One of the businessmen thinks we're running a scam here and wants proof you really are Murchison Whitaker."

Frances moved the phone away from her ear as though hot steam were pouring through it. When the static subsided, she continued, "It's Mr. Phelps from Phelps Precision Tools in Hartford. He wants to know who scored the winning touchdown in the final game between Essex and Andover in 1896."

She listened. "Do you want me to ask him?"

Frances looked over to where Mr. Phelps was preening at his cleverness. "Grandfather wants to know if *you're* legitimate. Were you ever known as Stinky Phelps?"

Laughter rocked the room. Mr. Phelps's face collapsed like a blown tent. He didn't need to answer.

Stinky walked over to take the phone. "Hello, Butch?" A long tirade followed that made Mr. Phelps blush like a kid caught in the cookie jar. "Yes, Butch. Yes. I'd heard you weren't well, see, so I just … Yes, Butch. No, Butch. It's a fair offer. Yes, she's doing a fine job. Right. Good to talk to you, too. I'll put her back on." He handed the phone back to Frances.

"Who *did* score the winning touchdown?" Frances asked into the phone, then she laughed. "Yes, grandfather. Sorry to disturb you. I'll keep you posted." When she hung up, every eye was on her. She left them in suspense while she walked back to her seat.

"Lateral from quarterback Butch Whitaker to halfback Stinky Phelps, who shook off three tackles and ran twenty yards into the end zone."

Applause filled the room. Stinky Phelps, having climbed out of the abyss, smiled a humbled smile.

30

BREAKFAST AT THE WALDORF

Lindbergh was isolationism's most potent weapon. His opinions had become as significant as bombs. The magic of his legendary name and the appeal of his personality persuaded millions of Americans that there was no reason for the U.S. to fight or fear Hitler.

(Olson, 251)

A Broadway show and a late supper were to be the Whitaker team's reward for a long day. Razor and Duke were more attuned to hoedown music, but this was, after all, New York. On the way down, the Waldorf elevator stopped at the 23rd floor, and two elegant couples in evening attire got in. Frances froze. A shapely young woman rode on the arm of a debonair older man while chatting to the other couple. The older man, elegant in white tie and tails, was Frances's father.

"Lovely suite, Grace," said the young woman, "but you must see the view from our penthouse. Tomorrow night the Lionels will host cocktail hour before the theatre. All right, Georgie?" she purred. He nodded imperceptibly.

"Wonderful, Daisy," said Grace.

In the quiet discomfort that sharing a small space with strangers brings, Frances and Georgie Lionel exchanged sidelong glances.

Did he recognize her with short hair and makeup?

Duke Dubois broke the silence. "Miss Whitaker, if you want to check the front desk for messages from head office, I'll pick up the theatre tickets from the bell captain and order a cab."

When the elevator reached the lobby, the gentlemen exchanged polite smiles while standing back to allow all ladies to exit. Duke's cowboy outfit was well scrutinized. Frances crossed the lobby on marshmallow knees, concentrating to keep from stumbling.

As soon as they got to the lobby bar of the Imperial Theatre, she fortified herself with a double Scotch. The lighthearted tunes of Rodgers & Hart's *Too Many Girls* were a comforting distraction. By the time they finished dessert at the Russian Tea Room, Frances's equilibrium was much restored. However, when they picked up their room keys back at the Waldorf there was a message for Miss Whitaker. Frances opened a sealed envelope to find a business card.

> George Lionel, Managing Director
> The Crocker Trust
> San Francisco, California
> 72 Market Street Mission 9179

On the back of the card was scribbled, "Breakfast? 7:00? Dining Room?"

Razor and Duke controlled their curiosity and she didn't meet their eyes. At her suite door, Frances said, "I'm meeting an acquaintance for breakfast. I'll be back up in time to dress for our ten o'clock meeting."

Frances had last seen her father during the Christmas holidays in 1932. Seven years ago. It was just before he left Toronto for a job in the St. Louis YMCA. He had given Frances and Elsa gorgeous Fair Isle sweaters as presents. Her mother scolded him for the extravagance. Then he was gone, emptiness and hollow pain his only lasting gifts. Did she *really* want to see him again? What would she say? Frances's curiosity overcame her pride. What would *he* say?

A few early risers were scattered around the restaurant when Frances entered. A distinguished-looking man in a dark three-piece suit was reading the New York Times with his morning coffee. When she approached, he stood and held out his hand. "Miss Whitaker? You're no relation to the Murchison Whitakers of Minnesota?"

Frances limply took the outstretched hand. "Mr. Lionel? You're no relation to the Lionel McFaddens of Ottawa?"

His eyes shot down and away. They stood frozen in this tableau until a waiter with a thermos interrupted. "Fresh coffee, Sir? Ma'am?"

Mr. Lionel took a deep breath, still shy of meeting her eyes. "Will you join me for breakfast? The eggs Benedict are the best in New York." He sank into his seat. Frances sat down. She was shaking, afraid to speak. She bludgeoned her coffee with cream and sugar. Eventually, the timid watery eyes she remembered so well crept across the table, finally gaining the courage to reach her face. "You're not making this easy for me," he said with a rueful smile.

"*I'm* not making it easy for *you*?" Frances snorted. "*This* wasn't my idea. Being abandoned seven years ago wasn't my idea, either."

They retreated into silence. At last, he said, "What can I say? 'I'm sorry' seems vastly inadequate under the circumstances."

Frances drew in a deep draught of coffee and leaned back to look at him fully. He had aged well. Silvery hair was now woven into his dark thatch. Trim body and a healthy tanned face. Finally she said, "I disagree. 'I'm sorry' is a *very* good place to start. What happened in St. Louis? Something come up? Mr. Lionel?"

The waiter took their orders and left. George Lionel's lips mouthed several false starts before words finally trickled out. "Your mother had many strengths, Frances. I wish no ill will to her memory, but she was not the easiest person to live with."

"No argument there, Mr. Lionel. Some of us stuck it out."

"I have no excuse. I'm guilty. As charged." The old look of defeat that she recalled from her childhood flooded his face. Skewered from the moral high road. What was it that Miss Briscoe had told her about not abusing power?

Breakfast arrived and they silently played with the food on their plates. Finally, Frances said, "Curiosity has always been a character flaw. I'm intrigued to know how a St. Louis YMCA clerk gets to a penthouse suite at the Waldorf Astoria. Shades of a Horatio Alger novel."

"It's a long story of happenstance, and, I suppose, of opportunity knocking."

"Mother's favourite aphorism," Frances chimed in. "That, and 'curiosity killed the cat.'" The memory of shared persecution lightened the mood.

"Curiosity must be hereditary. Frances McFadden, a High School of Commerce student from Ottawa turns into a Miss Whitaker with a penthouse suite at the Waldorf? Shades of Cinderella."

"I dropped out of high school. I can't discuss Miss Whitaker. I am willing to listen to a tale of happenstance."

"And abandonment?"

"I didn't say that."

"I know what you're thinking."

"I'm thinking that you're right about the eggs Benedict. Let's hear the story, Mr. Lionel. I have to leave in half an hour."

"A clerical error turned me into George Lionel. I needed an American work visa before I could take the job at the St. Louis Y. I printed my name "McFadden, George Lionel" on the application form and sent it in. Somewhere, the form got wet and "McFadden" turned into an illegible watery blot. The visa came back in the name of George

Lionel. The St. Louis Y needed me to begin immediately. It would have been a great paper chase to sort the name thing out, so I started work as George Lionel. I never got around to correcting the error."

"Mother sent mail to Lionel McFadden. I posted the letters myself."

"Yes. I explained the problem to the mail clerk at the Y. She thought it a great joke and passed along all mail to either name."

"I can't remember why you moved to St. Louis in the first place."

"My boss at the Toronto YMCA knew I had a family to support. When he heard about the St. Louis position, a promotion to a bigger facility with a better salary, he gave me a sterling reference. Your mother wasn't happy that I was moving farther away, but she was always worried about money, and the trade-off was a larger remittance."

"How did things go in St. Louis?"

"Wonderfully, until the board of directors decided they wanted a new building and started to push my boss, Mr. Taggart, into major fundraising. He had no gift for it. I helped him as much as I could. I learned of an organization called the American Association for Philanthropy. It holds a conference every year. Very hoity-toity. Mostly a chance for big-money people to pat themselves on the back for good works among the downtrodden. Mr. Taggart and I went up to Chicago to their conference."

"No trouble fitting in with the money crowd?"

"We rented tuxedoes. A poor man in a tuxedo looks much like a rich man in a tuxedo."

"A costume ball."

"Kind of. There were dinners and dances and presentations on fundraising and tax issues. At one of these dinners, we sat at a table with people from California. A Mr. Crocker and his niece, a Mrs. Sinclair. They were both on the board of a family trust set up by Mr. Crocker's grandfather, who'd made a whack of cash in railroads and hotels. The Crocker Trust doled out money every year to worthy causes. Mr. Taggart told them about what a great staff we had in St. Louis and if we only had a newer building we could serve thousands more in the community. His bragging about how good an accountant I was piqued Mr. Crocker's interest, as they had been having some problems with their investment portfolio. By the end of the conference, he had seconded me for three months to come out to San Francisco and help the Crocker Trust tune up their organization. Mr. Crocker allayed Mr. Taggart's temporary loss of an assistant manager with a nice cheque for the new building fund.

"I wrote to your mother. She didn't like the idea at all. She didn't want me to take the job, even though it was short-term at a handsome per diem." He paused. "I don't think she trusted the idea of my being a success. Of being sought after. It was at variance with her opinion of me.

"I wasn't in San Francisco three weeks before I discovered something very fishy with the organizational structure of the Crocker Trust. The day-to-day management was in the hands of Randall Gibbs, a long-serving family retainer. He'd been manager for thirty years. Set me up in a lovely office. Gave me a company car. Couldn't be nicer. But it was quickly apparent that there were some shenanigans with the books. They had millions invested in a wide variety of stocks and bonds and properties, but the interest payout, which funded the trust's philanthropic endeavours, had been declining for years. Mr. Gibbs blamed it on the Depression and fees charged by the financial institutions they dealt with. Things were so bad that he recommended they either cut support by 40 per cent or dip into the trust capital."

"Mr. Crocker didn't suspect?"

"Mr. Gibbs had worked for three generations of Crockers. The Crocker du jour wasn't really interested in the day-to-day of running a philanthropic organization. He put in maybe two days a month as chair of the Crocker Trust. He liked the dinners and the hobnobbing. He had a very healthy income from a separate trust and a passion for polo.

"There were five family members on the Board. Mr. Crocker's two cousins and his two nieces, Daisy and Judith. He was the only man, so they pretty well left everything up to him, which meant Mr. Gibbs really ran the show. Mr. Crocker's niece, Daisy—the Mrs. Sinclair I met in Chicago—was a divorcee twice over. Married first when she was twenty to a playboy after her money. He was faithful for about two weeks. She was too ashamed to do anything about it for a couple of years, but his philandering finally became scandalous, and the family bought him out. Daisy rebounded into the arms of a lout named Sinclair. The strong, silent type. Silent when he wasn't drunk and physically abusive. They had a child, a boy who drowned because Sinclair was too wasted to watch him at the pool. Divorce number two. Daisy Sinclair was a nervous wreck when I showed up.

"Now, I swear to God, Frances, I did not encourage her in any way. However, she began to form an emotional attachment to me. I was completely unlike the California glamour crowd. I was quiet and self-effacing. Honest and hard-working. Polite and deferential. There are thousands of Canadians like me, but these characteristics do not dominate Californian society."

"Didn't she know you were married?"

"Well, yes and no. I told her that I had been married in Canada and that I'd been separated from my wife for years. She took this to mean divorced. By the time I understood the misunderstanding, it was too late to correct things without a lot of embarrassment.

"It was immensely gratifying to have a rich, attractive woman interested in me after years of enduring your mother's dissatisfaction. A flame was lit. I didn't put it out. After I assembled clear evidence of Mr. Gibbs' extensive pilfering, I was the golden boy."

"Did he go to jail?"

"His car went over a cliff near Monterrey. Maybe he killed himself. I became the managing director of the Crocker Trust. A letter went back to Mr. Taggart at the St. Louis Y with my resignation and another big cheque.

"Once I cleared out the fraud and dodgy investments, the Crocker Trust started making money hand over fist. I put safeguards in place so that no one could ever siphon off trust funds again. Annual reports were audited by an outside agency. Every cheque needed two signatures.

"One day, Mr. Crocker invited me to his club for lunch. He told me that Daisy was in love with me, and was just waiting for the proposal. He thought I'd be a great addition to the family.

"I was floored. Daisy had a worshipful way of looking at me, but I didn't imagine she was thinking of marriage. She was fifteen years younger. He asked me what I thought of her. I said I admired her very much. So then, he said that settled it. He'd ask the board to double my salary and he would give me shares in the Crocker Foundation. He welcomed me to stay on as managing director for as long as I wanted.

"I didn't know what to do. I felt that I was responsible for a huge misunderstanding. I went to see Daisy, and she admitted confiding in her uncle about marriage. *That* would have been the time to say I had a family back in Ottawa.

"I ... I couldn't withstand the momentum. What I did say was that I was very fond of her, and felt honoured by her trust and that of her uncle. I'd been working very hard, and asked for a month's holidays.

"I wrote your mother that I wanted a divorce and was coming home to sort out the details.

"When we met back in Ottawa, she said that she didn't believe in divorce, but agreed to think about it as long as I did not try to contact you or Elsa. That was torture. I used to sit in a coffee shop on Bell Street and watch you and your friends come home from school. She put me off until the night I had to leave, then categorically refused the divorce. I gave her a cheque for two thousand dollars, and told her I would send monthly remittances as long as she lived. I told her that I would stop in Reno, Nevada, on my way back to California and get a unilateral divorce, freeing her from a bad debt."

Frances stumbled through the remainder of the day in a daze. Fortunately, Duke and Razor knew their business. By six p.m., they had signed off on twenty contracts worth eight million dollars. Duke was jubilant. "Couldn't have hoped for better," he said. "We can get the *20th Century* out of here tomorrow and head for home. Be back in thirty days to take delivery, cut the cheques, and ship the goods out."

31

MEANWHILE

From 1939 to 1945, the Canadian male population between 18 and 45 numbered 2,474,000 men. Of these, a total of 1,029,510 [41%] served in the Canadian armed forces.

(Stacey, 590)

"**W**ell, well," said Brendan McGuire. "Is this Ulysses, home at last from the Trojan Wars? No. I believe it's Miss McFadden! Bridget, Claire, Maddie—remember Miss McFadden?"

"Goodness, Mr. McGuire. An expert in Greek mythology in addition to all your other attributes? But Ulysses was a man, *n'est-ce pas?*"

"Yes. A wanderer. I suppose I could have compared you to Helen of Troy, another wanderer, although a little more notorious."

"So, my little Rascals, what have I missed over the past week?"

"It's been really cold," said Maddie, "but we don't hold you personally responsible."

Ottawa, the quaint, unassuming nation's capital, had become the fulcrum of the Canadian war effort. Khaki uniforms blossomed on the streets. Newspapers were flush with patriotic ads of businesses purchasing war bonds or proudly manufacturing war materials.

Scraps of life flitted in and out of Frances's consciousness like butterflies in a high wind. Controlling neither flow nor pace, these transitions had an unsettling effect. When she confessed this confusion to Arnold Heeney over lunch, he looked her straight in the eye and said, "I know *exactly* what you mean." Her secretariat crept forward on little cat feet, cautiously assuming greater responsibilities. It made Frances happy and a little sad. She found sanctuary in mundane office routine. Making the morning coffee became a calming encounter with the familiar.

Paul told her he had attended two movies in her absence. He didn't say if he went alone, and in a display of either tremendous curiosity control or cowardice, she didn't inquire.

"How did we do in New York?" Graham Towers asked. The governor had begun using the royal "we" when referring to the Bank of Canada, an affectation that slipped unseen into Frances's own usage.

"I just typed up a summary for Mr. Howe. We didn't get everything we wanted, but I think he'll be pleased."

"Did our money hold out?"

"We signed twenty letters of intent for just over forty million dollars' worth of goods. We will pay nearly eight million up front, with the balance mostly in ten-year bonds. The manufacturers have thirty days to get their products to the New Jersey docks. I'll return to New York at the end of March to write the cheques when we take delivery. It should be a quick trip. A day in transit each way, and two days for signing contracts."

Graham Towers arched a mischievous eyebrow. "It'll take you two days to sign your name twenty times?"

Frances countered with an ironic eyebrow of her own. "The Whitaker lawyer, Mr. Dubois, warned me there will likely be minor amendments to the draft contracts. He has to go over each change with a fine-toothed comb. We don't want any glitches. Then everything must be copied in triplicate."

"Nobody twigged to the shell game?"

"No. We caught them off balance. No Murchison Whitaker in person. Unusual sales terms. Too-good-to-be-true payouts in the contracts."

"Not to mention a mysterious beauty negotiating with them."

"Right. Our trump card. Strangely, no one proposed marriage. How did the secretariat hold up?"

"Brendan kept the circus running smoothly. Coffee was a little weak the first day, but I just had to mention it once."

"I've been meaning to speak to you about secretariat compensation," said Frances. "They moved into the outer office five months ago carrying their previous salaries. They've worked out well beyond expectations. They deserve a raise in recognition of their new responsibilities."

"Do they?" countered the governor. "I've worked here for six years and I haven't had a raise."

"Yes, but you're paid more than the prime minister. Nobody in the secretariat is earning a thousand dollars a year except for me."

"How do you know what I earn?" asked the Governor. "Not even my wife knows."

"I remind you, Governor, that I was here in the trenches before you arrived in Ottawa. When you signed for $35,000 a year, it fostered a little water cooler conversation."

"Really?"

"Few had ever heard of you. Everyone was impressed at the value Prime Minister Bennett put on your services."

Graham Towers's eyes twinkled. "Are Canadian taxpayers getting their money's worth?"

"They are. In fact, *I'd* give you a raise. But I'd like to look after my team first."

"Wouldn't that put noses out of joint among other Bank staff?"

"Everyone in the secretariat has mastered new responsibilities while learning to back up four other positions. They work hand-in-glove. No other support positions in the Bank demand that."

"Have they been lobbying for a raise?"

"No. They're too busy."

"Isn't this request a little premature?"

"Budget year starts April 1. The executive is already going over the draft figures. Now's the time to slip something in."

Graham Towers wavered. "How much are we talking about? I'd need details to justify any increases."

"I'll write up job descriptions and recommend a salary scale. Seniority should count for something. Brendan and Bridget have been with the Bank the longest. But pay should be harmonized over the next year."

"Is this preliminary to your own request for a raise?"

Frances gave him a flinty glare. "Is this the Spanish Inquisition? That's eight questions in a row. No. The Rascals deserve recognition for service beyond the call of duty, that's all, especially now that they've proven they can run the place without me."

Graham Towers laughed. "You are far from expendable, Miss McFadden."

"Thank you, sir. That's all the compensation I need." Frances stood to go. "By the way, do we care who wins the federal election on March 25?"

"Not really. The people of Canada will choose a government and we will serve it, regardless of which political stripe it wears."

"We don't have a preference?"

The governor smiled. "We are familiar with the Liberal cabinet ministers, but we could learn quickly to work with others."

"You don't have a preference?"

"The Spanish Inquisition, Miss McFadden? *I* have a slight preference for the devil that I know. *We* don't have a preference. We conduct ourselves at the Bank of Canada scrupulously free of political bias. There has been no difference in the way we have served either Prime Minister Bennett or Prime Minister King. Our job is to advise on monetary policy, not to win a popularity contest. We offer our best advice. Sometimes the government takes it, sometimes it doesn't. That's their prerogative in a democracy."

Anna Deloitte's sunny disposition had clouded in recent weeks. There may have been several causes, but the only concern she discussed with Frances was her eyes. "When I suddenly look left or right, I see these little black floating objects like tangled spider webs. I know they're not there, but I still see them. And I've also become tremendously sensitive to any bright light. I look like a movie star in these ridiculous dark glasses, but if I don't wear them outside I get a splitting headache. My doctor has referred me to an ophthalmologist in New York so I'm heading down at the end of March. You should come with me, Frances! See what mischief we can get into," she said with a conspiratorial wink.

"As a matter of fact," said Frances, "I have Bank business in New York on March 27. I'll be busy all day, but maybe we could meet up in the evening. You could show me what big city trouble really looks like."

"Oh, Frances, that would be wonderful! I'm staying at the Plaza close to my doctor's office. Does that suit you?"

"I'm already booked at the Waldorf. A little flashy for my taste, but that's where my meetings are. We could get together for dinner or see a play."

"You're a dear!" She hesitated, then added, "I *might* have a favour to ask of you."

Anna's hypnotic smile rendered resistance useless. "Teach me how to make those pumpkin muffins of yours and I'll do anything."

At the Metcalfe Street Bridge Club, no shortage of opinions existed on the progress of both the war and the federal election. Anna Deloitte might be wearing tinted glasses, but her vision of the war effort was crystal clear. "The whole affair is a foolish waste of life. Thousands will be orphaned and widowed. To what gain?"

"Surely you believe this Nazi tyranny must be contained?" demanded Margery Davis, who had seethed not-so-silently ever since

Germany won thirty-three gold medals at the 1936 Berlin Olympics to a paltry four for Great Britain.

"Of course," replied Anna. "By diplomatic means or economic sanctions. Not by guns."

"My vote is for Mr. Manion," said Betsey Knowles. "We need a Union government for a united front in the war effort."

"I think the Liberal government is doing quite well on their own," countered Agnes Dawes, whose second cousin once removed delivered milk to the prime minister's residence. "Is there one Conservative besides Mr. Manion who is cabinet material?"

Gladys Gilhooley, emboldened by a second glass of sherry, said, "The CCF is the only political party that has the interests of the common man at heart, the poor fellows who will be cannon fodder in this folly."

"Do you think Quebec voters will support a Union government, Audrey?" Debra Semple asked of the only French Canadian present.

"I live in Eastview, so I cannot really speak for Quebec."

"But you must have an opinion?"

"French Canadians lost the Battle of the Plains of Abraham in 1759. That soured them on warfare."

"Times change."

"Yes, but dying in battle is still dying in battle. I agree with Anna. Is this war really necessary?"

"Surely you bought Victory Bonds in the first issue?"

"I intended to. By the time I got to the bank, they were sold out."

"Frances, will the Bank of Canada be offering another issue of Victory Bonds?"

"The governor hasn't consulted me, but if the bridge club thinks it's a good idea, I'll put in a word."

Late Wednesday afternoon, Dorothy Deavy phoned Frances from the staff room at Cambridge Street Public School. "I'm going to throttle a nine-year-old if I don't escape from this mayhem. Would you be up for a girls' retreat this weekend at our Kingsmere cottage?" The four childhood companions had drifted apart lately, friendships being collateral damage of wars and marriages.

"What about your beau? Won't he be distraught without you?"

"Georgie will be in Cornwall this weekend leading a science workshop for elementary teachers. Kevin is up at Fort Coulonge buying lumber for D. Kemp Edwards, so Katie is at loose ends. And Mary tells me that Nat's father has the flu and he's off to Montreal on Saturday to cheer him up. That leaves you as the only love slave. Can you get a twenty-four hour pass? I want to try out our new sauna."

"What's a sauna?"

"It's kind of a hot closet you sit in to get steam cleaned. They're all the rage in Sweden."

"And your father, who irons tea bags to reuse them, sprang for a steam box at the cottage?"

"The hired man on the farm next to Uncle Walter is Swedish. In the off-season he does odd jobs for cash to help his younger brothers immigrate. Dad's a softy for a good cause. Katie got a cheap load of lumber seconds for the project, and Erik put the sauna up in three days. The whole shebang only cost twenty dollars. Saunas are supposed to be good for the soul. How's your soul these days?"

Frances's soul could use a refresher, but there was Paul to deal with. "Dorothy Deavy is angling for a girls' getaway up at their cottage this weekend. I told her you had first claim on my Saturday time."

"Yeah, right. For those Saturdays when you don't mysteriously disappear on secret missions regarding pressing affairs of state."

"My loyalty oath to the king requires me to accept work assignments. I have no loyalty oath to the Deavy sisters and I have a standing commitment to you."

"Tell you what, Miss McFadden. I'll trade off Saturday night this week in return for a double header next week: dinner at my place on Wednesday and a movie date on Saturday. Or is that too punitive?"

"Two dates a week? Next I'll be darning your socks."

"Have you ever darned a sock?"

"No, but I inherited my mother's sewing basket and I used her darning egg once to kill a spider."

"Can't cook. Can't sew. If the Bank of Canada goes out of business, better not consider switching into domestic service."

32

KINGSMERE IN WINTER

Slippery Slope Recipe

1.5 ounces amber rum
1 tablespoon of maple syrup
1 teaspoon of butter
1 cup of boiling water

Add the rum, maple syrup, and butter to a coffee mug.
Fill with boiling water. Stir.

Dorothy, the schoolteacher, was the only one of the group who didn't have to work Saturday mornings, so she did the grocery shopping. The friends met in the Byward Market and boarded the Gatineau bus at 1:00 p.m. sharp. At L'Épicier Laframboise in Old Chelsea, they rented ski equipment and haversacks to tote their supplies. Frances and Mary doubled up on Deavy laps and they all jammed into the front seat of the store pickup. Gaetan Laframboise drove them out to where the ploughed concession line crossed the end of the north lake road, a half-mile from the Deavy cottage.

"Going to join the army, Gaetan?" asked Katie.

"Nah," said Gaetan. "Luke is up in the bush nord o' Maniwaki cutting timber. Papa need me inda store. He have da arthritis bad. Can't 'ardly lift cornflakes box no more. Dis a man used to pick up anvil in one 'and. Besides, I'm not much interest in killing."

"But you hunt every fall, don't you?" asked Dorothy.

"Shoot da deer for winter food. Don't want to eat Germans. Too spicy."

"Don't you feel a duty?" asked Mary. "To fight for democracy?"

"Family is my duty. Germans invade Quebec, you betcha, I fight. Germans still long way away."

"But France is in danger."

Gaetan snorted. "France gave Quebec away in 1763. Left Quebecers fend for demselves. Now Frenchies' turn to fend for demselves." Gaetan pulled the pickup over and fished the skis and poles out of the back of the truck. He lent the girls a collapsible snow shovel. "In case da snow drift 'gainst da door," he said.

Only the Deavy sisters had ever skied before. Katie broke trail and Dorothy brought up the rear, with the novices sandwiched in between. The lake road, a winding slash carved through a forest of cedars and white pine, was awash with snow. It was hard work going uphill, and terrifying going down. Unbalanced by the haversacks, Frances and Mary fell often, giggling at their clumsiness. A three-foot drift of snow guarded the cottage front door and the shovel came in handy. Gaetan's thoughtfulness offset his lack of patriotism.

The pine frame cottage had no insulation. It was colder inside than out in the warm March sunshine. Dorothy quickly fired up the big Findlay Oval in the kitchen while Katie got a blaze roaring in the cobblestone fireplace. Frances cleared snow from the woodpile and brought in armloads of split oak and maple to feed both fires. The privy was another question.

"I hope your bums are ready for an outhouse seat at twenty degrees Fahrenheit," said Katie.

"It should keep the lineups short. Nobody will be loitering out there over the back pages of the Eaton's catalogue."

"Didn't I see a chamber pot under the bed? That would do in emergencies."

"We'll move the mattresses into the living room in front of the fire. The bedrooms will be iceboxes, but you can take the chamber pot in there if nature calls."

"Or you could exercise extreme bladder control for thirty hours," said Katie.

"I like choices," said Frances. "That's what democracy is all about."

Mary shovelled a path to the outhouse and came back with a trophy. "Hey, look at this!" she said, holding up a toilet seat. "It was just sitting there, unattached, over the hole in the bench. We can heat it up in here, and then if anybody needs it, they can carry it out with them."

"Where's your pioneer spirit?" said Katie.

"I think that's cheating," said Dorothy.

"Purists," concluded Frances, "can go without."

Dorothy sizzled grilled cheese sandwiches in the cast-iron frying pan while the others dragged the mattresses out of the small bedrooms. They built a campsite in front of the cobblestone fireplace, draping blankets over the open rafters to form a tent. Candles and the kerosene lamp made it a snug setting.

"Let's go for a ski on the lake while the cottage warms up," said Dorothy. "We can fire up the sauna now and steam our aching muscles later."

"Is the lake safe?"

"There's a good two feet of ice out there. Uncle Walt has no fear taking his team of horses onto the lake to cut ice for the summer."

It was much easier throwing a ski forward and gliding on the flat lake surface. The sun dazzled and they warmed quickly with the work. They gawked at Mackenzie King's cottage nestled in snow, and stopped to examine deer tracks under the cedars overhanging the shore. After an hour, they did the final turn at the far end of the lake, and Katie challenged them all to a race home.

The sauna was a small, shed-like structure built in a cedar grove by the dock. They stuck their skis and poles in a snowbank by the door and stripped in the change room before entering the hot chamber. Mary lit an oil lamp. Two seating platforms faced the stove. "Top shelf is for martyrs," said Dorothy.

"What's the diff?" asked Frances.

"Try it and see," she said. She pulled a dipper full of water from the galvanized pail beside the stove and threw it on the hot rocks.

"Yow!" exclaimed Frances when the wave of steam hit her. She retreated to the lower bench. "My nasal hairs are on fire!" They basked and when they felt brave enough, another dipper of water went onto the rocks. Katie went outdoors to relieve herself off the stoop. "You know," she said on returning. I'm out there stark naked in 20-degree weather and I don't feel cold. I bet we could make naked angels in the snow."

"It's broad daylight!" said Mary.

"And we're broads," replied Katie. "There's nobody on the lake. Not one of these cottages is winterized. We might as well be on the moon."

"Na-ked ang-els in the sn-ow!" the Crazy Deavy sisters started a rhythmic chant as they led the parade out.

"Cold on the tootsies," said Dorothy. "Gotta be quick."

"It's going to be cold somewhere else very soon," observed Frances.

Along the south side of the dock, the March sun had melted a two-foot snow-free path. They crept along it before stepping down to the frozen surface. The angels fanned out and dropped into a cross formation in the snow with their toes almost touching. Arms and legs flailed. In thirty seconds, their artwork done, they jumped up and retreated to the heat of the sauna.

"Wow!" exclaimed Mary, in surprise. "The heat opens your pores and the snow closes them up again, but it feels so clean! Like a baptism."

"Yah," said Katie. "We should suggest this at church."

Fifteen minutes more in the sauna warmed them so thoroughly they marched naked to the cottage to change into dry clothes. The big pot of snow that Dorothy had put on the back of the stove was now steaming melt water. She dug out mugs and poured buttered rum toddies laced with maple syrup. "Sun's past the yardarm," she exclaimed. "Time to fight pneumonia and fend off scurvy. Georgie calls this particular concoction a 'Slippery Slope.'"

"Slippery Slopes!" They toasted a bucolic cottage in spring sunshine and lifelong friendship. A generous hand on the rum bottle made the war disappear from consciousness.

After a second round, Frances became flushed and a little brazen. "How are the weekend widows getting along without their snuggle bunnies?"

"Well," said Katie, "Let me tell ya. Kevin comes home from work horny as a tree toad. 'If you really care about saving time,' he says, 'you should meet me at the door naked!'"

"What if it's the milkman?" asked Mary.

"Clarke's Dairy might give us a discount. Kevin's hung like a Brahma bull. Saslov's sells smaller salamis."

"Ouch! Does it hurt when you … when he …"

"It did at first, but I've learned to distract him with my pendulous bosoms—he's like a dog with a toy. That gives me a chance to warm up. How about it, Mary? Does ol' Nat have quite a passion built up after a day at the Bank? Take you right there on the doormat?"

"Katie!" Mary exclaimed. "Nat's a gentleman. He controls his emotions." She giggled. "At least until bedtime! Nat and I are desperate to have a baby, so we've been," she smacked her lips draining her second Slippery Slope, "experimenting."

"Beyond the missionary position?"

"Yeah. No luck with that approach, so we've branched out. One of Nat's frat brothers at McGill showed him a book called the *Kama Sutra*. Nat thought of it as just smut, but it discusses all these different positions. You know, the rocking horse, the crouching tiger, the splitting bamboo."

You know?

Blank stares all around. This was a new Mary speaking.

Outflanked on variety, Katie pressed on. "So ... how often do you split the bamboo, then?"

"Oh, we mix the techniques, but we're hard at it ..." she started to giggle ... "three times a night. Nat calls it 'the hors d'oeuvres course, then the entrée, then the dessert.'"

"You have sex three times a night!"

"We want to have a baby!" exclaimed Mary defensively. "That's the only way you get one, right?"

"Twenty-one times a week!"

"Sometimes we skip dessert."

Rather than admit that Kevin usually fell asleep thirty seconds after consummation, Katie switched topics. "How about you and young Roderick, Frances? Anything up there?"

"We're pretty tame by your standards. We mostly go to movies and get a soda and then he walks me home."

"Do you invite him in?"

"I didn't at first. I didn't want to show off."

"Your apartment or your body?"

"Don't you at least neck?"

"Is this the Salem witch trial? We have some tender moments. We both work long hours and are tired. He doesn't know whether to join the forces or not. He feels he should, but his boss wants him to stay. The whole Department of Agriculture has an exemption from military service. 'Got to feed the troops!' his boss says."

"Hasn't he at least slipped your brassiere off? Kevin had a terrible time with my bra clasp when we started dating. I just about had to draw him a manual. But Paul is a mechanical engineer, right? If I were Dean of Engineering, I'd teach disarming brassiere clasps first day. That'd get their attention. I certainly had no trouble mastering the fly, button, *or* zipper. Come on, Frances—you and Paul are in a passionate clinch, you're getting all steamy, don't you grab him in the crotch to see if your voluptuous body is having any impact?"

"I don't have to answer these questions!"

"You're blushing!"

"You've already answered!"

"I am *not* blushing!" said Frances, thankful for the dimness in the cottage tent.

"Truth or consequences! Truth or consequences!" sang the chorus.

Frances diverted the attack. "Now, Dorothy, tell us about your mystery man, Georgie Holland. He's not exactly a gusher with personal information."

"Can't talk. You wouldn't understand."

"Try us. We're smarter than you think."

"It's not a question of smart, it's ... well, you just wouldn't understand."

"Hey, give us a little credit. We've known each other since Grade 2."

"Yeah. We helped each other understand menstruation when we all thought we were dying."

"And we stood by you when Larry Boynton ditched you for the head cheerleader at Lisgar."

"Larry Boyton was shallower than a birdbath. And he did not 'ditch' me. I told him to get lost when I found out he collected pornographic post cards."

"We'd understand!"

Dorothy's jaw worked over the wording. "Okay," she said. "Brace yourselves." She fetched the saucepan off the stove and topped up each mug. "George is married."

The bombshell silenced the cottage.

"You're dating a married man?"

"I don't believe it!"

"Where's your moral compass?"

"There must be extenuating circumstances," said Frances.

"Thank you, Frances, for the benefit of the doubt. There are. But it's hardly worth wasting my breath on you doubting Thomases."

"Oh, come on!"

"Give us a try!"

Dorothy looked grim and sighed. "George's wife has been in the Brockville Psychiatric Hospital for two years."

"She's nuts?"

"That's not an expression they use at the Brockville Psychiatric. They use the term 'extreme derealization neurological disorder.'"

"What's that?"

"It means she has difficulty perceiving the world as it is. She might not recognize people she's known for years. She has debilitating panic attacks and violent outbursts."

"She's nuts."

Dorothy threw up her hands. "George put up with two years of craziness before he was able to get her committed."

"What kind of craziness?"

"Attacked him with scissors and badly cut his arm. It took twelve stiches to close the wound. She punched out the living room window with her bare fist and just stood there watching the blood pouring out."

"How do you know he's not making this up?"

"I saw the scars on his arm. And, he took me down to Brockville one Sunday for a visit."

"That must've been scary."

"They've tried all sorts of treatments—drugs and electric shock—to no avail. She's either in a screaming fit or heavily sedated. He'd say, 'Hi, Virginia, it's George. I've brought a friend to visit.' She'd say 'George? George?' with this absent look in her eye like she's searching for a memory. Very depressing. The doctors don't know what else to try. George's done all he can for her. It's not fair. He can't get on with his life."

"Isn't insanity grounds for divorce in Ontario?"

"Being institutionalized doesn't automatically mean a doctor will certify her as insane. They had happy years before she started to deteriorate. George would never abandon her. He doesn't have a cruel bone in his body."

"Would you marry him if he were … free?"

"In a heartbeat. He's so kind and gentle. I love him." Dorothy Deavy, the wisest, the strongest, the most mature of the foursome, started to cry. Her friends grasped for a part of her to hug, a meld of wet wool and tears.

"You're doing the right thing to stand by him."

"I'm sorry I questioned your integrity."

"It must be painful. Such a hopeless situation."

Dorothy blew her nose. "Thank you. It helps to be able to share this. Mom and Dad would be horrified. And I can't tell any of my friends from work."

"What can you do?"

"Bask in the glow of the magic little light that blooms every time we're together."

33

COURIER

The first federal anti-Chinese bill was passed in 1885 when the Canadian Pacific Railway was completed. The Chinese Immigration Act imposed a head tax of $50 on Chinese immigrants to Canada. In 1903, the amount was raised to five hundred dollars, the equivalent of two years' wages. The Crown collected $23 million [$308 million in 2016 dollars] *from 81,000 head tax payers while seriously constraining Chinese immigration. In 1923, the Canadian Parliament passed The Chinese Immigration Act,* [also known as The Chinese Exclusion Act] *that essentially banned Chinese immigration to Canada entirely.*

(Li, 29, 30, 38)

"**O**h!" said Paul over a toasted western at the Tic Tock on Saturday night. "I meant to tell you. I'm going to be away next weekend."

This was a relief to Frances, as it coincided with her second "Melanie Whitaker" excursion to New York. Still, she was surprised. "Business or pleasure?"

"Bit of both. My director has been asked to send me to Toronto Thursday and Friday for meetings. I'll be over halfway to the farm in Ilderton, so I'm taking a couple of extra days to visit my family."

"Is this about agricultural research? Better legumes or happier chickens?"

"Not exactly."

"I thought engineers dealt exclusively in 'exactlies.'"

"I can't discuss it. You know how that is. I just want to say goodbye to my folks in case I need to go away for a while."

"Away? Where?"

"Look, things are up in the air. When I learn more, you'll be the first to know."

On Wednesday, Frances returned from a meeting to find a message in Brendan McGuire's hand on her desk. It said simply: "Huey Foo" and gave a phone number.

"Mr. Foo? I meant to call and thank you. Your cleaning team has set a new standard at the Balmoral."

"Thank you, Miss Fran. Chinese New Year just pass. Very tasty chef's special tonight at the Bluebird Café to celebrate. Be my guest? Six thirty?"

It would be unfair to call the Bluebird Café a "greasy spoon." The cutlery, the tables, the floors—everything was spotlessly clean. Still, the Bluebird wore a tiredness that did not augur prosperity. At six thirty, the place was empty save for the ancient man behind the cash who looked up from his Chinese newspaper when Frances came in and gave her name.

The man gave a wordless nod, and led her to a back booth before disappearing through the swinging door into the kitchen. Huey Foo came out smiling in his cook's apron. "Ah! Miss Fran! So good see you. Dinner almost ready." He spoke in Chinese to the old man who walked to the front and flipped over the "OPEN" sign on the door to proclaim "CLOSED" to the outside world. The pert Chinese waitress covered the Formica table with a linen tablecloth, then laid two place settings with china that was well above restaurant fare. She lit a short candle that floated magically in a shallow bowl of water, then set three steaming platters on the linen. Huey Foo came out of the kitchen in a clean shirt and slid into the seat facing Frances. The waitress placed a large pitcher of beer and glasses down on the table.

"Your restaurant is licensed to sell beer?" asked Frances.

"No sell beer. This private party. Beer very good with Chinese food." The waitress dimmed the lights, then she and the old man left, locking the front door behind them. The glow from the floating candle warmed the booth like a campfire.

Huey served Frances generous portions. "Szechwan pork with snow pea. Spicy. Open taste bud. Peking Duck—northern delicacy. Moist, dark meat; crisp skin. Seafood and Shanghai noodle always delicious."

"Cheers," said Frances, raising her glass of beer.

"To Chinese New Year. Year of Dragon. Good luck to finish old year strong. Start new year fresh. Wanted celebration before you go New York on Thursday."

Frances's chopsticks stalled. Only two people in Canada—Graham Towers and C.D. Howe—knew she was heading to New York. She had told the secretariat that she would be away on Bank business for several days. The Rascals knew not to ask for details.

"Tell you story," said Huey Foo with a faint smile. "Very few Chinese in Canada. Like a family. Always help each other. Remember Chinese crew clean and paint your office in old building on Queen Street?"

"Yes."

"One cleaner, Wang Fung, now clean in Toronto airport. Surprised to see Miss Fran arrive there last month. Remember how kind you were years ago. Flight for Detroit leave and suddenly, Miss Fran gone. Wang Fung see passenger list when he empty wastepaper. Only two women. Melanie Whitaker and Mrs. Hastings. No Miss Fran. Very curious. Wang Fung worry. Tell me. Hope you okay.

"Yesterday, another my cleaner, Hop Lee, empty trash at Altman Travel Agency. See Melanie Whitaker book sleeper for New York on Thursday."

He set down his chopsticks and took a long drink of beer. "Your travel name not my business." He lit a cigarette.

"Why mention it then?"

"Need favour. Must get package to New York."

"What kind of package?"

"Small. Fit easy in suitcase."

"Small probably isn't the issue."

When Huey Foo exhaled cigarette smoke through his nostrils, he looked like a Chinese dragon. "Two type people in world," he said. "One type want *no* detail. Other type want *all* detail." He looked at her through the smoke. "Which type people you, Miss Fran?"

Frances laughed. "I guess I can be either type, depending on the circumstances. Because of the nature of my trip, I'd better know some details."

"Package is antique wooden box. Very handsome." He paused. "Has secret compartment contain diamond worth ten thousand dollar."

"You want me to smuggle ten thousand dollars out of Canada?"

"Smuggle bad word. Deliver good word."

"But it's against the law! The Bank of Canada put currency restrictions into place when the war started to preserve the value of the Canadian dollar."

"Diamond not currency."

"Ten thousand in diamonds is the same as ten thousand dollars, isn't it? This law helps Canada fight the Nazis. It's a good law."

Huey Foo's head tilted left then right as though he were balancing an equation. "Maybe good law for Canada. Bad law for Chinese."

"How so?"

"Nazi not only evil in world. Since 1885, any Chinese come to Canada pay head tax. Man come. Work hard many year. Save to bring wife, children to Canada. In 1923, new Canadian law. No Chinese allowed. None. Very sad family kept apart. Good people. Honest. Chinese still work hard. Save money. Hope law change. 1937, Japanese invade China. Bomb city. Kill children. Rape women. Many thousand die." Huey Foo paused to light another cigarette. "Canada big country. Room for many people. Chinese in Canada only want help family in China."

"How?"

"Snakehead lead family out of China by secret path. Cross Japanese line to Hong Kong, then Hawaii to pick sugar cane, then Mexico." He scoffed. "White men cannot tell Chinese from Mexican. Worker come to California, Texas, pick lettuce and strawberry. Then to Michigan pick cherry and apple. Then at night by boat cross lake to Canada. Long journey. Expensive."

"How much?"

"Five hundred dollar each. Snakehead office in New York. You take ten thousand in diamond there, save twenty Chinese from rape and murder."

Frances' throat went dry. "Look, I'd like to help, but the Bank of Canada is in charge of the Currency and Exchange regulations. I typed up those rules myself. I feel like I own them."

"Every day Japanese kill more Chinese. You want innocent women, children die?"

"Of course not! Can't you take the diamonds to New York yourself?"

Huey Foo scoffed again. "Chinese cook? Travel New York City? Very suspicious. Draw custom agent attention. Stop me. Search me. Passport examine over and over. Pretty white lady, nice dress, border police lift hat and smile."

"I'm sorry. Truly. But I work for the Bank and it's my duty to uphold those regulations."

"Understand Miss Fran loyal. Must obey Bank rule." Huey Foo closed his eyes and smoked silently for a long moment. "But Miss Fran *not* go New York City. Miss Melanie go New York City. Miss Melanie not work for Bank. Miss Melanie free of duty. Not so?"

Frances took a Yellow Cab from Grand Central Station to the Waldorf Astoria. She dropped her luggage with the bell captain, then headed for Mott Street in Chinatown. The taxi driver blasted a path with his horn through streets bustling with cart pullers and hawkers. At the Hop Sing Trading Company, a bay window was filled with boxes of unrecognizable items dusted with grit and dead flies. Inside the door, open wooden tea crates inked with Chinese characters lined a narrow path leading to a counter piled with bolts of cloth. Floor-to-ceiling shelving units stood behind the counter, separated in the middle by a curtain. After a minute, a sombre Chinese youth pushed the curtain aside and cocked his eye at her without speaking.

"Good morning," said Frances. "I have a package for Leong Ah Ken."

"So sorry. Ah Ken not here. May I help?"

Frances pulled out a folded piece of paper covered with Chinese characters and handed it over. The youth squinted at it and nodded his head. "Hao, hao." He held up an index finger to Frances and said, "Wait one moment," before disappearing behind the curtain. Frances walked around the store, skirting burlap sacks of rice and bags of unrecognizable substances. She was fingering a beautiful piece of yellow silk when the youth returned. "This way, please," he said, and held the curtain aside for her. A narrow passage led to a stairway so steep it was almost a ladder. They went up two flights to a small landing lit by a grimy skylight. The youth knocked a short rhythmic cadence on an old pine door. It was opened by a giant wearing a long braided queue. Behind an elaborate red lacquered desk by the window sat a man of indeterminate age. He looked at her patiently, but said nothing until the giant left, closing the door.

Then Frances spoke. "Some say that the mulberry bushes of Chekiang feed the happiest silkworms in the world."

The man smiled. "Some say that everything that counts cannot always be counted," he replied. "So Foo Hong Yee has always told me."

"Mr. Foo sends his greetings and a small token for his good friend Ah Ken to celebrate the Year of the Dragon. He apologizes for the late arrival." Frances handed over the antique box. Ah Ken admired it briefly, then pressed two carved lion's heads simultaneously and a small drawer at the bottom of the box popped open. Taking out several sheaves of red paper money and removing the drawer completely, he stuck a chopstick in the opening. There was a soft click and a panel on the back of the box slid left to disclose a brown paper envelope. The envelope was covered with Chinese characters and contained a folded piece of black velvet. Ah Ken unfolded the velvet to reveal a galaxy of sparkling diamonds. He took a jeweller's eyepiece from a drawer and examined several of the diamonds before shunting them across the velvet with a chopstick as he counted.

Ah Ken reached for a small paintbrush and, dipping it into ink, drew for a minute on tissue- thin parchment, then waved the paper back and forth to dry. "A receipt for Hsiao Foo," he said, handing the paper to Frances. "Tell him that the imports he requests will be sent for immediately."

"Thank you."

Curiosity kindled a thought in Ah Ken. "Is it not illegal in Canada for white women to work for Chinese men?"

Frances smiled. "Many things are illegal in Canada. I do not work for Mr. Foo. When we have common interests, we assist each other."

"Such happiness for Hsiao Foo to have this good fortune."

"Double happiness. The good fortune is equally shared."

34

SURPRISE, SURPRISE

Steve Jordan was the name of a minor character played by Humphrey Bogart in the 1930 John Ford comedy Up the River. *Although he didn't play the lead, it was Bogart's first role in a feature-length movie with sound.*

(Nollen, 42)

The Murchison Team at the Waldorf Astoria took on the manufacturers one at a time. "Divide and conquer," said Duke Dubois. Razor Rutledge nodded. Thanks to their advance paperwork, most contracts were ready to sign. There were a half-dozen tweaking skirmishes. Frances watched the tennis match from the sidelines while proposals and counter-offers volleyed back and forth. Duke was a good closer. "We're 98 per cent in agreement, Mr. Quimble. You want part of this gift horse, or you want to leave now for an early lunch?"

When final changes were inked, Frances signed the contracts in triplicate and issued cheques on a numbered account at the Union Bank of Switzerland. A young Union Bank executive named Marvin Pincus was on hand in the next room to set up numbered accounts for those businessmen who wanted their receivables deposited in Switzerland. By five o'clock, Frances had signed off eight million dollars and issued thirty-two million in Amazon Development Corporation bonds. High stakes for a bank secretary who earned a hundred and twenty-five dollars a month.

Frances begged off an invitation from Duke and Razor to catch the Rockettes at Radio City and took a Checker Cab uptown to the Plaza. She was early for her rendezvous with Anna and nestled into a lobby chair with a copy of *Life* magazine. An article comparing the orchestral styles of Count Basie and Duke Ellington had her attention when a vaguely familiar voice addressed her. "Hello, sweetheart. I see you survived Marseilles."

It was Humphrey Bogart in a three-piece suit and striking red tie. Frances had met him flying Pan-American to Europe the previous August. She was going to help Scotty Meldrum speed up the Polish gold transfer. He was travelling not-so-incognito with a small entourage. They had shared a few rubbers of bridge to pass the time. Frances smiled and rose to shake his hand. "Mr. Smith, I believe it was."

He laughed. "Mr. Smith passed away in Portugal, with no regrets. In New York, I use the name Steve Jordan—a minor character I once played in a very forgettable movie." He lit a cigarette. "And are you Miss Smith in New York?"

"East of the Mississippi, I'm Melanie Whitaker."

"Not your real name, by chance?"

"The whole world's a stage, Mr. Jordan. You're not the only one playing different roles. How was the road north from Lisbon? And how is Mrs. Smith these days?"

"Mrs. Smith and I lasted about a week together in Portugal. Joe Moss had to put her on a ship back to America before one of us resorted to homicide. Joe and I came back on the Queen Mary just after war was declared. Delightful accommodations. Superb food. Too much exposure for my taste. There are expectations in my business that you act as well in public as you do on the sound stage."

"You prefer to misbehave?"

"I prefer not to act when I'm not at work. What brings you to New York?"

"Business."

He had a knowing smile. "You're a busy woman."

"It keeps me off the streets and out of trouble. My mother's prescription for a virtuous life."

He looked over his shoulder. "I'd better get back to my party. Just wanted to say hello."

"That was kind. There must be legions who would love a 'hello' from you."

"They want to converse with the celebrity, not with the person. That makes you special. How's the bridge?"

"Getting better with practice. You?"

"Hardly play at all. It's not a prime Hollywood pastime."

"Not enough notoriety?"

"I guess. Does business ever take you to California?"

"You never know. Does business ever take you to Canada?"

He winked. "Are you propositioning me, Miss Whitaker?"

Frances smiled. "Just returning the serve."

He laughed his throaty guffaw and gave her a mock salute. "Safe travels, Miss Whitaker."

"You, too, Mr. Jordan. See you in the movies."

There was no answer to her knock at Anna's suite. Frances knocked again, louder, and was checking her wristwatch when the door clicked open. She lifted her eyes, then staggered backwards against the corridor wall. In the doorway was a handsome man whose left suit coat sleeve hung empty at his side.

"Ah! Miss McFadden," Max Kessler said. "Anna asked me to entertain you if she was late getting back from Dr. Magner's." He reached for Frances' trembling elbow and drew her into the suite. "Please understand. This little reunion was *not* my idea."

"I … I … I'm …"

"Speechless? Surprised to see me alive?" Max smiled. He deposited her in a chair before walking to the bar where he poured large Scotches over ice into Steubens crystal.

Frances teetered at the edge of the abyss. "I'm sorry!" she gasped. "I'm sorry! I didn't mean …"

"To throw me off that train in Poland?"

"I did *not* throw you! I stumbled in the dark. I didn't mean … How did you … ? Are you … are you going to kill me?"

He handed her a drink and raised his own. "Relax. Here's to old times." He smiled. "I never thought of you as the homicidal type. I'm not so sure about Mr. Meldrum when," he cleared his throat, "push comes to shove. However, you didn't stop the train to look for me, did you?" Max Kessler took a fresh cigarette out of a beautiful silver cigarette case.

"I … I couldn't think. Stopping seemed pointless. Falling from a moving train … what were the chances … ? How did you ever … ?"

"Come out alive? By the confluence of fortuitous circumstances. The train had slowed to go into the tunnel. The tunnel was under repair to correct a drainage problem. Because drainage tile is brittle, it's transported packed in straw. A huge pile of discarded straw cushioned my fall, although I dislocated my shoulder and knocked myself out. The train was long gone when I came to."

"Did you tell Anna … that we'd met?"

"What's the point? You'd obviously spared her."

"I've felt so deceitful," Frances held her head. "But I … I didn't know how to explain. She was getting your cheerful postcards from Western Canada."

"A conundrum. I suppose silence was better than lies."

"How did you ever escape the war zone?"

"I've been in war zones before. The best strategy is to head for the nearest good hotel."

"Really? I'd head for the hills."

"Ah, you see, I've been a German army officer. I knew they are quite partial to first-class accommodation, like, say, the Paplin Inn near Zukowa. On principle they wouldn't bomb such a quaint little place because they'd want to use it for their field headquarters. Much pleasanter than running a war out of a leaky tent, believe me. I was drinking in the bar when a colonel from the Twenty-first Panzer Division pulled up at the door. I didn't know him, but we had mutual friends. I confided that I had vital information about the Polish gold reserves, and he let me use his field communications to get in touch with military intelligence, the Abwehr, in Berlin. I told them to send a U-boat pack out to hunt down the *Mont Royal*."

"You betrayed us?"

Max Kessler had a generous laugh. "Spare me, Miss McFadden. You left me for dead in a Polish train tunnel with no gold and very few cards to play. Anyway, the north Atlantic is a vast space to track down a small Canadian freighter. They wouldn't have sunk you even if they had found you. They wanted the gold back. The odds were in your favour.

"The Abwehr didn't know whether to believe me or not. However, when they got to the Bank of Poland in Warsaw and found tractor parts in the vault, then the boxes of rocks in the Carpathian mines, my stock went way up. I suddenly became the Third Reich's expert on gold transport. The German high command wanted to get a secret shipment through to their bankers in Switzerland before the border closed. A brutish Gestapo major named Batz was in charge of the gold, and they asked me to ride along 'for insurance.' Keep an eye on each other and five million US in gold bars. Batz was a suspicious, stupid person. Insisted we ride in the freight car with the consignment and be on guard twenty-four hours a day. Needlessly uncomfortable, and his halitosis was poisonous at close quarters. He exhausted himself with vigilance.

"Before leaving Berlin, I passed the gold shipment information along to the British MI6 agent who had been my handler. Their people, dressed as Swiss police, boarded our train at a suburban stop outside Zurich. I had conveniently left Batz with the gold to visit the washroom. Batz was detained for questioning, and our "baggage" was offloaded. When I got into Zurich, I went straight to the German Embassy and told them my tale of woe.

"Diplomats *hate* all this intrigue. Gives their profession a bad name. The ambassador was concerned about the ramifications if a confession was forced out of Batz. He insisted that I leave Switzerland immediately." Max Kessler laughed. "I couldn't have scripted it any better. He had a young embassy secretary pose as my daughter to accompany me on the next train to the Italian border. The German Embassy got rid of a potential embarrassment and, more important for me, could vouch that I didn't leave Switzerland with any gold bars. From Como, I took the train to Brindisi, where I boarded an ocean liner to Buenos Aires."

"Penniless?"

"Not quite. I had negotiated a 10 per cent cut with MI6. What could they lose? No gold delivered, no commission. The British deposited the crates of gold with their Swiss bankers. They transferred my five hundred thousand into an account I've had there for years. I was able to get travel money wired to Brindisi, then most of the balance sent ahead to the Banco de Córdoba in Argentina."

"You didn't worry that the British would stiff you?"

"The British? With all that public school training? Character moulded on the playing fields of Eton? I never doubted their integrity for a moment."

"Why South America?"

"Argentina is a delightful distance from the war zone. I inherited a small estate there when my mother's brother passed away last year. Uncle Oskar was an ex-cavalry officer. Superb horseman when sober. He went down there in the 1920s, bought two thousand acres in the middle of nowhere and started a stud farm for Arabian horses. His first stallion and brood mares probably cost more than the land. He did well. His one fault was an abiding fondness for drink. Galloping drunk one day, his mount shied from a snake. He fell. Broke his neck."

"What happened to the place?"

"He had half a dozen servants—a trainer, some gauchos, a cook-housekeeper and a maid—likely his mistress. She cleared out after the funeral, but the rest kept the place running. They were very happy to hear I was coming down to secure their future."

"So, what about Anna?"

As if cued from backstage, a key scratched in the suite door lock and in came a smiling Anna Deloitte.

"Frances! Maxie! Wonderful news! Dr. Magner prescribed these new eyedrops that he assures me should clear up my problem in five days. Then bon voyage!"

Frances blinked. "Bon voyage?"

Anna gave Max Kessler a generous kiss. "Didn't Maxie tell you? We're getting married tonight and then we're sailing to Argentina to start a new life together." Anna looked at her watch. "The minister will be here in an hour. Remember that little favour I asked you about? You will be my maid of honour, won't you, Frances? Then we can all head out to the Rainbow Room and dance until dawn."

35

DESBARATS STABLES

The [Canadian] *election was on Tuesday, March 26. When all returns were in, the Mackenzie King Government had 184 supporters out of 245 Members of Parliament: the greatest majority given to any Canadian Government up to that time.*

Pickersgill, 72–73

In Sir Wilfrid Laurier's day, the Desbarats mansion in Sandy Hill was a social fulcrum in Ottawa second only to Rideau Hall. Careers could be advanced or lost there over tea and buttered scones. A staff of nine had cooked, cleaned, gardened, and served the home where prime ministers were regular guests. Times change, and old Mrs. Desbarats's patrician chins took to trembling for the first time in eighty-three years.

Three generations of Desbaratses had never visited a lawyer's office. The large drawing room served when necessity demanded discourse with barristers or solicitors. They were not required to use the trades entrance. George Perley, trustee of the Desbaratses' dwindling estate, was an old-school lawyer of courteous bearing. He did not begrudge a streetcar outing over to Daly Avenue. Back in 1937, he had recommended that the family's large country retreat in the Gatineau Hills be sold. Nature had run amok, and either serious investment or two sticks of dynamite were needed to render the decaying hulk harmless. Sixty years earlier, Mrs. Desbarats had honeymooned there with her shy groom, Edward. Mr. Perley nodded, observing that sentiment was a luxury that generated little income. The sale of the rambling cedar-shake property boasting a mile of lakefront and fifteen hundred acres of bush kept creditors at bay for two years.

By 1939, further economies were necessary. Reluctantly, Mrs. Desbarats ceased paying her pew rent at Christ Church Cathedral and suspended patronage of a dozen charities that she had sustained for half a century. The corporal's guard of servants required further trimming. The cook and housekeeper were asked if either would take on two jobs. The indignant cook packed her recipes and stormed out the kitchen door. Mrs. Dodds, now the cook-housekeeper, knew a great deal more about dust than she did about devilled eggs. Alice, the ancient maid, tottered precariously with the tea tray. A local youth subdued the once-manicured lawn with a rusty mower and occasionally threw a dull scythe at weeds in beds where prizewinning roses once bloomed.

If Mrs. Desbarats wished to shuffle off her mortal coil in the home that had housed her husband's family for eighty years, part of the property would need to be sold. Fortunately, the house sat on three double-depth lots that stretched right back to Stewart Street, where the stables still stood. In 1866, her husband's grandfather, George Édouard, a fancier of fine horses, had built the only brick stable in Ottawa to protect his mounts from fire and the fierce north wind. It housed an oak box stall for Jericho, his riding stallion, with standing stalls for the drive horses and the girls' ponies. A fifth stall sheltered the family cow. At the east end of the building, two sets of double doors provided access and egress for the Desbaratses' carriage and the buckboard. In the loft, large, central dormers facing north and south facilitated the hauling up of hay or oat bags. At the stair end of the hayloft was a workshop for the repair of harnesses and a small bedroom for the groom.

The stables had not been used in twenty years. The cow went when Clark's Dairy began home delivery. Mrs. Desbarats harboured a secret trepidation around horses, and discreetly sold them off when taxi service in Ottawa became reliable. Decades of dust crusted the family carriage, an ancient wagon, and an open four-seater sleigh.

Mrs. Desbarats hesitated to carve off lots beside the house, where new construction would compromise the natural light through her east and west windows. This left the back lots on Stewart Street. The stables would need to be torn down, although she loved the look of the weathered cupola through the second floor sun porch window. Sentiment again. D. Kemp Edwards had been purveyors of building materials to the Desbaratses for generations, and Mr. Edwards was summoned to the living room for consultation.

Wednesday morning, Katie Warren called Frances at work, voice a-tingle. "Frannie, you gotta meet me for lunch at the Honeydew! I have big news!" Could the stork be winging its way to the Warren household?

Katie's freckled face flushed around an impish grin. "Guess what!"

"You're pregnant?"

"*God*, Frances! *Must* you drag sex into every conversation? Kevin does *not* get near my naked body without his instrument safely sheathed in latex. We're far too immature to have children. They'd have to parent themselves. No! We're buying a home in Sandy Hill!"

Frances was dumbfounded. "I thought the influx of war workers had completely dried up the housing market in Ottawa."

"Well, it's not actually a house. It's the stables behind the old Desbarats mansion. A 'fixer-upper,' Kevin calls it."

"You're going to live in a stable?"

"It was good enough for Jesus, it's good enough for me."

"Well, congrats," said Frances. "So long to your walk-up over Warburton's Fish Market; hello to Sandy Hill and the carriage trade. Will I be required to curtsey when you pass?"

Katie socked her playfully on the arm. "The erstwhile carriage trade no longer uses carriages, thank the Lord, rendering stables surplus to their needs. Sandy Hill is a little down at the heels these days. The big money has all moved to Rockcliffe Park. Only relics of genteel poverty in need of a cash infusion are still rooted there. Hence the sale of the family stables."

"I didn't notice this treasure in the *Ottawa Citizen* classified ads."

"Nope. Old lady Desbarats phoned up Mr. Edwards for a cost estimate to dismantle the stables so she can sell the property. He was shaking his head about it in the office. Figured it would run her at least four hundred to tear it down and haul it away. Told her she'd be money ahead to sell it 'as is.'

"Kev and I hate the stink at our place. An hour after our clothes come in off the line, they reek of fish guts. Stray cats trail us everywhere. So we took the streetcar over for a look-see. The backyard is so overgrown that the stables are invisible from Daly Avenue. We walked around the block and stole a peek through the grimy windows that face Stewart Street. It's jammed with dust-covered junk, but I liked it! Very cottage-in-the-wood, even though it's not five yards from the sidewalk. Run down, but with the abandoned charm of a castle ruin. Has a cedar shake roof and dormers filled with broken windows."

"What does Kevin think?"

Katie smiled. "Kev is not given to emotional displays, except when I'm naked. Then the emotional display is quite localized. But he kept saying, 'Holy mackerel!' over and over.

"We talked to Mr. Edwards next morning, and he burst out laughing. Said the place would be a money pit, but we persuaded him to phone Mrs. Desbarats and set up a meeting for us. We got spiffed up in our Sunday best and went over to see her after work.

"Frances, you would not have believed this lady! It was Miss Havisham, except she was dressed in black, having been a widow for twenty years. Genteelly courteous. A little deaf. Living room dark as a cave. Frayed velvet drapes. Antimacassars on the backs of horsehair chairs. A doddering maid poured tea unsteadily and served little crustless cucumber sandwiches.

"Well, what woman could resist Kevin's smile? She gave us the key to the stable and let us out the side door under the porte-cochere. The laneway was completely overgrown. We couldn't see the stable until we were twenty feet away. The padlock was so rusted that the key wouldn't turn. The doorframe had dry rot and Kevin nudged the door open with his shoulder.

"The place smelled of mouldy straw and mouse poop. Two stair treads were broken, but we clambered up to the loft and frightened the bats. The roof leaks in one place, and a persistent drip of water had drilled a hole straight through a loft floorboard. Kev wants to ask Paul Roderick to check the place for structural soundness. Okay with you?"

"Why would you even ask?"

"Well, I know your relationship has been up and down. I didn't want to do anything behind your back. The way I categorize relationships, he belongs to you."

"Best not tell him that."

The next day, Paul phoned Frances at the Bank. "Good morning, Miss McFadden. The Warrens have asked me for professional advice on a property they're interested in. I have cautioned them that civil engineering isn't my specialty, but Kevin claims any engineer will do, so I'm meeting them Friday after work to check the place out. Care to join us?"

"That's very considerate, Mr. Roderick."

"I thought you might be curious."

"You know me too well."

The foursome explored the stables upstairs and down. While Paul poked around with a flashlight and a jackknife, Frances and Katie measured the interior dimensions. They clambered through the undergrowth to scout the exterior before walking down Daly Avenue to the Albion Hotel.

In the Ladies and Escorts section, Paul raised a draught to the Warrens. "I'd say go for it. Housing is scarce in Ottawa. It has good bones. Solid brick. Stone foundation. Sturdy beams. Leaky roof is easy to patch." He drained his glass. "That was my heart speaking. Now for the engineering report." He grabbed a napkin and jotted notes. "The place will need a hell of a lot of work. If you don't mind me asking, how much does Mrs. Desbarats want for it?"

"Three thousand cash."

"It will cost at least—*at least*—another five hundred to make it fit for human habitation."

Katie and Kevin shared unsettled looks.

"First problem: no furnace. Horses and cows throw off a ton of heat. As long as they're out of the wind and rain, they're comfy at thirty below. The human hide is a little more vulnerable. You're going to need a furnace and a coal bin or an oil tank. These take up space and coal is messy. If you don't want to sacrifice the ground floor, you'll need to dig out a basement."

"But there's a cement floor," said Kevin.

"Yeah, well, that means they poured half an inch of cement on top of the dirt to make the manure easier to clean out. Pick and shovel time. Secondly, the place has no insulation. You need to insulate the walls and ceiling or else the fuel bill would bankrupt you."

"There's running water," said Katie.

"Yup, that's a break, but there's no bathroom. Probably was an outhouse close by at some stage. I have a feeling that a woman as refined as Miss Katie," he said with a wink, "is going to want indoor plumbing.

"Thirdly, no electricity. You'll want it wired for lights, electric outlets, hot water tank, and a stove."

"Jeez," winced Kevin. "We shook out the piggy bank and went hat in hand to our parents to scrounge together fifteen hundred dollars. My cousin Pete works at the Royal Trust and thinks we can get a mortgage for the balance at 5 per cent. That doesn't leave a penny for repairs."

"Bankers are benevolent people," said Frances. "Get an extra five hundred on the mortgage to cover renovations."

"You guys are in the building trade," added Paul. "You must know plumbers and electricians who'll give you wholesale prices. Hammer and nail, shovel and pail—the sweaty stuff—I'm happy to help you with."

"You know," said Katie, "the guys at the lumberyard would pitch in on the grunt work if we put up a picnic lunch and a case of beer."

"You could talk to Mr. Morningstar about deeds and legal issues," said Frances. "I wasn't quite twenty-one when my mother passed away, so he was my legal guardian for a while. He was very supportive without being bossy."

Kevin's face sank. "Lawyers' fees. Tradesmen's bills. Appliances. Mortgages!" He tapped his empty glass absently on the table while his mind whirled, then he looked up hopefully for the waiter.

36

RESPITE

April 9:

> The *"phoney war"* ended suddenly when the Germans invaded Denmark and Norway on April 9. The humiliating defeat of the Allies in the brief Norwegian campaign that followed brought down the Chamberlain government in Britain.
>
> (Stacey, 31)

May 10:

> The German assault upon the Netherlands, Belgium, Luxembourg, and France [blitzkrieg] began.
>
> (Hastings, 53)

While major catastrophes stalked the world stage in the spring of 1940, Sandy Hill was the scene of a pleasant respite. Mr. Morningstar thought the Desbarats property a sound investment with one cautionary corollary. "You should get more than just the footprint of the stables," he advised. "When Mrs. Desbarats goes to her final reward, you don't want a new owner putting up an apartment building smack against the back wall."

Mrs. Desbarats had not envisioned selling more than the land where the stable stood. The Warrens were summoned to a second interview. Katie took an offering of homemade butter tarts. "You mentioned how fond you were of looking at the stables from the upper floors of your home," Katie said. "We don't want to alter the outside appearance at all. We just need some space out back where ..." she lowered her eyes demurely, " ... where the little ones can play." The image of frolicking children trumped the war gloom and completely melted Mrs. Desbarats. Almost completely. Mr. Perley advised her that five hundred dollars would be a fair price for the land fifty feet in from the stable's back wall and an additional fifteen feet on each side. Mrs. Desbarats graciously threw in the contents of the stable and undertook the survey costs.

On April 2, the Warrens signed the offer to purchase with $300 down, conditional on the severance and their mortgage approval by the Royal Trust. Mr. Perley and Mr. Morningstar kept the pressure on for their respective clients.

The deal closed on April 9, the day Hitler invaded Denmark and Norway. Denmark surrendered in three hours, less time than it took Paul Roderick to draft up architectural plans for the renovations.

Later that afternoon, as C.D. Howe was sworn in as minister of the newly formed Department of Munitions and Supply, the Warrens convened a meeting at the Albion Hotel to appoint their own war cabinet. As minister of Public Works, Paul would plan the renovation logistics. Kevin took on the Ministry of Labour, charged with recruiting an army of workers. Katie became minister of the Interior, and would seek a crew to scrub out the grit and cobwebs of twenty years. Dorothy Deavy was named minister of Finance to budget and track expenses. Frances was named minister of Revenue, chief fundraiser, as the cost of the additional property purchases had completely exhausted the Warrens' mortgage money. George Holland was given the External Affairs portfolio, agreeing to subdue the jungle engulfing the stable.

As 120,000 German troops swept into Norway, a routine developed at the Stewart Street stables. A gang assembled at one p.m. on Saturday after work and laboured until six, when they broke for a picnic of hearty sandwiches and iced beer. Refreshed, they soldiered on for as long as daylight lasted. The diehards returned after church the next day and worked until Sunday supper.

On April 14, when British and French troops began to land at Narvik to assist in the defence of Norway, George and the Science Department at Glebe Collegiate showed up with saws and shears and scythes to beat back the undergrowth as far as the survey pins. They uncovered an old biffy leaning precariously, door unhinged. A family of racoons was evicted, and Kevin patched it up to service the worker crew. Once everything movable was cleaned out of the stable, the stall walls came down and were stored for future use as wainscoting. There were some jurisdictional disputes. "Get your guys to smash up this old buggy and wagon," Katie told Kevin, "and we'll put it out for the garbage men."

"Wait a minute," countered Frances. "Cleaned up, I might be able to sell that stuff to an antique dealer." Even though her Little Rascals had never received their pay raise, they voluntarily logged overtime one Saturday afternoon to spruce up the carriage, wagon, sled, and assorted livery paraphernalia. Two antique dealers and a livery stable owner dropped by to look things over. They cleared $113.65, selling everything except for two horseshoes that were mounted over the door for good luck.

Katie's team dusted and swept, mopped and scrubbed. They puttied in new window panes and scoured every glass surface spotless with vinegar and newspapers.

Mr. Edwards was happy to loan Kevin shovels and picks and wheelbarrows as long as they were cleaned up and back at the lumberyard by Monday morning. "Can you borrow a couple of trucks if we pay for gas?" Paul asked Kevin. "We have to haul a lot of rubble off site." Mr. Edwards was compassionate.

A dozen lumberyard friends used picks and sledgehammers to break up the shallow concrete liner on the stable floor. Wheelbarrows carted the debris up ramps into a dump truck. As one full truck pulled out, another took its place. A foot of loam lay beneath the stable floor from centuries of decayed vegetation. Under that was the sand that made Sandy Hill famous. Easy shovelling. Frances was amazed at how quickly the excavation grew.

The footings were uncovered six feet down. Thick slabs of limestone had been laid below the frost line by masons that old Edouard Desbarats had brought from Quebec City long ago. "That's still a shallow basement," Paul said to Kevin.

"Is it deep enough for a furnace?"

"Yeah, but not much headroom. You couldn't stand up. We still want to lay a two-inch cement floor down here."

"So?"

"We could dig down another two feet, but we'd have to build a curb wedge inside the footing or the wall might collapse into the hole."

"Won't the floor joists cut into the basement height?"

"We can seat the floor joists on top of the foundation wall, giving you a one-foot step up from the ground outside. You'd want that anyway to keep rain and melting snow from seeping in. That still leaves you ten feet of clearance on the ground floor up to the beams holding the loft."

Kevin grimaced. "What the hell—it's only time and money."

On April 28, southern and central Norway were abandoned in the face of advancing German troops. King Haakon and the Norwegian government were evacuated north.

With the foundation dug, Kevin, Paul, George, and Nat came over three evenings in a row to build the curb framing. On Saturday, three teams mixed, poured, and levelled cement, while another team ran sewer and water pipes out under the footings toward Stewart Street so the city crew could hook in.

"It will be easier to install the furnace and hot water tank before we put the floor joists in place," Paul said. "If you want oil, we need to put the tank in now."

"Not many people heat with oil."

"That will change. An oil furnace fuels itself governed by a thermostat. Very convenient. You have to feed a coal furnace yourself. And, coal is messy. Dust everywhere."

"I vote for oil," said Katie, knowing who would do the cleaning.

After the floor was poured, Erskine Heating put in a hot water boiler system using radiators salvaged from a factory fire.

Following the German invasion of France and the Low Countries on May 10, the Allied task force in Norway was gradually reduced. On the day the retreating Norwegians surrendered Hegra Fortress to the Germans, Mr. Edwards drove the delivery truck over, carrying the floor joists and spacers. There wasn't much to show for a month's work—just a furnace on a cement floor in a cavernous hole inside an empty brick shell. Paul was impressed by the delivery. "These floor joists are grade-A lumber, warp free."

Mr. Edwards took out his pipe. "Kevin and Katie are my best employees. They deserve my best wood."

"We're going to frame interior balloon walls to hold insulation and back up the wainscoting. It's not structural and it will all be hidden, so we don't really need top-grade lumber. Any suggestions?"

"About 15 per cent of any wholesale delivery consists of seconds— warped and split boards. We usually cut them up for spacers. You can have them for ten cents on the dollar."

"Great! We also need tarpaper to mount inside the framing as a vapour barrier."

Mr. Edwards shook his head. "I've heard of tarpaper used on the outside of balloon construction. I don't know of any builder in Ottawa who mounts it inside."

"Do you know of any building in Ottawa that doesn't leak heat like a sieve in winter? The summer after my first year of engineering, I helped build a kitchen addition on our log farmhouse. My materials professor advised using a tarpaper vapour barrier and filling the joist walls with wood shavings. Mother was snug as a bug."

"I'll provide thirty rolls of tarpaper at cost. Wood shavings are a nuisance. We just burn them. Pay for the gas and you're welcome to all the truckloads you need."

On May 25, with French, British, and Belgian troops encircled by German forces at Dunkirk, King Leopold of Belgium notified King George of England that the Belgian forces were crushed. Two days later, Leopold surrendered to the Germans.

Paul pushed them forward at a punishing pace. Frances had been seeing a lot of him at the stables. She was impressed by his sense of order and his ability to keep people cheerful doing hard work. Still, she was worried he'd wear everyone out. "We've got all summer," she said.

"We need to get the work far enough along that Kev and Katie can carry on without me," he confided. "Something's brewing. I might have to leave Ottawa on short notice."

"Oh?" Frances's heart quickened.

"Don't tell a soul." He did not meet her startled eyes. "Wars can affect even insignificant lives."

There was something unsettling in this vagueness from someone usually so precise. Still, Frances had her own portfolio concerns. "Money is tight and bills are piling up. How much more do you think we'll need to get this place into move-in condition?"

Paul checked his clipboard and did some rapid calculations. "At least another five hundred."

Tough news for the Revenue minister. She set up an emergency Woolworth's lunch with Dr. Grace. "Kevin and Katie's home is their dream. They'd like to move before the summer heat stinks them out of their apartment, but we're running out of money."

"Can they get an advance on their salaries?" asked Dr. Grace.

"Mr. Edwards lends them equipment, loans them his trucks, and sells them lumber at cost or less. They can't in good conscience ask for anything more."

"Friends? Relatives? The banks?"

"All tapped out."

"What if you sold a series of stories about the renovation to the newspapers or *Better Homes and Gardens?* 'Young Couple Copes Imaginatively with Housing Crisis.' Great human interest story. Take some pictures. They'd love it."

"Katie's getting by on six hours' sleep. She has no time to write."

"I've always felt that you had a natural gift with the English language, Miss McFadden."

"Me?"

"Yes. You've had six years' experience rendering Bank of Canada meetings into brilliant prose."

Frances took her head in her hands. Dr. Grace laughed and slapped her on the back.

"Do your best. I have some savings that I didn't get into war bonds before they sold out. I could lend that toward the cause."

"They're not going to take money from you! They don't even know you."

"You're the minister of Revenue. Just tell them you arranged a loan at very good rates."

"How good? They don't even have enough to buy bubble gum."

"Say I loaned them five hundred dollars repayable at a dollar a week for ten years. Could they handle that?"

Frances did the math in her head. "That's not even two per cent. You're a saint!"

"Tell my mother. Ever since dashing her dream that I join the mission field in China, she's written me off as a sinner."

37

CORRESPONDENCE

At 8:30 p.m. on June 7, the British cruiser Devonshire depart-ed from Tromso for England with King Haakon, Crown Prince Olav, Prime Minister Nygaardsvold and most of the Norwegian Government. The next morning, [Norwegian] *General Ruge sent word to* [German] *General Dietl asking for a ceasefire. Negotiations for the surrender of Norwegian forces were concluded at Trondheim on June 10.*

(Haarr, 312–16)

Through the spring, the postman brought Frances a second respite from war. Vibrant multi-coloured stamps, which put the Canadian post office's monochromatic imprints of George VI to shame, adorned letters from afar.

Buckingham Palace,
London, England
March 15, 1940

Dear Miss McFadden,

Thank you for mailing the two packages of Canadian butterflies to me! They are so beautiful! The Tiger Swallowtail is my favourite.

Did you send separate parcels in case one met fate on the North Atlantic?

Father and Mother speak daily of the generous support we receive from Canada. (In addition to butterflies of course!)

Elizabeth <u>insists</u> that I pass along her warm regards, although I believe she is old enough to write her own letters.

Respectfully yours,

Margaret

The Crocker Trust
72 Market Street,
San Francisco, California
March 19, 1940

Dear Frances,

Meeting you again has been a great gift to me. I would like to invite myself back into your life if you are open to the idea.

Our long disconnection was a failure of my imagination. Having distanced myself through divorce and relocation, I thought I was doing you a favour by not imposing between you and your one functioning parent. How did your mother explain my disappearance? It would be in character for her to say nothing at all. Am I right?

If you wish to open a new chapter, you can write me at the above address.

Yours sincerely,

Father

The Plaza Hotel, Buenos Aires
April 10, 1940

Dear Frances,

We have arrived in Buenos Aires aboard the USS President Cleveland. Some restraint at the dinner table and brisk walks around the promenade deck have kept the worst aspects of seasickness in check.

Maxie and I were able to brush up our Spanish with daily tutorials from a fellow passenger, Father Joseph. I had Spanish friends at boarding school and Max is a natural polyglot, so the Good Father got us up to speed quite quickly. He is a Jesuit priest returning to his mission in

La Plata after his first holiday abroad in fifteen years. He refused to charge us for this service, but gracefully accepted a donation to support the girls' school at his mission.

Off the Azores we were "menaced" by a German U-boat! We came upon it suddenly out of the morning mist. They were repairing something having to do with their aerials and were unable to dive. America is a non-belligerent, so our ship really was no threat. We passed within three hundred yards. They waved. We waved. Isn't the use of the passive voice "to be menaced" quite a dramatic construct?

We are in Buenos Aires for a few days to sort out business issues and purchase supplies not so readily available further inland.

I visited an ophthalmologist who checked me out thoroughly. He was <u>supposed</u> to be interested in my eyes, but I found him leering quite shamelessly at other parts of my anatomy. South American men!

You can write to me care of the Banco Nacional on Calle Central in Córdoba where we should be in a week's time.

Much love

Anna

2112 Capistrano Drive,
San Diego, California
April 14, 1940

Dear Frances,

Thank you for your kind response. You have grown into a generous and forgiving adult, for which, I'm ashamed to say, I share no credit.

We are basking in beautiful weather down here. I recall the trepidation with which you "welcomed" the annual onslaught of winter in Ottawa. You really should come for a visit. I'd be happy to pay for your trip out. You'd be welcome to stay with us.

One thing I noticed right away in Southern California is that the weather, uniformly delightful, is never a topic of discussion. A Canadian here is handicapped at first for conversational gambits.

The Crocker Trust head office is in San Francisco and we have a substantial house there on Nob Hill. We also have a property on the coast here at San Diego where my wife likes to spend the cooler months. It can be damp in San Francisco, although the California winter doesn't hold a match to Canada. It gives women an excuse to wear their fur coats when the mercury plunges to 50F.

Affectionately,

Father

The Windsor Hotel, Cordoba, Argentina
April 22, 1940

Dear Frances,

Your letter was waiting when we arrived in Córdoba. I am delighted to hear that your friends Katie and Kevin were able to purchase their very own home. I well remember Mrs. Desbarats, as I dined in her Daly Avenue home many times in the 1920s.

A steamer transported us up the Paraná River as far as Rosario and from there we took a quaint little train west to Córdoba. What a surprise! Here in the middle of nowhere is a metropolis of nearly three hundred thousand people with magnificent buildings that date to the seventeenth century.

Fashion trends are somewhat behind New York and Buenos Aires, but women still dress with flare. There is a surprising British influence in Argentina (note The Windsor Hotel stationery) due, I am told, to substantial British investments here over the last sixty years in railways and trade.

We have a lavish old-fashioned suite where breakfast in bed consists of extremely strong coffee and a bounteous fresh fruit medley with hot croissants. Maxie attends to financial and legal affairs during business hours, which frees me up for sightseeing. (My eyesight has improved dramatically!)

On Friday, we take a train north-east about fifty miles across the pampas to Santa Rosa. You can write to me there care of General Delivery.

Much love

Anna

The Crocker Trust,
72 Market Street, San Francisco
May 4, 1940

Dear Frances,

Thank you for your recent letter. I certainly do remember the Deavy girls and am amazed to learn that little Katie is now married and renovating a home in Sandy Hill! It sounds so adult! Dare I ask if you have a young man in your life these days? Oh, and could you please send me a recent photograph? My wife is curious to see what you look like.

How goes the war? The conflict barely receives mention in the local newspapers. Almost everyone here is an isolationist and a staunch fan of Mr. Lindbergh.

Some of the businessmen see opportunities in profiting from "the European situation," as they quaintly refer to it (in order to keep any unpleasantness remote). The German war machine is held in very high regard here. There is anti-Semitism as well (mostly unspoken) although many Jewish men have been quite successful in the film industry.

Another curiosity is that the local wealthy class, almost exclusively Anglo-Saxon, have such little sympathy for the fate of the United Kingdom.

Fondly,

Father

Casa Nueva,
c/o General Delivery, Santa Rosa, La Pampa,
Argentina
May 14, 1940

Dear Frances,

Thank you for your latest note. I'm delighted (and a little surprised) at the speed of mail delivery. Most aspects of life work at a much slower pace down here. "Mañana" seems to be the perpetual delivery date for every service.

Santa Rosa is little more than a rail junction. It has a tiny train station, a general store, and a very seedy two-story building that passes as a hotel. A scatter of adobe shanties house the citizens. Three of Max's gauchos met us at the station. One drove a kind of enclosed carriage (like a stagecoach) for us, and the others managed two wagons for our luggage and the material we've shipped up from the coast.

It's a bumpy ride of more than an hour out to the ranch. Our property, which is an estate of two thousand acres, is called "la estancia." Spanish words roll off the tongue with such a delightful cadence!

The first thing you see when you drive up is a long impressive building with dormer windows twinkling in the sun. It was the stables (los establos) of course, as Max's uncle, Count Gorka, treated his horses (caballos) like royalty. By comparison, our house (casa) is a simple affair with wide porches to shed the heat. It is built right on the lip of a valley overlooking a shallow river, el Río Primero, which winds lazily into the haze.

There are high hills in the distant west. Max says they are just like the foothills of the Rockies. Very few trees, except down by the river. Not another building is visible in any direction, although I'm told there are neighbouring estancias within a few miles.

We are now five hundred miles from Buenos Aires and easy access to the western world. As long as the western world is consumed by warfare, I don't mind at all.

You can write care of Pensión Rosetta, the seedy hotel cum post office (and likely bordello) in Santa Rosa. A gaucho rides in once a week for supplies (and perhaps to use the services at la pensión) and will pick up the mail.

Much love,

Anna

The Crocker Trust,
72 Market Street, San Francisco
May 21, 1940

Dearest Frances,

I was heartened to hear that you have "a gentleman friend" in young Mr. Roderick. I was just your age when I married your mother during the last war. Perhaps we would have been wiser to wait, as our characters did not weave well into an enduring partnership. I guess the uncertainties of world turmoil thrust us into a shaky alliance.

I believe you to have sound judgment, and although I do not know this young engineer, I fully support you in whatever direction this relationship might take. I left you unsupported for so long that it is time I made up for lost ground.

Everyone here has been quite nice to me, and it would be ungracious to speak ill of those who have contributed to my elevated standard of living. However, our social set, all wealthy for generations, bring to mind the Eloi in H.G. Wells' novel *The Time Machine*. They are completely given over to pleasurable pursuits. Parties until all hours, sailing, horseback riding, the theatre, concerts, tennis, polo. The concept of work is almost foreign.

I actually enjoy work, the rewarding challenge in solving a complex problem, or the satisfaction in seeing a project move forward. I am indulged as quite the eccentric, like someone who collects antique snuffboxes. Should these darling people ever be thrown onto their own resources by some awful quirk (like a hostile invasion) I do wonder if they could actually survive.

Love,

Father

Casa Nueva, Argentina
May 28, 1940

Dear Frances,

Thank you for all the news from Canada. I miss you, of course, but I am not saddened that the war is so far away. Soon after arriving at Casa Nueva, every neighbour within twenty miles dropped in to welcome us. Maxie's uncle, Count Gorka (originally Gorszczynski) was an excellent horseman. This trait is revered like gold here, so people were predisposed to like us. They brought all sorts of housewarming gifts to cover their curiosity.

There are about a dozen estancias in the neighbourhood—a surprisingly polyglot crowd—half old Argentinian families augmented by British, Italians and Swedes. Some came to Argentina for adventure. (Two are remittance men who are sent quarterly cheques as long as they stay away from home!)

Twice a month someone hosts a Saturday social open to everyone. This is usually a long lunch (called el almuerzo largo) that lasts from 10:00 a.m. until 4:00 p.m. On special occasions, this is upgraded to a banquet beginning at four and running until midnight, (called el banquete de noche) where wonderful foods are served, including little pies (empanadas) and lots of meat cooked on a barbecue (asado). People camp overnight and head home following a hearty breakfast the next morning.

Quite a change from the Balmoral Arms! Of the fifty apartment-dwellers there, only you and Betsey Knowles ever invited me in. With the rest of the tenants, it was just a nod and a quick comment on the weather as we waited for the elevator.

Here, the estancias are huge and spread over hundreds of square miles, yet everyone is tightly linked and interdependent. My apartment in Ottawa, which I thought of as cosy, was isolated compared to the sense of space and ironic intimacy here.

Max's uncle died without issue, so along with the property, he has inherited the title "Count Gorka." Maxie is not pretentious, but he thought that living as a Polish Count in exile rather than a retired German cavalry officer/farm implement salesman might leave us less exposed to political issues. So I am now the Countess Anna Gorka, mistress at Casa Nueva! Tell that to Betsey Knowles!

Much love

Anna

38

PLAN B

The Dunkirk evacuation of 338,000 Allied troops was completed on June 4. The British Expeditionary Force [BEF] left behind in France 64,000 vehicles, 76,000 tons of ammunition, 2,500 guns and 400,000 tons of stores. Britain's land forces were effectively disarmed.

(Hastings, 67)

We shall go on to the end, ... we shall defend our Island, whatever the cost may be, we shall fight on the beaches ... we shall fight in the fields and in the streets ... we shall never surrender, and even if, which I do not for a moment believe, this Island or a large part of it were subjugated and starving, then our Empire beyond the seas, armed and guarded by the British Fleet, would carry on the struggle, until, in God's good time, the New World, with all its power and might, steps forth to the rescue and the liberation of the old.

Winston Churchill
British House of Commons, June 4, 1940

B ack on Monday, May 13, two days after Winston Churchill became prime minister of the United Kingdom, Frances had taken a message from the French Legation in Ottawa. M. Bozonnet, the French envoy, wished an audience with Graham Towers at his earliest convenience. While Governor Towers never literally rolled his eyes, a pained incredulity could flash across his face to much the same effect. Nevertheless, M. Bozonnet was invited to attend the Tuesday morning executive meeting.

The French envoy extraordinaire and minister plenipotentiary bore an uncanny resemblance to Groucho Marx. A triangular face sported a drooping moustache. Unruly eyebrows looked like wings about to fly away with his nose.

"The French government is confident that the Nazi aggressors will be thrown back soon," he confided with Gallic nonchalance. "However, M. Fournier, the governor of the Bank of France, has anxieties about our gold reserves and the considerable Belgian and Dutch reserves being held at the request of their governments. He has convinced Premier Reynaud that it would be prudent to move the gold out of the country.

"Personally, I view this as defeatist and completely unnecessary. However, as a servant of the government, I am obliged," he said with obvious distaste, "to follow directions. The Bank of England is out of storage space, so I was instructed to convey the request for accommodation here." A curious aura of ambiguity emanated from M. Bozonnet, begging a favour that he clearly didn't want.

"How much gold?" asked Mr. Marble. As Bank secretary, he would be tasked with finding the space.

"All in all, about twelve billion francs. Five hundred million American."

Scotty Meldrum gave a low whistle. Mr. Marble scribbled madly. "About thirty-six thousand bars?"

"About."

"I'm happy to oblige if we have the space," said the governor. Concurring nods from Scotty Meldrum and Mr. Marble contrasted with an expression of profound disinterest from M. Souliére. One might have thought a shared French heritage would have bonded the two men. One would have been mistaken. M. Souliére surrendered a neutral shrug, much in line with his enthusiasm about the war.

"We have to bear in mind other obligations," said Mr. Marble obliquely, "but we could do it."

"If France can get the gold to Halifax, I can organize armed trains to bring it to Ottawa," said Scotty Meldrum.

"Fine, then," said the governor. "Your Excellency, please convey our receptiveness to M. Fournier. He can contact me directly to work out the details."

On the day the 10th Panzer division surrounded the port of Calais, French light cruisers *Émile Bertin* and *Jeanne d'Arc* departed from Brest with two hundred million dollars' worth of French gold. They arrived in Halifax on May 29. The cargo was unloaded at night onto four heavily guarded trains that trundled to Ottawa while the cruisers sped back to France for a second shipment.

The day after the Dunkirk evacuation, Paul phoned Frances at the office. "I have news," he said.

Frances's heart skipped a beat. "Good or bad?"

"Didn't Hamlet say, 'there is nothing either good or bad, but thinking makes it so'?"

"All right, Shakespeare, what are you thinking?"

"I'm thinking that we should have dinner tonight. Say the Chateau Laurier at six thirty?"

"The Chateau? Is the news that bad?"

"Our last dinner there was a disaster. Why don't we try for a fresh start?"

Graham Towers was pathologically cheerful no matter the circumstances, but he returned from a late afternoon meeting with the war cabinet looking as though his dog had just died.

"Better drop everything, Miss McFadden," he said with a stark despondency. "It's going to be one of those days." Frances telegraphed a silent charade to Maddie to cover her desk and grabbed her notepad.

In a rare tribute to the humid day, the governor took off his suit jacket but left his tie and vest in place as he explained. "Quite frankly, the current situation in Europe is beyond the comprehension of our leaders on Parliament Hill." He spoke slowly while lighting a cigarette. "These men are not stupid, but the world has never before seen a situation like this.

"I believe that the Allied cause is just. I hope and pray for success." He inhaled deeply, reverentially. "However, hopes and prayers may not be enough. Duty dictates that we now consider a Plan B."

"Plan B?"

"France is about to collapse. The United Kingdom just got beaten out of Norway. It lost all its military equipment at Dunkirk and now has only the English Channel and an unarmed scraggle left to defend the nation.

"I just asked the prime minister what he imagined would happen if the United Kingdom fell to the Germans. He indignantly maintains that it will not fall. I envy his optimism, but our duty is to prepare for all scenarios. In 1937 we began to plan for foreign exchange controls in the event of war. We did not wish for war, but those preparations saved our bacon when war came."

"And now?"

"Well, first of all, we need to overcome the emotional feelings around the 'Mother Country,' the seat of Western democracy, being conquered by a tyrannical power. We need to consider the consequences for Canada should such an event transpire."

"Surely the British navy would still protect us," said Frances.

"Mr. Churchill would die before surrendering the British Navy to the Nazis. But suppose he does die? Would some other British leader, gun to head, bargain away the navy in return for a peaceful occupation that would spare civilian lives?"

"Never!"

"No? That's exactly what happened in Denmark, Norway, Holland, and Belgium. Their choice was capitulate or be destroyed. Anyway, the navy is not our concern. The Atlantic Ocean will protect us from invasion for quite some time. However, the economic consequences of England's defeat would be ... well, somewhere between traumatic and catastrophic."

There were times when Frances painfully recognized the limits of her Grade 11 education. "I don't understand," she said.

Graham Towers ticked points off on the fingers of his left hand. "First off, the United Kingdom is our largest trading partner. Trade would end immediately, grinding the Canadian economy to a virtual halt. Second, without the protection of the British navy, our ability to ship products to other markets around the world would be seriously compromised. Third, the British pound sterling is the international currency of the British Empire. The Reichsmark is not going to replace it. So, as the senior Dominion, does the Canadian dollar become the new Commonwealth standard? And would Australia and South Africa and Ceylon accept it? We don't have the reserves to finance that possibility. I'd have to go down to Washington and firm up lines of credit with the Federal Reserve." He jotted a note. "I should set that up regardless of what else happens.

"Fourthly, what would we do with our excess inventories? Our swelling unemployment if factories can't sell their products? Trade with the Americans is seriously compromised by their Neutrality Acts. Would they trade with us at all? The Canadian dollar would surely depreciate, making imports prohibitively expensive." He leaned back in his chair and stared at her. "The Canadian economy could be destroyed without the Nazis firing a single shot at us."

"What's the prime minister's response to all this?"

Graham Towers shook his head. "Mr. King likes to keep costs down and government small, but beyond that he doesn't really engage intellectually in the economics of nationhood at peace or at war. And he shelters behind this belief that England will never fall."

Frances's mind raced through a labyrinth of dead ends. "So ... ?"

"So, we have four tasks. We need to describe a complex economic situation in terms simple enough that the war cabinet can
understand it. Second, we need to make clear that we are not nay-
sayers, attempting to undermine confidence in the war effort. A man
does not buy fire insurance hoping his home will burn down. The
insurance protects the asset against unknown perils. Canada needs
an insurance policy.

"Third, we are the experts in monetary policy. We need to provide
the government with a range of alternatives, detailing the risks and
benefits of each choice. Finally, and most important, we need to do
this today. We are ... we *could be* on the brink of a cataclysm. Every
minute lost reduces our options as external events overtake us."

Frances was momentarily silenced as the impact of all this sank
in. "What do you want me to do?"

Graham Towers looked at his watch. "Contact the Executive
Committee and summon them to an emergency meeting in the boardroom for four thirty. See if you can get Sandy Skelton from Research
to attend and Clifford Clark from the Department of Finance if he's
available. Add that new fellow, Walter Gordon. Bright chap. Get
Mr. Rollins from Currency in on it, too.

"Have the secretariat comb through our files for everything on
the Bank of England and Imperial trade and commerce. Please do not
share with them the direness of the situation. Get ready to burn the
midnight oil."

Everyone was able to attend except for M. Souliére, who was in Quebec
City. Brendan ordered in sandwiches and coffee. Frances typed up
an agenda with all the points the governor wished to cover. What
impressed her most at the meeting was that no one was given to
emotional outbursts. They all treated the situation as a series of problems to be solved. No chaos. Only "if this, then that." The meeting
lasted for three hours. She could hear the phones ringing unanswered
in the empty outer office. Debate and counterpoint ... and finally a
plan hammered out.

The governor excused everyone except Frances, who drafted the
top-secret report, reducing the fundamentals to two typed pages. He
would personally deliver a copy to the prime minister at Laurier
House on his way home.

Just as Frances put the dust cover over her typewriter at nine
o'clock, she remembered her dinner date with Paul. *Oh, God!* She
phoned his apartment but there was no answer. She phoned the dining room at the Chateau Laurier. Émile told her that Paul had dined

alone but had left a message and a package for her. Frances hurried guiltily up Wellington Street to the hotel.

The message was brief.

> Sorry to have missed you. Tried phoning your office and your home.
>
> Something has suddenly come up. I depart Ottawa tonight and don't know when I'll be back. Left detailed instructions for Kevin on finishing the stable renovations.
>
> Could you water the plants in my apartment? There's a secret key hidden on the ledge over the front door. No snooping!
>
> Au revoir,
>
> Paul

The package was a long box holding a dozen pink roses. The note said simply,

> All my love,
>
> Paul

39

DOUBLE BLOW

The Desbarats stable was metamorphosing into a home. The plumbing was hooked up and the electrical wiring completed. Oak planking covered the floor joists. Tongue-and-groove pine installed over the interior framing hid the insulation and gave the place an intimate, cottagey feel. Only cabinet work in the kitchen and some painting remained. Katie and Kevin hoped to extricate themselves from the fish stench of their apartment on the July first long weekend.

Gladys Gilhooley's bachelor brothers were in distress back east on the Nova Scotia farm. A serious stroke had felled Matthew and he was in intensive care in the Kentville hospital. Gladys, ever the picture of emotional reserve, was clearly anxious.

"Matthew is a silly fool and has spent a lifetime overworking himself, daring God to strike him down. Well, God has acquiesced. Matt didn't return for lunch yesterday and Mark went searching to give him what-for. He found the draft horses wandering by the creek trailing their reins. Backtracking across the lower meadow, he came across Matthew lying unconscious in a furrow. He managed somehow to carry him back to the house. Doc Watson took one look and sent for the Kentville ambulance. Matt is still unconscious and Mark is a wreck. They've worked that farm like a married couple for fifty years. One would be lost without the other." She shook her head. "I'm booked out on the four o'clock train."

"What about your classes?"

"Things at the High School of Commerce are essentially wrapped up for the year. Just doing review, then we're into exams. A substitute teacher will cover for me. Typing exams are easy to mark."

"Can I help?"

"Pray. For all the Gilhooleys. And give my regrets to Betsey. I'll be in Dutch for prioritizing my brothers over a night of bridge."

June 10 was muggy. Frances and Maddie were holding down the office while the rest of the Rascals took lunch. Frances's phone rang and a hoarse voice whispered, "Frances? Jack Pickersgill. I'm going right down to the United Cigar Store on Sparks Street to pick up the noon editions of the newspapers. Meet me there."

"I can't leave Maddie holding down the office alone. How about in half an hour?"

"Now, Frances."

"I can't just …"

"Tell her you've got diarrhoea. She won't ask for details." The line went dead.

Jack Pickersgill was not a man given to thespian tendencies. What didn't he want to say on the phone? Insatiable curiosity has its drawbacks. She picked up her purse and walked over to Maddie's desk. "Can you hold the fort alone for fifteen minutes?"

Maddie saluted. "Aye, aye, Captain. Fear not!"

A noon-hour crowd milled around in the United Cigar Store, but the stocky figure in the rumpled brown suit was easy to spot back by the magazine rack. He was examining a folded copy of the *Ottawa Citizen* and aimed an elbow at *The Ladies' Home Journal*. "Pretend you're reading that," he whispered. "Don't want anybody to think that we're talking."

"Why not?"

"Because I'm about to break the Official Secrets Act."

If Jack had said, "Because I'm opening a nudist colony on Parliament Hill," Frances wouldn't have been more surprised. She scanned a recipe for rhubarb crumble. "No one would ever call you loose-lipped."

"It's a terrible day," he said in a tone so flat you could bowl on it.

"The sun's shining. The sky's blue. What's wrong?"

"Two pieces of bad news will be made public when the House of Commons meets at 2:00 p.m."

"If it would ease your conscience, I can curb my curiosity until then."

"Your curiosity and my conscience are small potatoes. I'm worried about the Bank of Canada."

"Oh?" was all Frances could think to say as she flipped through an article on summer wardrobe alternatives.

Jack's eyes slid left and right before he whispered, "Mussolini is set to make a broadcast at 1:00 p.m. Ottawa time. He's going to declare war on France. Then invade."

"Not very sportsmanlike with France reeling."

"Mussolini, apparently, is willing to sacrifice a shot at the Lady Byng Trophy in return for the easy pickings. The French army has completely collapsed."

"Does a declaration of war on France automatically extend to us?"

"It does."

"Ugh. Was that the 'good' bad news or the 'bad' bad news?"

"You decide. Norman Rogers was flying down to Toronto this morning to deliver a speech to the Empire Club. His plane went down near Newcastle in a thunderstorm. No survivors."

"Oh, God!"

"At a very dark time in the war, with a fresh new enemy, we are bereaved of our Defence minister. These items taken together might well have a negative impact on the stock market and cause a run on the Canadian dollar. It seemed prudent to inform someone at the Bank of Canada."

"Why doesn't Mackenzie King just call Governor Towers?"

"He's on his way to Rockcliffe right now to break the news to Mrs. Rogers and their sons."

"There's a job I don't envy. It's not the first thing you think of when contemplating a prime minister's workday."

"Mr. King was particularly close to the Rogers family." Jack checked his watch. "I have to run. Do what you like with this information. You just never heard it from me."

Having wrung the *Ladies' Home Journal* into a tight baton, Frances purchased it before racing back to the Bank. The governor would be having his post-lunch nap, from which Miss Briscoe said he should never be disturbed. She hurried down the hall to Scotty Meldrum's office. His secretary, Clara Hewitt, had technically been Frances's boss until Frances leapfrogged into the governor's office. This altered power structure had produced a disquieting few days before they settled into a wordless accord, like symbiotic animals.

"Hello Clara, is the deputy governor in?"

"No, Frances. He's out with Mrs. Meldrum buying birthday gifts for their boys. He was supposed to do this last week and is in the doghouse."

"Please have him give me a call when he returns."

Frances thought for a moment, then crossed the hall to knock on the door of the associate deputy governor. His secretary, Manon Labelle, smiled sweetly. "*Oui?*"

"*Est M. Soulière dans son bureau?*"

"*Non, Mademoiselle. Il est malade, chez lui.*"

There was something almost mystical in the way M. Soulière managed, *always,* to never be around when needed. Would it have mattered? He weighed every aspect of Bank governance by how it contributed to Quebec interests. He saw little benefit to his home province in a European conflict between imperialist powers. At executive meetings, a passionate lack of interest in the war seeped from him like the smell of sour milk.

Frances could hear the staccato attack of Maddie's typewriter as she headed back up the hall to the outer office. "Any problems on the home front?"

"Piece o' cake. Could've done a load of laundry."

"Brendan and Bridget and Claire should be back soon. I need to slip into Miss Briscoe's office for a quiet minute." She gave Maddie a knowing nod and a polite but knowing nod was returned. Frances marvelled that the secretariat could turn off their curiosity like a spigot. She could learn a lot from them.

The great debate. Miss Briscoe had said she wouldn't interrupt the governor's nap unless the building was on fire. Frances wished she understood enough about the stock market to know if Jack Pickersgill was overreacting. She checked the governor's agenda for the afternoon. Nothing much that he needed to be fresh for. Well … why not? There was no response to her knock on the connecting door to the governor's office. She opened it and tiptoed across to the door to his bedroom and knocked again.

"Yes?" came a groggy voice.

"Governor? It's Frances. Sorry to disturb you. Something's come up."

"Come in." Governor Towers had his suit coat and shoes off. His tie was loosened, but he wasn't wearing pyjamas, thank God.

"Just give me a moment, Miss McFadden." He swung his feet to the ground and picked up his glasses from the bedside table.

"Sorry, sir. An emergency and I couldn't find Mr. Meldrum."

"Did you try M. Soulière?" he asked.

Their eyes met in silent conversation.

"Manon said he was home with the 'flu," she replied, before sharing her news.

"Where did you hear this?"

"A reliable source."

Graham Towers raised his eyebrows.

"I promised confidentiality. A *very* reliable source." She felt guilty keeping secrets.

"Hm. This is a double-barrelled blow," said the governor, straightening his tie. "It's not so much the acts taken separately, but the psychological impact of cumulative events adding to our war burden. Can you round up the executive for an emergency meeting in the boardroom?"

"No one's here. Mr. Meldrum's out shopping. Mr. Marble is in Kingston getting an honorary degree. And M. Soulière is sick."

"Well, then, Miss McFadden," said the governor, smiling his number two smile and reaching for a cigarette, "I guess it's up to us. What do you think we should do?"

Ah! The glory and the cataclysm of the inclusive "we." Frances gulped. "I suppose we need to warn the stock markets and chartered banks as well as our regional offices that there might be panic selling or a run on the dollar. But how do we do that without actually breaking the news?"

"A good test of your memo writing skills, Miss McFadden. It's your secret, but unless we share something …" he trailed off. "Give it a shot."

Frances was back in eight minutes with a draft.

Most Urgent:

Breaking news from Europe this afternoon negatively impacts the Allied cause. As well, a senior Canadian official has just met with a serious accident.

Taken together, these events could undermine the Canadian dollar and may cause disruption in the stock market.

"Excellent! Can you add these two short sentences?

"'Canadian interests are best served by carrying on business as usual.

I recommend a calm demeanour and accommodation of any draw-downs on bank deposits.'

"Cable this out immediately under my signature to the presidents of the chartered banks and the stock exchanges. Copy all Bank regional directors and department heads."

He smiled and looked at his watch. "Since you have everything under control, Miss McFadden, I might as well finish my nap."

40

ÉMILE BERTIN

According to the Bank of Canada's inflation calculator, the Émile Bertin's 1940 cargo would be worth $4.8 billion in 2016 Canadian dollars.

(http://www.bankofcanada.ca/rates/related/inflation-calculator/)

Eight million French people abandoned their homes in the month following the German assault. The massed flight of civilians impacted as disastrously on military communications as upon soldiers' morale. The people of eastern France had suffered German occupation in 1914; they were determined to escape another such experience.

(Hastings, 59)

O n June 14, a cryptic nine-word telegram arrived for Frances at the Bank.

Nightingales actually do sing here STOP

Travel imminent mademoiselle STOP Paul

What was that song? *"A Nightingale Sang ... in Berkeley Square"?* In London, England? Paul's in England and about to travel to ... ? mademoiselle? He'd never called her "mademoiselle." *Surely ... surely he's not going to France?* The guilty flush of the missed dinner date surged again. His veiled hints about having to leave Ottawa had conjured thoughts of Montreal or Halifax. *England! France?* The distance increased as each petal wilted and fell from the long-stemmed roses.

Later in the afternoon, Frances was helping Governor Towers sort files for his Washington trip when Claire knocked at the door. "Sorry! Incoming call from the prime minister. "

Frances rose to leave, but the governor waved her back to her seat. His part of a sixty-second conversation went, "No. Yes. Good Lord! No. Of course." Then the phone dropped like a guillotine back onto its cradle. "Paris has been declared an open city," he said.

"Open for … ?"

"The French army will not defend Paris and is retreating south. 'Open city' is code to your enemy that 'the place is yours, no need to blast the architecture or the civilians to smithereens.' The army leaves the front door unlocked and sneaks out the servant's entrance." The governor reached for a cigarette. "Mr. Churchill has just informed Mr. King that the collapse of France is imminent."

Cue the organ music.

"How … imminent?"

"Churchill thinks about a week. The French government is scrambling south, working out of suitcases. The Nazis might pause for a quick glass of champagne in Paris, but they'll be right back on the chase. Roads are jammed with refugees, slowing both the retreating French and the advancing Germans. Remember Colonel Vanier whom we met at the Canadian High Commission in December? He was appointed Canadian Envoy to France in the New Year. He's trying to get the embassy staff to Bordeaux and safely out of the country before the Germans nab them."

"Wouldn't they have diplomatic immunity?"

Graham Towers smiled. "Diplomats caught behind enemy lines are very much dependent on the good will of their new hosts. Canada no longer has diplomatic representation with Germany, so a neutral party like Switzerland would need to act as an intermediary. Exchanges can be arranged, but the Nazis have an excellent bargaining position— say, fifty captured German officers for one minister? Best just to scram.

"Lead elements of the French government have reached Bordeaux. The *Émile Bertin* has been dispatched to Halifax with the last of the gold reserves." The governor exhaled two perfect smoke rings. "I hate to leave in the middle of this mess, but it's essential that we nail down the Federal Reserve's support to prop up the Canadian dollar. I have complete faith in the deputy governor to run things here in my absence."

"Will you be in Washington long?"

"Marriner Eccles at the Fed will be no trouble, but he'll need help placating isolationist elements in Congress. I'll be trotted out for lunch or cocktails with Senator X and Congressman Y to show how harmless Canadians are and why all this financial jiggery-pokery is in the best interests of America." The governor cleared the ash from his cigarette. "I'd like to take you to Washington, but you're more valuable here helping Mr. Meldrum get the last of the French gold tucked safely into the vault downstairs."

A rose-hued dawn announced the summer solstice on the twenty-first of June. Wafers of sunlight slipped through the Venetian blinds in Frances's bedroom, tracing zebra patterns across her sheets. A chorus of larks sang in the tree beneath her window. They triggered thoughts of nightingales singing elsewhere.

Since the governor had been away in Washington, Frances grabbed coffee and toast to go at Tamblyn's Drug Store. She read the *Globe* at her desk until Claire and Brendan arrived at 7:45. In return for their early start, Frances made allowances later in the day. Claire played shortstop on the Bank's baseball team and left early two nights a week to race home for a wardrobe change and a quick bite to eat. Brendan could just squeeze in a round of golf at McKellar Park before dark if he got away from the Bank by 4:15.

At eight, Frances left to see Rose Malone at the Department of Finance. Rose had been Clifford Clark's secretary for over eight years and had initially invited Frances to join the Momsie meetings. J.L. Ilsley was about to become the new minister of Finance, and a quick refresher on Finance–Bank protocols had been requested.

"Mr. Ralston was *most* reluctant to leave Finance to replace poor Mr. Rogers as minister of Defence," confided Rose. "The prime minister must have put him in a hammerlock, pleading duty to a nation in peril. Mr. Ilsley's bringing his secretary over from National Revenue, a Miss Endicott, but she won't know a thing about the Finance Department's relationship with the Bank of Canada. I want to make sure I have all my ducks in a line." She gave a beleaguered smile. "This is my fourth Finance minister in six years. They each like their sandwiches sliced a little differently."

By 9:30, Frances was crossing back to work under the umbrella-shaped elms lining Wellington Street. From this perspective, the Bank of Canada building looked omnipotent, like a classic Greek temple. She ducked a territorial red-winged blackbird that swooped within inches of her face, warding her away from an unseen nest. Birds seemed to be speaking to her today. Her mother would have read it as an omen.

Back in the outer office, she found the secretariat clustered around Maddie Hall, whose pretty face was contorted, barely holding back tears.

"What's wrong?"

"Mr. Meldrum stormed in here five minutes ago looking for you," said Bridget. "He was *hoppin'* mad. Red as a beet. Wants to see you *im-mediately*."

Frances winced. "Any hints?"

"He was pretty clear," replied Brendan, looking down at an imaginary note pad. "He said 'Goddam! Sonofabitch! Shit!' Did I get that right?"

"Maddie took both barrels in your absence. I'm sure it was nothing personal."

"Yeah. Like a typhoon is nothing personal."

Frances took a deep breath and picked up her steno pad.

"This is what you're paid the big bucks for, Miss," said Brendan. "Oh, um, if you get sacked, can I have your desk?"

Frances walked down to Clara Hewitt's office next to the deputy governor. Clara, not usually given to acts of collegiality, hushed Frances with a finger to her lips, then mimed an explosion and pointed at the connecting door to Scotty's office. Frances knocked, heard a bark, and entered. Scotty Meldrum was pacing back and forth like a caged gorilla.

"Where ya been, lass, for God's sake!" His Scottish brogue flared most when exasperated.

"Good morning, Deputy Governor. I was over at the Department of Finance helping Rose Malone prepare for Mr. Ilsley. Something come up?"

Scotty Meldrum looked like he was about to have a heart attack. His mouth opened but no words came out. Exceptional times call for exceptional measures. "Would a wee Macallan refresh the senses?" Frances asked. The weight of his nod sank the deputy governor into his desk chair.

Frances went to the emergency rations hidden in the bottom drawer of his filing cabinet and poured him a generous libation. The deputy governor turned the crystal Old Fashioned glass slowly, examining it as though it were some puzzling artefact from an Inca tomb, before setting it down.

"So? Has the governor been kidnapped by enemy agents?"

Scotty gave a dismissive half-chortle before words came to him. "By the way, where, may I ask, *is* the governor these days?"

"He's in suite 314 of the Willard Hotel in Washington."

"He is not. I phoned three times and he doesn't answer." He glared at her. "You've lost him, it appears."

"Sorry," Frances replied, in a tone completely bereft of sorrow.

"The *Émile Bertin* arrived in Halifax yesterday with three hundred million in gold."

"Wonderful! Were our trains ready for it?"

"Yes, goddamit! The trains were ready. The longshoremen were ready. The Mounties, all in plain clothes with Thompson submachine guns hidden in potato sacks, were ready."

"And … ?"

"And that sonofabitch captain refused to unload the gold!" Scotty smashed his fist down on his desk with a force that sent ripples rebounding in his tumbler of Scotch. He picked it up and drained it in one motion. "Burns, the Bank's regional director in Halifax, went on board this morning to make arrangements for the transfer. Captain Battet rebuffed him."

"Why?"

"Claims that he's had 'further instructions' from the French Admiralty."

"Further to … ?"

"The change in government in France. The *Émile Bertin* cast off from Brest on June 14. Premier Reynaud resigned on June 16 when his cabinet wouldn't support carrying on the war. Pétain is now Premier of France. He's seeking an armistice with the Germans. May well want to use the gold as a bargaining chip. Battet says he's been directed to leave Halifax immediately and take the gold to Fort-de-France, Martinique."

"It *is* their gold."

Scotty smashed his fist down on his desk a second time. "The Bank of Canada promised the Bank of France, *in writing*, that we would shelter their gold reserves. If this … this weasel Pétain surrenders to the Germans, he's as good as handing them that gold to use against us. I *will not let this happen!*"

"What can we do?"

"See if you can get through to Commodore Reid at Halifax Central Command. I've tried twice." Scotty reached for the Macallan and poured a booster shot that would have fuelled a rocket.

There was some considerable static on the line and a distant ringing, then a voice answered, "Halifax Central Command. Able Seaman Porter."

"Hello. Frances McFadden here at the Bank of Canada in Ottawa. The deputy governor urgently needs to speak with Commodore Reid. Could you connect us, please?"

She passed the phone to Scotty. "Reid? Where have you been, man? This is Meldrum at the Bank of Canada. That French cruiser at your dock is carrying three hundred million in gold destined for our vault. It cannot be allowed to leave Halifax until that cargo is off-loaded. Understood?"

There was a frosty pause on the line before Commodore Reid responded in measured tones. "Meldrum, I control only the movement and disposition of Canadian ships here. French naval vessels operate under the direction of the French Admiralty."

"Listen, Reid! The Bank of Canada has undertaken an obligation to the Bank of France to store their gold reserves for the duration. We have armoured trains at dockside right now, but this Captain Battet refuses to unload. We will not default on our responsibilities. A promise made is a debt unpaid."

Frances had heard that line somewhere before. *Oh, yes.* Miles, her doorman, quoted from "The Cremation of Sam McGee." Funny to think of Miles Treleaven and Scotty Meldrum sharing an appreciation of Robert Service. Perhaps the doorman and the deputy governor rub elbows at poetry readings. Perhaps not.

"This is *not* your problem, Meldrum. Nor is it mine. It is a French problem. I suggest we let the French resolve it. We have problems enough of our own."

"Reid, we have guaranteed the protection of that gold. It *must* be unloaded. Arrest that goddam captain if you have to! Do I make myself clear?"

Scotty pulled the phone away from his ear and stared at it. "That son of a bitch hung up on me! I'll have him court-martialled if he lets that ship go." He slammed the receiver down. His eyes bugged out and spittle frothed on his usually immaculate moustache.

"God damn it to hell!" He stood up. "I'm going up on the Hill to see if I can scare up Rear-Admiral Nelles or Mackenzie King to throw this tinpot captain in irons."

He jabbed a finger at Frances. "You call that bastard Reid right back. Tell him emphatically that the *Émile Bertin* cannot be allowed to leave. The Bank of France is on record requesting that the Bank of

Canada protect that gold. We have received no instructions to the contrary."

Another thought struck Scotty Meldrum and he furrowed a brow. "How legitimate is this Pétain regime, anyway? France is a democracy; who elected him, for God's sake? And even if he were legitimate, he's under duress with a German army camped in his living room. In law, a contract entered into under duress is not valid. The only logical thing to do in the circumstances is to protect the gold until the situation clarifies. Now, get hold of Reid and rattle his cage. Do not let that gold leave Halifax harbour, McFadden, or we'll be takin' it out of yer wages."

Frances went back to the outer office to update the secretariat. Brendan did some quick calculations. "If you don't eat or have other expenses, Miss, you could have it paid off in two hundred thousand years."

41

ALL NECESSARY STEPS

*The National Resources Mobilization Act became law June
21. It conferred upon the government special emergency
powers to mobilize all human and material resources for the
defence of Canada. The Act made 802,000 single men and
childless widowers between the ages of 21 and 45 liable for
military service in Canada.*

(Granatstein, 99)

While giving Commodore Reid a few minutes to calm down,
Frances phoned Jack Pickersgill. "Big problem here at the Bank,
Jack. All very off the record. Does the name *Émile Bertin* mean any-
thing to you?"

"The French light cruiser in Halifax harbour carrying a secret
cargo?"

"You know the secret?"

"Yup."

"The Bank promised to safeguard the cargo, but the captain is
refusing to unload. Says he has new instructions to sail directly to
Martinique. Governor Towers is in Washington, so Deputy Governor
Meldrum is in charge here, and he's charging around like a wounded
bear. Just stormed up to the Hill looking for a posse to lynch this
French captain."

"Very bad timing, Frances. Busy day up here. The Earl of Athlone
is getting sworn in as governor general at noon in the Senate Chamber.
The prime minister is all a-flutter over protocol and the details of the
reception. Napkins must be folded just so, apparently, lest British
aristocrats think us colonial bumpkins. And right after Question
Period in the House of Commons, the National Resources Mobilization
Act goes to a vote."

"What's that?"

"The NRMA will require *all* persons to place themselves, their services, and their property at the disposal of His Majesty—i.e., Mr. King's government—for the successful prosecution of the war. Unquote."

"Sounds draconian."

"Wars aren't for sissies."

"Well, the deputy governor wants *somebody* up there to give this Captain Battet quick and pointed encouragement to off-load that gold."

"Quick and pointed would not be adjectives I'd use to describe Mr. King's normal mode of behaviour."

A sudden thought occurred to Frances. "The French envoy to Canada initiated this gold storage request. Could he help?"

"Pierre Bozonnet? *Not* the sharpest knife in the drawer. Snails race faster than Pierre thinks."

"Could he at least tell Captain Battet to unload the gold?"

"I don't think Pierre could tell the time from the Peace Tower clock. He's a rule-follower, to boot. God only knows who's making up the rules in France these days. The country's being run from a card table in the lobby of the Hotel Bordeaux."

At noon, Maddie put through a call to Frances, who was working in Miss Briscoe's office. An angry female voice hissed, "Where is he?"

"He who?"

Scotty Meldrum? Vice-Admiral Nelles? Captain Battet?

"Graham, you little guttersnipe! Where's my husband?"

Frances silently counted to five. Then she continued counting to ten. "Good afternoon, Mrs. Towers. Governor Towers is in Washington staying at the Willard Hotel. Suite 314."

"Don't get cute with me! That's where he's *supposed* to be. I've left five messages for him and he hasn't replied. Where is he *really*?"

"Mrs. Towers, I spoke with him yesterday morning in room 314 at the Willard Hotel."

"You're covering for him, aren't you?" she exclaimed, her voice rising. "He's with *her*, isn't he?" She slammed the receiver down in Frances's ear.

With the Peace Tower clock striking two, Scotty Meldrum was back, drenched in sweat.

"Have you ever seen Mackenzie King in court dress with his cockade hat? He looks like a gilded pork chop, for God's sake. I had to wait interminably through all the pomp and circumstance of Lord Athlone's investiture to get a word in his ear. He was irked at having his tea party interrupted. I finally got his attention by telling him that this cargo represents more than the entire Canadian gold reserves. He agreed in principal that we should keep the *Émile Bertin* from sailing, but he is absolutely against any use of force. He told Arnie Heeney to cable Captain Battet that should the *Émile Bertin* attempt to leave, the Canadian government would regard it as 'an unfriendly act.' Jesus H. Christ! Won't *that* shiver his timbers? No more invitations to tennis for him!

"Chubby Power is our only friend up there, even though he's just acting minister of Defence. He agrees that 'all necessary steps' should be taken to stop the cruiser from sailing."

"You mean ... use force?"

"All necessary steps."

"Fire on an allied warship?" Frances felt like Alice floating down the rabbit hole—out of control and way out of her depth. She tried playing the French minister card again.

"Bozonnet?" Scotty scoffed. "A banana has more brains. I saw him at the reception on his fifth glass of champagne. Mumbled he's 'not sure of his own authority' anymore. What's left of the French government is huddled in Bordeaux in complete disarray, and who knows where the loyalty of the navy resides. Bozonnet thinks—and I use the term in the widest possible sense—that the *Émile Bertin* should be allowed to leave Halifax if it wants. How helpful." Scotty kicked the filing cabinet. "Have you got through to Reid yet?"

"He's out of the office. I'll keep trying."

Brendan bounded in waving two telegrams. "This just in from Montague Norman at the Bank of England ...

> "Urge most vigorously that immediate action however strong should be taken to prevent the *Émile Bertin* from leaving Halifax for time being STOP

"... and this from Anthony Eden, British secretary of state for war:

> "The British government continues to hold the French government to all its treaty obligations as an ally STOP Their navy their colonies their gold will continue to be used to carry on the conflict STOP"

"Hurrah!" shouted Scotty, grabbing the telegrams from Brendan. "I never thought I'd say it, but God bless the English! I'm going right back up to Parliament Hill and pummel the prime minister with these."

He turned and shook a finger at Frances from the doorway. "Call Reid again, McFadden, and clear the decks. Your sole job is to keep that cruiser tied to the Halifax dock until I get back with reinforcements. I'm deadly serious," he said, looking deadly serious: "as goes that ship, so goes your career at the Bank."

He stormed out. The secretariat, God bless them every one, studiously pretended not to have heard a word. Frances wandered back into Miss Briscoe's office, the good ol' MBO. She wondered if they would name a room after her when she was gone. A phone call to the Willard Hotel in Washington found no response from the governor's suite. She left the "Culloden File" message for him at the front desk and redialed Halifax Central Command.

"Commodore? This is Frances McFadden at the Bank of Canada. I apologize for the deputy governor's tone on his last phone call. He is not usually emotional, but he sees it to be his duty to protect that gold. He is most anxious that you hold the *Émile Bertin* until it unloads."

Commodore Reid spoke in the gentle cadence of a grandparent. "Miss McFadden, I appreciate that Mr. Meldrum is only trying to do his duty. Please understand that I'm only trying to do mine. I'm sure that duty is Captain Battet's sole motivation as well."

"But France has sent their gold reserves to the Bank of Canada for safekeeping. That's the only reason that the *Émile Bertin* is in Halifax Harbour."

"Granted, but that French government resigned, and a new French government has directed Captain Battet to Martinique."

"Commodore, the new French government has clearly fallen under the influence of the German army. French assets are now essentially German assets. Surely you can see the wisdom in off-loading the gold to protect it?"

"Wisdom has nothing to do with it, Miss McFadden. I follow orders from Rear-Admiral Nelles. He takes direction from the acting minister of Defence, Mr. Power, who in turn reports to the prime minister. Please note: The deputy governor of the Bank of Canada is *not* to be found in that chain of command. I have no orders to restrain the *Émile Bertin* from sailing."

"Commodore, we just received a telegram directly from the Bank of England insisting, and I quote, that 'immediate action, however strong' be taken to prevent that cruiser from sailing."

There was a long pause.

"Commodore?"

"*However strong*? Are you suggesting, Miss McFadden, that I open fire on a light cruiser?" He laughed. "The Halifax harbour defences consist of three surplus WWI howitzers. They *might* actually work, if I could find ammunition that still functions after twenty years in storage. *If* they did work, and *if* the untrained militia that man them could manage to aim well enough to hit this French cruiser, they might scrape the paint in a few places. Should the *Émile Bertin*, which has nine six-inch guns, decide to return fire in its own defence, a single broadside could level the city of Halifax. I was a midshipman here in 1917 during the Halifax explosion. Two thousand were killed and twelve thousand buildings damaged or destroyed. Is any amount of gold worth repeating that?"

Silence.

"Is it, Miss McFadden?"

"No, Commodore. It is not. But what if you were ordered to open fire?"

Commodore Reid replied tangentially. "Did you know that Admiral Nelson was blind in his right eye? At the battle of Copenhagen, his commanding officer hoisted a signal for him to withdraw from action. Nelson felt the correct strategy was to attack, so he held up his telescope to his blind eye, and didn't 'see' the signal. He attacked and won the battle." Commodore Reid let that thought sink in for several seconds. "Well, I'm deaf in my left ear."

"The deputy governor has just gone up to Parliament Hill to get the support of the prime minister and Vice-Admiral Nelles. Is there any possible way you can delay things at your end?"

"I can see the *Émile Bertin* through my office window. It's not five hundred yards away. A beautiful fighting ship," Commodore Reid said with admiration. He took a deep breath. "Tell you what. I will contact Captain Battet. I will present your request. However, I seriously doubt that Mr. Meldrum is in his chain of command, either."

42

END GAME

Mackenzie King had always been a little wary of the Bank of Canada, which he regarded as a [Prime Minister R.B.] *Bennett creation, and King had been subjected to the Deputy Governor in the midst of a crisis.*

"Those people at the Bank—they're mad!" he confided to Jack Pickersgill.

(Schull, 44)

Commodore Reid got back to Frances in less than twenty minutes. "Your lucky day, Miss McFadden. You should buy a ticket on the Irish Sweepstakes. Captain Battet is willing to give the Canadian and French governments three more hours to sort things out."

"Praise the Lord! How did you manage that?"

"Partly professional courtesy to a fellow naval officer, partly due to the fact he's still taking on stores of water and oil. Anyway, the *Émile Bertin*'s here until five-thirty. The ball's back in your court."

Miss Briscoe had maintained that "real differences were achieved by small increments." She hadn't explained how you incrementally stop a warship.

Frances phoned several offices on Parliament Hill, shadowing places that Scotty Meldrum had just left, just called, or just walked by. She tried Dr. Grace, her so-often saviour. His secretary said he had left for the Five Lakes Fishing Club right after the governor general's reception. Then, the Willard Hotel in Washington again. The phone rang and rang in Governor Towers's suite until the front desk cut in.

"May I take a message, Ma'am?" asked a courteous southern drawl.

"Please. Governor Towers needs to call his office in Ottawa at his first opportunity."

"Certainly. And the call is pertaining to … ?"

"The Culloden File."

"Wasn't a similar message left earlier?"

"It was. Please leave it again."

Frances had continued to work out of the MBO so as not to distract the Rascals from their normal duties. It wasn't a member of the secretariat who walked through the open doorway, snatched the phone out of her hand and slammed it down.

"All right, where is he? *Really?*" demanded Molly Towers, eyes filled with lightning. "He's with *that woman*, isn't he?"

"Good afternoon, Mrs. Towers, I was just trying to get in touch with the governor myself."

"To warn him?"

"To advise him that Mr. Meldrum is having some difficulty dealing with the prime minister's office on a pressing issue."

"Balderdash! You're either a liar or completely incompetent. Or both. That old bag Briscoe *always* knew where he was. *Always!*"

The Rubicon had been crossed. Frances's face hardened.

"And did she always tell you?"

Short staccato intakes flared through Molly Towers's nostrils. "I will *not* stand for back talk from a … from a two-bit clerk who whored her way into the Balmoral Arms!" She strode to the credenza and swept the sherry decanter and four crystal glasses crashing to the floor. "You're fired!" she shouted, before whirling around and out the door.

Trapped behind her desk, Frances's only resort was to grab an ashtray and hurl it at the retreating dragon. It smashed against the door frame, exploding into pieces that cascaded to the floor. By the time she scrambled around her desk to the doorway, Molly Towers had disappeared down the hall. The eight eyes of the secretariat stayed discreetly averted as they typed away.

At 4:30, Bridget rang through to Frances in the MBO. "Do you know a guy named 'Colonel Vanier'? He's calling from France, for goodness sakes!"

"Hello, your Excellency. I'm sorry, but Governor Towers is in Washington."

There was a crackling static on the line, through which a scratchy voice could barely be heard. "Good evening, Miss McFadden. It is you I wish to speak to. Mr. Roderick asked me to pass along a message."

"Paul Roderick?"

"Yes, and I must say his French is surprisingly good for someone from southwestern Ontario. He has been immensely helpful as we dismantled the Paris Embassy, destroyed our coding equipment, and burned the files. He single-handedly kept two decrepit cars running as we crawled down here to Bordeaux. Could not have made it without him. As soon as the moon is down, I'm catching a sardine trawler for England with the last three members of the embassy staff."

"Oh, thank God!"

"Mr. Roderick asked me to inform you that he has decided to stay in France."

The last five words echoed in Frances's head. "What! The French are capitulating! Isn't that why you're leaving?"

"Yes, the Pétain government is seeking an armistice. However, there are elements in France that will continue to resist the Germans. Mr. Roderick hopes to help. You can contact him through the High Commission in London, if you like. We have a communications network set up."

"But he tests farm equipment! How can he help a retreating army?"

"My question exactly. He believes he can assist in keeping French military machinery functional, as well as contribute to making German machinery dysfunctional. Is that a word? It was his expression. Now I must ..." The static reached a crescendo, and then the line went dead.

A numbness overwhelmed Frances. Nothing had prepared her for the sense of loss that suddenly engulfed her.

It was after five thirty, and Scotty Meldrum had not returned or called. Frances phoned Commodore Reid for the third time that day. "Commodore, Frances McFadden. Any instructions from the prime minister or Vice-Admiral Nelles?"

"No, ma'am."

"Can you hold the *Émile Bertin* just a little longer?"

"Too late, Miss McFadden. Captain Battet gave us three hours, true to his word. Time's up. The ship has just cast lines off. There are two tugs nudging her around toward the harbour mouth. There she goes, heading east past Georges Island."

Frances's heart sank.

"If it's any solace, the British Admiralty cabled me. Their cruiser *Devonshire* is waiting outside Halifax harbour and will trail the *Émile Bertin* to Martinique."

No solace at all.

Frances barely remembered to thank Commodore Reid before hanging up. The room swayed as dizziness overtook her. Had she eaten any lunch, she might have thrown up. Finally she stood and walked unsteadily to her desk in the outer office. All typing came to a halt.

"That's it," she told the secretariat. "The *Émile Bertin* just left Halifax with the gold." She paused to gain composure. "I'm sure you all overheard the deputy governor say, as goes that ship, so goes my career at the Bank. I'll be clearing out my desk."

The Rascals rose to their feet as a unit. "We would like a word, if we may, Miss McFadden," said Brendan. For the first time she could remember, there was no irony in his voice. His stilted formality registered on her in spite of a calamitous day.

"Yes, Brendan?"

"First of all, I apologize for that wisecrack about wanting your desk if you were fired." He bit his lip. "I thought the comment so ludicrously farfetched as to be humorous." With that, Brendan, Claire, Maddie, and Bridget formed up in a neat row in front of her. They each carried a single piece of paper. Claire, Maddie and Brendan laid theirs face up on her desk. They were identical, except for the names.

> June 21, 1940
>
> Please consider this notice of my resignation from the Bank of Canada effective the date of Miss McFadden's departure from the staff.
>
> Respectfully yours,
> Brendan McGuire

"What's this?"

"If certain parties believe that you are no longer good enough for the Bank, then clearly, neither are we," said Claire.

"We're not going to give them the pleasure of firing us, too," said Maddie.

"They wouldn't dare!" said Frances. "They need you here to win the war."

"Correction," said Brendan. "They need *you* here."

"They're too goddamn dumb to know what they need," said Bridget.

Frances shook her head. "Look, you've all helped to make the Bank of Canada a world-class institution. World class. Institutions carry on after individuals depart. Witness Miss Briscoe. Worthy work is being done here."

"'Worthy?' Firing their best employee over petty issues?"

"Because you couldn't overpower a French cruiser?"

"Because Governor Towers doesn't answer his wife's messages?"

"As goes Miss McFadden, so goes the secretariat," Brendan paraphrased. "Anyway, it wouldn't be any fun here without you. Who would give us tummy rubs and feed us treats? Oh! Bridget has something to say in private."

Bridget followed Frances into the MBO and closed the door. Her eyes were wild. "Oh Miss, please forgive me! I agree *completely* with the others." She fought for control of her voice. "It's just that … if … if I don't bring my paycheque home, my little brother and sister don't eat. My father drinks up all the relief money. I know I can find another job in a week, so my resignation is for seven days from now. Please don't think me disloyal." Tears crept down Bridget's freckled cheeks. She placed her resignation letter on the desk and left.

Now what?

Gold gone. Job gone. Boyfriend gone. Who said, "Bad things come in threes"?

Frances went into the supply room and found an empty cardboard box. She placed it on her desk and began emptying her desk drawers of personal items. There wasn't much. An extra blouse and a clean pair of underwear. A fountain pen Miss Gilhooley had given her. A few photographs. A bottle of aspirin. Spare menstrual supplies. Her logbook of overtime hours. Seven thousand three hundred and fourteen hours at time-and-a-half plus 3 per cent on the unpaid balance. $11,263.

Two chances of collecting that.

The secretariat observed and wordlessly followed suit. Claire and Brendan usually left at 4:15 for baseball or golf. Bridget and Maddie normally departed at 5:30. Once packed, no one moved. A tableau of silent figures sat at their desks, hands folded, behind mournful cardboard boxes.

The phone rang in Miss Briscoe's office, and Frances dragged herself up to answer it. "Bank of Canada secretariat," she said wearily. "May I help you?"

"Hello, Miss McFadden. How are things in Ottawa?" asked a chipper Graham Towers.

For the second time in a catastrophic day, Frances completely lost control. "Where have you been?" She spat the words like a scolding parent.

There was a momentary silence on the line, then a contrite response. "I just returned to the Willard to find two "Culloden File" messages. Is something the matter?"

"There was. Something the matter. Nothing matters anymore. And I've been fired twice in the last three hours."

"Twice? You must have been very naughty, Miss McFadden," the governor chuckled. "That explains your Culloden File messages."

"Not at all. No, it was Mr. Meldrum in a complete frenzy, running amok on Parliament Hill that I thought you should know about."

"What happened?"

"The *Émile Bertin* captain refused to unload the French gold. Claimed he had new orders to take it to Martinique. Before racing off to Parliament Hill for help, Mr. Meldrum delegated to me responsibility for contacting Commodore Reid in charge of Halifax harbour and demanding he fire on the cruiser if it tried to leave. Mr. Meldrum said that if we lost the gold, he would take the three hundred million out of my salary. Brendan calculates that I could have it paid off in two hundred thousand years. Then Mr. Meldrum stormed up to Parliament Hill to find someone to force the captain to change his mind. His parting words were 'As goes that ship, McFadden, so goes your career at the Bank.'"

"And?"

"Commodore Reid was understandably reluctant to engage a well-armed French warship in the confines of his harbour. The *Émile Bertin* sailed twenty minutes ago."

"Unfortunate. But clearly beyond your control."

"That is not how your deputy governor sees things."

"So he fired you again?"

"No, your wife fired me next."

"My wife?"

"Yes. She had tried and failed to get in touch with you at the Willard Hotel. Thought I knew where you really were. Claimed Miss Briscoe always knew where you really were. Then she called me an incompetent liar and a whore. And fired me."

"Dear God in Heaven!"

"Where *were* you, by the way?"

"Marriner Eccles was called to New York for some Federal Reserve crisis that he was cagey about explaining, so I had a free day. I went over to Virginia to visit old friends."

Female, perhaps?

"Why didn't you tell me?"

"I didn't wish to trouble you."

No trouble at all.

Frances exhaled slowly. "Actually, being fired from this madhouse is a huge relief."

"Now, just a minute. Did the deputy governor hire you?"

"No."

"Did my wife hire you?"

"No."

"Correct. I hired you. Only I can fire you. It's one of the few perks of being governor of the Bank of Canada. You are not fired."

"Then I quit," said Frances. I am *not* staying where I am not wanted. I cannot abide it here for one more second. Mr. Meldrum is an insufferable bully and your wife ... your wife is a bitch."

It was the first time in her life that Frances had ever used the word "bitch."

Truth to Power? It felt wonderful!

There was a long silence on the line from the Willard Hotel.

"You're upset."

"That's remarkably perceptive for someone who left me here with a madman and a crazy lady, then vanished completely. So, toodle-oo. I have absolutely no wish to be an ongoing source of friction between you and your wife or you and your deputy governor."

"Miss McFadden, you know Mr. Meldrum as well as I. A good soldier. A loyal servant of the Bank. His one fault is that he occasionally lets his emotions get the better of him. When he does blow up, it is usually ill-directed and always out of proportion to the circumstances. He did not really mean to fire you."

"'As goes that ship, so goes your career at the Bank.' His exact words. Sounds clear enough to me."

"You are not fired. He will be contrite when he calms down."

"And your wife? My competence may be debatable. I am *not* a liar or a whore."

"A very bitchy thing for her to say. Here's a secret. Molly has a mental disorder called manic depression. She suffers from extreme mood swings. Her doctor has prescribed pills that moderate her condition but they have uncomfortable side effects. She sometimes skips her medicine and slips into a dangerous zone marked by paranoia. I'll call her right now. I will remind her to take her medication and to lie down for two hours. Her conversation with you will be an indistinct memory."

Frances's voice ratcheted up a notch. "Well, *I* won't forget being called a liar and a whore. Or being fired by Mr. Meldrum—because the French government changed its mind about a gold shipment? I lack the patience of Job. I'm fed up dealing with lunatics."

"Abandon your secretariat?"

"They've all resigned. Their letters are on your desk. I tried to dissuade them, but they've had no recognition for their increased workload over the past eight months, so I can't really blame them.

Bridget will stay on for a week to smooth the transition. The rest of us are packing up and will be out of here in five minutes."

There was a long silence on the line from the Willard Hotel.

"Miss McFadden, you and the secretariat are indispensable to the operation of the Bank of Canada. The Bank of Canada is indispensable to the successful pursuit of this war. What would it take to persuade you to stay?"

There was a long silence on the line from the Bank of Canada.

"Do you want me to fire Mr. Meldrum and divorce my wife?"

Frances burst out laughing.

"I was thinking more along the line of a firing squad and a burning at the stake. But I'm open to negotiation."

Governor Towers laughed. "Listen. I apologize. You have my word that I will never again slip away without telling you where I am. This misbehaviour of my wife and the deputy governor is really my responsibility. I chose them both—for their strengths. It was their weaknesses—their fears—that overcame them. They succumbed to the pressure, but you … you did not. They're both astute enough to recognize that glaring fact when they come to their senses. Neither will ever dare to cross you again. I won't even have to mention whose side I'm on. This puts you in quite an enviable position, Miss McFadden. And I believe that position deserves a new title. How does 'Executive Assistant to the Governor' sound?"

The thought sank in for a long moment.

Now that small increment would have pleased Miss Briscoe.

"Think about it—if you did quit the Bank, who wins? Or more significantly, who loses?

"Miss McFadden, no one in the service of his Majesty's Governments anywhere in this war-torn world could have done more than you have done today. If it were up to me, I'd give you a knighthood.

"Please take a memo."

Frances automatically reached for her notepad. "Shoot."

"To members of Bank of Canada Executive Committee

"c.c. Human Resources Director:

"Due to heightened responsibilities and the interlocking nature of their duties, all five members of the governor's secretariat are to receive a 20 per cent pay raise retroactive to January 1, 1940."

Frances stopped writing. "Twenty per cent?"

"Oh, all right. Thirty per cent."

"Can the Bank afford it?"

"The Bank can't afford *not* to afford it."

The governor paused. "Think of it as enlightened self-interest, Miss McFadden. Now you'll be able to pay off the gold debt in just a hundred and forty thousand years."

43

PERSPECTIVE

Your perspective on life comes from the cage you were held captive in.

Shannon L. Alder

"**A**h! The mystery woman!" exclaimed Dr. Grace from across the table in the Canadian Grill as Frances sat down to join him. Tousled hair framed a face well tanned from a weekend at the Five Lakes Fishing Club. Although pushing forty, his carefree smile endowed him with a boyish, wholesome look. "So? Why is the impecunious Frances McFadden footing the bill for Sunday dinner in the Chateau Laurier's opulent dining room? Have those penny-pinchers at the Bank of Canada finally granted you the recognition you so richly deserve?"

"Nothing quite whets the appetite for fine cuisine as getting sacked," Frances replied with a smile of her own. "I was dismissed Friday afternoon for dereliction of duty."

Dr. Grace choked on his Macallan. "Graham Towers fired you?"

"No. Scotty Meldrum did the deed at about two o'clock. Governor Towers phoned later from Washington, offering to hire me back."

"You accepted?"

"Haven't decided. After the shock wore off, I had this levitating sense of … relief! Like I'd been acquitted of a crime or freed from a cage. Mr. Meldrum's intention was to punish me, but, ironically, I experienced this incredible feeling of release."

"But you love that job to a fault!"

"All too true. Sadly," agreed Frances. "The 'to a fault' part has given me cause to take long, reflective walks over the weekend. And to seek a consultation with the good Dr. Grace." She paused for a long sip of white wine. "It has dawned on me that the Bank of Canada is no longer enough."

"Not enough money? Not enough interesting work?"

"The money's fine. The work's gratifying."

"So ...?"

"Friday was the worst day of my life. The chaos set me thinking."

"About?"

"About the bloom of my youth sacrificed to twelve-hour days at the Bank of Canada."

"But you're making such a huge contribution—to both the Bank and the war effort."

Frances yawned. "Maybe the Bank benefits. Maybe the war effort benefits. The fundamental question is, if I may be so selfish, 'Does Frances McFadden benefit?'"

Henri scooted by to replenish drinks, and they ordered dinner before Frances continued. "A startling revelation struck me ... that I'm becoming Miss Briscoe. The Bank eclipsed every aspect of her life. Family. Friends. Her reward? Five days of retirement before she entered the hospital where she died. I admired Miss Briscoe. I do not want to become Miss Briscoe."

"You have friends. You have family. You have a delightful collegiality with your Little Rascals that Miss Briscoe never had."

"My friends have all passed me by. Katie and Kevin own a home in Sandy Hill. Mary and Ned are anxious to start a family. Dorothy would marry George Holland in a heartbeat if he were available."

"He isn't?"

"He has a wife in a straightjacket in the Brockville Psychiatric Hospital."

"Ouch."

Anyway, they're all settling into partnerships, working toward a future together. I'm going nowhere."

"*Nowhere?* Chief factotum to the second most important man in Canada?" Dr. Grace raised his eyebrows, but Frances did not bite. "What about your young engineer?"

She grimaced. "Ah, yes, Paul. Paul volunteered for some secret assignment that has taken him to France. Would he have marched off so blithely if marriage were in the offing?"

"Is it?"

Frances held her head. "He's so wonderful in so many ways. But I treated our relationship like a hobby, for God's sake. Something to do in my spare time when I wasn't at the Bank. I thought nothing of traipsing off to England and New York on Bank business. Nary a thought as to how that might affect him. Now he's done the same to me ... and I feel abandoned. And he's in a war zone where ... well, bad things can happen easily." Tears slipped down her cheek, and Frances blotted them with her napkin.

"And my father—my only living relative! Yes, I was angry and hurt when he popped back into my life. But I didn't fully appreciate that he's been through some craziness himself. He apologized profusely and reached out with warm letters from California. His sincerity and his hope were genuine. I've been very half-hearted in response."

"So, you've done an inventory of your ambitions?"

Frances sighed. "I know what I don't want. Forty years from now, I don't want my life summed up by a pen set flanking a little silver model of the Bank of Canada."

"What do you want?"

"You know, Black Friday at the Bank produced another epiphany. I realized that intimacy frightens me. I didn't learn anything about affection at home. My mother wasn't a bad person, or mean, just not at all demonstrative. I've been kind of using the Bank of Canada as a place to hide from my emotions."

"Don't be so hard on yourself! You jumped from being a school kid right into an adult job, without much chance to establish perspective. You proved yourself so competent so quickly that you were deluged with added tasks. It would be easy to lose your bearings in that labyrinth."

Frances looked him in the eye. "This was not the fault of the Bank. I dove in willingly. I was not a victim."

"So, must you give up the Bank to save yourself?"

"Don't know."

They ate in silence for a while. Excellent food has a delightful restorative effect.

"I could ... write to Paul. I could tell him ... that his absence has made me realize how important he is to me. I could say that I would like to explore a permanent relationship."

"You could tell him that you love him."

Frances grimaced. "Love was not a word lightly bandied about where I grew up. It seems boastful and overly dramatic."

"Try it. What do you have to lose? Now, how about your father?"

"He offered to foot the bill for a visit to California. Maybe I should go. I haven't taken any holidays in two years."

"Why not?"

"No time! We lurch from crisis to crisis. When the governor is in the office, he wants me in the office. When the governor is out of the office, he wants me in the office to keep things running."

"Seems a little selfish."

"I saw it as a huge vote of confidence. I was necessary! The Bank would grind to a halt without me."

"Yeah, until Scotty Meldrum gave you the axe. What heinous sin did you commit, by the way?"

"I didn't prevent a French cruiser from sailing out of Halifax harbour."

"Bad you!"

"Yeah, well, Mr. Meldrum's ego was on the line. He felt it was his duty to keep the cruiser tied up. He was up racing around on Parliament Hill, trying to get support. Left me in charge. I failed."

"Left *you* in charge? Not the associate deputy governor, M. Soulière? Not Mr. Marble, secretary of the Bank? That clearly shows where Scotty places you in the Bank's hierarchy of talent." Dr. Grace drained his second Macallan. "You can't seriously believe that this ship's sailing showed any deficiency on your part."

"Mr. Meldrum and I have been through a few scrapes together. The real failure, to me, was that he didn't understand that I had done everything possible."

"And Graham Towers did? "

"The governor is far less emotional than Scotty and he was six hundred miles away from the crisis. Still, I have no wish to be a source of friction between them. It's probably best if I just 'fold my tent like the Arabs, and silently steal away.'"

"Wordsworth?"

"Longfellow."

"Anyway, I must beg to differ. You may be right to focus more on your personal life, but you shouldn't abandon all your good works over this little tiff. Back to your father ..."

"Yes. My blood. My only kith and kin. Mother dead. Sister dead. Not many wagons left to circle in the ol' McFadden family. Maybe the survivors should stand by each other."

Dr. Grace signalled Henri for coffee and the dessert menu. "You invited me here for my advice?"

"I did."

"Then let me earn my dinner. You know the old homily 'Nothing ventured, nothing gained'? Be strong! Write to Paul Roderick. Apologize for holding yourself aloof. Tell him you have trouble with emotional attachments, but that you're ready to make a commitment. For the cost of a stamp, you'll find out if he shares the feeling. Then take a vacation. Go out and visit your father. See first-hand if blood is thicker than water. The worst that can happen is that you get a holiday and you set your mind at ease.

"Whatever you do, for God's sake, don't quit your job at the Bank. It's a priceless gift to work at something you love. And, you're a perfect fit there, Miss McFadden, whether you believe it or not."

"Is that strength?" Frances asked. "Imploring Paul? Excusing Scotty? Absolving my father?"

"Is taking a chance weakness? Is forgiveness weakness? Is empathy weakness?"

Henri poured hot coffee and left. Frances looked at her cup for a long moment, then picked it up and inhaled the tangy aroma deep into her lungs before she drank. It was bitter and mellow. Robust and soothing. Pungent and pleasant. Like life. It tasted of the future and the promise of a fresh start.

Frances looked over at Dr. Grace and smiled.

ACKNOWLEDGEMENTS

Writing takes patience, time, and curiosity abut the human condition. Although it is a solitary vigil at the keyboard, this novel was greatly enhanced by a number of people.

Heartfelt thanks to:

Amelia Hope

Bridget Hall

Ann Hyland
Rhoda Diebel
Lise Bazinet
Bob Nielson
Charis Wahl
Ros Nielson
Terry West

Herb Batt
Sylvia Warsh
Carolyn Harris
Geoff Collins
Magda Seydegart
Charles Marriott
Jane Naisbitt
Carla Hall

Don Hall
Don Ray
Dudleigh Coyle
Dan Way
Jack Nield

Steven Poloz
Jane Boyko
Shannon Worek
Sylvie Peterson

Tim Gordon
Jane Karchmar
Wendy Clements
Chantal Duguay-Hyatt

Book Clubs everywhere!

HISTORICAL PERSONALITIES

This novel is a work of fiction wound loosely around historical events and personages. Although many figures in the novel are based on real people, most characters, places, and incidents are either the product of the author's imagination or are used fictitiously. This appendix briefly describes historical characters up to and including the period in which the novel is set (September 19, 1930–June 23, 1940).

NOTE: For ease of reference, members of the nobility are indexed under their title as they appear in the novel, rather than alphabetically by their legal name (e.g., "Earl of Athlone," rather than "Cambridge, Alexander Augustus, first Earl of Athlone").

Batten, Captain: commander of the French light cruiser *Émile Bertin*.

Bogart, Humphrey: American stage and screen actor often typecast as a gangster during the 1930s.

Brox sisters: American trio of singing sisters popular in the 1920s and 1930s. They appeared in the film *The Hollywood Review of 1929*, in which they performed "Singin' in the Rain."

Campbell, Captain Harold: private secretary to the Duke of York (1933–36). When the duke became King George VI, Campbell was appointed his equerry (an office or honour, senior attendant to a sovereign).

Cardin, Arthur: Liberal Member of Parliament (M.P.) from Richelieu–Verchenes. Influential minister in the Mackenzie King cabinet from Quebec. Held the portfolios of Fisheries, then Public Works, then Transport. Helped fellow Quebec Ministers Lapointe and Power rally support to defeat Premier Maurice Duplessis in the October 1939 Quebec election.

Churchill, Winston: British Conservative politician, First Lord of the Admiralty in the Chamberlain cabinet from September 3, 1939, to May 10, 1940. Prime minister and minister of Defence of England from May 10, 1940.

Clark, Clifford: seconded from the Political Economics Department at Queen's University in 1932 by Prime Minister R.B. Bennett to serve as deputy minister of Finance. Supported the establishment of the Bank of Canada. Though initially cautious, he began to see an expanded role for the state in economic planning.

Crerar, Jessie: wife of Thomas Crerar.

Crerar, Thomas: Liberal M.P. from Churchill, Manitoba, minister of Mines and Resources in the King cabinet from December 1, 1936, to April 17, 1945. As a cabinet minister from Western Canada, he was charged with keeping Western wheat farmers happy.

Cripps, Sir Roger: president of Canadian Steamship Lines in 1939.

Dandurand, Raoul: Quebec corporate lawyer appointed to the Canadian Senate in 1898 by Sir Wilfrid Laurier. Speaker of the Senate from 1905 to 1909. From 1921 until his death in 1942, Leader of the Government in the Senate, serving in every cabinet formed by Mackenzie King.

Desbarats, George–Edouard: influential Canadian printer and inventor. As Queen's printer in 1864, followed the new Canadian government when it set up in Ottawa in 1867. Built the mansion in Sandy Hill at the corner of Chapel Street and Daly Avenue.

Dickens, Charles (1812–70): British author and social critic. The Prelude is based on lines in the first chapter of his novel *The Tale of Two Cities.*

Drew, George: Conservative leader of the opposition in the Ontario Legislature (1938–43) and later premier of Ontario (1943–48).

Duff, Sir Lyman Poore: puisne justice of the Canadian Supreme Court from 1904 to 1933. Chief justice from March 17, 1933, to January 7, 1944. Administrator (acting governor general) between the death of Lord Tweedsmuir on February 11, 1940 and the swearing-in of the Earl of Athlone on June 21, 1940.

Duke of Richmond, Charles Lennox: Fourth Duke of Richmond, appointed governor general of British North America in 1818. Died August 28, 1819, near Richmond, Ontario, of hydrophobia from a rabid fox bite. Interred in Quebec City.

Dunning, Charles: former premier of Saskatchewan, minister of Finance in the King government from 1935 to September 5, 1939, when he resigned due to ill health. In 1940, he became chancellor of Queen's University.

Duplessis, Maurice: Union Nationale Premier of Quebec from August 17, 1936 to November 8, 1939, then leader of the opposition in the Quebec Legislature.

Earl of Athlone (Alexander Cambridge, 1st Earl): born in 1874 as Prince Alexander of Teck, was a British military commander and major-general. Served as governor general of Canada from June 21, 1940 to April 12, 1946.

Eccles, Marriner: successful American economist and banker. Chairman of the United States Federal Reserve from 1934 to 1948.

Eden, Anthony: British Conservative politician, secretary of state for Dominion Affairs in the Chamberlain government from September 1939 to May 1940, then secretary of state for war in the Churchill government from May to December 1940.

Fournier, Pierre: governor of the Bank of France from July 1937 to August 1940.

George VI: king of the United Kingdom and the Dominions of the British Commonwealth from 1936 to 1952. Married to Elizabeth Bowles–Lyon. Father of Princess Elizabeth and Princess Margaret.

Heeney, Arnold: Rhodes Scholar from Manitoba, Civil law degree from McGill, practised law in Montreal until appointed principal secretary to Prime Minister King in 1938. Became secretary of the War Committee in 1939 and clerk of the Privy Council in 1940.

Hepburn, Mitchell (Mitch): Liberal premier of Ontario from 1934 to 1942, fierce adversary of McKenzie King.

Howe, Clarence Decatur (C.D.): Liberal M.P. for Port Arthur from 1935–57. Minister of Transportation in the King cabinet. Appointed minister of Munitions and Supply on April 11, 1940, where his powers were so far-reaching that he was known as "Minister of Everything."

Ilsley, James Lorimer: Liberal M.P. for Digby–Annapolis–Kings, minister of Revenue in the King government from 1935 to 1940, minister of Finance from July 8, 1940 to December 1946.

King, William Lyon Mackenzie (1874–1950): B.A. 1895, M.A. 1997 University of Toronto; L.L.B (Osgoode Hall) 1896; M.A. in political economy from Harvard (1898). Appointed deputy minister of Labour in 1900, elected to Parliament as a Liberal in 1908, appointed first minister of Labour in 1909. Ph.D. from Harvard in 1909. Published the far-sighted book *Industry and Humanity: A Study in the Principles Underlying Industrial Reconstruction* in

1918. Chosen leader of the Liberal Party of Canada in 1919, served as prime minister (1921–26, 1926–30, 1935–48). Also held the External Affairs portfolio until 1945.

Lapointe, Ernest: Liberal M.P. for Kamouraska (1904–19) then Quebec East (1919–41). Minister of Justice (1924–30, 1935–41) in successive King governments, and senior Quebec lieutenant in cabinet. Mackenzie King did not speak French and relied on Lapointe to handle important matters in the province.

Laurier, Sir Wilfrid: Liberal prime minister of Canada 1896–1911.

Leopold III: King of Belgium (1934–51). As commander of the armed forces, he assumed the right to surrender unilaterally to the Germans on May 27, 1940, believing his army was crushed. As he did not consult the Belgian Parliament in seeking the surrender, this act led to a constitutional crisis after the war and his abdication.

Lindbergh, Charles: famous American aviator, strong supporter of the isolationist America First movement, which advocated American neutrality during World War II until the Japanese attack on Pearl Harbour on December 7, 1941.

Lord Riverdale (Arthur Balfour, 1st Baron): British industrialist, sent to Canada by the British government in late 1939 to negotiate the funding of the British Commonwealth Air Training Plan. Clashed with Mackenzie King.

Lord Tweedsmuir (John Buchan, 1st Baron): prolific Scottish novelist. As Lord Tweedsmuir, served as governor general of Canada from November 2, 1935 to February 11, 1940. Died February 11, 1940, in Montreal due to complications following a stroke. Cremated and interred at Elsfield, Oxfordshire.

Manion, Robert James: Conservative M.P. for Fort William–Rainy River, later London. Served in the Meighen and Bennett cabinets. Chosen leader of the Conservative Party in 1938 to succeed R.B. Bennett. Lost his seat in the 1940 election and resigned as party leader.

Marble, Douglas: secretary of the Bank of Canada from 1938.

Massey, Alice: wife of Vincent Massey.

Massey, Charles Vincent: son of Chester Massey, owner of the Massey–Harris Company. Strong Methodist. Ran unsuccessfully as a Liberal in the 1925 federal election. Served as Canadian envoy extraordinaire and minister plenipotentiary to the United States for Canada 1926–30. From 1932 to 1935 served as first president of the National Liberal Federation of Canada. Appointed Canadian High Commissioner to the United Kingdom in 1935.

Nelles, Rear–Admiral Percy Walker: chief of the Canadian Naval Staff 1934–44. Oversaw the wartime expansion of the Royal Canadian Navy and the transformation of Canada into a major player in the Battle of the Atlantic.

Norman, Montagu: English banker, governor of the Bank of England from 1920 to 1944.

Pearson, Lester (Mike): diplomat, second secretary at the Canadian High Commission in London, England.

Pearson, Maryon: wife of Lester Pearson.

Penfield, Dr. Wilder: American-born Rhodes Scholar, moved to Montreal in 1928 to teach at McGill University and became a leading Canadian neurosurgeon. In 1934 appointed first director of the Montreal Neurological Institute and Hospital. Operated twice on Lord Tweedsmuir in February 1940 but was unable to save his life.

Pétain, Philippe: retired marshall of the French army, joined the government of Premier Paul Reynaud on May 18, 1940. On Reynaud's resignation on June 16, became premier and set about negotiating an armistice with the Germans that was signed on June 22.

Pickersgill, Jack W.: third secretary in the Department of External Affairs, seconded to Prime Minister Mackenzie King's Office in 1938.

Power, Charles Gavin (Chubby): Liberal M.P. for Quebec South, joined the King cabinet in 1935 as minister of Pensions and Health, then postmaster general, then minister of National Defence for Air. Served as acting minister of Defence between the death of Norman McLeod Rogers on June 10, 1940 and the appointment of James Ralston on July 5, 1940.

Princess Elizabeth: born April 21, 1926, eldest daughter of the Duke of York and Elizabeth Bowes–Lyon. Became heir presumptive to the throne in 1936 when her uncle Edward VIII abdicated and her father became King George VI.

Princess Margaret: born August 21, 1930, younger daughter of the Duke of York and Elizabeth Bowes–Lyon. When her father became King George VI in 1936, she became second in line to the throne.

Queen Elizabeth (Elizabeth Bowes–Lyon): queen consort of the United Kingdom and the Dominions. Wife of George VI and mother of Princess Elizabeth and Princess Margaret.

Ralston, James Layton: served in the army during World War I and subsequently rose to the rank of colonel before entering politics as a Liberal. Retired from politics in 1935 to practise law in Montreal. Appointed minister of Finance on September 6, 1939. Elected MP for Prince (P.E.I.) on January 2, 1940. Appointed minister of Defence on July 5, 1940.

Reid, Commodore: commanding officer of Halifax Naval Station in 1940.

Reynaud, Paul: maverick French politician and lawyer, minister of Finance 1938–40, premier of France from March 21, 1940 until he resigned on June 16, 1940. Arrested and incarcerated for the duration of the war.

Roach, Hal: American Hollywood producer who created a series of 220 short films between 1922 and 1944 known variously as *The Little Rascals, Hal Roach's Rascals or Our Gang.* The films were about a group of poor neighbourhood children and their adventures with snobbish rich kids, officious adults, parents, and other adversaries. The series included black and female children in leading parts at a time when discrimination against both groups was commonplace.

Robertson, Norman: American isolationist, executive director of the America First Committee, whose sole aim was to keep America out of World War II.

Rogers, Norman McLeod: Rhodes Scholar, professor of History at Queen's University, Kingston, elected Liberal MP from Kingston in 1935, minister of Labour until September 18, 1939, then minister of Defence until his death on June 10, 1940.

Roosevelt, Franklin Delano (F.D.R.): Democratic president of the United States from March 1933 until his death April 12, 1945. Although he strongly favoured the United Kingdom in the war, he was up for re-election in November 1940, and strong isolationist elements in the USA made him cautious to publicly support intervention in the war.

Skelton, Alexander (Sandy): Rhodes Scholar, economist, director of research at the Bank of Canada, eccentric son of O.D. Skelton.

Skelton, Oscar Douglas (O.D.): M.A. Queen's, Ph.D. University of Chicago, professor of Political Science and Economics at Queen's

University. Served as dean of Arts from 1919 until his appointment as undersecretary (deputy minister) of Foreign Affairs in 1925 by Mackenzie King. Trusted advisor to Mackenzie King on domestic and international issues. The leading Canadian civil servant of his time. Credited with creating the modern Department of Global Affairs.

Stuart, Robert Douglas: American. While a law student at Yale, organized the America First Committee to support enforcement of the Neutrality Acts and to oppose the United States' intervention in World War II.

Stuart, Ronald Niel, VC: commodore of the Canadian Pacific Fleet and commanding officer of the *Empress of Britain.*

Towers, Graham: born in Montreal in 1997. Served in WWI, graduated from McGill in 1919. Rose to be assistant general manager of the Royal Bank of Canada. Appointed first governor of the newly formed Bank of Canada by Prime Minister R.B. Bennett on September 8, 1934. Appointed chairman of the Foreign Exchange Control Board in September 1939.

Towers, Mary (Molly): nee Godfrey, middle daughter of Charles and Emily Godfrey of Montreal. Married Graham Towers on February 1, 1924.

Vanier, Georges–Philés: served as an officer with the French Canadian 22nd Battalion of the Canadian Expeditionary Forces in WWI. Wounded in action at Chérisy in 1918 and lost his right leg. Served as the first secretary in the Canadian High Commission in London, England from 1930 to 1939. In 1939, he was appointed envoy extraordinaire and minister plenipotentiary to France. Left France in June 1940 as armistice arrangements were being made with the Germans.

Wilson, Cairine (nee MacKay): daughter of Liberal Senator Robert Mackay, wife of Liberal M.P. Norman Wilson, mother of eight children. First woman appointed to the Canadian Senate, on February 15, 1930.

Wilson, Janet: daughter of Cairine and Norman Wilson.

Wilson, Norma: daughter of Cairine and Norman Wilson.

GLOSSARY OF TERMS

Abwehr. German military intelligence organization from 1920 to 1945.

British Commonwealth Air Training Program (BCATP). A massive joint military aircrew training program created by the United Kingdom, Canada, Australia, and New Zealand in December 1939. It trained nearly half of the pilots and aircrew who served those countries in World War II. Canada was chosen as the primary site for the BCATP because of weather, open space, and proximity to the European theatre without threat of attack. By the conclusion of the war, 167,000 students had been trained, including 50,000 pilots.

The Co-operative Commonwealth Federation (CCF). A social democratic party founded in Calgary in 1932. The CCF contested their first federal election in 1935 and elected five members of Parliament. Their leader, J.S. Woodsworth, was a dedicated pacifist and opposed on principle Canada's entry into World War II.

Chinese Immigration Act of 1875. A Canadian Act of Parliament that placed a head tax of $50 on all Chinese immigrants coming to Canada. It followed the recommendations published in the *Royal Commission on Chinese Immigration* in 1885. The intention of the Act was stated explicitly in its heading, reading, "An Act to restrict and regulate Chinese immigration into Canada." The Act was a reaction to the 17,000 Chinese immigrants who came to Canada in the early 1880s to work as labourers building the Canadian Pacific Railway. In 1903 the head tax was raised to $500.

Chinese Immigration Act of 1923 (also known as the Chinese Exclusion Act). A Canadian Act of Parliament that effectively closed off Chinese immigration to Canada except for diplomats, students, and "special circumstances." Between 1923 and 1946 only fifteen Chinese immigrants were accepted into Canada. The law was repealed in 1946 because it contravened the newly signed United Nations Charter of Human Rights.

Culloden. A battle on Culloden Moor near Inverness, Scotland, on April 16, 1746. It was the final confrontation of the Jacobite rising of 1745, which was an attempt to place the Stuart line back on the British throne and replace George II of the Hanoverian line. The catastrophic defeat of Bonnie Prince Charlie's forces by the Duke of Cumberland ended the Stuart claim to the British throne. In the novel, "Culloden File" is used as code for "dire emergency—respond immediately."

Defence of Canada Regulations. A set of emergency measures implemented under the War Measures Act. These extreme security measures allowed the waiving of habeas corpus and the right to trial; bans on political and religious groups and certain publications; restrictions on free speech; and the confiscation of property. The Regulations were used to intern opponents to World War II (real or perceived), particularly fascists and Communists, as well as opponents of conscription.

deputy minister (DM). The highest-ranking public servant in a government department, serving directly beneath the cabinet minister (an elected Member of Parliament) in charge of the department.

Émile Bertin. A French light cruiser used to bring two cargoes of gold to Halifax in May–June 1940.

envoy extraordinaire and minister plenipotentiary (known as envoy or minister). A diplomat of the second class, ranking below ambassador. Up until World War II, only a few major nations exchanged ambassadors, so most diplomatic missions were headed by envoys (see high commissioner).

Foreign Exchange Control Board (FECB). Regulations drafted by the Bank of Canada that became law on September 15, 1939, naming Graham Towers as chairman. The board's purpose was to maintain balances of foreign exchange and marketable foreign securities as well as control imports and exports in order to shield the Canadian economy from the disruptive effects of war.

Garnons, Herfortshire. A convalescent hospital for Canadian officers during World War II set up and financed by Vincent and Alice Massey through the Massey Foundation. It was located in a fifty-room country house set on six thousand acres 150 miles west of London, England.

governor general (GG). The viceregal representative of the Canadian monarch who carries out most of the monarch's constitutional and ceremonial duties. Primary residence is Rideau Hall. The governor general is appointed by the monarch on the advice of the Canadian prime minister, usually for a period of five years. Until 1952, Canadian governors general were members of the British nobility.

high commissioner. The title given in the British Commonwealth to the senior diplomat in charge of the diplomatic mission of one Commonwealth government to another (ranks as an ambassador).

Jeanne d'Arc. A French light cruiser, sister ship of the *Émile Bertin;* brought one load of French gold to Halifax in the spring of 1940.

Lady Byng Trophy. A trophy presented each year to the National Hockey League player adjudged to have exhibited the best type of sportsmanship and gentlemanly conduct combined with a high standard of playing ability. The trophy was donated in 1925 by Lady Byng, an avid hockey fan and wife of Canadian Governor General Viscount Byng of Vimy.

Laurier House. Home of Prime Minister Sir Wilfrid Laurier from 1897 until his death in 1919. His wife, Zoé Laurier, willed the house to Mackenzie King upon her death in 1921. King lived there from 1923 until his death in 1950. Upon King's death, he willed the house to the people of Canada.

McKeller Park. A public golf course opened in Nepean township on the outskirts of Ottawa north of Carling Avenue in 1928 and closed in 1952. Golfers could play all day for a flat rate of $1 or pay $35 per season.

National Resources Mobilization Act. An act of the Canadian Parliament passed on June 21, 1940. It represented a much more active war effort in the wake of recent German victories. The Act enabled the government to requisition the property and services of Canadians for home defence. (Note: Although a form of conscription, there was no conscription for overseas service.) The act appeased the conscriptionists without antagonizing the anti-conscriptionists.

Neutrality Act of 1935 (USA). American legislation that imposed a general embargo on trading in arms and war materials with all parties in a war. This act, spurred by the growth of isolationism and non-interventionism, was supported by powerful forces in Congress, but was criticized by President Roosevelt, who felt it restricted the administration's options to support friendly nations.

Official Secrets Act (Canada). An act based on the Official Secrets Act legislation of the United Kingdom (1911, 1922, 1939) providing for the protection of state secrets and official information, mainly related to national security. People working with sensitive information were commonly required to sign a statement to the effect that they agreed to abide by the restrictions of the Official Secrets Act.

pro bono. Work performed without charge to the recipient.

PMO. The political staff of the Prime Minister's Office.

Rideau Hall. Since 1867, the official residence in Ottawa of the Canadian governor general; and the social centre of official Ottawa. It is located at 1 Sussex Drive.

Rockcliffe Park. The wealthiest neighbourhood in Ottawa and one of the most prosperous enclaves in Canada. It is located on the south bank of the Ottawa River and abuts on Rideau Hall, the governor general's estate.

Rosedale. An older, affluent suburb in Toronto, Ontario. It is home to "old money" and some of Canada's richest and most famous citizens.

Sandy Hill. An older neighbourhood of Ottawa located close to downtown, south of Rideau Street between the Rideau Canal and the Rideau River. During the nineteenth and early twentieth century, it was Ottawa's wealthiest neighbourhood.

Union Nationale. A conservative and nationalist political party in Quebec founded and led by Maurice Duplessis in 1936. The party supported the Catholic Church, was tough on communism, and opposed women's suffrage. Duplessis' government was defeated by the provincial Liberals under Adélard Godbout in the 1939 Quebec election, largely due to the efforts of federal Liberal cabinet ministers Cardin, Lapointe, and Power.

War Committee (War Committee of Cabinet). A small cabinet war committee of six cabinet ministers created by Mackenzie King in 1939 to coordinate war activities. Membership increased to nine during the course of the war. Though not officially called the "War Cabinet," it was the effective wartime government of Canada.

War Measures Act. A federal statute adopted by Parliament in 1914 after the outbreak of the First World War. It gave sweeping emergency powers to the federal cabinet, allowing it to govern by decree when it perceived the existence of "war, invasion or insurrection, real or apprehended." It was used to limit the freedom of Canadians in both world wars.

BIBLIOGRAPHY

Note: Works cited in the novel to introduce chapters are denoted with an asterisk (*).

Ahamed, Liaquat. *Lords of Finance: The Bankers Who Broke the World.* New York: Penguin, 2009.

*Anonymous, "Loan Response Pleases Ralston," *Ottawa Journal*, January 17, 1940.

Babad, Michael, and Catherine Mulroney. *Where the Buck Stops: The Dollar, Democracy, and the Bank of Canada.* Toronto: Stoddart, 1995.

Bissell, Claude. *The Imperial Canadian: Vincent Massey in Office.* Toronto: University of Toronto Press, 1986.

———. *The Young Vincent Massey.* Toronto: University of Toronto Press, 1981.

*Bothwell, Robert, and William Kilbourn. *C.D. Howe.* Toronto: McClelland and Stewart, 1979.

*Bryce, Robert B. *Canada and the Cost of World War II.* Montreal and Kingston: McGill–Queen's University Press, 2005.

———. *Maturing in Hard Times: Canada's Department of Finance through the Great Depression.* Kingston and Montreal: McGill–Queen's University Press, 1986.

*Cook, Tim. *Warlords: Borden, Mackenzie King and Canada's World Wars.* Toronto: Penguin, 2012.

Curtis, Monica, editor. *Norway and the War, September 1939–December 1940.* Documents on International Affairs. London: Oxford University Press, 1941 (reprinted in 1965 by Johnson Reprint Corporation, New York).

Daniélou, Alain. *The Complete Kama Sutra: The First Unabridged Modern Translation of the Classic Indian Text.* Rochester, Vermont: Park Street Press, 1994.

Davies, Norman. *Heart of Europe: A Short History of Poland.* Oxford, England: Oxford University Press, 1984; reprint 1987.

Edwards, Todd L. *Argentina: A Global Studies Handbook.* Santa Barbara, California: ABC–CLIO, 2008.

*Fullerton, Douglas H. *Graham Towers and His Times.* Toronto: McClelland and Stewart, 1986.

Gibbons, Alan O., David Kirkwood, and Blair Seaborn. *Five Lakes Club 1940–2000* (formerly *Five Lakes Fishing Club*). Ottawa: self-published, 2000.

Granatstein, J.L. *The Ottawa Men: The Civil Service Mandarins 1935–1957.* Toronto: Oxford University Press, 1982.

*———. *The Politics of the Mackenzie King Government, 1939–1945.* Toronto: University of Toronto Press, 1990.

*Haarr, Geirr H. *The Battle for Norway—April–June 1940.* Barnsley, U.K.: Seaforth Publishing, 2010.

*Hastings, Max. *All Hell Let Loose: The World at War 1939–1945.* London: Harper Press, 2012.

Hennessy, Elizabeth. *A Domestic History of the Bank of England, 1930–1960.* Cambridge, England: Cambridge University Press, 1992.

*Knowles, Valerie. *First Person: A Biography of Cairine Wilson, Canada's First Woman Senator.* Toronto: Dundurn Press, 1988.

Lennon, Mary Jane, and Syd Charendoff. *On the Homefront.* Erin, Ontario: The Boston Mills Press, 1981.

*Li, Peter S. *The Chinese in Canada.* Toronto: Oxford University Press, 1988.

Maxtone–Graham, John. *The Only Way to Cross.* New York: Macmillan, 1972.

*McIvor, R. Craig. *Canadian Monetary, Banking and Fiscal Development.* Toronto: Macmillan, 1958.

*Musk, George. *Canadian Pacific: The Story of the Famous Shipping Line.* Toronto: Holt Rinehart & Winston, 1981.

*Nolan, Brian. *King's War, Mackenzie King and the Politics of War 1939–1945.* Toronto: Random House, 1988.

*Nollen, Scott Allen. *Three Bad Men: John Ford, John Wayne, Ward Bond.* Jefferson, North Carolina: McFarland & Company, 2013.

*Olson, Lynne. *Those Angry Days: Roosevelt, Lindbergh, and America's Fight Over World War II, 1939–1941.* New York: Random House, 2013.

*Patenaude, J.P. *Defence of Canada Regulations.* Ottawa: King's Printer, 1939.

Pearson, Lester B. *The Memoirs of the Right Honourable Lester B. Pearson,* Volume I, 1897–1948. Toronto: University of Toronto Press, 1972.

*Pickersgill, J.W. *The Mackenzie King Record,* Volume I, 1939–1944. Toronto: University of Toronto Press, 1960.

*Powell, James. *A History of the Canadian Dollar.* Ottawa: Bank of Canada, 2005.

Power, Charles G. *A Party Politician: The Memoirs of Chubby Power,* edited by Norman Ward. Toronto: Macmillan, 1966.

*Pigott, Peter. *Sailing Seven Seas: A History of the Canadian Pacific Line.* Toronto: Dundurn Press, 2010.

*Schull, Joseph. *The Great Scott: A Biography of Donald Gordon.* Montreal: McGill–Queen's University Press, 1979.

Speaight, Robert. *Vanier: Soldier, Diplomat and Governor General.* Toronto: Collins, 1970.

*Stacey, C.P. *Arms, Men and Governments: The War Policies of Canada 1939–1945.* Ottawa: The Queen's Printer for Canada, 1970.

———. *Six Years of War,* Volume I. Ottawa: The Queen's Printer for Canada, 1955.

Watts, George S. *The Bank of Canada: Origins and Early History.* Ottawa: Carleton University Press, 1993.

*Williams, David Ricardo. *Duff: A Life in the Law.* Vancouver: University of British Columbia Press, 1984.

ABOUT THE AUTHOR

Ian McKercher lives in the Glebe area of Ottawa with his wife, Amelia. His apprenticeship to writing began accidently at age thirteen when he was given a day-diary for Christmas. Teaching English at Glebe Collegiate for twenty-five years amid thoughtful colleagues and curious students kept him engaged with the printed word. His writing flows from a belief that Canada has an esteemed but undiscovered history that is ripe for acknowledgement.

The popular response to his first novel, *The Underling* (published in 2012), encouraged him to write *The Incrementalist* as a sequel.

TO ORDER MORE COPIES:  **Burnstown Publishing House**   5 Leckie Lane, Burnstown, ON K0J 1G0
www.burnstownpublishing.com
613-509-1090